Soiled Doves

Linda Daly

Artistic Endeavors

First Edition

Editing by:
Shelly Brown
Shawn Guideau, *MA, LPC, NCC*
Nancy Lepri

Formatted by:
Linda Daly

Cover designed by:
Linda Daly

ISBN-10: **0-9817654-8-3**
ISBN-13: **978-0-9817654-8-8**
Published by Artistic Endeavors, LLC
www.lindaldaly.com

Printed in the United States of America

*Beloved grandma, Berta Emma Anna Stoehr, you were right…
"Positive thinking makes it so".*

Linda Daly wishes to thank all of her friends, family members, and colleagues who have generously offered their support and expertise in helping to keep her dream alive, as she continues the Doves Collect series, book 4 – Soiled Doves. Especially:

Marie Fernandez
Sharon Boury
Jane Ellen Harris
Micki Peluso
Stacie Coller
Anne-Marie McCormack
Catherine Zayak

Doves Collect Family Tree

English Cast of Characters

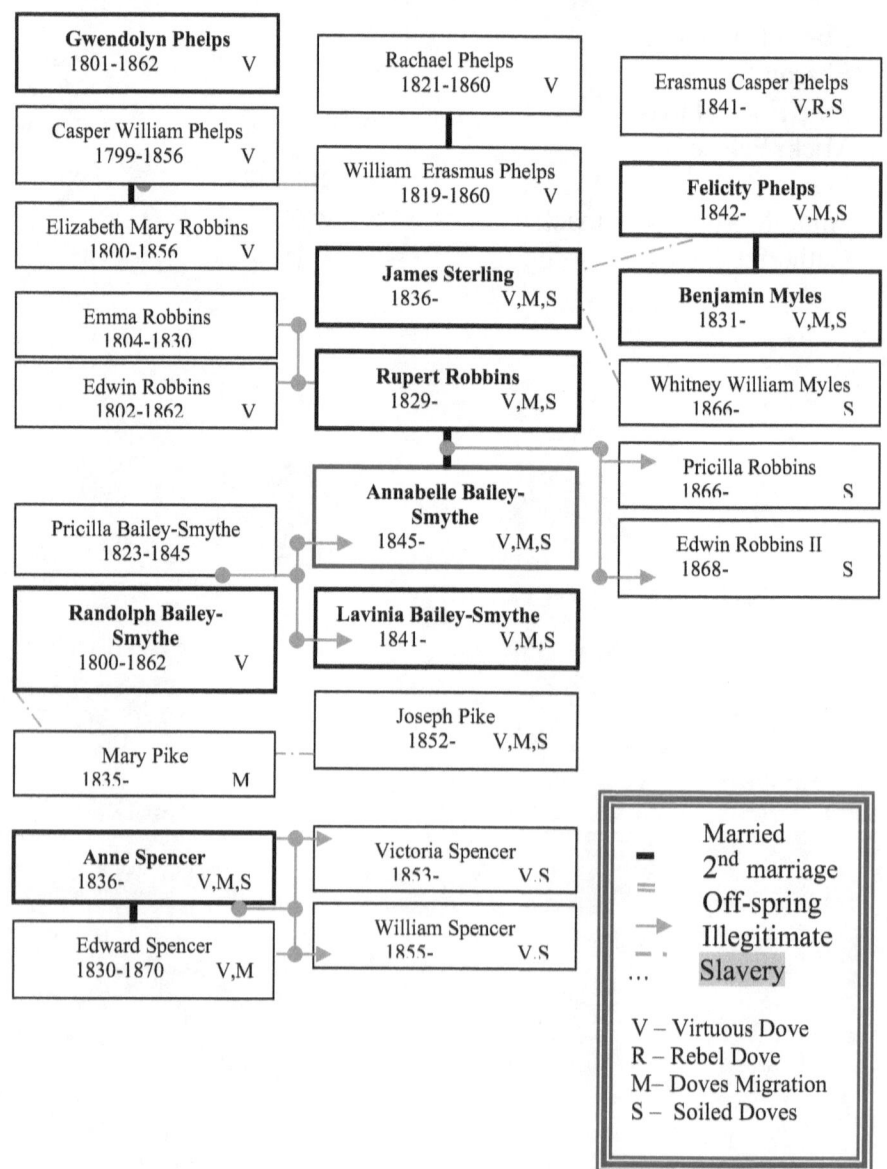

Gwendolyn Phelps
1801-1862   V

Casper William Phelps
1799-1856   V

Elizabeth Mary Robbins
1800-1856   V

Emma Robbins
1804-1830

Edwin Robbins
1802-1862   V

Rachael Phelps
1821-1860   V

William Erasmus Phelps
1819-1860   V

James Sterling
1836-   V,M,S

Rupert Robbins
1829-   V,M,S

Erasmus Casper Phelps
1841-   V,R,S

Felicity Phelps
1842-   V,M,S

Benjamin Myles
1831-   V,M,S

Whitney William Myles
1866-   S

Annabelle Bailey-Smythe
1845-   V,M,S

Pricilla Bailey-Smythe
1823-1845

Randolph Bailey-Smythe
1800-1862   V

Lavinia Bailey-Smythe
1841-   V,M,S

Pricilla Robbins
1866-   S

Edwin Robbins II
1868-   S

Joseph Pike
1852-   V,M,S

Mary Pike
1835-   M

Anne Spencer
1836-   V,M,S

Edward Spencer
1830-1870   V,M

Victoria Spencer
1853-   V,S

William Spencer
1855-   V,S

▬	Married
═	2nd marriage
	Off-spring
→	Illegitimate
...	Slavery

V – Virtuous Dove
R – Rebel Dove
M– Doves Migration
S – Soiled Doves

American Cast of Characters

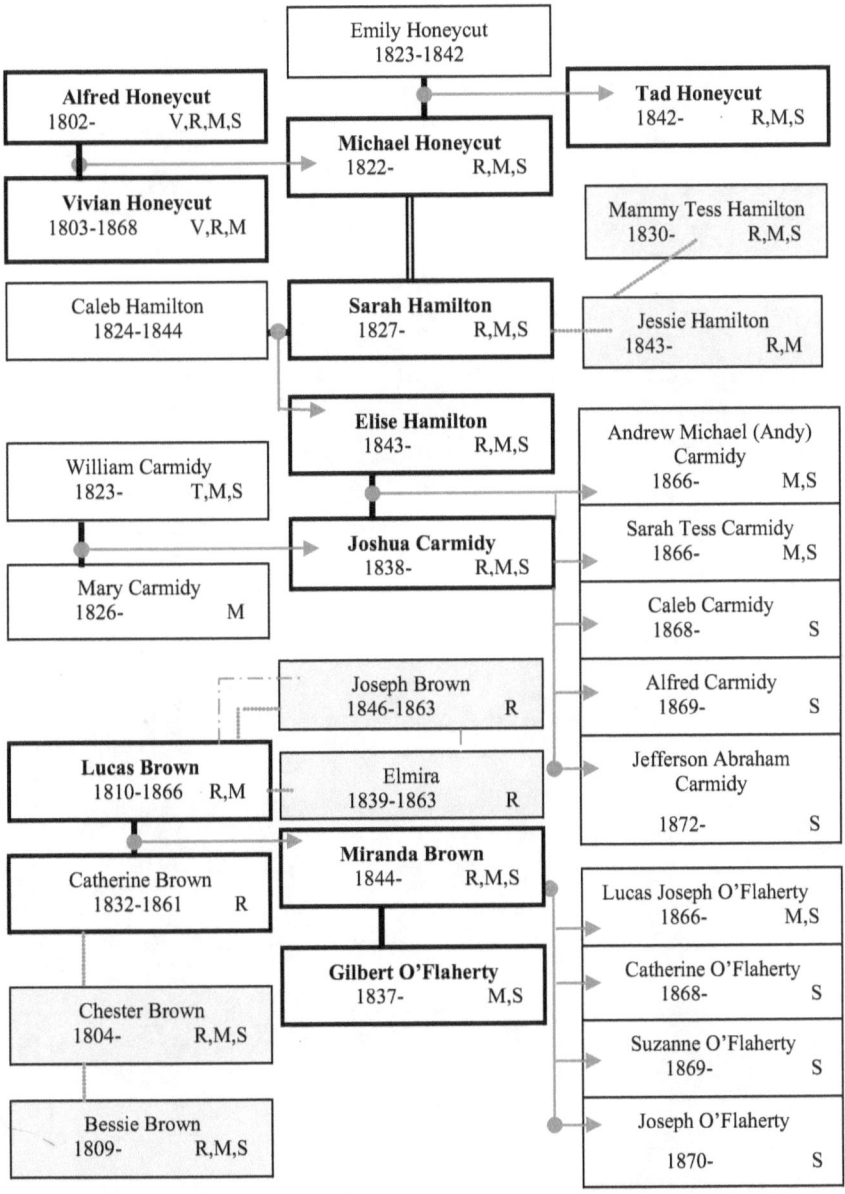

Emily Honeycut
1823-1842

Alfred Honeycut
1802-   V,R,M,S

Tad Honeycut
1842-   R,M,S

Michael Honeycut
1822-   R,M,S

Vivian Honeycut
1803-1868   V,R,M

Mammy Tess Hamilton
1830-   R,M,S

Caleb Hamilton
1824-1844

Sarah Hamilton
1827-   R,M,S

Jessie Hamilton
1843-   R,M

Elise Hamilton
1843-   R,M,S

William Carmidy
1823-   T,M,S

Andrew Michael (Andy)
Carmidy
1866-   M,S

Joshua Carmidy
1838-   R,M,S

Sarah Tess Carmidy
1866-   M,S

Mary Carmidy
1826-   M

Caleb Carmidy
1868-   S

Joseph Brown
1846-1863   R

Alfred Carmidy
1869-   S

Lucas Brown
1810-1866   R,M

Elmira
1839-1863   R

Jefferson Abraham
Carmidy

1872-   S

Catherine Brown
1832-1861   R

Miranda Brown
1844-   R,M,S

Lucas Joseph O'Flaherty
1866-   M,S

Gilbert O'Flaherty
1837-   M,S

Catherine O'Flaherty
1868-   S

Chester Brown
1804-   R,M,S

Suzanne O'Flaherty
1869-   S

Bessie Brown
1809-   R,M,S

Joseph O'Flaherty

1870-   S

~ One ~

November 1872
New York

"Fiddlesticks!" Elise exclaimed under her breath, reading the article in Harper's Weekly regarding the arrest of Susan B. Anthony, after casting her vote in the presidential election in Rochester, New York. "And to think I could have been there," Elise muttered, while sighing heavily.

Shaking her head disapprovingly at her daughter, Sarah said, "Elise Carmidy, how can you even say such a thing? Why if I didn't know better, it sounds to me like you would have rather given birth to this wonderful grandson of mine in some nasty old jail, rather than in the comfort of your own home." Holding little Jefferson Abraham protectively in her arms, she added, "Now that would have been a fine how-do-you-do, named after two presidents and entering the world in such an abominable place. Not to mention that Alfred would probably have had a stroke explaining to his business associates down at the club that his granddaughter is an emancipated woman, who gave birth to his grandson while serving jail time." Glancing down lovingly at her youngest grandchild, just a week old, who lay contentedly in her arms while sucking on his fist, she cooed. "That would never do, would it little Jefferson."

"Abominable place, indeed. Lest you forget, President Jefferson was incarcerated for two years following the war."

"Let's not go bring that up, Elise. You know how I feel about that whole situation. Why, I still cannot believe you would name this fine grandson of mine after a man who was captured in such an unsavory and cowardly manner, as was Jefferson Davis—dressed as a woman…why, I never!"

"That was never proven and you know it, Mama."

"Well, as Lucas always said, 'Where there's smoke, there's fire'."

"I swear Mama, how you go on, sometimes. Of course, I wouldn't have intentionally wanted little Jefferson to be born in some old nasty jail, but if it had happened that way; I would not have been ashamed. I could think of whole lot worse than a jail. Besides, Grandfather would not have had a stroke. He supports my beliefs in the movement. And for your information, I see nothing wrong in letting my children know that their mother believes strongly in women's equality."

"Now don't get yourself all riled up Elise, and sour your milk. Think of the baby...."

"Yes, Mama," she said obediently, while rolling her eyes and picking back up the newspaper, as she lay in her bed. "Sometimes I swear, you and Joshua are conspiring to keep me in the family way, just so I can't be active with such an important cause."

Sarah chuckled, while continuing to rock her grandchild. "Sweetheart, after giving birth to five children, I would have thought by now, you knew how babes were made."

Unaccustomed to her mother making such a comment, even as subtle as it was, Elise glanced over the top of her paper, blushing. "Mama, is that any way for a grandmother to talk? Why I never...." Her voice trailed off, seeing Joshua walk into the room with Sarah Tess by his side.

"Never what, my beautiful pearl?" Joshua asked, as his little daughter ran over to her grandmother, her blonde curls bouncing with every step she took. Carefully leaning over her little brother, Sarah Tess kissed her grandmother delicately on the cheek.

"Mornin' Grammy. Mammy Tess was looking for you. I told her you were busy with Mama and little Abraham."

"Sarah Tess, your brother's name is Jefferson Abraham. And please, don't run indoors. Now come over here and give your mama a kiss good mornin'."

Pouting, the petite blonde, begrudgingly lifted herself slightly over the bed and kissed Elise's cheek. "Mornin' Mama. I don't know why I can't call my little brother Abraham, instead of Jefferson. After all, they are both his names. And you said you even met Old Abe once."

Joshua and Sarah exchanged glances, finding it hard to conceal their amusement at how persistent little Sarah Tess was. Elise, noting their amusement and not sharing their opinion, shook her head disapprovingly. "Honestly you two, why do you insist on encouraging her? And you wonder why she acts like this."

In the sweetest of voices, Sarah Tess looked innocently up at her mother. "Like what, Mama?"

"Never you mind, Sarah Tess. You go on now and help Mammy Tess with Caleb and Albert."

"Yes Mama, but Andy is down there helpin' out and I'd only be in the way...." Sarah Tess's voice trailed off as if just realizing something. Cocking her head and raising her eyebrow, just as she had seen Elise do countless times, the willful child asked innocently, "Mama, why do we call Andy that? After all, his name is Andrew Michael."

"Sarah Tess, don't upset your mama this morning, by asking so many questions you already know the answer to."

Hearing Joshua call her by her name, rather than his pet name, Sarah Tess's smile faded and she whimpered up at him, "Yes, Papa. I'm sorry."

"No harm done, sweet pea. Do what your mama asked."

Turning her attention back to Elise, Sarah Tess looked pleadingly at her. "Mama, can I please stay here with Papa, before he goes to the office? I'll be good, all day. I promise."

Seeing Elise was not yielding to their precocious daughter's request, Joshua intervened on her behalf. "Sweet Pea, you go on down stairs and help out for a while, then before I go to the office we can have breakfast together, just you and me. How does that sound?"

Hearing her father's comment, Sarah Tess beamed and ran over to him. "Oh Papa, thank you."

Lifting her into his arms, Joshua hugged her tightly while kissing her on the cheek, then placing her back on the floor, Sarah Tess skipped merrily out of the room. Noticing the look of disapproval on Elise's face, Joshua shrugged his shoulders. "Don't be angry Elise, I can't help myself. Every time I see Sarah Tess, I imagine that's how you must have been, at her age."

Not amused by Joshua's comment, Elise directed her attention back to her paper. Sarah nodded her head, and gingerly stood up to bring little Jefferson, who was still contentedly sucking his fist, to Joshua. "I know exactly what you mean, son. Little Sarah Tess is her mother's daughter, that's for sure. So quick and spirited."

"Too spirited if you ask me," Elise chimed in. "And don't you think for one moment, that little girl doesn't already know how to wrap her father around her baby finger."

Joshua, taking his son in his arm, smiled lovingly at him then glanced at his wife. "Just as her mother always has, since the first moment I saw her."

Elise, trying not to smile, seeing the love in Joshua's eyes as he gazed down at her, said, "Oh, pish posh. No need to sweet talk your way out of this one, Joshua Carmidy, since we all know differently."

Sarah gave Elise a stern look, as only a mother can to her child when she disapproves. "Now don't be getting yourself upset Elise, you remember what happened after little Alfred was born...."

Cutting her off, sounding far harsher than she intended, Elise snapped, "Mama please, you reminding me all the time is what's upsetting to me."

Kissing her tenderly on the cheek, Sarah said, "Well, I think I better be getting on soon. I've promised Alfred to ride out to the cemetery this mornin', to place flowers on Vivian's grave and tend to the plot some."

Nodding her head, Elise said in a gentler tone, "Thank you Mama, for coming by this mornin'. Even though I was a might sour, it was so good to see you. Send my love to Grandfather and thank him again for the additional servants; and let him know Joshua and I will get back to him regarding his kind offer. Although, I can't for the life of me understand why on earth, he would want us all to come live with him. Does he understand just how noisy five children can be?"

"You know Alfred, darlin', he never does anything haphazardly. In truth, Michael and I believe that since he's always had a particular fondness for you, and now with Vivian gone, rambling around all alone in that big old home of his must be terribly lonely for him. I personally think it would benefit all of you greatly, and since you have to move anyway, why not move into the Honeycut's? God knows it's big enough for ten children." Glancing up at Joshua and feeling as if she were overstepping her bounds, Sarah hastily said, "Just listen to me go on like some interfering mother-in-law. I have no doubt Joshua; you will do whatever is best for you and your family."

"Thank you, Mother Honeycut. And for the record, I've never thought of you as interfering in our lives. On the contrary, I've always valued your opinion."

Smiling, Sarah peeked at her grandson, nestled in Joshua's arms and cooed, "Your papa is such a smooth talker little Jefferson, he should go into politics."

Hearing Sarah's comment, Elise glanced away from the newspaper and said firmly, "Oh no he shouldn't! We hardly see enough of Joshua as it is, and I'm far too selfish to share him with anyone else other than his clients."

Chuckling, Joshua winked at Elise. "My pearl, selfish? Why banish the thought. Need I point out, I'm here now?"

"Hmm, but not for very long," Elise mumbled under her breath. Then glancing back at her paper, she asked nonchalantly, "Joshua, was I mistaken or didn't you say that once the baby was born, you'd take some time off?"

Aware where the conversation was headed, and knowing only to well that Joshua was the only one who could appease his wife when she was in such a state, Sarah took the opportunity to make her leave.

"Well, since you two have such little time together, and I have things to attend to this mornin', I'll be on my way." Bending over to kiss her daughter's cheek, and brushing away a strand of hair from her brow, Sarah whispered, "Be nice, Elise. You know how much Joshua loves you."

Smiling insincerely at her mother, Elise said, "Thank you for comin' by, Mama. Will we be seeing you and Michael, after dinner?"

"Of course. And if I know your grandfather, Alfred will want to stop by and see you, Joshua, and the children as well."

As Sarah left, Joshua rocked his son gently in his arm as the baby began to fuss slightly, no longer appeased by sucking only on his fist. Joshua sat beside Elise on their bed. "Well, it appears little Jefferson is no longer satisfied with a substitute, darling."

Without hesitation, Elise placed the paper on the other side of her and began unfastening the drawstring to her gown, to nurse her son. As she lovingly took their son in her arms and guided him to her nipple, Joshua smiled lovingly at his wife. "Now tell me dearest, what has made you sour today."

Glancing over at him, her lips pert, she asked, "Sour? Why, I don't know what you're talking about, Joshua. I'm not sour. And I do wish you wouldn't speak to me as if I'm a six-year-old child, like Sarah Tess."

Tenderly cupping her face in his palm, Joshua huskily whispered, "Darling, look at me and tell me. Do you honestly believe I think of you as anything but a beautiful, vibrant, woman who I love with all my heart?"

Elise, speechless, leaned forward slightly so Joshua could place his arm around her. Waiting until his frame was nestled next to hers on their bed, Elise leaned into his shoulder as she continued nursing their son. Tenderly, Joshua rubbed Jefferson's back while the child took his mother milk, and lovingly kissed Elise's forehead. "Sweetheart, allowing me to share this special moment before going to the office, means more to me than you'll ever know. Never have I seen you look so beautiful nor have I loved you more, than at this very moment."

Clearly, Joshua was choked by emotion and Elise felt her earlier tension ease. "Oh Joshua," she whispered. "You say that every time we have a new child."

Kissing her tenderly again, he whispered, "And every time I mean it. Now tell me my pearl, what had you so tense?"

"Oh nothing really, it's just when I read about Susan B. Anthony being able to vote, I wondered if I or even Sarah Tess, would ever truly experience such equality. Then reading how Miss Anthony and some of her other followers were placed in jail, I felt ashamed. Here I was, worrying if we should leave our lovely home, when those women have sacrificed what little freedom they have, for the good of all women."

Pulling her even closer to him, Joshua took Jefferson from Elise and leaned his son tenderly into his free shoulder, while Elise tenderly patted his back to burp him.

"Darling, I know how difficult it is for you to stand on the sidelines and only watch as others fight the battles for women's rights. As soon as you are able, I was thinking we should take Alfred up on his offer, and move into the Honeycut mansion. It makes good sense. God knows, we need the room, and he the company; and with such a grand home, you could have a number of parties to generate support for your cause."

Excitedly, she responded with a squeal. "Really darling? You wouldn't mind?"

"Anything to make you happy, darling. Besides, I've come to realize, equality shouldn't be just about race but gender too."

Lovingly she gazed at him. "Oh Joshua, you really are such a wonderful man. Have I told you recently, how much I love you?"

"Not so far this morning. Which is passing by quickly and I still have another little miss I must tend to, smoothing out her ruffled feathers, before getting to the office."

"Oh Joshua, must you go in today? Can't you stay home, just this once?"

"Darling, I promise over the holidays I'll take off a few days, and come summer if you and the children are up to it, I was thinking, we could all take a trip to England."

"England!" she squealed in stunned disbelief, then quickly showering him with kisses, mindful the baby was still in Joshua's arms, Elise said, "Really? Oh, darling could we? Maybe Miranda, Gilbert, and the children could join us also. Wouldn't that be wonderful?"

Chuckling, he kissed his wife's head, then leaning down, Joshua tenderly kissed Jefferson's head before placing him next to his mother to feed on her other breast. "It does indeed. Let's hope Felicity and Benjamin have room for all of us. Four adults, nine children, along with the servants and nannys, is a lot to house for an entire summer."

"Oh, I'm sure that won't be a problem for the Myles's. I'll write both Miranda and Felicity today. Thank you, Joshua."

"Thank you my darling, for giving me another son."

~

Devonshire, England

Sitting close to one another to assure their children could not overhear them, were Felicity Myles and Annabelle Robbins. Both women, obviously upset, spoke in hushed whispers, glancing at the three children from time to time as they played quietly. Mrs. Duncan, their housekeeper, watched the children close by.

Annabelle took in a deep breath and leaned closer to her dearest friend, her husband's cousin. "Are you certain? Poor Anne must be devastated. It's one thing to lose your husband to that dreaded disease, but quite another to find out he contracted syphilis from one of our own. And by Lavinia no less...." Her voice trailed off, thinking of her sister. "That explains why Lavinia made a sudden trip to Lourdes last September. And to think, we believed she had gone with Francois on a pilgrimage to be healed by the waters of the grotto, so he could paint again. Do you think Francois has the disease, as well?" she asked solemnly, her eyes wide with fear.

Felicity nodded her head gravely, obviously uncomfortable answering such a question. "Quite possibly. After all, both he and Lavinia made no attempt to conceal their torrid love affair. They lived shamelessly in her townhouse in London, and in France at Elaine's villa north of Bordeaux, these past few years. According to Anne, she has reason to believe from a reliable source that when Edward was in Plymouth a few years back, presumably to meet with James on business, is when he and Lavinia took up. More than likely, Lavinia was using Edward to make James jealous."

Annabelle gasped, raising her voice slightly. "What! No one spoke of Lavinia being in Plymouth then. Rupert would have told me, if she were there." As she processed this latest piece of news, Annabelle asked, "Why would Lavinia come to Plymouth, to see James of all people? You don't suppose she found out about Whitney being James's son, and has told him? Is that why you asked to see me today? To see if it was Rupert or I who told her? I can assure you, we have never breathed a word of it to anyone, and especially not to Lavinia."

Reassuringly, Felicity patted her friend's hand, and consolingly said, "Of course you didn't. That thought never entered my mind. In truth, I don't believe anyone had to say anything to Lavinia. Just one look at Whitney and it's obvious he looks nothing like Benjamin, nor even me for that matter. And as hard as it is for me to admit, Whitney is the spitting image of that man. Those in our set who know James, surely must have noticed the resemblance, but have been gracious enough not to mention it. Well, at least not directly to my, or Benjamin's face, that is. I can only imagine what has been said behind closed doors, I though." Sadly, Felicity shook her head and added hastily. "It seems to me, for a decade now, either Benjamin or me have been the topic of gossip in our set. When do you think this nightmare will ever end? Wasn't it enough that the church upheld their decision, not to allow Benjamin from being a reverend over a congregation? Why must God still continue to punish us for loving one another, by now going after our son?"

Shocked by her friend's comment, Annabelle tenderly took Felicity's hand in hers. "Felicity, God hasn't punished you. Despite everything you and Benjamin have been through, you have managed to remain truly devoted to one another. And although Benjamin can't preach any longer at the Church of England, he's done wonderful work with the Salvation Army. Saving countless poor souls. As for Whitney, just look at him. Even if you don't see it, I think he favors you, not James. He has blond hair, but many children are fair in their youth. Although he may not look like Benjamin, he has what truly matters, and that is Benjamin's tender heart. Never have I met such a loving and caring little boy. Why, I have often wished little Edwin would be as gentle with Pricilla as Whitney is. So my dear friend, as I see it, you are not being punished, but rather, have been blessed."

Glancing over at her son and seeing him interact with Pricilla and Edwin, Felicity smiled. "He does have Benjamin's disposition, doesn't he?"

"He does indeed. And when Benjamin returns from London next week, I'm sure he'll know the truth about Lavinia as well. Knowing my sister as I do, I'm sure she wouldn't miss an opportunity to hurt Benjamin, by flaunting it in his face. I would even hazard to guess she tried to state it was your fault, leading her husband astray, having to have what was hers again. This of course is ludicrous, as we all know. And as painful as it is for me to have to bring this all up again, although I have no respect for James Sterling, I honestly believe Lavinia drove him insane. After years of telling him, that Benjamin had forced himself on her. Then seeing how his marriage was in ruination, compounded by how he had treated poor Rebecca to be with her, I somehow can understand, how this tormented him. Not that I abide in what he did, mind you. Because I hate him for that! However, from personal experience, I know just how maddening Lavinia can be. Why as a child, I often wondered if she would drive me into complete maze myself."

"Oh Annabelle, as hard as it is to believe, seeing Whitney grow, loving him as I do, over time, somehow the pain of that dreadful night he was conceived, the nightmare of the whole incident has faded. Yet, saying that, I will never allow that man to set eyes on my son. Ever! He has no right to such a fine son as Whitney. Moreover, as God is my witness if Lavinia has told James of Whitney, for whatever sick reason she may have, I will do whatever it takes to keep that depraved bastard far away from my son. Even leave England, if necessary. I mean it Annabelle, no matter what you,

Rupert, or even my darling Ben has to say; as long as I have a breath in me, Whitney will never know what a vile man sired him."

Never had Annabelle seen Felicity react in such a way and it frightened her. Even following the attack at her and Benjamin's home at the orphanage years prior, and how brutal James had been to her, Felicity had never shown such hatred toward him as she did now. Realizing Felicity was reacting as a mother bear would to protect her cub, Annabelle searched for the appropriate words to console her friend's troubled mind. Finding none, she quickly changed the subject.

"Felicity dear, not that I doubt what Anne has told you, but I'm curious as to how is it that, if Lavinia gave Edward this disease, then why are she and Francois still alive, and Edward died so suddenly?"

"Don't you recall the doctor telling Anne he could try and treat Edward for the cholera? However, for the syphilis lesions on his genitals, there was little he could do, since he could not administer mercury while Edward had cholera."

"Ah yes, I had forgotten Edward had cholera and syphilis. It was such a dreadful time for poor Anne. Having to send away her children and the servants to our home, to keep her and Edward quarantined to prevent an epidemic like in London. Even after Edward died, Anne remained locked up for several weeks by herself, to be certain she hadn't caught the illness. So how can you be certain it was Lavinia that Edward contracted this dreadful disease from? I heard that was only common with prostitutes and those men who favored such improprieties. Surely, you are not suggesting Lavinia has lowered herself to…"

"Not that I wouldn't put anything past Lavinia, especially if it would benefit her monetarily. However, in this instance, I believe she actually contracted it herself, through Francois. You told me yourself, how you had witnessed him at his late sister's home with a number of such immoral women. And although I have no proof of this, to my way of thinking, it makes sense that Francois unsuspectingly passed it on to your sister."

"Dear God, how dreadful for both of them. I understand this is a painful way to die. Wasn't it Benjamin who said he went to the insane asylum in London to help save the immortal souls of those who were locked away inside?" Not waiting for an answer, recalling the incident clearly in her mind, Annabelle hastily added. "As I recall, he said a number of those poor souls had deterioration to their faces and limbs, and their teeth had rotted from their mouths, even having lost the majority of their hair." On the verge of tears, Annabelle pulled her hand to her mouth and pleadingly looked over at her friend for any sign that she was mistaken. Seeing Felicity offer none, Annabelle softly wept in denial. "Surely, you must be mistaken about Edward catching it from Lavinia. Dear God no, all she has left is her beauty. We would have noticed such a condition, wouldn't we, Felicity?"

"Dear, please don't cry. As you know, we haven't been in actual contact with Lavinia in over a year, and even then, it was from a distance. It was at Edwards's funeral, don't you recall how she arrived unexpectedly, never leaving her carriage? Don't you remember how we commented at how she was behaving, not even raising her net veil as she watched from the window of her carriage, then leaving before the service was even completed?"

Nodding her head, dumbfounded, Annabelle murmured, "Yes...I remember. We all thought she was still angry that Rupert had given Joseph Pike such a large portion of Father's holdings, after his mother had come forward and confessed that Joseph was my father's illegitimate son. However, if she had it then, how could she have taken up with Edward when James was in Plymouth two years back? Surely, Edward would have noticed such a disease?"

"My very question to Anne. According to what the doctor told Anne, the signs of the disease come and go. Oftentimes someone will look as normal as you and I, thinner perhaps, showing no outer appearances that one can see. So it's quite possible, Edward took up with Lavinia, not knowing. However, according to Anne's source, Lavinia knew precisely what she was doing. Anne even thinks Lavinia deliberately set out to infect Edward, knowing how contagious the disease is, in hopes it would spread to us, as well."

"Us? Oh, you can't be serious! How is that possible? And who is this source?" Annabelle asked, her voice becoming more agitated, and Felicity nodded toward Mrs. Duncan, to move the children farther from them.

"Annabelle, Elspeth told Anne everything. As for deliberately infecting us, from what I understand, a rash forms, oftentimes on the arms and palms of the infected person, which is highly contagious. With our families interacting as we do, it could have happened quite easily, in fact. Without us being aware, we could have spread it amongst ourselves, thinking it was something the children picked up from school. What better way to get back at us, than to infect us with this age-old source of shame, scandal, and suffering?"

"Lavinia is insane! So is that all of it? Or is there more?"

Taking Annabelle's hand in hers, Felicity leaned closer, while speaking softly. "Dear, your assessment of Lavinia isn't far from the truth. This morning, I received a telegraph from Rupert, advising me that Francois passed last week and he's been laid to rest."

"Oh no." Fear gripped at her heart and she hesitantly asked, "And what about Lavinia? Was she there with him, in Paris?"

"No. It appears Lavinia has locked herself up in the townhouse, in London. Rupert is on his way to have her committed to an asylum. It appears Lavinia has become a helpless maniac, prone to bouts of violence, brought on by the disease and a vast consumption of alcohol."

Unable to control her anguish any longer, Annabelle wept softly in Felicity's arms, while the children looked helplessly over their little shoulders as Mrs. Duncan scurried them from the room.

~ Two ~

Late November 1872
Fairfax, Virginia

As the sun set over the Allegheny Mountains, Miranda and Gilbert, having returned from their evening walk, nestled contentedly in each other's arms on the back porch of their home adjacent to Glenbrook.

"Are you cold, Mandy girl? Should we go in?"

"Not just yet, darlin'. Just got a chill is all."

Wrapping his arms more tightly around his wife, Gilbert gazed over the horizon. "This time of night, I can almost smell yer Da's cigar smoke coming from the study. I half expect him to call out for me to join him in a bourbon."

"Funny you should bring Papa up this evening. I was thinking about him and Mama most of the day. Wondering what they would think of the children and the changes at Glenbrook."

"Never havin' met your mother, I can only speak for yer Da, and judging by the way he looked at Lucas after he was born, all I can say is he'd love Joey, Katie and Peanut just as much."

Giggling under her breath, Miranda rubbed her hand over Gilbert's arm, wrapped tightly around her waist. "Are you ever going to call Catherine and Suzanne by their Christian names, Gilbert? Even in private."

"Nah, can't say I will. Katie suits Catherine and well, Peanut is such a wee lass, she'll probably never grow into such a big name."

"Hmm, I suppose you're right, she is petite isn't she? But she sure is a feisty little thing. Just like her papa."

"Me? Why the way she balls up her fist and stomps her foot, I'd be saying she's mimicking her Ma rather than her Da. That one I'll be keepin' a close eye on, rest assured. Won't be havin' her undress down to her petticoats in front of some bloke before she's wed. That's for damn sure."

"Is that right? Well her mother did all right by herself, I'd say. Not only are you a wonderful husband and father, but you've managed to make quite a handsome profit from Papa's inheritance."

"Lass, there was no skill involved there. The saints were shining down on me that day and we both know it. No, if I have anything to say about it, me girls are going to latch onto a learned man. And if'n he be in favor with the angels, I won't be complainin' none."

"Well let's not be thinking about that just now, shall we dear? After all, they're only five and four. We've got a few years yet to enjoy them."

Again, she felt a chill run through her bones and just as before, Gilbert drew his body closer, suggesting they go in. Not wanting to end their time alone together, Miranda convinced him to wait a few more minutes. As they stood holding one another, Miranda thought of what Gilbert had said and a great sadness filled her. As much as she had tried over the past six years, the one subject she and Gilbert could never agree upon was the value of a learned man. Rather than point out the obvious that Tad was a learned man and it did nothing to improve his character—she held her tongue. Years of experience had taught her to pick her battles wisely when discussing something the two of them didn't agree upon, especially where Tad was involved.

Miranda avoided bringing up "Black Friday" and her conviction that Tad had prior knowledge that gold prices would drop dramatically on that day in particular. Perhaps his advice to sell gold had been a coincidence, but Miranda could never shake the feeling that Tad had deliberately set out to discredit Gilbert, again.

As she stood enjoying her husband's protective arms around her, Miranda recalled a rare evening at Tad and Constance's home. They'd been unable to avoid the occasion, as it was the celebration of the anniversary of the founding of Fairfax. With her great-grandfather having been one of the original settlers, it was expected that she would, of course, attend.

Returning home from the party, Gilbert had mentioned that he had overheard Mr. Hildebrandt—Constance's father and Tad speaking about a tip Tad had received from a friend in New York. According to Gilbert, Tad had revealed that gold prices would soar the following Friday.

After Miranda and Gilbert had discussed selling their gold to reinvest their earnings into a company Gilbert felt more at ease with, Gilbert had arranged with his broker to sell on Friday September 24, 1869. The precise day he had overheard Tad speaking of with Mr. Hildebrandt.

Fortunately, for Gilbert, his gold had sold at $160 an ounce, minutes before the market crashed to $133, providing Gilbert with a substantial gain. While the rest of the country dove into a depression caused by the price of gold dropping dramatically within fifteen minutes, the O'Flaherty's earnings multiplied and multiplied yet again, when Gilbert reinvested their earnings in Amour and Company. Amour, a plant in the Chicago Union stockyards, proposed using ice year-round to keep perishables from spoiling during rail transport, rather than continuing to use the old method of curing meat with salt. Recalling Gilbert's years working at an ice company in New York, Miranda had readily agreed to allow her husband to invest her inheritance however, he wished.

Although selling the gold had been a very fortunate move, Miranda suspected that Tad had deliberately allowed himself to be overheard that night, hoping that Gilbert would act on his tip. At the time, she could never fully understand what Tad's motive was, or why he would help a man he despised, secure more wealth. However, this past January, following the sudden death of Erie Railroad owner James Fisk, Miranda came to understand that Tad had not planned for Gilbert to profit, but actually intended for him lose a fortune; perhaps drive she and Gilbert into financial ruin, even.

She listened intently as the rumors unfolded regarding Fisk and his partner, Jay Gould. It was said that the two railroad tycoons were responsible for causing the market to crash following their run on gold in September of '69, with the aid of President Grant's brother-in-law, Abel Corbin. Knowing that the Honeycut's, Tad in particular, had ties with Fisk and Gould, Miranda viewed this as more than coincidental. Yet, she had no proof that Tad, again, had tried to destroy Gilbert. Rather than bring her suspicions out into the open, which would have only resulted in more bitterness between Gilbert and Tad, Miranda repeatedly tried to tell her husband that luck was an important element in any undertaking.

Unfortunately, Gilbert maintained that she was wasting her breath speaking of such things to a man that didn't have the education to understand that kind of logic. All the while, he was continuing to educate himself by reading throughout the day.

Miranda watched in silence as her husband, now an accomplished reader, pushed himself daily, to become well-advised on a number of subjects. She knew his motivation originally had been to prove he was worthy of being with her; she recalled how Gilbert had detested that Tad had read to her while they had been courting back in New York, when he, Gilbert O'Flaherty, couldn't read nor write.

Although she had tried to reassure Gilbert there was no need for him to push himself so hard, loving him for the man he was, Gilbert continued his quest. Of late, Miranda found herself wondering if Gilbert had surmised on his own that Tad had duped him into selling on "Black Friday" as well, giving him yet another reason for becoming a learned man.

Whatever the reasoning behind Gilbert's thirst for knowledge, Miranda took great pleasure in seeing how her husband applied his newfound education to their family life. Following the evening meal, it was customary for all four children to gather around Gilbert, usually with Suzanne on his lap, as he read great works of literature to them, while Miranda worked on her needlepoint. Even though the children did not understand fully what their father was reading, never had Miranda felt such peace and happiness as when she watched her children look up at their father with such admiration.

Yet recently, despite the contentment she felt most of her day, she found herself periodically, for no apparent reason, suddenly feeling anxious, as if her happiness was about to end. Even in her dreams, she found herself increasingly agitated by nightmares that Tad was lurking in the shadows, ready to strike again. Although her nightmares varied in content, the result was always the same. She would hear her mother crying, unable to find her and then coming out of nowhere was Tad, hell-bent on making sure that if he could not have her, then no one would. This resulted in Miranda sleeping less every day, too frightened to witness her demise by the hands of the man she despised.

Compounded by having to face the heart-wrenching decision of either to close down the school her father had founded, or rebuild Glenbrook according to the guidelines set forth by Reconstruction requirements for private learning institutions, Miranda was consumed with worry. Although she understood the necessity of the guidelines, which prevented anyone from opening a building and calling it a school, the decision to either close Glenbrook or comply with the new government rules was a difficult one for Miranda to make. Her father, Lucas Brown, she often thought, was probably rolling over in his grave at the thought of the government telling him what he could or could not do with his own property.

After an exhausting search to find an architect willing to keep the majority of Glenbrook intact rather than tear down and rebuild, Miranda then had to get her plans approved. Thankfully, Joshua pulled in some favors and helped push her request through government channels, eliminating the anticipated years of bureaucratic delays that had been foretold to her by Verus Wiley, Fairfax's newspaper editor and trusted family friend.

"What ya thinkin' about, Mandy girl?"

Glancing up at her husband with a smile, she said, "How good it was of Joshua to help us out like that."

"Aye. I like him and Elise very much. If you'd like, we could make a trip up north to see them and Alfred over the holidays."

"Hmm, as lovely as that sounds, now that they're going to be living with Alfred, do you think that's such a good idea?"

"Miranda, we can't be living our lives in fear we might run into that man. We manage nicely to avoid him here in Fairfax most of the year, and I'll be damned if..."

"Darling," Miranda interrupted Gilbert. Although the possibility of running into Alfred's son Tad was, indeed, the primary reason Miranda hesitated, she offered her husband a different explanation. "I was thinking it would be too much a strain on Alfred, with nine children running around."

Gilbert's tone softened and he calmly said, "Forgive me lass, for jumping to the wrong conclusion. Perhaps Joshua would be good enough to open up their home since it will be vacant, and we can stay there instead. Being around friends will do you some good, especially around the holidays. And with any luck, perhaps it will snow and we can bundle up the children and take a drive through Central Park."

Thinking of no valid reason to refuse that would appease Gilbert without alerting him of her real reasons for hesitating, she shook her head and smiled. "That sounds perfect, darling. I'll wire Elise in the morning."

"Good. I honestly think the scenery will do you some good. You look so thin lately."

"I do? Why, I was just thinking how fortunate I was to have kept my girlish figure after giving birth to four children."

"Lass, you're thinner now than when we first met. Not that I'm complaining mind you, but I'd like a little more meat on them bones of yours so you don't blow away on me."

"Not to worry, I'm not going anywhere, Mr. O'Flaherty."

"You'd better not, Mrs. O'Flaherty. I can't make it without my Mandy girl."

Turning around to face him, she gazed lovingly up at him and brushed her slender fingers through his thick hair. "Oh Gilbert, we've come so far haven't we? Have I told you lately just how happy you've made me?"

Taking her hand in his, he tenderly kissed the tips of her fingers and huskily whispered, "When you look at me, just as you did that first night you became mine, I know my Mandy girl."

His mouth came crushing down on hers and just as it was that first night, Miranda eagerly returned his affection, kissing him passionately.

Seeing Miranda and Gilbert in each other's arms, Bessie sheepishly cleared her throat. "Excuse me, Miz Miranda but the chilrens waitin' at the table for you and their papa."

Pulling slightly away from Gilbert, Miranda smiled over at the elderly woman who had been with her family since Miranda's mother was a child. Since the war and the end of slavery, Bessie had been not only their hired servant, but also a beloved member of the O'Flaherty family.

"Thank you kindly Bessie, but you didn't have to come look for us, that's what we have Trudy and Sissy for."

"It weren't no trouble at all Miz Miranda. Needed to walk a bit anyway; my rheumatoid's a might cantankerous tonight."

Gilbert went over to the heavyset woman, offering her his hand. "Why not come sit out here for a spell Bessie, and I'll have Trudy bring you a plate."

"Aw, Massa Gilbert, you don't need to be fussin' over me like that."

"Oh, but I do. I promised Chester when he passed that I'd take good care of his Bessie and I never break a promise."

Miranda watched silently as Gilbert tenderly helped Bessie to a seat beside the window, and then dragged over a table, placing it in front of her so she could eat in comfort.

"How's that, Bessie?"

"Mighty fine, Massa. Mighty fine, indeed."

Nodding, Gilbert looked at Miranda who joined her husband, and they entered the dining room where their four children sat waiting patiently for their dinner. Seeing their parents, all four of them smiled brightly, calling out their greetings.

"Evening, Papa."

"Evening, Mama."

Just as every night, Miranda and Gilbert walked around the table and individually greeted each with a kiss, asking how their day had been. Lucas, the only one old enough for school, would speak of what he had learned, while the other three told of their adventures with their nanny. Even Joseph, the youngest at age three, would speak of his day playing with his marbles or wooden paddle and ball, while Miranda and Gilbert listened intently, giving each child special attention, never making them feel unloved or unnoticed as Miranda had felt as a child. Once satisfied that all was well with his children, Gilbert would help Miranda to her seat. After taking his place at the head of the table, he would then nod for dinner to be served.

Gazing at the family she and Gilbert had created, Miranda tried to recall when this particular ritual had begun. Unable to remember the actual first time Gilbert delayed dinner to inquire about the children's day, she knew it had stemmed from her expressing to him that as a child, she dreaded meals with her parents the most, always feeling left out, unnoticed, and especially unloved.

Just as he tried to please Miranda over the years in other ways, Gilbert subtly, without prompting, also tried to erase the pain of her youth and bring joy to their children's lives in the process. As she glanced over at him, directing the servant to tend to Bessie, her heart overflowed with love for the man she had married—a man of great contradictions.

To everyone outside his family and circle of trusted friends, Gilbert appeared to be a cold and untrusting man with an unyielding temper. However, to those he cared for, he was tender and compassionate.

Hearing him announce that the family would be going to New York on a train, the children erupted with enthusiasm. Unlike her childhood memories where children were to be seen and not heard at the dinner table, Gilbert encouraged conversation amongst his family, claiming this was their special time together. Wondering if this was a family tradition, he had brought with him from Ireland, she smiled, glancing over at their oldest son Lucas, as he asked his father a question.

"Da, is New York by England? We're still going there too, ain't we?"

"Aren't we," Gilbert said, correcting his son's language, determined that his children would be learned persons who spoke proper English. "New York is far away from England. Two different countries, son."

Catherine, looking confused, asked her father, "Will we like New York, Papa?"

"Aye, lass. New York is a fine place. Your Mamma and I met there. Don't you remember me telling you about the big park and all the people that live up there? Aunt Elise lives there and you like her don't you, Katie?"

Their oldest daughter looked at her mother with a frown. "Mama, can I bring Lucy with me? And do I have to share her with Sarah Tess? She's so bossy."

"Catherine, be nice. Sarah Tess is a lovely little girl who is headstrong is all," Miranda softly scolded her daughter. "And yes, you can bring your doll to the Honeycut's, if you promise to share."

"Hmm…then I'll bring another dolly. Lucy doesn't like to play with strangers."

Suzanne taking a bite of her food, and hearing what her mother and sister were speaking about boldly spoke out. "Hush up Katie; it's you who don't like strangers!" Turning to her mother, she asked, "Mama, why did you say the Honeycut's? Isn't that the man we saw in town today who said you weren't very social for being practicably related?"

Without looking at Gilbert, Miranda knew he was staring at her. "Suzanne, not 'practicably;' practically. And yes, the man we saw in town this afternoon does have the same name as where we are going to visit Aunt Elise. That man is Aunt Elise's half-brother."

"So you saw Tad this afternoon?" Gilbert asked.

From his tone it was clear, even to the children, that he was angry, and they glanced down at their plates; except for Catherine, who was still obviously upset by her younger sister's comment. Defiantly, she said, glaring at Suzanne, "See, Mama don't like strangers either. That's why she wouldn't speak to him."

Miranda sheepishly looked over at Gilbert and said, "Yes, the girls and I ran into Constance and Tad at the General Store."

Suzanne, unwilling to let her sister get the upper hand, snapped, "See, that man isn't a stranger. Mama just don't like him is all or she would have been more friendlier." Turning her attention to her mother, she said, "Why don't you like Aunt Elise's stepbrother? And what's a stepbrother?"

It was clear that Gilbert was amused by his daughter's questions, even though he tried to conceal it. "Mandy girl, aren't you going to answer Peanut?"

Taking in a deep breath, noting that Gilbert had left it up to her to explain such a peculiar situation, Miranda smiled patiently at her daughter. "My, but aren't you the curious one tonight, Suzanne. A stepbrother is…let me see how I can explain. A long time ago, Grandma Sarah's husband died when Aunt Elise was just a baby. Then several years later, when Aunt Elise was a grown up girl, Grandma Sarah met Grandpa Michael and they fell in love and got married. Grandpa Michael had a son, Tad, who is that man we saw today. So that makes Tad Honeycut your Aunt Elise's stepbrother. Understand?"

The little red-haired girl thought pensively for a while, then asked, "Does that mean we should call that man Uncle Tad, like we call Aunt Elise, 'Auntie Elise'?"

"No!" Gilbert and Miranda said simultaneously.

Suzanne glanced quickly at her parents, obviously confused and fearful that she had said something to anger them. Meekly, she asked, "Papa, are you angry with me? Did I say something wrong?"

"No. Da could never get angry with his little peanut," Gilbert soothingly said, pasting a big grin to his lips as he looked around the table. "So children, aren't you going to ask when we're going on the train? Lucas and Joey, if you boy's like, maybe we could get you hats like the conductor or engineer wear?"

At once, the mood changed around the table as the children fired their concerns at Gilbert.

"Da, when are we to go?"

"Can we ride a train?"

"Where is New York?"

"Will I like it there, Da?"

As Gilbert answered his children's questions, only Miranda saw the look in his eyes as he briefly glanced in her direction. His eyes let her know that the discussion about her running into Tad wasn't over. Dreading the conversation that she knew would come later in the privacy of their bedroom, Miranda suddenly lost what little appetite she had. She put down her fork, having eaten only a few bites of her pot roast, and listened as her family spoke of snow in New York.

~

Honeycut Mansion
December 28*th*, 1872

Riding to the train station to meet the O'Flaherty's were Sarah, Michael and Alfred on one seat; and facing them on the other sat Joshua and Elise. Adjusting her lap-throw tightly around her, Elise said absentmindedly, "I do hope the children won't be too cold here in New York and come down with something to spoil their trip. That's all Miranda will need, tending to a bunch of sick children."

"Nonsense!" Alfred spoke sternly. "Children have a way of adjusting to their climate far better than adults do, it would appear."

Looking up, Elise smiled lovingly at her grandfather. "Point taken, Grandfather. I'm just anxious, is all. With good reason, I might add. This is the first time that Miranda and Gilbert have made the trip to New York; and wouldn't you know it, Tad and Constance had to be here, too."

Clearing his throat, Michael raised his brow. "Elise, are you implying you're not enthusiastic that your brother has come to be with his family during the holidays?"

Blushing, Elise said sheepishly, "Oh Michael, that didn't come out right, did it? You know how pleased I am that you and Tad are able to spend some time together. It's just, I can't believe that after all these years the two of them finally make a trip up north and it's at the same time, no less. Mama, you understand, don't you?"

"I do understand darling. I'm just surprised we haven't had a similar situation arise these past six years. It is rather ironic though, that both couples would come to New York at the same time, don't you think? Especially since they reside in the same small community and manage to avoid being around one another."

Alfred glanced over at Michael. "Ironic indeed, considering Tad and Constance made the trip at the last moment."

"Father, as I told you, Tad thought a change of scenery would do Constance some good since she lost another child. That was why they came unexpectedly. Believe me, them coming when Miranda and Gilbert are here is mere coincidence. You saw how surprised Constance was, hearing the O'Flaherty's were on their way as well."

Raising his brow, Alfred said, "Yes, she was surprised, wasn't she? Such a pity the two of them are having such a hard time starting a family. And to lose another baby in such a way...." Shaking his head sadly, he added, "What possessed that young woman to go riding when she was in the family way, anyway?"

"Grandfather, Constance has always been an accomplished rider and I'm sure she didn't think anything could happen to the baby. It was just a tragic accident that the strap gave way, and she fell. Accidents happen; don't you remember when I fell down the stairs when I was carrying the twins?"

"Let's not bring that up," Joshua said, gravely shaking his head. "That was the scariest time of my life. To think I could have lost you and the twins.... Hell, it still frightens me when I think of it, and I can tell you, I don't frighten easily."

Elise smiled lovingly at her husband, and they all sat silently for the remainder of the trip, each of them deep in their own thoughts.

As Sarah glanced between Elise and her husband, she recalled the weeks that followed Elise's accident and how distraught Joshua had been. He was definitely a man in pain, anguishing over his wife and unborn children; so unlike Tad's reaction, which had been distant. Although he had spoken the appropriate words, Sarah could not detect any true grief in his tone or in his eyes as he spoke his word of insincere sorrow. What was even more alarming to her was the way Tad and Constance interacted with each other. Never once had she detected any depth of tenderness between Constance and Tad as was obvious between Elise and Joshua.

From the moment she had heard they were courting, Sarah wondered if her stepson was actually in love with Constance or had he found a way to remain conveniently near Miranda. Even at the elaborate wedding that the Hildebrandt's had given their daughter, Sarah couldn't help but notice the absence of bliss between the bride and the groom.

Elise, never being one to shy away from speaking her mind, and able to read her mother's thoughts by the expression on her face, wasn't surprised that Sarah purposely gazed out the window, avoiding Elise. *Fine Mama, try to pretend that all is well, but you feel the same way about Tad and Constance being here, as I do.* Reluctantly, Elise followed her mother's lead and spoke not a word as her mind re-examined the countless conversations she and Sarah had shared regarding Tad and Constance.

From the onset of discovering that Tad was courting Constance, Elise made no attempt to conceal her displease and mistrust of Tad's motives. She was convinced he was merely trying to taunt the O'Flaherty's out of revenge, because Miranda had chosen Gilbert over him. With Constance having lost the love of her life, Thomas Hastings, and frightened she would end up a spinster, out of sheer desperation she had married Tad. After all, what alternative did she have? As Elise pointed out on numerous occasions, having Tad Honeycut arrive in Fairfax must have been viewed as a blessing by the Hildebrandt's. He was handsomely rewarded by James Hildebrandt, who opened a law office for his son-in-law. Using his connections, he had persuaded several of his friends to transfer their business to Tad's firm.

After all, it wasn't every day that an eligible, well-bred, educated bachelor, who just happened to be the grandson of a wealthy business tycoon, came to town. And since he was the son of Michael Honeycut, a trusted friend of the community, Tad wasn't viewed as an outsider trying to worm his way into the close-knit community. Instead, welcoming him into the inner circle of their small-town society seemed the natural thing to do.

The only fly in the ointment to this perfect union, was Constance. From the onset of their courtship Elise, who knew her childhood friend quite well, saw that Constance held no genuine love for or interest in, Tad Honeycut. To Constance's credit, she never tried to pretend there was, at least not to Elise. Instead, she would speak of their new home, or ask about Elise's growing family when they were alone.

Not wanting to cause any problems between her and Michael, Elise never pressed Constance on why she would settle for a man she obviously didn't love, surmising that Constance probably felt she didn't have any other recourse but to do as her father wished. Even if for no other reason than to save face in the community.

Saddened for her friend, Elise looked to her mother for comforting words, and seeing the same sadness in Sarah's eyes as she felt in her own heart, Elise said, "My goodness Mama, you look so sad. Is something wrong?"

Sarah, engrossed in her own thoughts about Tad and Constance, and Miranda and Gilbert, didn't realize that Elise had spoken to her. Feeling a gentle nudge from Michael, she turned and smiled.

"Elise just asked if you were all right. Are you, darling?"

"Yes, of course. I was just thinking we really ought to make this a special time for Miranda, despite the awkwardness of Tad being here. We all have the luxury of having one another, but who does Miranda have? Or for that matter, Gilbert? Besides one another? And no matter how full and happy a life they have built together, having a family, even if we are an extended one, is special too."

Alfred, clearing his throat, nodded his head in agreement. "Here, here daughter. I couldn't agree with you more. What can I do to assure their visit will be memorable?"

For the remainder of the ride, the five of them put their heads together, eventually deriving a tentative plan to keep their house guests sufficiently amused, while keeping them separated as much as possible.

~

Following dinner, with Tad and Constance at the opera with Sarah and Michael, and Gilbert chatting with Joshua and Alfred in the study, Miranda and Elise went to retrieve some of her old art supplies from the basement. As they entered the familiar dwelling that had once housed Gilbert as he convalesced after being run down in Central Park, Miranda was flooded with the memories. Especially by memories of the night, she and Gilbert had declared their love for one another.

Never before having fully explained how Gilbert and she had met, and the circumstances that led to them running off together in secrecy, Miranda finally shared with Elise every event as it had unfolded. Enthralled by Miranda's tale, Elise asked, "So there you were, living a lie, pretending to still be interested in Tad's advancement's, all the while arranging to travel with Gilbert to San Francisco! Without Gilbert even knowing your plans, nor declaring his love for you? Oh my goodness Miranda, I had no idea how brave you were—please, go on."

Shaking her head, Miranda said with a smile, "Trust me, I didn't feel very brave. As a matter of fact, I recall asking myself several times 'what would Elise do?'."

Obviously pleased by her friend's comment, Elise smiled. "What a kind thing for you to say. But please; tell me what happened next before the children need something and they come in search of us."

Well, that evening following dinner, I came down here just as I always did after everyone retired. Just as we did most every night, Gilbert and I ended up having heated words. Hearing something upstairs, and afraid that Gilbert would be discovered, we stood over there...." Miranda paused, pointing to where she and Gilbert had stood, that night long ago."It was there that Gilbert kissed me for the first time."

"Oh my, that must have been some kiss considering you ran off with him."

"It was, but there's more. You see, Gilbert stopped himself and said we weren't suited for one another, and I should leave."

"What?"

"Oh yes. You see, Gilbert felt he was unworthy of me; that I should be with a learned man who could give me a life I was more accustomed to."

"How unselfish and chivalrous of him," exclaimed Elise.

"It was. However, when you desperately need to know that you are loved, especially having made the decision to cast aside my birthright, family and friends to be with a man, an encouraging word would have been welcoming. To make matters worse, as I passed by Alfred's study and seeing that he was up, my heart leapt in fear. After Alfred invited me in for a chat, it became clear to me that somehow Alfred had heard our spat."

"Oh no!"

Shaking her head, Miranda continued. "Oh yes. Despite him trying to be subtle, Alfred even called me the pet name Gilbert used."

As shocked as Elise was, she giggled. "Don't you just love Grandfather? He's so crafty and devious at times."

"He is indeed, but that night I can assure you I did not find his slyness the least bit amusing. Not only did I fear that he would expose Gilbert, I was more ashamed that I had done such a thing without his permission. After being reassured that he had known Gilbert was there right from the onset, knowing how Tad had deliberately tried to kill Gilbert, Alfred and I had words. In a heat of anger I told him despite what he thought, I was going to San Francisco to be with Gilbert."

"Oh you didn't. Knowing Grandfather, that must have not set well with him."

"Actually, Alfred was wonderful. Of course, he tried to discourage me, pointing out the obvious, like what if Gilbert didn't love me. What would I do alone in a city thousands of miles from friends and family? After explaining I loved Gilbert enough to take such a risk, I went upstairs, distraught, and even starting to doubt myself. Was it really Gilbert I loved or was I attracted to him since he was everything my father and society loathed?"

"You poor dear," Elise said sympathetically. "So what happened next?"

"As I entered my room, crying, there sat Montgomery."

Shocked, Elise asked, "Montgomery? In your bedchamber? Whatever for?"

"I had arranged for him to meet me there after I had seen Gilbert that night, for the sole intention of learning more about a passageway that he had spoken of that led to each of the rooms on the second floor and connected to the kitchen and here in the root cellar."

"What passageway? Do you mean the dumbwaiter?"

Nodding, Miranda said, "Yes. You see, all the time I had lived there I never knew it existed. Which, as it turns out, was how Tad had access into my room at night, without me knowing."

Elise gasped. "Oh you can't be serious? How unscrupulous! Go on, what happened next?"

"Let's see, well, Montgomery sent me down to the root cellar using the dumbwaiter and when I got down here, much to my surprise and horror, I heard Alfred and Gilbert talking."

Putting her hands to her face, Elise exclaimed, "Grandfather came down here? Oh my goodness, what happened next? The suspense is killing me."

Smiling at how dramatic Elise was, Miranda continued. "Alfred had apparently offered Gilbert a job in San Francisco and proposed that he should marry me."

Elise's eyes widened and her jaw dropped. "Alfred never ceases to amaze me. How did Gilbert react to his suggestion?"

"Nothing was said since the two of them had seen me. Alfred, politely excused himself allowing Gilbert and me to talk things over. And at first, our conversation was anything but pleasant given the fact that Gilbert assumed I had sent Alfred down here. So again the two of us had words. And given the fact I was in a state of shock, finding out that Tad had been watching me while I slept in my locked room for years, but the man I loved was speaking to Alfred regarding such personal matters, no less, compounded with the strain of harboring Gilbert for all those months...well, I was beside myself."

"'Beside yourself' would be an understatement. Why, I can tell you I would have been plum loco about then."

Smiling at how Elise could always cut right to the heart of the matter, Miranda nodded in agreement. "I was. Without thinking, I accused Gilbert of caring more about his injured pride than for me, who had been fiendishly watched by Tad in my sleep. Gilbert got so angry I thought he was going to burst, needing to know what I was talking about. Then, after finding out Tad had seen me in my nightdress, he calmly walked away, unwilling to discuss anything with me any further; acting almost as if I was soiled or something. Well, I was outraged! I was not going to be dismissed like that, and even as he began to undress, I stood my ground and Gilbert sat right here as a matter-of-fact, with his head in his hands refusing to speak with me."

"So what did you do?"

"Elise, it was so strange, all I kept thinking was Gilbert and Tad viewed me as nothing more than a prize to satisfy their egos and it made me angrier than I had ever been in my life. Then Mama's voice kept ringing in my ears, telling me to 'be a good girl, do what you're told'. As if claiming my independence, I refused. Before I even realized what I was doing, I decided that if it meant more to Gilbert that Tad had seen me in my nightgown, then I'd give him something to even the score. So I undressed, right down to my petticoats."

"Miranda! I can't believe it. That's something I would do, but never you. What can I say, other than I'm shocked!"

"Apparently, so was Gilbert. You should have seen him when he looked up and saw me standing defiantly in my under garments, demanding to know if the score was even. Or if he was ahead, since I willingly undressed for him."

Giggling, Elise said, "I can only imagine. So, what happened next? Did you and him…I mean…you don't have to tell me if you don't want to."

"No, I want you to know. Gilbert declared his love for me, and then promptly told me to get dressed and go back upstairs to the life where I belonged. Explaining if I did not, he'd be doing a lot more than just watching me as Tad had. There we stood and I couldn't leave. I didn't want to and I told him that I *was* where I belonged. Knowing what I meant, he took me in his arms and told me that after that night, in the eyes of God we would be one. Tenderly he carried me to his bed and I did become his. Without fear or reservation. And although we celebrate our anniversary on the date that Benjamin performed our wedding nuptials, in my heart I think of that night when we began our lives together here in this dungeon—as he used to call it—as our true wedding night."

"Oh Miranda, I don't know what to say other than thank you so much for sharing with me just how special yours and Gilbert's love was."

"*Is*, Elise. From that night to this day, never once have I regretted, not even for a minute, choosing Gilbert. He has made me happier than I had ever dreamt possible. To be loved with such intensity by one so tender and caring, I still find amazing. Do you know that every day we take a walk together before dinner, then afterward, before dinner can be served, we walk around the table, kiss our children, and hear the news of their day? This family ritual began after Gilbert found out, how as a child, I dreaded having dinner with Mama and Papa, never knowing when they were going to begin fussing with one another and always feeling unloved and in the way. So not only has he healed that painful memory of mine, but has also set a strong foundation for our children, leaving no doubt in their minds as too how much they are loved."

"Oh Miranda, no wonder your father said what he did, then."

Unsure what Elise meant Miranda asked, "I don't follow."

"When Michael told us how Gilbert had brought little Lucas to him before he died, I distinctly remember Michael saying that when your father heard Gilbert announce his grandson's name, Lucas said, 'Thank you, Gilbert for naming him after me. You're a good man, better than I deserve. You make damn sure he grows up to be like the fine man his father is and not like his namesake, hear ?'"

Stunned, Miranda wide-eyed, said, "Papa said that? Why, Gilbert never said a word...."

"Well, after everything I've heard tonight, it doesn't surprise me, dear friend. Your husband is too fine a man to need praise. If I haven't told you lately, I'm sure glad you married such a fine and wonderful man."

As the women continued sharing intimate stories of their lives, in the shadows, hidden from view, stood Tad, clenching his fists; barely able to control the rage he felt. *You'll pay dearly for choosing that lowlife Irishman over me, you whore!*

~ Three ~

Hearing the front door open, Alfred, who had been talking in private to Joshua regarding information that Gilbert had shared with them about the tip he had overheard from Tad concerning "Black Friday", looked up. "Who could that be?"

Seeing Michael and Sarah entering the parlor, Alfred said, "What a surprise. I thought you were going to the opera tonight."

"So did we, Father. Unfortunately, Constance wasn't up to it so we'll have to go another night."

Frowning, Alfred looked suspiciously between his son and Sarah. "I see, and where are Constance and Tad now, Michael?"

"Following dinner, Constance wasn't feeling well so she retired early, and once we were certain she was resting, Sarah and I came over here to gather my wayward son. However, from your surprise, I gather Tad's not here."

"No, he's not here...." Alfred paused, obviously unnerved by the latest development and glanced at Joshua. "Son, we had better find Elise and Miranda."

Gilbert, entering the parlor, said, "Sir, they're in the basement reminiscing."

Not asking Gilbert how he knew, surmising he had overheard the two women while reading in the study, Alfred smiled and said, "Well I'll send down a servant then."

"No need," Gilbert interrupted calmly. "I've sent Montgomery to fetch them. With it getting so late, perhaps it would be best if we called it a night, sir."

Hearing the soft chattering of Elise and Miranda coming from the hall, Alfred glanced at Sarah, who up until then hadn't said a word. "Daughter, after Elise and Joshua see that our guests are well settled for the night, perhaps you'd be so kind as to help me plan a special menu honoring Gilbert and his family."

Knowing the arrangements had been planned the day they received the wire that the O'Flahertys were visiting, Sarah nodded and smiled. "Why certainly, Father Honeycut. I'd be delighted."

Seeing the puzzled look on Elise's face as she walked in, obviously having heard the comments exchanged between her mother and grandfather, Joshua spoke quickly, to prevent Elise from saying anything. "What do you have there?"

"Some old paint supplies of Miranda's that she wanted to take back home."

Seeing a canvas already painted, Gilbert smiled at Miranda remembering it well. "Ah, an original from the artist. We'll have to display it proudly over the mantel."

Blushing, Miranda said, "Oh Gilbert, surely you jest."

As they made small talk, it was clear by the look on Elise's face that she suspected something was wrong, but rather than alarm Miranda and Gilbert, she said nothing. Anxious to get the O'Flaherty's settled in for the night, Elise suggested they attend to the children before traveling in the bitterly cold night air.

Within the half-hour, Elise and Joshua escorted the O'Flaherty children to the coach, without Montgomery, who Alfred had asked to remain behind to get reacquainted. As Gilbert left, although he appeared jovial and in good spirits, from the look in his eyes it was evident that he was equally concerned about Tad's whereabouts.

"I'll have Montgomery at Joshua's home within the hour, lad," Alfred said, as he shook Gilbert's hand.

"Aye. Thank you, sir."

Seeing the carriage leave, Alfred turned around and looked at the others. "Let's have us a nightcap, shall we? In my study." Nodding to Jerome, he added, "Have Matilda get the children ready for bed. I'll serve my guests."

Obediently the butler turned and climbed the stairs leading to second floor, as Alfred watched Sarah and Michael head toward the study. Pulling Montgomery to the side he said, "Discreetly check the house and the grounds. I have reason to believe my grandson is on the premises. Find him, but don't let him know we're on to him."

"Yes, sir."

Patting his former trusted employee on the back, Alfred said, "Good man."

Entering the office, Michael said, "Father, I'm sure there's a reasonable explanation...."

"Michael, sit down," Alfred cut him off sternly, closing the door behind him. "Son, I know that you probably think I'm overreacting, and that what happened six years ago is in the past. But I can assure you; Tad and Constance's sudden trip was not coincidental. And I believe Tad is in serious trouble, perhaps even requiring mental care." Reaching into his pocket, he pulled out a letter. "Read this. It's a letter from James Hildebrandt. A rather disturbing letter I might add, which I received this very afternoon following the O'Flaherty's arrival."

Suspiciously, Michael took the letter from his father and began reading it. Clearly, by the look on Michel's face, he was agitated by the contents. Finishing it, Michael folded the letter and glared at his father as he returned it.

"Clearly it is not my son who is in need of medical attention, but Hildebrandt, the old coot, for implying such preposterous accusations against Tad. Surely you can't believe that Tad would want to harm his own wife?"

Hearing Michael's last comment, Sarah gasped and Alfred looked over at her sympathetically. "My dear, forgive me if what I'm about to say is upsetting to you.

"According to Hildebrandt, he has reason to believe Constance's accident was deliberate. Without accusing him out right of course, he has suggested that Tad, being less than enchanted with his wife's condition, showed no remorse. In addition, Hildebrandt has asked that I take full responsibility for his daughter's welfare, since it was at Tad's insistence at the last minute to take this vacation when his wife was clearly not up for traveling."

"Oh dear. Why do you suppose James would write such a letter?"

"Because he's a damned fool!" Michael snapped. "How dare he imply Tad would not care for Constance properly."

Without raising his voice, he looked gravely over at his son. "Michael, you said yourself that Constance was not well enough to attend the opera tonight. Where is Tad? Wouldn't you think he would be by her side, so soon after losing a third child?"

Before Michael could respond, Montgomery entered the study after a brief knock. "Sir, may I have a word with you in private."

"That won't be necessary, Montgomery. Please come in and tell us what you've discovered."

"Just as you suspected, sir. Mr. Honeycut was indeed here. I spotted him leaving through the servant's quarters."

Clearly shaken by Montgomery's report, pale as if the blood had drained from his face, Michael asked solemnly, "How can you be certain it was my son?"

"I saw him exiting my old living quarters and get into a Hansome cab parked at the end of the road, sir. Tad was in such a hurry, he never even saw me standing by him in the gardens."

Inhaling deeply, Alfred said, "Thank you, Montgomery. Please do me another favor, if you would. When you return to Mr. Carmidy's home, please inform Gilbert precisely what you witnessed this evening and inform...."

Hearing his father's comment, Michael interrupted. "Father, are you certain that is wise? Why alarm him needlessly if Tad was here...."

Ignoring Michael, Alfred continued speaking to Montgomery. "As I was saying, inform Gilbert that I am taking the necessary precautions to ensure Tad has no way of entering my home again without being detected, and that first thing tomorrow morning, the dumbwaiter will be disassembled as well. No one, and I do mean no one, will ever be able to use that device again to violate another's privacy."

"Yes, sir. Am I to assume that Miss Miranda is to know nothing of this?"

"That is correct. If Gilbert chooses to speak of this matter with his wife, that is entirely up to him, but she'll hear nothing of this matter from us. Please relay my sentiments on that as well. Oh, and one last thing Montgomery, please extend an invitation for Gilbert to join me for an early breakfast. I trust, Montgomery, you won't leave Miranda and the children alone while he meets with me."

"Oh that's ridiculous, Father," Michael scoffed.

Again ignoring Michael's comment, Alfred said, "I'll have a driver pick Mr. O'Flaherty up at 7:30."

"Yes, sir. If there's nothing else then, I'll make my leave."

Walking him to the door, Alfred shook his former employee's hand. "Thank you again, Montgomery. I'm indebted to you."

Shaking Alfred's hand vigorously, Montgomery said proudly, "Think nothing of it, sir. You know how I feel about Miss Miranda."

Nodding his head, Alfred said, "A feeling that we both share, old friend. Tomorrow afternoon, when Gilbert and I take the children to the park, why don't you come along? Tad and Joshua will be busy at the law firm, and Elise and Miranda are planning a shopping trip. I'm sure Michael won't mind escorting them, will you son?"

Having no alternative but to agree, Michael nodded. "Fine, Father. As you wish."

Extending her hand to Michael's arm, Sarah stopped when he turned and said sternly, "I'm not a child who needs consoling, Sarah."

Hurt, she quickly rested her hand in her lap and watched as Alfred returned, having said his good-bye to Montgomery.

"No, you're not Michael; and neither is Tad," Alfred said sternly as he reentered the room. "You seem to forget I love him, too. However, I am not blinded by his faults any longer. Six years ago, he nearly killed an innocent man out of his desire to get what he thought he deserved. I'll be damned if I'm going to give him another opportunity, right under my own nose!"

"Father, I know perfectly well what my son did. And he paid the ultimate price for his mistakes—losing the one thing he valued most in this world. But he's moved on. He has a wife and a blossoming career, with well-respected clients. Do you think he would risk everything for a past obsession?"

Seeing his father ready to object, Michael took a new approach and hastily added, "Father, I don't want to argue with you. I know what my son is capable of. *Was* capable of. All I'm asking is for us, his family, to give him the benefit of the doubt. No matter how suspicious this all looks on the surface, Tad *has* changed. He means no harm to Gilbert or Miranda. For God's sakes, he lives in the same town as them. If he wanted to cause either of them any harm, surely he would have ample opportunity there and not have to come to New York to do something dastardly."

"Michael, don't you think I know that? But what you have failed to take into consideration is that the O'Flahertys are here in New York as our guests and deserve to have a measure of security as well as a pleasant visit. Haven't you noticed how thin Miranda is? Why, I'm sure having Tad living in Fairfax, seeing him wherever she goes or bumping into him socially in such a small town, is in part the reason for her strain. I can't imagine how it must be to have that constant reminder hanging over her head. And if Tad is here for anything other than sinister motives, then why sneak around as he just did? Michael, as hard as this may be to accept, despite what you feel for Tad, you must come to terms that your son came here to New York for the sole purpose of being close to Miranda. You lived in that small town, I'm certain it wouldn't be too difficult to find out what they were planning. For all we know, the telegraph operator told him or little Lucas mentioned it to one of his school chums, and somehow it got back to Tad. However he found out, there is no denying that Tad has no business being here with his wife as weak as she is."

"If I may say something?" Sarah spoke before her husband had a chance to reply.

"Yes, of course," Alfred said as Michael nodded.

"As you know Father Honeycut, I've promised Constance that we'd spend the day together tomorrow, to become reacquainted. I'll see if I can get her to confide in me regarding her marriage, which shouldn't be too difficult, since I've known Constance all her life. However, I must say this beforehand...James and Louise have always been rather protective of Constance, as to be expected since she is their only child. And if her marriage to Tad is not working out, surely you can understand they wouldn't blame Constance, or even take responsibility themselves for arranging such a union. Before you say anything, I know of several marriages that were prearranged, for convenience, and they worked out and eventually couple grew to love one another deeply. However, there are just as many that don't."

"Dearest Sarah, I appreciate your insight on this matter. And I'm sure in part you are right on both points you have made, regarding the Hildebrandts pointing the blame toward Tad, and that arranged marriages are a gamble. Given Tad's history though, tell me why he had to marry a woman and live in the same town where Gilbert and Miranda are trying to make a life for themselves? And more to the point, why did he come here tonight and never alert anyone of his presence? If you can get that information from his wife, in one afternoon, then by God, dear daughter-in-law, you need to go to Washington and see how you can put this nation back on course."

Before Sarah had an opportunity to respond, Joshua returned and opening Alfred's study door, said, "Forgive the interruption, sir. Since you're speaking of Washington, if Gilbert's suspicions regarding Tad prove to be factual, do you realize what could happen to the Honeycut name?"

Michael, hearing Joshua's comment, jerked his head around and said, "That's a rather ominous comment Joshua, especially from you, son. What do you mean?"

Alfred, gesturing for Joshua and Elise to take a seat, said, "Come in please. I've not even had an opportunity to discuss that bit of information we uncovered yet, with everything else that had happened tonight." Looking gravely over at Michael, he said, "Son, when I said earlier that Tad was in trouble, perhaps I should have said, we are all in trouble. It appears Tad, in his quest to destroy his enemy, could bring shame and dishonor down around us all."

"Not to mention financial ruin. Tell me Alfred, did you by chance do any trading on 'Black Friday'?"

"Why yes of course, but not in gold!"

Immediately Joshua and Alfred were besieged with questions as Elise looked over at her mother, who was obviously upset. Judging by the way Sarah avoided looking at Michael, Elise surmised her mother's current state must have something to do with Tad. Knowing firsthand how often they had quarreled over Michael's son, Elise nonchalantly reached over and comfortingly took her mother's hand in hers. No words were needed. Sarah's smile of gratitude as she squeezed her daughter's hand spoke volumes.

For the better part of an hour, the events that had taken place since the O'Flaherty's arrival were discussed with Michael and Sarah barely saying a word. When Michael stood, saying it was getting late and that he wished to see if his wayward son had returned home, Elise noted the tension between him and his father as Alfred asked for a private word with him. Michael did not attempt to conceal his displeasure at such a suggestion, and reluctantly agreed.

Waiting in the parlor for Alfred and Michael to finish their business, while Joshua checked in on the children, Elise leaned close to her mother to be certain they wouldn't be overheard. "Mama, I think I know why Tad came here tonight, sneaking around as he did."

"You do? Then why didn't you say anything?"

"You know men; they wouldn't have listened to a woman. Not really listen."

Nodding her head, recalling Alfred's comment earlier and as well meaning as it had been, she couldn't help but detect the underline sarcasm in his words. "Yes. Even the finest of men have a way of being rather condescending at times."

Sighing, Elise said, "At times? Best not get me started on that subject or I'll go off on a tangent." Pausing to gather her thoughts, she continued, "The thing is this Mama. From the time we all sat around and heard how Miranda had run off with Gilbert, never once do I recall Tad fully appreciating why she had chosen Gilbert rather him. I mean, he was scolded plenty by Alfred and Michael all right, and then as if the matter was resolved, he went on down with Michael to Fairfax as if to forget the whole matter and begin anew. As it turned out, he suffered no real consequences for what he'd done. Then when Lucas persuaded Gilbert and Miranda to settle in Fairfax, not knowing that Tad was there of course, I believe my stepbrother decided right then and there to get back at the both of them. This time though, he would have to do it in such a way that he wouldn't get caught, which is why he tried to ruin Gilbert financially. When that failed, it probably ate at his craw, knowing that Gilbert not only had the woman he wanted, but was a financial success too, in part due to him. Can you imagine the rage this must have caused him? Let's face it Mama, even with him in Fairfax, there would never be a way of him finding out first hand why she had betrayed him as she did, unless he heard it directly from Miranda herself. Knowing that Miranda was visiting her oldest friend and knowing this house as he did, I'm betting he came here to find out the truth once and for all. If Grandfather was right and Tad was hiding in the shadows, then he got himself an ear full."

Putting her hand over her mouth Sarah said, "Oh no, what do you mean?"

"Mama this is strictly in confidence. I mean it Mama, don't you dare even breathe a word of it to Michael."

Nodding her head, Sarah said, "I promise."

Taking in a deep breath and leaning even closer, Elise said in a hushed whisper, "Tonight, when we were retrieving Miranda's art supplies from the cellar, she told me that Gilbert had never showed his true feelings toward her all the while she tended to his wounds. In fact, he kept her at bay. This of course troubled Miranda deeply, feeling he was doing it for her sake, certain that he felt he was not good enough for her. He even arranged to leave New York altogether, without her. That all changed though when Miranda...well let's just say, Miranda convinced him otherwise and gave herself to him, heart and soul, down there in that cellar before they were ever married. And trust me, Miranda held nothing back as she described the events that brought her and Gilbert together."

"Oh no!" Sarah gasped. "Don't get me wrong Elise, I'm not shocked that Miranda and Gilbert...well I am shocked, but what I mean to say is, if Tad overheard...." Sarah's voice trailed off as her eyes widened in fear. "Can you imagine hearing in such intimate detail how the woman he loved had betrayed him not once, but twice? Why, I can't imagine the anger he felt. Feels."

"I know. And given what we know Tad is capable of, I can tell you true Mama, I'm worried sick that this time Tad won't be going after Gilbert, but Miranda instead."

~ Four ~

"Oh Mother Honeycut; thank you so much for being so kind to me today." Constance whimpered through her tears as Sarah consoled the distraught woman. "I just don't know who to turn too anymore or what to do. It's so awful now…I'm so frightened of him. You can't imagine the hate I see in Tad's eyes sometimes. Why it's almost like looking into Thomas's all over again, and you know what happened to him."

"Yes dear, sadly I do. Now try and calm down some so you can tell me what's happened to make you fear Tad so much."

Pulling away from Sarah, Constance blew her nose. "What if he finds out?"

"Sweetheart, I gave you my word. Nothing that you and I speak of today will go outside these four walls. And just as I told you before, I may be Tad's stepmother, but I am also your friend and have been since you were just a babe. Besides Constance, if it's as bad as you are leading me to believe, who would be better able to help you than a member of Tad's own family?"

"That's just it. You can't help Mother Honeycut, no one can. I swear he won't stop until I'm six feet under."

Without showing her surprise and horror at such a comment, Sarah said calmly, "Sweetheart, surely you can't mean that. Try to stay calm and tell me everything, dear."

As Sarah held Constance's hand, the distraught woman began speaking freely. From the beginning of their courtship, Tad had made it no secret he was not interested in Constance romantically. Rather, he made it clear he was still in love with another woman from New York. Constance, understanding how he felt, loving Thomas as she did and knowing they would never be together, found the proposed agreement acceptable. Following their marriage, which had been arranged by her father, Constance had hoped they could comfort one another's broken hearts and in time, even find love. All that changed though, following a town dance where Tad had consumed far more alcohol than normal.

"It was that very night that I lost our first child," Constance whimpered. "And it was Tad's fault."

Not being accusatory, Sarah urged her to continue. "What are you saying, dear? Did Tad harm you?"

Nodding her head, she said, "But it was an accident that time."

"Sweetheart, you're not making any sense. Either it was Tad's fault, or it was an accident. Which one was it, Constance?"

"Both, I suppose. You see, that night he came home very late—drunk. While he was satisfying his manly needs, he called out Miranda's name."

Constance paused and looked at Sarah as if to judge her surprise. Since Sarah was not willing to comment, Constance continued. "You can't imagine my shock, hearing the father of my child call out another woman's name as he was lying on top of me. In my anger and hurt, somehow I managed to get him off me and I started yelling. We made such a fuss that night, I'm surprised half of Fairfax didn't hear. He confessed that it was Miranda he thought of as he made love to me, ever since we were wed, and I slapped him. There he stood, laughing at me, telling me over and over again that it was Miranda he loved and I had better get used to it. As I lunged to hit him again, I fell into the arm of my chair, straight into my abdomen. That night I lost our first child."

"Oh darling, I'm so sorry. So you never knew that Miranda and Tad had a history with one another until that night?" Sarah asked.

"Never. I knew that she had lived with his grandparents of course, but the two of them were so unfriendly when they did see one another, it never occurred to me that Miranda was his lost love. Afterwards, I would watch them whenever they were together. Sarah it was awful—Miranda wouldn't speak to him unless it was impossible for her to avoid, while Tad watched her every move. It was clear to me that Miranda was not the problem in our marriage, that she genuinely loved Gilbert, so I tried desperately to have Tad fall in love with me, to forget Miranda. And for a time, he was kinder to me. Until he found out how much money Gilbert had made from selling that old gold mine of his. The way he acted, you would have thought Tad had lost a fortune, rather than increasing his holdings by selling some of his own gold that day, too."

"Excuse me for interrupting dear; am I to understand that Tad traded gold that day, too?"

"Why yes. He and Papa both did rather nicely for themselves, from what I understand."

Smiling insincerely, Sarah said, "How nice for them both. Go on dear, what happened next?"

"Well, as I said, Tad was in such a foul mood all the time. Nothing I said or did was pleasing to him. Even when he learned we were to have another child, he still was hateful. Becoming increasingly agitated with me, saying the nastiest things when he was liquored up, like; 'How disgusted he was by how fat I was becoming', or that 'he could never love me or my child.' I was devastated. Even after he was sober and I would cry and beg him to stop being so cruel, he never apologized for what he said or tried to make amends. It was as if he didn't care how much he was hurting me. As a last resort, I went to Papa and told him everything, hoping that Papa could make things better between us. Instead, Tad became even uglier and that afternoon after speaking with Papa, I fell down the stairs after one of our arguments."

"Oh Constance no," Sarah whispered, unable to hold back her emotions any longer. "Did Tad push you or did you fall?"

Constance looked at Sarah, tears streaming down her cheeks, her lips quivering, unable to speak.

"Sweetheart, you must tell me," Sarah said, softly coaxing the distraught woman.

"After I yelled, 'No wonder Miranda loved Gilbert as she did' and that he was a better man than Tad could ever be, he...he...pushed me." Sobbing uncontrollably, Sarah reached for her daughter-in-law and they wept softly in each other's arms.

"Oh you poor thing. I'm so sorry that you've had to suffer so much pain, Constance."

"It was partially my fault, Mother Honeycut. I should have never said such a hurtful thing."

Pulling away from her, Sarah cupped Constance's chin in her hand. "Don't you even think such a thing. It most certainly was not your fault. No matter what was said, Tad had no right to ever use violence against you. Have you told anyone of this? Your father or mother?"

Shaking her head she said, "No. After I fell, Tad calmly walked down the stairs and said that if I ever spoke a word of what had happened, he would have me committed to an asylum. Coldly smiling he added, 'There would be nothing my father could do to stop him'. Then he calmly went back to the office and left me lying at the bottom of the stairs, crying. Sometime later, a servant found me and I told everyone that I had tripped on my skirt. With Tad gone, no one, not even Father, suspected Tad had anything to do with my losing our second child."

"Sweetheart, I don't know what to say."

"There's nothing to say. Mama used to always tell me as a child, 'if you make a hard bed, remember that you're the one who has to sleep in it.' Well, that is exactly what I did, all right. I married Tad so others wouldn't think I was an old maid; and now I'm forced to live with the man I thought was refined and educated, but has turned out to someone else entirely."

"Go on dear, what happened next?"

"From there on, Tad never hid his disgust for me while in private. When he needed to have his demands met as a man, he simply took me by force. After a while, I stopped fighting, praying instead that I'd become pregnant so he wouldn't want me that way anymore. You see, I knew how it disgusted him when I was in the family way. At last, my prayers were answered. And as I had predicted, as soon as Tad was told, he no longer visited my bed. What I had not counted on was the hate in his eyes every time he looked at me. It was precisely the same as the night I confessed to Thomas that I was an Abolitionist."

"Oh you poor dear."

"There were advantages so please don't feel sorry for me. For instance, weeks passed and we hardly spoke to one another and when we did, he was civil. In return, I stayed clear of him the best I could, being extra careful never to do or say anything that would provoke him. I was bound and determined to have that baby, thinking at that least I'd have a child to love. Then early one morning in late November before going to the office, Tad said, 'You need to get out and get some exercise, like Miranda did when she was in the family way'. Never had I been more hurt, him comparing me to Miranda even then, when I was carrying his child. Rather than saying anything, I told him I'd take a ride around the grounds if he'd like. Pleased by my response, Tad said he'd get my horse ready and then left for the office. Later that mornin' I fell off my horse and a few days later I lost our third child."

Horrified by what she had just heard, Sarah found it hard to accept that anyone could be such a monster, especially her husband's son. Hesitantly she asked, "Constance, last night when you said you were too ill to attend the opera, was that the truth or was it at Tad's insistence?"

"It's true that Tad said he didn't want to go to the opera. However, I really wasn't in the mood to go. Especially when I found out that Miranda was here in New York. Suddenly it was very clear to me why Tad insisted we come here out of the blue, and I just couldn't bring myself to act like the happy couple for you and his father."

"Well it's no wonder, my dear. What I can't fathom is that a member of our family has endured the hardships that Elise so often speaks of after one of her meetings; telling tales of women who have suffered needlessly at the hands of their husbands. And to think Tad is the one responsible is inconceivable to me. Oh Constance, surely there has to be something I can do, to help you? I can't bring myself to think of you living such a hellish existence with that monster another day, and stand by and do nothing. Please dear; you must allow me to speak with Tad's father on your behalf. Surely between the two of us, we can think of something, without letting Tad know that we are aware what he has done to you."

"No! Please, you mustn't!" Constance begged. "Otherwise, I can't bear to think what he'll do to me. Please Mother Honeycut, you promised."

Becoming hysterical again, Sarah held Constance protectively in her arms, reassuring her that she would keep her word. All the while, Sarah tried to think of a way to inform Michael without actually speaking to him directly. Remembering she had said, 'that nothing they spoke of would leave these four walls', but never having said anything about not telling someone else, Sarah decided that she would speak with Joshua when he dropped Tad off. If Michael just happened to overhear, then she had not actually broken her word.

Knowing the lateness of the hour, and expecting Tad and Joshua home soon, Sarah softly said to Constance, "Dearest, Tad will be back soon. Don't you think it would be wise if we were dressed, so you and he can go to dinner at his grandfathers without looking as if you have been crying all day?"

Nodding her head, she held onto Sarah for a while longer. "Thank you, Mother Honeycut. You don't know how much this helps, not carrying the burden alone."

Kissing Constance's cheek, Sarah said, "Sweetheart, I promise you this, you will never have to face another day alone. I am always here for you. Somehow, between the two of us, we'll figure out how to make Tad stop hurting you."

~

Later that afternoon, after they had changed for dinner, they sat chatting quietly in the parlor. Sarah braced herself, hearing the door open. Glancing over at Constance, she smiled warmly at her then called out to Michael, "Darling, we're in here."

Surprised that Joshua and Tad were with him, she said, "I wasn't expecting to see you two for another half hour or so. What a pleasant surprise."

As Michael approached, Sarah noticed how drawn Michael looked, and knowing it had nothing to do with taking the women shopping, she teased him as he kissed her cheek. "Now don't you try to worm your way out of babysitting tonight. I'll need your help with nine children, husband of mine."

Smiling wearily, Michael said, "Fear not, my dear. A little rest and I'll be as good as new."

Tad, who had kissed Constance's cheek, glanced over at his father. "I half expected you to bring Elise and Miranda back to show Sarah and

Constance all they had found today. How many shops did they drag you to, Father?"

"I lost count son, after the first five or so. My goodness, I had no idea there were so many shops. It's such a shame you couldn't join us, Constance."

Smiling politely at her father-in-law, Constance said, "Perhaps another time. Besides, Mother Honeycut and I had such a wonderful visit it was worth missing a little shopping."

Suspicious, Tad glanced between his wife and Sarah. "Oh really? Why, I can't imagine how anyone could find that much to talk about to fill a day. Even you, Constance."

Ignoring Tad's sarcasm, Sarah stood and walked over to the liquor decanter to pour Michael a drink. Seeing how nervous her daughter-in-law was, she hastily said, "My, but the time just flew by. It was so heartwarmin' to hear about everyone from back home. Son, your dear wife has been so patient with me today. She even allowed me time to reminisce about the days before the war. Joshua, as I recall, you had dinner once at the Brown's, where Constance and her family also attended, isn't that right?"

"I recall that evening quite well."

Constance, smiling fondly over at Joshua, said, "As do I. Why, I thought you and Mr. Brown were going to have it out, right there and then at the dinner table."

"Lucas was just toying with me that night. Sizing me up, I suspect. And I can tell you, he kept me on my toes all night."

"That was Lucas all right. How he loved to spar with a formidable opponent, especially about politics." Michael raised his glass and toasted his old friend. "To Lucas, may he rest in peace."

Everyone chimed in and said, "Here, here."

Sarah, still trying to keep the conversation light so as not to alert Tad that Constance had confided in her, said, "Constance, I just thought of another time. Do you remember when you, Miranda, and Elise were catchin' crawdads down by the stream at Glenbrook? There we were, sitting in Catherine's rose garden, and here comes you, in a brand new blue cotton dress, soaked in mud. I thought your father was going to have himself a stroke."

Constance nervously chuckled, glancing over at Tad then at Sarah. "Why, I had forgotten all about that day. As I recall though, we weren't trying to catch the crawdad's Mother Honeycut. Elise actually pushed me into the creek and one just happened to end up in my pocket. Don't you remember me screaming and hollering when it crawled out?"

"Oh my, I do remember that now. You and Elise were such spirited children at times."

"Seems to me, my wife still is." Joshua chuckled. "And I wouldn't have it any other way."

Smiling, she handed Michael a snifter of brandy and then another to Tad. "My, it was so nice reminiscing all day. I hadn't realized how much I miss Fairfax." Turning to Joshua, she handed him a drink as well. "Son, before I forget, don't you run off till you pick up some of the tomatoes I setup for your mother. How are William and Mary, by the way? I'm sure they are busy planning for Charles's wedding."

Obviously not interested in hearing about Joshua's brother's wedding, Tad belted back his brandy and said, "If you'll excuse me, I'll change before dinner. Grandfather hates to be kept waiting."

Constance, beginning to stand to accompany her husband, stopped, hearing Tad say, "You stay here Constance, and visit with everyone. I won't be but a moment."

Sarah returned to her seat smiling warmly at Constance and patted her knee. "Things have a way of working out." Sarah glanced at Joshua, as if addressing him rather than Constance, in case Tad was able to hear them. "Just look how wonderful your wedding was, Joshua."

As the four of them conversed politely, Joshua speaking in depth of the wedding plans of his brother and Julia, a local girl, Sarah could feel Michael's eyes on her. Fearful she would not be able to keep up the charade if she looked at him, Sarah continued to focus on Constance and Joshua, all the while patting Constance's knee reassuringly. Feeling the girl tremble but masking it well, Sarah smiled at her.

Within minutes, Tad returned, anxious to be on his way. As they bid farewell to Constance and Tad, Sarah gave Constance a kiss on the cheek and smiled lovingly at her. "Have a wonderful evening tonight, dear. I'm sure we'll see you both after dinner long before you've finished visiting with Alfred."

"That will be nice. Are the O'Flahertys coming with you tonight? Pity I've not even seen them since they've arrived."

Sarah, glancing over at Joshua, said hesitantly, "Why, I'm not sure. I suppose it will depend on the children; and whether Miranda and Gilbert are up to it. If not tonight though, tomorrow for sure. As I recall, we're all having dinner with one another. Isn't that right, dear?" she asked, glancing over at Michael.

"Near as I recall, unless you and Tad would rather go to the opera since we weren't able to attend last evening. Why not make a night of it and go out for dinner; then afterwards take in the sights of New York? I'm sure

Constance would love to see the city at night, son," Michael asked Tad enthusiastically.

"Let's give it some thought," Tad replied, placing his hand on the small of Constance's back. "Come along, Constance. We can't have Grandfather waiting, now can we."

After the two of them left, Michael looked suspiciously over at Sarah. "Why do I get the feeling something more went on here today than simply reminiscing?"

Turning, Sarah called out as she headed back to the parlor. "I have no idea, dear. Joshua, will you join me in the parlor?"

The two men, mystified by Sarah's behavior, glanced at each other. Joshua, extending his arm out, said, "After you."

Hesitating, seeing Sarah shake her head, Michael said, "No. I think I'll head to my study for a spell." Glancing over at Sarah, as if asking for permission and seeing her nod, he added, "I'll see you before you leave."

Sarah, smiling reassuringly at her husband, said, "Dear, please do keep your door open. It's rather stuffy in there today."

Puzzled by Sarah's sudden need to speak privately with Joshua, while at the same time making it clear that she wanted Michael to overhear, rather than question his wives motives, Michael walked into his office as Joshua stepped into the parlor.

"Shall I close the door, Mother Honeycut?"

"No, dear. That won't be necessary," Sarah said, politely.

Glancing at Sarah, Joshua's frown turned to a wide grin. "And to think I always thought Elise inherited her spirit from her father."

"Why son, whatever gave you that impression? Come sit down, Joshua. I've asked to speak with you this afternoon alone, regarding a very serious matter." Waiting until he was seated across from her, and to make certain that Michael could overhear, she began speaking more loudly than usual. "It has come to my attention that an old friend of the family has suffered greatly at her own husband's hands. I'm seeking legal advice as to what can be done to prevent him from continuing to harm her."

"Well ,ma'am, as you know, that depends on the degree of the harm and in what state the couple reside. Has she proof that her husband intentionally set out to cause her bodily harm? And to what degree her injuries were, must be taken into consideration as well."

"The young woman has suffered horrific acts of brutality by the hands of her husband," Sarah said gravely. Hearing Michael's footsteps leave his office, she glanced to the doorway. Once Michael was in sight, she hesitantly added in a soft voice, "She has lost three children, two due to 'accidents' which her husband deliberately caused; and all three conceived by force."

Barely able to find his voice, pale and visibly shaken, Michael asked, "Are you certain of this, Sarah?"

"Quite certain, darling. Please Michael, you mustn't come in here. I've given my word that I would not speak with you regarding this matter. However, I never promised not to get help for our daughter-in-law, nor can I be faulted if you overhear my conversation with Joshua."

Nodding, he glanced over at Joshua, who was staring at Michael, as if asking how to proceed. "Son, please advise my good wife."

After ascertaining more details, Joshua explained that there was little anyone could do. Being extremely careful not to use Tad's nor Constance's names, Joshua explained that a husband could in fact, have his wife committed without question, and that the woman's family could not by law prevent such an act.

"Furthermore," he added, "having three miscarriages, it would seem understandable to some, that a woman might need the kind of medical attention that an asylum could offer.

"Mother Honeycut, as you know, a wife must resign herself to her husband's demands, by law. If she feels this is no longer to her liking, her only recourse is to divorce her husband. Of course, since there are no children, she will only have to leave her husband's home, rather than face leaving her children as well. In this instance, I presume the woman does have family she can return to? In either case, this woman and of course her family, will have to live with the stigma of such actions. Society as a whole, is not forgiving when a woman leaves her husband. Which as you know, is not a life most women can bear, despite being justified in leaving their spouse. My advice to you, to help this woman short-term, is to be as close to her as possible. Solely as a means to prevent such acts of violence to continue. Of course, there are no guarantees that her husband couldn't still have her committed, if he felt provoked, simply out of the necessity to protect his name and standing in the community."

"I see." Sarah looked helplessly over at Michael.

Michael, coming into the room and placing his hand on Sarah's shoulder, spoke softly, while extending his free hand to Joshua.

"Son, thank you for your advice. I trust what you and my wife have discussed this afternoon will be held in the strictest of confidence."

Standing, Joshua accepted Michael's hand and shook it, saying, "I give you my word. I just wish there was something I could say that could ease both your minds."

Nodding, Michael leaned into Joshua and hugged the man he thought of as a son. Then patting him on the back, he said, "We've kept you long enough. Elise will be wondering what has detained you and we don't need to arouse her suspicions."

Joshua, nodding his head, bent over and kissed his mother-in-law's cheek. "Mother Honeycut, if there is anyone who can figure out a way to make this whole matter more tolerable that would be you. I have no doubt that given time to think on it some, you'll come up with a solution."

Patting Joshua on the cheek, Sarah smiled lovingly at him. "Thank you, son. Tell my daughter we'll be around in an hour or so."

Nodding, Joshua shook Michael's hand again and left telling them both he knew the way out. Hearing the door close, Sarah, who had been holding back her tears, looked up at Michael sheepishly. Seeing the hurt in his eyes, she started weeping. "I'm so sorry darling that you had to find out this way, but I didn't know what else to do."

Taking her in his arms, he whispered, "Nonsense, you did fine." Holding her more tightly than he had in years, they clung to one another, as they wept softly, thinking of the horrors Constance had endured at the hand's of Michael's only child.

"Darling, I can't bear to hear the details of what Tad has done."

"I know, my dearest. I could hardly get through it myself as Constance told me. What are we going to do, Michael?"

Pulling away slightly from her, not concealing his tears, he said, "Why, we're going to Fairfax of course. Didn't you just say earlier how homesick you were?"

~ Five ~

Just after the clock struck eight, with smiles pasted on their faces, Michael and Sarah entered the Honeycut mansion. Surprised to see them so early, Alfred said, "Well for goodness sakes, I didn't think we'd see you for at least another hour or so."

"Well, we were rather anxious to share our news with you, so we asked the kids to make it an early night." Michael, glancing down at his wife, said, "Shall I tell them, or would you like the honors, my dear?"

Smiling sweetly, Sarah said, "By all means, you go ahead."

Curious about his father's enthusiasm, Tad glanced at him. "Why Father, just look at you; a far cry different than when I left you a few short hours ago. What has put you is such high spirits?"

"Why, a trip to Fairfax, son! It suddenly occurred to me that with Sarah so homesick, and me hating to see you leave next week, not having a long enough visit. Well, we decided nothing was keeping us here, so we're coming to my son's home for a spell! That is, if you don't mind extending your humble abode to your father, Tad."

Obviously surprised, Tad said, "We'd be glad to have you come stay with us, it's just...."

Michael, not giving Tad a chance to make an excuse not to travel back with them, went over and hugged his son. "Thank you, Tad. You know, it's always troubled me that we left Fairfax to be here with you and Elise, and then you moved down there." Patting Tad on the back and gripping his shoulder, he added, "If I didn't know any better, I'd think you were trying to get away from me."

After the two of them chuckled, Michael continued. "Seriously, now that Elise doesn't need Sarah anymore and I can write anywhere, I really would like to spend more time with you, son."

"I'm touched, Father. The thing is, Constance and I are returning home the day after tomorrow."

Sarah moaned her disappointment, glanced over at Constance, and seeing the surprised look on her daughter-in-law's face she said, "Oh really? Why so soon? We didn't even get a chance to go shopping."

Tad took this opportunity to interject, dramatically shaking his head. "I know, but in my haste to have Constance get away from Fairfax, to help ease her troubled mind, I never took into consideration how depressing it would be for her to be around all these children. Which obviously *has* had an adverse effect on her." Speaking of Constance in the third person, as if she wasn't even the room, he continued. "Why, she couldn't even go to the opera last evening. So I've decided to leave the day after tomorrow."

"My, that is sudden. No problem though, we can be ready by then. Can't we, dear?" Sarah looked lovingly at her husband as she went to sit by her daughter-in-law. "Besides, nothing is better for what ails you than to be surrounded by those who love you. And I've loved Constance since she was just a wee thing."

Smiling warmly at Sarah, Constance said appreciatively, "I love you too, Mother Honeycut."

Alfred, uncertain as to why it was necessary for his son and Sarah to make such a trip, but alerted by Tad's reaction to hearing of it that something was afoot, hastily reaffirmed Michael's and Sarah's need to travel to Fairfax. "Well then, it's settled. See Tad; Constance looks better all ready. I have no doubt, with Sarah by her side our Constance will be in the pink in no time at all."

Smiling insincerely over the rim of his glass as he sipped at his brandy, Tad nodded. "Yes, Sarah is a wonder, all right. We wouldn't dream of letting you stay away from your Doves Landing on our account, knowing how much it means to you. Would we, Constance?"

"Nonsense, why I wouldn't stay there even if Constance didn't need me. With Mama Tess here, tending to the children, and with the Faradays overseeing the boarding house, it just wouldn't be right. Besides, I haven't thought of Doves Landing as my home for quite some years now."

Before anyone had time to respond, The O'Flahertys and Carmidys joined them, much to Tad's surprise, judging by the look on his face. At once, Elise's four older children came running into the house, well accustomed to their surroundings by now.

"Grandpa, did you hear the news?" exclaimed Sarah Tess.

Alfred, bending over to face the little girl, said, "Why yes, I did." Spotting Miranda's littlest daughter following closely behind, Alfred said, "Well hello again there, Peanut. What a lovely dress you are wearing this evening."

Smiling broadly, she came over to him and politely curtsied. "Why thank you, Grandfather Honeycut. My papa picked it out special for me to wear tonight."

"Ah, is that right?" Seeing Miranda's shyer daughter enter the room with Andy, Alfred greeted both of them. "Hello Katie, did Andy help you find your doll's missing shoe?"

"Yes, sir." She smiled shyly before going back to her mother who was helping the remainder of the children with their winter coats.

Alfred, taking Andy's hand, shook it, and then leaned closer to him. "Fine job, lad."

"Papa says it's better to be nice to the ladies than to make them cranky."

Alfred broke out laughing, and nodded over at Joshua. "Your son here is letting us in on your philosophies toward the fairer gender."

"Hmm, is that right?"

As the adults made their way into the parlor, Elise, with Jefferson Abraham in her arms, she took her seat beside Constance after exchanging greetings with Alfred. "My, I do hope you weren't planning on a quiet evening, Constance. With nine children about, I'm afraid quiet is out of the question."

Miranda, nodding politely over at Tad, sat in the chair next to Constance after kissing her friend on the cheek, while Katie stood by her side and Gilbert directly behind her. "Catherine, why don't you go and play with Sarah Tess and the other children."

Shyly, the girl shook her head and looked up at her father. "Papa, can I please stay here with you and Mama?"

Since Jerome had brought more chairs into the parlor, Gilbert nodded his head while taking a seat between Miranda and Alfred. "I suppose that will be all right, Katie, for a wee bit."

Joshua, who had taken a seat next to Tad and Michael, facing the women, made room for his daughter on his lap, as Suzanne snuggled up on her own father's lap. Within seconds, she was busily rubbing Gilbert's ear lobe with one hand while sucking her thumb with the other, as if this were the most natural thing to do.

Joshua nodded over at Gilbert and chuckled. "Ah, another ear tweeker. Between Sarah Tess and Elise it's a wonder my ears haven't grown to the size of one of those elephants of Barnum Bailey's."

"Aye. I never could understand the attraction to ears."

Elise, glancing over at Miranda, shook her head. "Oh you men, how you go on so. Why, someday you'll miss these times."

Nodding his head, Alfred, making room on his lap for his namesake said, "That they will indeed." Patting little Alfred's back as he lay his head on his shoulder, he said softly, "You tuckered out this evening, little Alfred?"

Nodding his head, he rested on his great-grandfather's lap.

"They all are," Miranda said, bringing her youngest son Joseph onto her lap. "It must be this northern air. Why, I had forgotten just how cold it gets up here."

Looking over at Miranda, Constance said, "Even when we do get snow, it doesn't seem this cold."

Sarah, smiling over at her husband as she picked up Caleb and placed him on her lap, said, "Well, if nothing more than to have a mild winter again, the trip to Fairfax will be most welcoming."

"What do you think of your mother and Michael making a trip back to Fairfax?" Tad asked, glancing over at Elise, before resting his eyes back on Miranda and Constance.

"I think it's wonderful. We'll all miss Mama and Michael of course, but going back to visit all their friends will do them good."

Hearing the baby stir in Elise's arms, Constance leaned over and smiled at him. "Only you Elise, would name your son after two men with such opposing viewpoints."

"Why, I like to think little Jefferson Abraham here, is a perfect name for our son. It's only befitting, considering our histories, that we would name our son after two presidents who served their countries proud."

"Well, that still remains to be seen. I'd love to see what they write about both men in the history books in a few decades."

"Aye." Gilbert nodded in response to Constance's comment. "Perhaps they'll continue to praise Old Abe as the great emancipator and Davis as a man with a vision that led the Cotton States into rebellion."

"Why Gilbert, if that's the case, then I'll be even prouder that we named our son after such fine presidents. Two men who had the courage to live by their convictions, is a strong foundation for any young man. Don't you agree, Joshua?"

"I do indeed."

Alfred, looking over at Gilbert, said, "Why Gilbert, it shames me that you are so well-versed on our politics and I know so little of your homeland."

"My politics, too. I've been a citizen of this country going on twenty years, sir. Until Miranda and I wed though, the war, or the southern states in particular, held little interest to me. All I cared about was making sure I earned me three hundred dollars to avoid the draft." Directing his attention toward Joshua, he added, "Beggin' your pardon Joshua, but I had no desire to fight in a war that had nothin' to do with me. Had me own war to fight right here, to make sure me and my sister didn't end up in five-points."

"No offense taken, Gilbert. Many natural born citizens felt the same about the war, without as noble of reasons as you. So I take it you did manage to dodge the draft?"

"Aye. I won it playing poker."

Hearing Gilbert's remark, Tad, who had been taking a sip of his brandy, started coughing. Glaring over at his rival, he stood up and walked angrily over to the liquor cart and poured himself another brandy.

Watching Tad, a hush fell over the room. Only Constance, unfamiliar with Tad and Gilbert's history, spoke.

"My, but we are a diverse group, aren't we?" Gazing once more at the baby in Elise's arms, she said, "Come to think on it Elise, I think your little Jefferson Abraham has a perfect name. If nothing more, than to represent how your families, despite such different backgrounds, were able to make peace. Do you think it would be all right if I held him for a spell?"

As Elise transferred the sleeping child carefully into Constance's arm, Alfred spoke softly to the child he held.

"Little Albert, I have a surprise for you and the rest of the children in the top drawer of my desk."

Hearing his great-grandfather's comment, little Alfred perked up, wide-eyed. "You do?"

"I sure do. Be a good boy now, and go and fetch it. Don't touch anything else, here?

At once, the Carmidy children headed toward Alfred's study. Andrew stopped, seeing that the other children weren't following, and waved his hand. "Come on Lucas, it's candy."

Sheepishly, the O'Flaherty children looked anxiously at Gilbert and seeing their father nod his head, they eagerly followed, their laughter filling the halls.

"Grandfather, you spoil them. I think you get more pleasure seeing their faces light up than they do eating the candy," Elise said, straightening her gown.

"A handsome dividend to my investment, I'd say."

As Joshua and Michael joined Tad to freshen their drinks, Alfred lingered for a minute to look at his latest grandson, sleeping in Constance's arms. "He's a handsome boy, Elise. Pretty soon, I'll be needing more licorice sticks for this little tyke."

Constance, smiling up at him, waited until he had joined the others and whispered, "I like Mr. Honeycut. He's a kind-hearted man."

"That he is. I have always have been very fond of him, thinking of him as a second father," Miranda spoke softly. "But I can assure you, he is as shrewd and perceptive as anyone you will ever meet. I know I'd never want to get on the wrong side of him, that's for sure."

Catherine entered the parlor again, a pout across her face. Returning to stand next to Miranda, she sighed.

"Why such a sour look, child. Didn't you like the licorice?" Miranda asked her oldest daughter.

"I did. But Sarah Tess gave me the broken one. Look!" Lifting two strings of candy to show her mother, she said, "Everyone else got a long one but me. Even Joey. Sarah Tess said since I was the oldest I had to be nice. Mama, Lucas is a lot older than I am, and he didn't have to get the broken one. Sarah Tess just likes him more, the old bossy thing."

The three women found it hard not to laugh at the younger girl, and looked over at Elise for her reaction to hearing her daughter being called bossy.

"Catherine, sugar, you are the lucky one. Put that one piece of candy in your pocket like you already ate it, and when the rest of them have none, you can pull out your saved one. But don't eat up the other piece real fast, now. Just suck on it some, real slow, so no one knows. I know Sarah Tess, she'll have already eaten all of hers and she'll want some of yours, too. That will teach her not to be so mean, not taking the broken one herself."

"But it'll get all sticky and gooey in my pocket," the little girl exclaimed.

"Not if you wrap it up in my handkerchief, it won't." Pulling out a lacy starched hanky from her sleeve, Elise handed it to the little girl. "Here ya go, sugar. Now run along and play with the other children and mark my words, Sarah Tess will be in here in a few minutes complaining to me that you tricked her."

"But Auntie Elise, isn't that what I'd be doin'? Mama and Papa don't take kindly to us being mean to others."

"Sugar, it's not really being mean now is it, if you were smart enough to keep a little something for later?"

The little girl thought for a moment then smiled, taking the handkerchief from Elise's hand. After wrapping the licorice carefully inside the hanky, she skipped merrily back to the study.

"Elise Carmidy, as sorry as I am for Catherine calling Sarah Tess bossy, I'm not so sure you teaching my daughter how to be deceitful was such a wise thing either."

"Why I did no such thing! Is she lying, or taking something that isn't hers? Course not! All I'm doing is teaching both girls a mighty important lesson in life. Little Catherine is so meek and sensitive, just like you were as a child; and well, Sarah Tess is so...."

Elise, glancing between her two friends and mother and seeing their eyes dancing, said, "What? You don't think I realize my child is like I was when I was her age? Oh trust me, I know Sarah Tess, better than anyone here does—and it scares me. Why, that little girl not only has managed to wrap Joshua around her baby finger, but most of the boys in her class, too. You should see them all following her around like little lap dogs. It's pitiful! Of course it riles up most of the little girls in her class, too."

Constance, looking over at Miranda with a wide grin, said, "Sounds familiar, Doesn't it Miranda?"

"Oh wipe those silly grins off your faces; I know what you're thinking. Unlike me learning the hard way and almost losing my Joshua, Sarah Tess needs to learn from an early age that there are consequences to her actions. Besides, to my way of thinking, it wouldn't hurt little Catherine none, if she finds out there's another way to skin a cat." Glancing over at Sarah, Elise asked, "It'll do both girls a world of good, don't you agree, Mama?"

"You know Elise, only time will tell. But one thing's for sure; seeing those three girls interact as they do is like stepping back in time and watching you three all over again."

"Hmm, I suppose you're right. I do hope though, that it doesn't take something as awful as a war to make them truly become friends." Elise, looking over at Constance, said, "I'll never forget how you came to see me most every day when I was in bed, after my unfortunate accident."

Smiling, Constance nodded her head. "Well, it did us both some good, as I recall. Why I even forgave you for tripping me that night in Miranda's bedroom."

"Tripping you?" Elise said coyly, recalling the incident well, but pretending she didn't know what Constance was speaking of. "Why, I don't recall any such incident."

As the three of them reminisced about the night Joshua had escorted Elise to the Brown's dinner party, uninvited, they laughed amongst themselves, oblivious to Tad's close watch and obvious displeasure with his wife's enjoyment of the moment.

Seething inside, he turned to Alfred. "Well Grandfather, it's getting late. I should get Constance home soon. I'm sure it's troubling for her to be around so many children. No need to cause her any strain."

"Nonsense. She's enjoying herself. They all are, so why spoil their fun?"

~

Later that evening, in the privacy of his old room, Tad took out his frustration. After Constance had repeatedly tried to reassure her husband that she had nothing to do with Sarah and Michael's decision to return with them to Fairfax, Tad ordered her to undress down to her pantaloons and camisole. As Tad discarded his own clothing, and fearful that they might be overheard, Constance stood in silence as he approached her. Even as his hands gripped at her breasts, tearing her camisole so that he could feel her nakedness in his hands, she made not a sound. Feeling no enjoyment as Tad sucked at her nipples until they were raw, like a wild beast nursing, she stood motionless. He bit them and she winced, which seemed to arouse him further, and he forced her to the floor. Tearing at her pantaloons, he entered her with such force, she gasped.

"Shut up, you whore," he spat in a hoarse whisper. Grasping her hands, he pulled them above her head, thrusting more deeply inside her as Constance wept in silence, until his needs were met. Immediately, his body went limp and he lay over her, breathless, as Constance stared up at the ceiling waiting for the violation of her body to end.

Catching his breath, Tad pulled himself up and stood hovering directly above her. "Tomorrow, you and that busy-body stepmother of mine can go shopping to replace your torn clothing. Be sure no one sees them. Understand?" Seeing her nod, he said coldly, "Hurry up and clean yourself up. I'm tired and want to go to bed."

Saying not a word, trying to cover her nakedness with her ripped undergarments, she rose from the floor and went to the wardrobe. Peeling the torn garments from her body, Constance quietly slipped into her robe and went to the dry sink. Seeing the tips of her nipples bleeding, she winced as she washed them. Then, after cleaning the remainder of her body, she closed her robe, and quietly slipped into bed. Saying not a word, Tad blew out the kerosene night lamp and rolled over, as Constance lay still next to her husband while tears rolled down her cheeks.

~ Six ~

Late March 1873
Fairfax, VA

While Gilbert and the children were in town running errands so Miranda could have a few hours alone, she walked into her childhood home. Seeing the condition of Glenbrook, now only a ghost of what it had once been in her youth, Miranda was heartsick.

No longer was it the grand plantation that had been in her mother's family for generations. Although the architect had been able to salvage most of the front of the original structure, a great deal of the back, including her father's office, had been torn down due to dry rot and termites. The only rooms unaffected were the foyer, parlor, and lounge on the lower level; and her room on the second story, along with two guestrooms. Even her father and mother's separate bedchambers had been unsalvageable.

Walking through the foyer and down the hall to the room that had once been the kitchen, Miranda closed her eyes. For a second, she could almost hear Bessie humming as she prepared the evening meal. Walking around the gaping hole in the middle of the floor that had once been the family's root cellar, Miranda pushed aside the tarps that led to what remained of the second story.

With no handrail, the wall having been torn down when the kitchen had been taken out, Miranda took the steps cautiously. Reaching the landing, and seeing only three rooms remaining intact on the second level of her childhood home, she sighed heavily.

"Dear God, it's almost as if Mama and Papa were never even here."

Forcing herself to continue, she stepped into what had been her childhood room, and gasped at seeing a portion of the wall torn away. As she looked through the opening, she could see through to the two guestrooms, which were to be combined with her room to make a large dormitory for the boarding school.

The room looked so ominous, with old pieces of scrap lumber scattered around. Walking to the one piece of remaining furniture, a small table upon which a kerosene lamp sat, Miranda quickly lit the lamp and looked around the partially wallpapered space. As she stood in the corner of the room, her mind was flooded with childhood memories.

There before her in her mind, sat the lonely girl who would listen to her mother crying from down the hall. She closed her eyes, and it was almost as if she heard her mother again. As the scene played out in her mind, just as it had so often as a child, she could hear her father yelling.

"Damn you, Catherine."

Miranda closed her eyes tightly, and whispered, "Please don't holler at Mama, Papa."

For a moment, the past and the present seemed to collide, and Miranda closed her eyes, her body jerking as she heard a door slam shut, just as she had heard many times as a child, when Lucas had slammed Catherine's bedroom door years earlier.

"Don't leave me, Papa," Miranda whispered, able to hear his footsteps on the stairs. This afternoon though, the familiar sound of her mother's gut-wrenching sobs echoing throughout the halls of the grand plantation didn't follow, and Miranda opened her eyes, feeling the presence of another.

Seeing Tad standing before her, Miranda jerked in fear.

"What are you doing here?" she asked, her heart racing. "Please leave, Tad; Gilbert is due home any minute and he will be angered."

"Do you think I give a shit what that lowlife Irishman thinks?" he yelled, cutting her off, his voice echoing throughout the empty building.

"Tad, please leave. You're frightening me."

Mocking her, he repeated her words. " 'You're frightening me…Tad, I can assure you, my feelings for you are just as strong…' Wasn't that what you said to me the night I met you in the drive of Grandfather's house, or were you deceiving me? Allowing me to kiss you on the cheek or the forehead as if you were a sacred gem, all the while you were bedding that Irish scum, you whore!"

Gasping, Miranda stepped back. "How dare you speak to me like that."

"I'll speak to you any way I damned well want to, you *whore!*" Grasping her arm, clenching it tightly in his hand he yelled, "Tell me you didn't sleep with him, Miranda, before your were even wed, all the while lying to me."

Struggling to be free from his grip, she yelled, "Tad, stop it! I owe you no explanations, after what you did."

"What I did?" he spat. "Why, all I did was love you, and tried to keep what was mine. And what did I get for my trouble? You, stripping down to your pantaloons and exposing yourself to that bastard."

Gasping at his words, and realizing that he must have overheard her and Elise when they were in New York, Miranda began hitting and clawing at him to be free. Making contact with his face, she clawed at his flesh, while trying to bite the wrist of his hand that held her firmly. Balling up his free fist, he punched Miranda in the abdomen.

Feeling as if the force of his blow had crushed her bones, Miranda screamed out in agony, experiencing more pain than she had ever before known.

Hunched over, unable to breathe, gasping for air, she felt Tad's hand release her arm and tightly grasp her neck, pressing her firmly against the wall. Inside her torso, it felt as if a knife had just punctured through to her back and she struggled for air, the piercing pain gripping inside her chest.

"I can't breathe." she murmured. "Help me." she tried to scream out.

Feeling his free hand tug at her clothing, she tried to kick him while pulling at his hand to prevent him from touching her breasts. Scratching at his arm, and kicking him near his groin, Tad winced and struck her in the stomach again causing Miranda to yelp in pain as she tasted blood in her mouth. Knowing she was no match against his strength, she slid her hands along the wall she was pressed up against, looking for a weapon with which to defend herself.

"I'm taking back what you and that bastard stole from me."

"Tad, please don't do this...I loved you once...."

"Is that why you seduced that lowlife into marrying you? Because you loved me?"

With her breasts fully exposed and his hands pawing at her, even as much pain as she was in, Miranda could not allow Tad to rape her without a fight. As he began unfastening his trousers, she stretched out her hands, knowing she must do something to prevent Tad from what he was about to do. His hands tearing at her pantaloons, she suddenly felt something sharp with the tips of her fingers. Stretching her hand out further, she managed to grasp hold of it.

"When I'm finished with you, if that Irishman still wants his precious 'Mandy girl', then he can have you."

"No!" she yelled, raising her hand which now held a jagged piece of wood, and striking Tad against the side of his head.

His hand released her neck and he lost his footing, knocking into the table beside them, spilling the lamp onto the floor. As the glass base of the lamp hit the floor, it shattered, kerosene flowing out onto the floor. Tad, dazed by the blow, angrily rubbed his face and seeing blood, he lunged back toward Miranda.

Struggling to breathe, feeling deep pain inside her chest cavity, Miranda managed to stand her ground. Holding the piece of wood before her, she yelled, "I mean it Tad. I'll run you clean through, if you come even one step closer."

As he lunged toward her, the pool of kerosene around his feet ignited, setting Tad's shoes and trousers on fire. Thrashing about, partially undressed with his trousers around his knees, Tad struggled to extinguish the fire that was spreading up his leg. Losing his balance, he fell backward into the glass window and called out as his fiery body fell from the building.

Screaming at the sight, she looked around the room, dazed. Realizing that the flames were spreading rapidly across the dry wood floor and onto the walls, Miranda tried desperately to escape.

Weak, and in severe pain, she leaned against the only wall still untouched by the fire, for support. Every movement caused excruciating pain in her chest. Rubbing the blood from the sides of her mouth, she leaned against the wall to brace herself, and tried to shield her bare chest from the intense heat. Inching her way closer to the doorway, she felt her legs begin to give out beneath her and despite her efforts, she slid to the floor.

On her side, she continued to scratch her way from the blazing room, which was filling with smoke, causing her to cough even more. Unable to breathe or move any further, her body too weak, Miranda gazed out at the thick black smoke and bright flames as they burned nearer. Raising her head slightly, she whispered hoarsely, "Gilbert...." Then Miranda's head dropped as darkness overtook her.

~

"Mandy girl, I'm here." Gilbert whispered, as he tenderly wiped the blood from the corners of her mouth. Helplessly, he looked over at the doctor. "Can't you please help her?"

"I'm sorry, Gilbert. There is nothing we can do for her now, except try to make her as comfortable as possible. Miranda is bleeding internally. She has several broken ribs, which punctured her lung, judging by how hard it is for her to breathe. You have to be strong Gilbert, for the children's sake."

Dazed, he gravely turned and took her frail hand in his and kissed it softly as he knelt beside her.

"Gilbert," she whispered, her voice barely audible. Struggling to breathe, she said, "I'm...sorry...."

"Shh lass, you did nothing wrong. I love you, my Mandy girl."

"He didn't get to..."

"Shh, I know darling. You were so brave."

"How...did I...get here?"

"I brought you home, lassie. To our bed," he whispered, kissing her cheek while stroking her smoke-filled hair.

A faint smile crossed her lips. "I love you."

"My Mandy girl, I love you. I always have, since the moment I laid eyes on you."

A tear streamed down Miranda's cheek and she whispered, "Please darling...take the children to...Ireland...and England...this...summer. Go with...Elise...and...Felicity. She'll help...to...raise...our...children."

"Shh, don't be thinking about anything but getting better, darling. When you're well enough, we'll all go together."

Her breathing becoming shallower. Miranda whispered, "Come hold me."

Gingerly, he slid next to his wife and raising her head, he protectively held Miranda in his arms. Faintly she whispered, between her raspy gurgling, "Promise me...take them to Felicity. She'll...help you."

With tears running down his cheek, wiping the blood from her lips, Gilbert whispered, "I promise."

"You are...a...good man. I...love...you." With that, Miranda's head rolled to its side and she breathed no more. Grasping her lifeless body closer to him, Gilbert sobbed uncontrollably.

Saying not a word, Doc Wade turned and left the room shaking his head gravely at Sarah and the stunned Michael, who were waiting outside the door. "I'm sorry. Miranda's with her maker."

Clenching her fist in her hand, Sarah shook her head. "No, not her, too!" Giving into her tears, she wept as Michael, devoid of emotion said, "I'll wire Father and Elise and tell them what has happened. You stay here and tend to getting Miranda ready to be viewed, so her children can say goodbye to their mama."

"What about Constance, she has to be told about Tad...?" Her voice trailed off, fearful to mention that Michael's son had been killed trying to attack Miranda.

"I'll take her to the Hildebrandt's then arrange for Tad's body to be sent back to New York."

"Michael, I'm so sorry."

Cutting her off, Michael said coldly, "For what? My son was a depraved monster who killed an innocent woman."

Shocked by his words, realizing the depth of his pain and knowing there was little she could do to ease his heavy heart, she said, "Darling are you sure, you don't want me to come with you?"

Shaking his head, he looked at the closed door where Gilbert's crying could be heard. "No, Sarah. That man needs you. I can't imagine what he must be going through right now. It's not bad enough that he found his wife suffocating—in a fire that my son no doubt caused. But to see her dress torn as it was, and knowing it was probably caused by Tad trying to rape her…then having to carry Miranda over Tad's body to get her home...." Michael's voice cracked, remembering the gruesome details of the earlier events.

Michael had arrived at Glenbrook just as Tad's flame-engulfed, partially dressed body spiraled out of the window of the two-story building. He'd watched in horror as Tad landed straight onto his head, his neck breaking on impact. Michael recalled his son's scream as he fell, then later how he had tried desperately to put out the flames that were ravaging his son's body, while Gilbert's voice rang out from inside Glenbrook, calling for Miranda.

Looking at Sarah, Michael said, "The pain that man has had to endure at the hands of my family is inconceivable. The least we can do now is to try to ease some of his burden and tend to his children as they grieve the loss of such a fine woman as Miranda. Please, Sarah, don't fret about me. The O'Flaherty's need you now."

Holding Michael for a moment longer, she said, "I love you, darling. Will you be back this evening? I think Gilbert will need a man near, that he trusts."

With tears streaming down his face, he looked at his wife. "I don't know if I can. What if he doesn't want me here? What if he blames me for what my son has done?"

"Gilbert has never held you or Albert responsible for Tad's actions in the past, and I doubt even in his grief if he will now. What he needs now is a friend, someone to lean on. He has no one else to turn to, Michael. Please darling, I know how much you are suffering too, but can you please try to come by? Not for my sake, but for yours and Gilbert's."

Nodding, he kissed Sarah's forehead. "When Gilbert comes out, tell him I'll be back before sundown. I'll take Tad's body into town, so he doesn't have to see it."

~ Seven ~

Joshua tenderly holds his wife as she says her final good-byes to Miranda. Unable to believe that her dearest friend, who she loved as a sister, was truly gone, Elise stood beside the casket and placed her shaking hand over it. "I'll always love you, little sis. And don't you worry, I'll look after your babes and your beloved Gilbert, I promise."

Through her tears, Elise kissed the casket one last time, before Joshua helped his wife from the graveside funeral, located in the Brown's family cemetery, next to Lucas and Catherine Brown.

Taking Catherine and Suzanne in her arms, she tenderly kissed each of Miranda's distraught daughters on the head. "Your mama's in heaven with her mama and papa, little ones. But she'll never be far from you. I promise. She loved you all so much."

Suzanne looked up at Elise and asked, "Auntie Elise, what's going to happen to us without Mama?"

"Why sweeties, you and your papa and brothers are all coming to live with us in New York for a spell, then we're all going to go see your other aunt in England. Do you remember your mama speaking about Auntie Felicity?"

Catherine, wide-eyed, said, "Yes. But she's not our real auntie, is she?"

"No. Not in blood, but she loved your mama just as much as we all did. Besides, you will be with your papa and all of us. And that's what your Mama wanted. Now we can do that for her, can't we girls?"

"I suppose, but it's so hard." Suzanne whispered.

"I know sweetheart, but we must be strong for your papa."

Catherine, looking up at Elise said, "Papa is stronger than we are."

Bending over so that she was eye level with the young girl, Elise smiled tenderly at her. "Catherine, men may look bigger than woman do, but their hearts can be hurt just as badly as ours, even if they don't show it like we do. Especially when a man like your papa loses the woman he loved so much. So sweetpea, we as women, must learn how to put our own feelings aside, and take care of the men we love. By taking care of your papa and being very brave and strong, not only are you helping him, but you are making your mama very happy too. Do you understand?"

Both girls nodded their heads and hugged Elise tightly. Joshua, who had been listening to his wife while fighting back his own tears, smiled lovingly down at Elise. Glancing over at Gilbert, who knelt solemnly by Miranda's casket, Joshua bent over and whispered, "Darling, let me take you over to your mother and the rest of the children while I go help Gilbert."

Nodding, Elise glanced back at Miranda's casket, and seeing how distraught Gilbert was, closed her eyes to prevent herself from crying. "Go ahead, Joshua, I'll be fine. That poor man needs you."

Taking the girls over to her mother and the rest of the children, Elise leaned in closer so as not to be overheard. "How are Michael and Alfred holding up?"

"Poor Michael and Alfred are not taking losing Miranda, who they both loved as one of their own, well. They are guilt-ridden, blaming themselves for not being able to stop one of their own from committing such a heinous, unthinkable act, while grieving their own loss. I honestly wonder if the two of them will ever be the same."

"And Constance; how is she holding up?"

"The poor dear has done nothing but cry since Michael told her. Just look at her." Sarah paused, nodding over at Constance, standing by her parents. "It's the strangest thing I've ever seen. Here stands the widow of the man who killed her friend, and I don't know if her tears are out of remorse for her friend or relief that her own nightmare has finally ended."

"Maybe a little of both, Mama. What is she intending to do following the funeral? Surely she won't want to stay in Fairfax; the shame of what Tad has done will be too great. Not to mention the stigma that poor child she is carrying will have to live with once it's born."

"Precisely why Michael and I were going to ask you if she could have Michael's old house to raise her and Tad's child."

"Of course, Mama. The house is Michael's. It's only right his grandchild should be born there. Perhaps now, one of Tad's children will actually have a chance to live."

Nodding, Sarah shuddered as Alfred and Michael joined them.

"God, how my heart aches for that poor man. He loved her so...." Alfred's voice trailed off, unable to finish his sentence.

"Father, we all loved Miranda. She was truly special."

Seeing Joshua walk Gilbert away from the gravesite, the group of mourners followed in silence as Gilbert headed toward his and Miranda's home.

Turning one last time, watching as they lowered her casket into the freshly dug earth, Gilbert whispered, "Da, take care of my Mandy girl, better than I did."

Tenderly, Joshua placed his hand on Gilbert's shoulder and said, "Gilbert, you mustn't blame yourself for what happened. You were a very good husband to Miranda. A day never passed when she didn't know how much she was loved and cherished. And that in itself should make you proud, since not every man can say he was able to make his wife so happy."

Looking over at Joshua, Gilbert nodded gravely. "I'll always love her."

~

Devon, England

Standing behind the doorway, Felicity smiled through her tears of sorrow as she listened to Whitney and Benjamin discuss him spending the evening at Rupert's and Annabelle's.

"Very well Father, I understand. Please tell Mother how sad I am to hear of the passing of her friend."

"I will, son."

"Father, you will have the tailor send over my trousers as soon as he arrives, won't you? You promised I would not have to attend church another Sunday in knickers."

"Why certainly, son. A man is only as good as his word."

After shaking each other's hands as adults would do when they take leave from one another, Benjamin tugged slightly on Whitney's arm and brought the seven-year-old boy closer to him, to give him a hug. Patting him on the back, Benjamin said, "I love you, Whitney. You do your mother and I proud."

Whitney, seeing Jimmy Bartlett watching their exchange, said embarrassed, "Father, not in front of Mr. Bartlett."

Smiling down at his son, he said, "Right. I shall have to be more careful of that in the future. Well, run along and I'll pick you up in the morning before church."

Nodding his response, he started to go down the stairs then turned back and flung himself into Benjamin's arms.

Patting the boy on the head, feeling his son squeeze him extra tight, Benjamin, said, "Don't worry son, your mother and I aren't going anywhere, God permitting."

Looking up at Benjamin, Whitney said shyly, "How did you know that's what I was thinking?"

"It's only natural for a fine young man like yourself to worry about your parents after hearing how tragically a mother left her four children to meet her maker, well before her time."

Nodding, Whiney looked innocently up at Benjamin. "Father, why would God take a mother from her husband and children like that?"

"Son I honestly don't know. However, know this; I truly believe that God must have had a very good reason to take her so soon into His Kingdom. And we mustn't ever question His actions, just believe He is doing what is best for all of His beloved flock."

"Yes, sir. You will take extra good care of Mother this evening, won't you?"

"Of course I will. Now, off you go and enjoy the company of your cousins."

Hugging Benjamin again, he whispered, "I love you, Father."

Genuinely touched by the love that her beloved Ben and Whitney exhibited to one another, Felicity brought her hands to her face and wept softly. *What a wonderful father you are.*

Edging her way closer to the doorway, still out of view, she watched as Whitney greeted Jimmy.

"Master Myles, how'd you be this fine and glorious day?"

"Why fine, thank you, Mr. Bartlett," Whitney said politely, not the least bit intimidated, and extended his hand to the driver. "And how are you and the missus?"

"Why we'd be fine as rain, young sir. Thank ya kindly for askin'. I'll be sure to tell Fannie you were askin' about her."

"Yes, please do and send our regards." Stepping into the coach and taking his seat, he tapped on the hood of the coach and as it pulled away, Benjamin chuckled under his breath. "A chip off the old block."

Turning, he was caught off guard by seeing Felicity standing inside the doorway.

"That he is, Ben. Why, he's so polished, and he's not even out of knickers yet. Why, some would think Whitney is a gentry."

"He is my darling, lest you've forgotten he comes from two of the noblest families in western England. A Phelps and a Robbins—a thoroughbred if ever there was. And as for his knickers, well that will soon change. He intends to wear trousers to church in the morning."

"I heard. I do wish he'd wait; he's trying to be grown up so fast."

Walking arm in arm, the two of them went to their favorite room in the house, the conservatory. As soon as he took a seat, Benjamin reached for Felicity's hand, and she took her seat as she often did, on his lap, resting her tear-stained cheek on his shoulder.

"Oh darling, I still can't believe Miranda's gone."

"I know, dearest. What pain Gilbert must be going through. When my time comes, I hope God will allow me to go first. I truly couldn't make it without my Felicity."

"Don't say such a thing. It's I who couldn't make it without you."

Smiling at her, he said, "Of course you would, you have always been stronger than I, my dearest."

"Please let's not speak of such morbid things." Nestling deeper in his lap, she asked, "Ben, why do you suppose Miranda asked Gilbert on her deathbed to have me of all people, help with their children? Why, I haven't seen her in years."

"You and she became very close working at the orphanage all those years. Knowing firsthand how loving and nurturing you are to children, I suppose she never forgot."

"Perhaps, yet she and Elise were like Annabelle and I are. More like sisters than friends. I would have thought she would have wanted Elise to help with them. All I can think is that Miranda wanted her children to be close to Gilbert's homeland, rather than in New York."

"It's possible dearest. Miranda was never fond of New York, so is it surprising she would not want her children raised there, despite her closeness to Elise? From her letters, it sounded as if Gilbert and Miranda lived a quiet existence in Fairfax, building a life around one another and their children. With so few friends and no family there, I'm sure Miranda must have been worried that Gilbert would have nothing there, but a house of memories."

"Yes, but surely she had to remember how Gilbert despised the English? How will he possibly find any peace here, surrounded by those he despises and doesn't trust?"

Felicity paused in deep thought, then added, "Don't get me wrong, I will be more than happy to help Gilbert in any way I can; that is if he'll even allow me to. You know how stubborn he can be?" Felicity asked, raising her head slightly to look at Benjamin.

"Indeed I do. I'll never forget the day of their wedding. Yet, even then, I knew what a loving and kindhearted man he could be, too. And I was right; just look how happy he made Miranda all these years. Besides, as I recall, he liked you. So perhaps in time, and given the right circumstances, he'll warm up to the English as well. That is, if we can persuade him to stay on for a spell following their summer holiday."

"What? Here in the house with us, as our houseguests? Oh, I can't see that ever happening, knowing how proud a man he is. Can you, Ben? A summer holiday is one thing but to live indefinitely? I just don't think that will be pleasing to him."

"I agree. However, what if we built a guest cottage down by the stream? Just as we have always said we wanted. That way, while he and the children are here, Gilbert can feel as if he is on his own, beholden to no one. To come and go as he pleases, answering to know one, but knowing he is always welcome. Then later, when the O'Flaherty's have no more use of it, you can convert it to a working studio to paint and dabble with your sculpturing."

A smile crossed her lips. "What a kind and wise man you are, Benjamin Myles. A cottage for the O'Flaherty's is perfect."

"Glad you think so, Mrs. Myles."

~ Eight ~

April 1873
Medoc, France

Anticipating Joseph Pike's arrival, Victoria Spencer, in a mauve, laced gown, looked anxiously at her reflection in the mirror. "Mother, are you sure this gown doesn't make me look fat? Just look."

Anne, tending to her grandson, turned and glanced over at Victoria, and saw her poking at the tops of her breasts that showed above the squared-off cut of her gown.

"No Victoria, you don't look fat! If anything, you look very alluring, perhaps too alluring. Now stop poking or you'll be all red and blotchy."

Seeing her continue despite her warning, Anne scolded, "Victoria, are you listening to me? Why must you always be so difficult?" Seeing her daughter pout, Anne sighed and added in a strained voice, "Please Victoria, today is far too important a day for you to carry on with such shenanigans. Honestly, who is the baby here? Do you honestly think for one moment, we are going to persuade that heathen to marry you, if you're acting so immature?"

"Mother, Joseph is not a heathen, and don't you dare act superior to him, today of all days!"

Hoping to avoid another argument regarding her low opinion of Joseph Pike, Anne quickly apologized to defuse her daughter's temper, which she knew only too well was prone to tantrums. "You're right, Victoria. Everyone, especially Joseph—having been robbed of his heritage for so long—deserves a new beginning. Besides, just look at what a lovely son he has." Lovingly looking at the toddler, who was now able to walk on his own, and seeing him toddling toward the terrace, Anne said, "Dear, you need to keep the doors closed when little Edward is in here. You know how he loves the outdoors."

"Yes Mother, but it's so warm today, I needed some air."

Ignoring her daughter's lack of motherly instinct, Anne said, "Why don't you and little Edward go out back as we discussed. A man, even one who has shown no interest in his child, cannot resist a woman who is doting on his own flesh and blood. And seeing you looking as lovely as you do today, I'm sure I'll have no trouble convincing Mr. Pike what a benefit it would be to take you as his wife. Now remember what we discussed; do not appear too eager or needy. We don't want him to think you are desperate."

"Even though that's precisely what I am, and we all know it."

"Nonsense. Joseph Pike is like any other man; he may suspect it, but it's up to us to convince him otherwise. Now hurry along, and please, Victoria; when you see him, be tender and especially attentive to Edward's every need. And don't forget to be especially nice to Jacque Paul; otherwise I'm warning you, you'll never have Joseph. Now it's all right to let Joseph know how much you missed him, but don't make it out that you can't live without him. And above all, when he persuades you to marry him, don't allow him to have his way with you again. Not until you and he are wed! Why should he marry you and take you away, if he can have it for free?"

"Mother, please! Must you speak like that? Give me some credit; I know what I need to do. Just worry about what you need to do."

Wanting desperately to point out that if she had known what she was doing before, none of this would have happened to begin with, Anne nodded her head. "Of course, run along and I'll wait here until James and Joseph arrives. Make certain that you remain in clear view, so he can see what he has missed out on."

As she knelt down to pick up her child, Victoria defiantly said, "Fine, Mother. I just wish you didn't make me feel as if Edward and I are some prize to be won."

Knowing what measures it already had taken to get Joseph to agree to come here today, Anne turned and wearily looked at the gardens below. Absentmindedly she rubbed her brow, thinking of the past few years filled with endless heartache and betrayal. Taking in a deep breath to steady her nerves that were beginning to falter, she hoped that James's plan would work. She tried to block out the irony of her predicament; that she now looked to the husband of the woman who had wreaked havoc on her life, to help resolve her latest calamity. Knowing she could not lock Victoria and Edward away forever, this was her last hope to save face.

"Edward Spencer, if you can hear me, you had better do something to help your daughter after putting us through such pain and misery, or so help me, I'll defecate on your grave, you spineless coward!"

The bitter resentment she had harbored for her dead husband hung in the air and she quivered, thinking of him fornicating with Lavinia. The thought was never far from her mind, haunting her day and night. "How could you, Edward? And especially with her!"

Needing to draw on any strength she could muster to get through the next few hours, she forced herself to imagine Edward and Lavinia enthralled in the depths of a seedy night of passion. As her vision came more clearly into focus, she could hear Lavinia's voice, enticing Edward to take her, knowing she was that much closer to infecting those she wanted to make suffer. Sufficiently outraged, Anne then transferred her anger and disgust to that of self-determination, and in her tormented mind, she envisioned what Lavinia must look like now.   She envisioned a Lavinia no longer beautiful with flawless skin, but rather, a wretchedly ugly woman, whose face was scarred with pockmarks. Even though the vision wasn't as clear as she had wanted, Anne noticed that Lavinia's teeth had rotted away from her receding gums and her once beautifully immaculate hair was gone. What remained were lifeless, straggly strands of brittle hair that could not hide a decaying skull; and Anne smiled wickedly.

"Well, you didn't succeed you vile, evil woman; but we will. All those who you despise—Felicity, Benjamin, James, Annabelle, Rupert, their children and the remaining Spencer's, shall continue to live, content to know you got exactly what you deserved." Snickering to herself, Anne added, "How it must eat at you to know you failed, having nothing to show for your life, as you rot away in that hellhole you so richly deserve."

Feeling strong again, Anne stepped away from the window and waited in her favorite fireside chair, which afforded her a look of distinction without openly flaunting it to a man she viewed beneath her, and especially her only daughter. "I'll be damned if another Bailey-Smythe will succeed in discrediting and humiliating another Spencer. So help me God, as long as there's a breath in me, you'll rue the day you ever tried to ruin my daughter's reputation, you greedy peasant."

As far as Anne was concerned, Joseph was no better than the dirty, vile peasants she had seen in London, and no amount of soap and fine clothing would ever improve his lack of character and decency. Having Randolph as his natural father may have afforded him the opportunity of advancing his class, but from where Anne stood, she saw the same despicable nature of Lavinia and Randolph live on through him.

Determined to make sure that Victoria would not live with the stigma of having a child out of wedlock, multiplied by the humiliation of being cast aside by the likes of Joseph Pike, Anne had to prepare herself to deceive him. Just as he had set out to deceive her daughter.

Thankfully, James had told Anne how such a feat could be achieved. And who better to know how the wicked and cunning mind of a Bailey-Smythe thought, than one of their victims? All Anne would have to do was make Joseph want Victoria as a possession, something he felt he was entitled to, and then make him believe it was his idea.

As much as Anne didn't want to see her daughter and grandson leave Europe, she knew that if she left for America, no one would be the wiser as to what really had transpired. Once Joseph and Victoria were wed, she would announce to her set that they had been secretly married two years earlier and he had left for America to secure a good life for his beloved wife and child.

To solidify her story, she would have to paint him as a decent, caring, and responsible young man, which might prove difficult, since she despised everything about him. Yet, if she was successful, not only would Joseph look as if he favored Annabelle's character, which was well received and respected in society, Anne could also act as a victim herself. The poor helpless matriarch of society, who had yet again been the victim of a Bailey-Smythe, this time affecting her daughter, who had been forced to leave her beloved country to avoid ridicule by the elite of society.

Anne had to admit the plan was flawless, even affording her a believable reprieve when Victoria grew tired of him, as she knew her shallow daughter would. All Anne would then announce is that the Bailey-Smythe true character had reared its ugly head once again. Leaving the devastated Victoria no other recourse but to flee from the wretched bastard-son of Randolph and the life her mother had tried to build for them, for her sake, as well as their child.

Relatively certain that Annabelle and Rupert would not deny her story, anxious to avoid another family scandal, and protect a direct heir of Randolph's, and his inheritance, Anne knew James's scheme was perfect. All she had to do now was see to it that Joseph was willing to restore Victoria's life to respectability. Knowing firsthand from years of being Lavinia and the squire's friends, she agreed with James; what was needed now was to entice Joseph with something even more precious than money; and that was having something someone else wanted. Randolph only wanted Pricilla when he had discovered Edwin's son, Rupert, was in love with her. And years later, when Lavinia lost James to Rebecca, when the squire refused to set him up in business, Lavinia vowed to have him anyway. No matter what it cost her.

So now, Anne decided to outwit the bastard-son of Randy by dangling Victoria and little Edward in front of his face. Explaining to the cold-hearted, manipulative bastard that at one time she had been prepared to offer him any amount of money he required, to begin a new business and life with her daughter and their child. However, now that an eligible, respectable bachelor, with no stigma attached to his name, had replaced him in her daughter's heart, she had sent for him so he could view firsthand what he had given up. And then she would offer to pay him a hefty sum to renounce being the Edward's father so that Jacque could claim him as his own. Which proved he was indeed his father's son, willing to give up his own flesh and blood. The trick was to make certain she would be able to point out that the squire was a lot wiser than he, knowing the value of respectability and a good trade that would secure long-lasting wealth.

With Jacque arriving at the most opportune time, in plain view, where Joseph would be sure to witness him playing with Edward, and observe how familiar he and Victoria were with one another, Anne knew she would succeed in outwitting this amateur. Now, all she had to do was make certain that not only would Joseph beg for her to reconsider, but she would have him believing that he was a master in getting what he wanted, and that it was all his own idea.

Hearing the sound of the knocker, she knew her guests had arrived. Glancing at the clock and seeing James was precisely on time as agreed upon, Anne closed her eyes. Spontaneously calling upon the disturbing image of Lavinia and Edward again in her mind, she felt her veins pump with the anger and venom required to see her scheme to fruition.

"Come in," she called. As she had seen her Aunt Gwendolyn do countless times, Anne remained in her seat, raising her hand for her guests to kiss, setting the tone that her guests were in the presence of a matriarch of society.

As expected, James came to her at once and bowed respectfully, taking her hand in his, and kissing it. Smiling warmly at him, she waved him to take a seat, purposely placing her hand in her lap, not offering Joseph the same privilege of kissing her person.

"How good it is to see you, James." Turning to Joseph with a noticeably different tone she added, "Thank you, Mr. Bailey-Smythe for seeing me today; please, take a seat. This won't take long."

Noting how he reacted when she addressed him as Bailey-Smythe rather than Pike, she waited until he had taken his seat, strategically placed so he could view Victoria and Edward in the gardens. As his eyes trailed outdoors following the laughter of a young child, she masked her amusement at how predictable he was by clearing her throat.

"I trust, Mr. Bailey-Smythe, that your voyage here was agreeable to you, as was the generous purse I paid to assure a few moments of your valuable time?"

Judging by the look on Joseph's face, her tone and attitude was not what he had expected, and she noted his hesitation in responding. "Yes, quite agreeable, Mrs. Spencer."

Giving him an insincere smile, she said, "Good. Then forgive me if I come directly to the point, since I do not wish my daughter to be further upset by accidentally seeing you this afternoon. With a toddler, one never knows how long he will remain amused."

As if she had preplanned it, Edward squealed in delight, followed by Victoria's soft laughter. Anne took the opportunity to allow Joseph a long look at her daughter, playing with his child, by addressing James.

"Will you be a dear and hand me those documents?" she asked, noting that Joseph was still watching Victoria and Edward.

"I've taken the liberty of having my solicitor draw up the necessary documents that will ensure at no time in the future would you, for whatever reason you might deem necessary, hold any claims or inheritable rights to my grandson, Edward. Please read them fully, and then sign where designated." Turning her attention to James, she said, "Understandably James, I'll be requiring a witness to this. I trust this will be agreeable to you?"

There was no denying Joseph's look of shock as he glanced between Anne and James, the smug look in his eyes that she had seen as he entered the room, now vaporized.

"Edward, you say? Interesting." Accepting the documents from James, he directed his attention back to Anne, who had not masked the contempt she felt for him. "Not to say this is not to my liking, Mrs. Spencer; but I am curious as to why you deem such action necessary, and as you pointed out, paid me handsomely to ensure that I sign them."

"Quite simple really, Mr. Bailey-Smythe. Victoria and little Edward have an opportunity for true happiness, and I want to be certain that no one…" Anne paused to make her point, then continued, "and I do mean *no one*, stands in their way. As you have made it abundantly clear you wish to detach yourself from both Victoria and your son, I've taken the proper measures to ensure that you and my daughter get what you *both* want. Rather than be negligent, as Randolph was when he allowed another man to raise you as his son, I've rectified that by having my solicitor draw up these papers for you to sign so your son can be legally adopted by another."

As planned, Jacque arrived, and Anne coolly said, "Fear not Mr. Bailey-Smythe, your son will be well cared for. If I'm not mistaken, the man who wants to make a happy and respectful life for both my daughter and grandson has just arrived. I planned for him to be here today, not to flaunt their happiness in front of you, but so that you could view, from a distance of course, how well the three of them get along. Feel free to go and look closely if you'd like. However, I must insist that you remain up here and not let your presence be known."

As Joseph grasped the document tightly in his hand, fearing he would just sign the paper and leave, Anne's heart began to race. *What if this scheme backfires, then what?*

Thankfully, James spoke up. "Anne, did I hear right, did Victoria just call that man Jacque Paul? Could that be Jacque Paul Freeport, by any chance?"

"Why yes, James it is. I hadn't realized you even knew of him."

"Why of course I've heard of him, the name is such an unusual one. As I recall, didn't I hear that he was sent to India after his brother died? Wasn't that quite some time ago?"

"Yes it was. Now let me see if I remember what he told me…." Again, Anne deliberately paused long enough to allow Joseph the opportunity to gaze out the window. Knowing he had, she continued, not wanting to arouse Joseph's suspicion. "Yes, as I recall, Jacque said he left for India shortly after his brother died. I believe he was eight years old then, and he's thirty-six now, so let's see, that must make it twenty-eight years ago, I believe."

"Twenty-eight, and he's just now returned? I'm curious as to why he would leave India after so long?"

Nodding, aware that Joseph was hanging on their every word, she said, "I was curious of the same thing myself. I've learned through Rupert, that following Francois's death, all of Elaine's inheritance—the house, her holdings, everything—reverted back to the Freeports, Elaine's late husband's family. And because Jacque is the only living relative, he received it all. Not that he needed it mind you, being quite established in his own right."

Joseph, obviously upset at hearing the details about his replacement, stood and walked over to the terrace. James, recognizing jealousy in the younger man's eyes, as only one who knows such emotions could, winked discreetly at Anne as he reassuringly patted her hand. "Isn't that something. And he never married while in India?"

"From what I understand, he lost his family in a tragic accident, and so he's taken to Victoria and Edward. And they to him, as you can see."

Turning, Joseph asked, "If I agree to this arrangement Mrs. Spencer, what guarantees will I have that my son will be taken care of properly? Especially by an older man who has lived his life in a foreign land."

Taking great pains not to sound as cold and foreboding as she had when he arrived, she stated, "Well in truth, none. Without trying to sound offensive, Mr. Bailey-Smythe, I was under the impression you cared nothing for your son. So what should it matter if my daughter finds comfort from another man who wants to give both she and her son the respectability that they both so richly deserve? After all, it's only natural for Victoria, being so young, to want to feel needed and loved. And if she can ensure this, through a man who appreciates her beauty and good breeding, won't your son then be happy as well?"

Before Joseph had a chance to respond, James added more to drive home Anne's point, without being too obvious. "Ah, respectability. If I learned anything from my ill-begotten marriage, it was the value Randolph placed on being clever enough to make a good business transaction and the sense to know the importance of respectability. And although he forgot the latter from too much drink, and ruined a lifetime with one foolish act, I'll always be reminded how earlier in his life, those two factors were what he built his empire on. Why, just look at whom he married? Pricilla, a woman well beneath his stature, yet, was possessed with the grace and elegance of the elite. Which, I might add, he paid her father quite handsomely for the right to marry his daughter. In return for his investment, she added respectability to a tarnished reputation, and he could proudly parade her around in front of his business colleges as a trophy of great achievement that he deserved. And as if that wasn't enough, look who he left his vast fortune to? Annabelle, the daughter of refinement, to be overseen by Rupert, the very man who had exposed him for being the unsavory character he had become. Clearly the old coot valued wealth, power and respectability equally."

Glancing at Joseph, and seeing he was haphazardly looking at the documents, James discreetly motioned for Anne to continue. Taking his cue, she turned her head and called to Joseph, "Mr. Bailey-Smythe, not that I'm trying to rush you, but time really is of the essence. Is there something in the documents that you find disagreement with?"

Joseph, seeing Victoria being kissed on both cheeks as the man left, said, "No." Then giving his full attention back to Anne, he hastily added, "What I mean to say is, I still require a little more time to finish reading them."

Anne, nodding as if understanding, turned back to James, and said, "So tell me James, how are your business dealings going these days?"

"Not bad. Since the war, people are moving outside the original colonies, which means construction is on the rise. I was just telling Joseph on the voyage how I am in need of expanding my import and export business to another port in the states. I have looked into a perfect location in Massachusetts—Boston to be exact."

"Boston? I don't believe I've heard of such a city. But then again, I know so little of the colonies."

"Sure you have Anne, don't you recall the 'Boston Tea Party' from school?"

Nervously, she discreetly glanced over at Joseph to see how he was responding to their conversation. Noting that the unsuspecting man was obviously upset, she smiled while answering. "Ah yes, vaguely. So tell me, what is it about Boston that you find so enterprising?" Her jubilation that things were going even better than she had hoped was hard for her to contain, and she took in a deep breath as James continued, calmly. Obviously, her partner in collusion was far more experienced in masking his feelings then she.

"Well, if I had the right partner, we could begin transporting wood by ship from Maine and Canada, which is at a premium. All that would be needed then is to rail them to major metropolises and make a large profit. Pity I haven't found the right man, though."

"Ah, well, I'm afraid you've confused me…by rail you say…?"

Before she could complete her question, Joseph obviously becoming more agitated, interrupted them. "Excuse me Mrs. Spencer; I was wondering if I might have a few minutes alone with you."

Seeing Anne's hesitation, James said, "I'm sorry old chap, to avoid Mrs. Spencer's solicitor from being in attendance this afternoon, I gave my word that I would remain here with you both at all times. I do hope you understand, but considering the delicacy of the matter and since we knew one another so well after the long voyage, I thought it best for all concerned."

"Yes, of course."

Seeing the young man needed the opportunity to persuade Anne from him signing this document, James offered him an alternative. "I can offer an amicable solution to you, though. Why don't I stand over where you are and give you and Mrs. Spencer some privacy."

Within seconds of Joseph sitting down, James listened as he leaned on the railing overlooking the gardens and smiled. Just as he had predicted, Joseph tried to convince Anne what was best for Victoria and Edward would be with the boy's natural father.

"What you say, Mr. Bailey–Smythe, does hold merit. However, you seem to forget the decision doesn't rest solely on me. Victoria would need to be persuaded, and after all that she has been through, I honestly don't know if you could win her heart again. Besides, even if you managed to convince my daughter to trust you again, I could never allow a member of my family to endure the humiliation of someone in our set discovering Victoria had a child out of wedlock. No, after all that has happened, I believe your son being tagged a bastard, even if it were only discussed behind closed doors, would be far too detrimental to him. And you of all people know just how harmful being shunned by others can be to a vulnerable and innocent child, having had lived through that nightmare yourself."

Anne dramatically paused and forced herself to look sympathetically at him, before continuing. "Surely you wouldn't want your own flesh and blood to experience such pain, even if it would be better for him if his biological father raised him? It's not that I want to deprive you of your rights, but considering it was you who turned me down when I offered to help you begin a new life for my daughter and your son, I see no other alternative."

Anne strategically paused, waving her hand just as she had witnessed her aunt Gwendolyn do whenever she wanted to drive home a point. "Where as, if Victoria married a widower with a child, those in our set would think how wonderful it was that she was so devoted to *his* son. And little Edward would remain an elite member of society, which is his birthright—unscathed by malicious and slanderous gossip."

With a wistful smile, Anne added, "As I see it, by you signing that document, everyone benefits. As you wanted, you'll be guaranteed that you will never have to be involved with any of us again, and Victoria and Edward will live as they deserve; perhaps not as my daughter had originally hoped, but nevertheless, content. All I'm asking you to do is finish what you began, and make it legal for all of your sakes."

"And what if I told you I still loved Victoria, and always have? That what I said and did was foolhardy, and now I regret my actions? Surely you can understand that in part I was acting out of revenge, lashing out at Victoria for the life of misery and shame I had been forced to live by my own father. Secondly, as you have said, I know how cruel others can be. And in truth, I feared that by marrying me, Victoria would have to endure such misery and pain, and loving her as I do, I just couldn't allow that to happen."

Sighing, Anne said, "Well, if that's the case that was very noble of you. As I said though, it's not I you would have to convince. And even if by some miracle you were able to win Victoria's heart again, which I seriously doubt you could, what about everything else I just said? You wouldn't want people to know what has happened, and believe you me, no matter where you and Victoria settled in Europe, one of our set would eventually run into you and then Victoria and Edward's reputations would be ruined."

"Not if we were wed now, and you told them we were secretly married two years ago."

Sighing heavily, trying desperately not to reveal her jubilation that James's scheme was working, Anne rubbed her hand over her mouth and closed her eyes for a second as if in deep thought. "Oh, if only you had realized this before, you could have started a new life for all of you in America."

"Mrs. Spencer we still can. If I can persuade Victoria to marry me, I'll take her and my son to America at once. To Boston, and I'll become that partner Mr. Sterling was in search of. That way no one need know what has happened in the past."

"Mr. Bailey-Smythe…."

Interrupting her, he said, "Please call me Joseph. And I prefer Pike."

Acting embarrassed, as if she didn't know he went by Pike again, Anne said, "Not saying I agree, but don't you think, *Joseph*, it would be wise to check with Mr. Sterling, if this is agreeable with him?"

"Leave it to me, I'll take care of everything. How much can I offer him to buy into his business?"

Sickened by how readily he assumed she would honor her original agreement when she was desperate, Anne said, "Oh Joseph, I really don't like to discuss money openly, it's so vulgar, don't you agree? Besides, this is probably far too premature. After all, Victoria has been badly hurt, and I don't know if she will ever be able to forgive you. Why don't I ask her if she'll even consider seeing you."

"No. Please Mrs. Spencer, allow me to go to her. And if I can convince her, perhaps you will be kind enough to allow myself and Mr. Sterling, of course, to remain here this afternoon until I have a chance to work out all the details."

"Well, I suppose it would be the best for Victoria and Edward. Are you sure this is what you want?"

"Never have I been more certain of anything," he said firmly, his eyes glistening as he stood to leave to claim his prize. Anne had succeeded in out maneuvering a Bailey-Smythe, yet it was a hollow victory.

With Joseph gone in search of recapturing Victoria's heart, Anne sat numbly and watched as James came to sit beside her. "Well, you got what you wanted Anne. I would have thought you would be happier."

"Happier, you say? I feel no joy in having to humiliate myself in order for that despicable man to think he is worthy to even speak with my daughter, let alone be a part of Victoria's life. Yet what other recourse did I have?"

"None. And I do know precisely what you feel. To agonize and plot for something you want only to discover that once you have it, the victory has left you empty."

Anne noted that after James spoke, he absentmindedly brushed the scar on his cheekbone, and she said, "You mistake me James, the victory indeed is hollow, but I feel anything but empty. The sheer thought of that man, coerced into marrying my daughter so he can again feel superior, as he must have when he enticed her into his bed, sickens me. Almost as much as the thought of Edward and Lavinia engaged in a seedy night of passion does. Moreover, to know it was I who has made this possible, so he can have his way with her any time he chooses, and worse, possibly continue the vile line of Bailey-Smythe is maddening, to say the very least."

There was no mistaking the anger and disgust in Anne's eyes as she spoke in a controlled tone. Before him sat a bitter, scorned woman, and James knew it. "So now what, Anne?"

"Now? Why James, you of all people know how we English, with our proper upbringing and rearing, handle any situation—we bide our time. Then when that future son-in-law of mine least expects it, I will strike and be avenged."

"I see, and what of Victoria? What if she truly loves him?"

"Love, you say? Oh James, don't tell me that all of a sudden you believe in such trite sentimentality where love conquers all?" Snidely snickering, she added, "Why, that scar on your face should be proof enough that love is nothing more than and illusion we pathetic mortals try to convince ourselves exists."

Judging by the look on his face, Anne realized that James had offered his services, believing she wasn't aware of what he had done to her cousin. "Why James, is it possible you believed I knew nothing of what transpired between you and dear Felicity in New York? Although my dear cousin never saw fit to include me in her secret, I assure you; her lack of enthusiasm during Whitney's pregnancy did not go unnoticed. And before you assume I sought you out to assist me in my hour of need was in part, retaliation for being excluded, as Felicity only confided in the Robbins's...let me state here and now, it was not."

Hesitating for a moment, James looked at the woman beside him before answering. "Well Anne, do go on. I must say, not only have you surprised me with your candidness, but I must say, I am extremely interested as to why you called upon me for assistance, if you knew that your cousin's child was mine."

Not expecting him to admit Whitney was his son so readily, Anne stood, and walked over to a cart where refreshments had been placed prior to his and Joseph's arrival. "Considering all that has happened this afternoon, would you care to join me in a drink, James?"

"I'll have whatever you are, Anne."

Remembering his drink of choice was brandy, Anne lifted a crystal decanter and said, "I took the liberty of having a rather expensive bottle of cognac opened from Rupert's collection. I trust that will suffice, rather than brandy."

The thought of drinking one of Rupert's finest prized bottles of cognac amused him. "Yes, indeed it would, Anne. However, I find myself wondering what it is precisely that you will require of me in the future. To openly afford me the opportunity to discuss my son, and have the luxury of drinking from the private collection of my nemesis, surely must be a means to entice me into something rather unsavory."

"Why James Sterling, what a low opinion of me you must have to think I'm capable of such a thing. Have you considered that through my ordeal these past few years, I have not had the time to understand that even the best of people can react completely out of their character when they have become victims of a Bailey-Smythe?"

Anne, having poured the cognac and returning to where she had been seated, paused momentarily to see her daughter speaking with Joseph as their child played contentedly nearby. Filled with utter disgust, she motioned to the three of them in the garden. "Trust me James, I know firsthand the detrimental mental anguish you must have experienced being married to Lavinia."

Taking her seat, she sipped at her cognac, aware that James was watching her every move, and listening intently to her words. "You see, I've come to believe that at one time, you were probably foolish enough to think you loved her. Just as Victoria believes she is in love with that vile, bastard son of Randolph's, no doubt. Although I will not pretend to understand fully why either of you allowed yourselves to come under their spell, I will say this James; I no longer will condemn you for what you did to Felicity. Just as I have learned to make allowances for Felicity not confiding in me, her true affection for Benjamin before their marriage, and even afterwards, welcoming them back into our fold, I am prepared to do the same for you. But before that takes place, I have a few things I need to explain and then I have questions that will need to be answered truthfully by you."

Seeing him nod his response, Anne took in a deep breath before continuing. "I realize by me speaking to you now, you may misconstrue my motive as that of revenge or jealousy, but I say to you James, that simply is not so. Although I will admit it pains me greatly that my cousin's opinion of me was so low that she didn't confide in me as to her true feelings for Benjamin before they were wed. Obviously, she must have believe I was so close-minded that I would never have understood or believed that there had never been any improprieties between either of them prior to that dreadful night of her debut. That hurt will never go away.

And my pain was only deepened when I learned that Aunt Gwendolyn risked her own life by traveling to America only thinking of Felicity's happiness, without so much as a thought as to how it would affect me. Yet, even then, I put my own feelings aside and forgave Aunt Gwendolyn and Felicity by welcoming my dear cousin back into our lives openly and without hesitation, which ultimately opened the door for her acceptance back into our set."

Anne paused to take a sip, and stared for a few minutes into the glass, as if reliving the painful past all over again. Inhaling deeply she directed her attention back to James. "Even upon Felicity's return, and witnessing the strain between her and Benjamin and how unhappy she was to be with child, I never once pried into her privacy asking her why having a child was so troubling to her. I did, however, take notice of how she, Rupert, and to a lesser degree Annabelle, reacted so adversely to even hearing your name spoken. It wasn't long before I began putting the pieces together. Then after seeing Whitney, I knew the depth of Felicity's pain. And, although I shall never forgive you for what you have done to her, after my own hellish nightmare, I've come to believe there must be more behind Whitney being your son, not Benjamin's, than you just being a barbarian."

James, leaning closely to Anne, said firmly and without hesitation, "That is were you are wrong, dear lady. I was a barbarian, a crazed and despicable barbarian, and for that I don't believe I will ever learn to forgive myself."

Anne sat in stunned silence as James explained the events leading up to the night he had taken Felicity as his own without her consent, and by such force. He held nothing back, beginning before Lavinia had married Benjamin, and how he and Lavinia had a shameless, ongoing affair while he was married to Rebecca. The only time Anne interrupted him was when he explained how Lavinia had told him that Benjamin had forced himself on her savagely when they were married.

"Surely you know now that Benjamin could never have done such a thing, James."

"Yes, now I know, as a part of me knew all along, this was yet another of an endless stream of lies that Lavinia used to manipulate me to get what she wanted."

"I see, go on," Anne said calmly, showing no emotion as he continued to speak of the intimate details of his life while being married to Lavinia. It was no surprise to her, knowing Lavinia as she did, how she had excused her bouts of temper tantrum to Benjamin and Felicity. James relayed how she had repeatedly taunted him. Almost daily, pointing out 'the injustice of the Myles's living a loving and peaceable existence' when Benjamin had caused her such inner pain. Then always adding that 'Felicity, the tart,' had only wanted Benjamin because he had once been hers.'

"You have no idea how hearing something day in and day out, even despite your better judgment…you begin to believe it," James said sincerely. "I grew to despise Benjamin, viewing him as a manipulative swine who jumped from one heiress to another. The only difference between he and I was that he had Felicity and I had what he had cast aside. Then as I became closer to Felicity for the sole purpose to avenge what Lavinia claimed Benjamin had done to her, I became obsessed with Felicity, loving her more as every day passed."

"Then why…"

Before Anne had a chance to finish her question, James interrupted. "You have no idea how many times I've asked myself that very question these past seven years. A moment doesn't go by that I don't think of what a monster I was that night. How could any man do the things I did to her, and love her as I do?"

"You said 'do', rather than 'did'. Am I to assume then, you still feel the same toward my cousin?"

"Now more than ever before, knowing what an amazingly strong woman she truly is after putting her life together and giving birth to a child I'm certain she did not want."

"And Benjamin, what do you think of him?" Never had Anne been so direct in her life, and surprised that she was capable of such a thing, felt empowered to ask another question before he had a chance to speak. "Before you respond, bear in mind that if you are not entirely truthful with me and I find out, I shall not hesitate to close any doors that I've opened for you. This, as you probably already have surmised, will result in you being silently banished from those of the upper class, without another chance. And please don't for one moment think I'm incapable of doing precisely as I say. Or that I won't find out, because James—after what I've had to endure at the hands of your ex-wife, I am more than capable of doing that, and far worse."

Leaving no doubt in his mind that she meant everything she said, and with so much at stake, far more than she could even fathom, James said, "After today, I don't doubt you in the least, Anne. And although I never intended to lie to you to begin with, I shall heed your warning for future endeavors that we may encounter. Now, in response to your question regarding Benjamin—No, I do not hate him any longer. It is rather difficult to hate a man who has raised your son as a member of the English gentry, but then to be forgiven for the sins I've committed against him and his wife is more than I deserve."

"How is that possible if he hasn't been in contact with you?"

"I never said he hadn't been in contact with me. This is something that you must have assumed, knowing how Felicity and Rupert felt."

For the first time since they'd begun speaking, Anne exhibited even the slightest expression as she shook her head and smiled wearily. "Now why should this news surprise me, knowing Benjamin as I do? So you say he's forgiven you. Should I then assume he's allowed you to look upon your child, as well?"

"I would rather not answer any further questions regarding Benjamin Myles—other than to say, I have since been enlightened regarding the truth about the incident Lavinia repeatedly taunted me with throughout our marriage, and we've come to terms with the past."

"Of course." It was clear to Anne by his unspoken words, that he had seen Whitney, and Anne was equally convinced, that only he and Benjamin knew of such a meeting.

"Well James, let me state here and now, I shall never forget what you have done for me and my family. And to show my appreciation, once Victoria and Joseph are safely on their way to America as husband and wife, I look forward to having you attend a party at Pixie Halt."

"Not as much as I will, being graced by such an invitation, but before that can happen, there is the matter at hand. Which, if I'm not mistaken, the happy family are on their way to announce their engagement. As short-lived as it will be."

Turning slightly, she saw Victoria pick up their son as Joseph placed his arm around her lovingly. Sickened by the sight, Anne took in a deep breath to brace herself for their return. "Right. The happy family, indeed!"

~ Nine ~

June 1873

After a busy day picking up their guests from Plymouth, followed by making sure they were settled in and freshened up before dinner, Whitney sat inside the stone porch gazing out over his mother's flower garden. While Felicity busily attended to last minute details with the servants, Benjamin joined his son.

"I thought I would find you here. Well, what do you think of our friends from the States?"

"Quite nice, Father. I especially like the baby, little Jefferson, and of course Andrew and Lucas. Why is it that they both have different accents if they come for the same place?"

"Well, son; in America, depending on where you live you may acquire a different accent. Much like when we travel to London. In their case, Andrew is from the north—New York, and Lucas is from the south, from a state called Virginia."

"Virginia, you say? Isn't that where Mother was born as well?"

"Indeed she was."

"Hmm, then why is it Mother no longer speaks with such an accent?"

"Oh, I don't know. Perhaps over time it's faded. When she first arrived here though, back in '61, she had a very distinct southern drawl as I recall."

"Like Mrs. Carmidy?"

"Precisely like Mrs. Carmidy's. Do you recall me telling you that Elise was born in Virginia, but now lives in New York? And how she and Mr. Carmidy met while their country was at war against itself?"

"Yes. Seeing them though, it's hard to picture Mrs. Carmidy as a spy. Why, she looks like a mother to me."

"A mother you say? Ah, and what does a mother look like exactly, by your definition?"

"Someone soft and pretty, who smiles a lot at her children. In Mrs. Carmidy's case, she was smiling at a whole lot of children, hers, and Mr. O'Flaherty's. Why did they have such large families and we only have us three, and Cousin Rupert and Annabelle have only four? Even cousin Anne only had two children."

Chuckling at his observations, Benjamin said, "I suppose that is what God intended, son." Seeing the boy frown in silence, Benjamin asked, "What seems to be troubling to you?"

"Nothing really Father. I was just thinking of Mr. O'Flaherty. He's not anything like I expected."

"Right. Well, Mr. O'Flaherty, as I explained to you before, has been through a lot in his lifetime. Not only has he just recently lost his wife, whom he loved very much, but also before that, Gilbert had suffered great injustices trying to build a new life in America after leaving his homeland. Being an Irish immigrant in New York was not an easy task. Why, I'd even say it was something I could never do. You recall how I told you how some people treated the colored and the Irish as if they were different races, and in return were very cruel to them?"

"Yes, sir."

"Good, lad. Well son, my advice to you would be to get to know Mr. O'Flaherty before you draw any conclusions as to his character. Because I discovered a long time ago, that under his gruff exterior there is a fine man. One that I admire a great deal."

"Is that true, Father? Or are you saying that to be polite?"

Unable to control his amusement at Whitney's directness, Benjamin chuckled. "Son, you are definitely your mother's son. So forthright and direct." Patting Whitney's head affectionately, he said, "In answer to your question, though, I'm very serious. Any man who can overcome the adversities and disadvantages that Mr. O'Flaherty has, is a man that not only do I admire, but one that I respect as well and aspire to be like." Seeing the confused look on Whitney's face, Benjamin explained. "You see son, it takes a great deal of inner strength, determination and courage to alter your life as Mr. O'Flaherty has done. And what's more, he did it unselfishly. Not just for himself, but for those he loved. To make their lives better. Any man who can do this is one that should be admired. Don't you agree?"

Nodding his head as if in deep thought, Whitney said, "Well Father, I shall definitely try to get to know Mr. O'Flaherty better. Perhaps after dinner, you and I could take him and his family to the cottage we have built for them."

"A walk down to the cottage might be nice. However, Whitney, why don't we just show him the cottage rather than spring it on him that it was built for them? A proud man like Mr. O'Flaherty may think we are trying to interfere in his life."

"Yes, but wouldn't he appreciate what we have done for him and his family, and be happy that we cared so much about them and that they are welcomed here?"

"In time he'll come to realize that all on his own, son. We don't need to tell him the first day they arrive, now do we?"

Frowning, Whitney looked over at his father. "I suppose not. Can we at least show them the fishing poles we made for all the boys, though?"

"Yes, I think that would be fine. Just remember Whitney, mum's the word regarding the cottage."

"I promise, Father. Can I go see if the boys are ready yet so we can walk the grounds?"

"Yes, and do check on the young ladies as well, and be sure to invite them to come. Remember they are your guests as well."

Rolling his eyes, he said, disappointedly, "Yes, Father." Running from the porch and through the hedges to the back entrance, he stopped abruptly and said, "Ah Mr. O'Flaherty, I didn't know you were taking a walk."

"Aye, needed a wee bit of fresh air, lad."

"Right. May I invite the children for a walk as well? We'll stay close to the house so as not to miss out on tea."

"That'll be fine, lad. I'm sure they're all waitin' on ya by now."

Hearing Whitney and Gilbert conversing, Benjamin walked out of the porch and headed toward them. "Ah Gilbert, how good of you to join me."

"I was a wee bit restless and thought I'd give me legs a chance to stretch a bit."

"Funny you should say that. I was just telling Whitney that after tea, I mean dinner..." Correcting himself, knowing Gilbert probably referred to the evening meal as dinner, since he had been in America for so long, Benjamin continued, "Getting back to what I was saying, if you and the boys are up to it, perhaps we could take a walk down by the stream and do a little fishing before sundown. By then Joshua should be back from visiting Rupert and Annabelle."

Nodding his head, Gilbert looked over at Benjamin sheepishly. "Beggin' your pardon, it wasn't intentional mind ya, but I overheard you and your boy talking."

Opening his eyes wider and feeling the blood rush to his cheeks, Benjamin said, "Right. Well, that is most unfortunate. Please allow me to explain."

"No need. That was mighty fine what you did for us, and what you said about me as well. It's no wonder your son is such a fine lad, havin' a father like you to look up to and get advice from."

Extending his hand for Gilbert to walk with him, Benjamin said, "What a generous thing to say Gilbert, thank you. I noticed how well your children have adjusted after the loss of their mother, obviously due to your rearing as well. I commend you; it surely couldn't have been easy going on without dear Miranda."

Seeing the children running alongside of Whiney as he walked towards the gardens, Gilbert nodded his head gravely. "Every day, I wake up and still can't believe she's gone. If it wasn't for the children, I don't know what I'd do. The letter you sent helps more than you know. Thank you, I read it often. As for the children, well, the credit goes to Elise. I honestly don't know what I would have done without her. She's taken all of us under her wing as if we were her own kin. A finer woman I've never met, besides your missus and my Mandy girl, of course."

"Miranda was a special woman. Again, let me say how truly sorry I am for your loss. To lose her as you did, well, I can't imagine the depth of your sorrow. And then to go to the Honeycut's following her death.... In truth Gilbert, I don't know if I could have been as forgiving and generous as you have been."

"Nah, you give me too much credit there, Parson. It wasn't Alfred or Michael who took me Mandy girl from me, now was it? Now if that bastard were still alive, it would be a different matter altogether."

Hearing the hatred in Gilbert's voice as he referred to Tad, Benjamin said, "As you say, it wasn't Michael or Alfred's fault, yet with all your grief, no one could fault you if you did hold resentment toward them."

Shaking his head while walking slowly beside Benjamin, Gilbert said, "Those two men did a lot for Miranda and me. During the war, if it hadn't been for Michael, Miranda and her Da might have been killed, if'n he hadn't got them safely to New York. And well, you know how much Alfred helped Miranda and me. It just didn't seem right to blame them for what, his lordship did. As I see it, there wasn't nothin' to gain in reminding them what a depraved bastard he was. Besides, Michael already blames himself enough for the both of us."

"Right. I'm sure having you with them through their grief, knowing you didn't hold either of them responsible, must have helped to ease some of his guilt."

"Or be a constant reminder..." Gilbert's voice drifted off sadly. "Whatever the case, Alfred loaned me a lot of his books, which helped to get through the last few months."

Nodding his head, his arms clasped behind him as he walked slowly over the grounds, Benjamin said, "Ah yes, I recall he has a fine selection. I do hope you will take the liberty of browsing through my library as well."

"Thank you. I may take you up on that since I just reread Hugo's work, *The Hunchback of Notre Dame,* and have nothing else to keep me mind off..." Gilbert's voice trailed off, and instinctively Benjamin knew what he was intending to say. Rather than continue speaking of Miranda, Benjamin directed the conversation elsewhere.

"Ah Quasimodo...." A smile crossed his lips as he recalled how years earlier Francois had tried to convince him that Hugo's work was that of a romantic nature. "I haven't thought of the hunchback for years. An old friend of the family and I would debate this work quite frequently. I'm curious what you thought of it. Obviously you must have liked it, if you've reread it."

"Not really. When I read it before, I thought Hugo was trying to make the point that loving someone from a different class would never work out. Now though, it strikes me that perhaps the hunchback would have been better off if he had never loved at all."

Realizing Gilbert was not just referring to the book, and hearing the laughter of children, Benjamin looked over at the O'Flaherty's children. His eyes were immediately drawn to the youngest girl who held onto Montgomery's hand tightly while eating a sugar cookie and scolding her sibling. Watching the petite little girl, Benjamin was reminded of Miranda, and said, "Well, you took something from the book that neither Francois nor I had thought of. What does strike me though, from your comment, is how truly sad it would have been if the hunchback had never experienced love at all. Even as painful as it was for the hunchback, it allowed his soul to grow."

Gilbert glanced over at Benjamin, knowing neither of them was discussing a fictional character in a book any longer and stubbornly, Gilbert pressed further. "Aye, it grew all right. The poor bastard didn't have it bad enough; he had to learn a new depth of pain as his heart was ripped from his chest! And knowing that he would never have what he needs and wants to be happy again. I say he was better off never to love at all."

"I see your point, Gilbert, even though I don't fully agree with you. Let me explain...A long time ago, I pointed out to a friend that the true meaning of life was when a man and a woman could love one another and live as God had intended. Now however, I find loving someone fully and without reservation, as you and Miranda did, was only a small fraction of the wondrous blessing God brought to your union. The proof is right over there. Miranda's beauty, warmth, and inner strength lives on, through them. And as painful as it has been for you to pick up the pieces of your shattered life since her death, have you considered how utterly sad it would have been for Miranda, if she hadn't met you? She would have never had the opportunity, or been blessed to experience the love you two shared. Her death was a horrific travesty, one that you will never fully understand, I'm sure. However Gilbert, as someone who knew Miranda, long before she met you, I say to you, as her friend and hopefully yours as well, you and the love you two shared together, fulfilled her. Never had I seen her happier or more content as the day you two wed. And by looking at her children and the zest they have for life, even during such a painful time in their young lives, I thank God that the last years of Miranda's life were filled with such love and warmth."

"Hmm, I'll need to think on that some, Pastor...er...Benjamin."

From the second story window, Elise watched Benjamin and Gilbert walking the grounds as the children played nearby and shook her head in wonderment. "That man never ceases to amaze me. There he is, walking around with an Englishman, chatting back and forth as if they were old friends, when everyone knows how much the Irish hate the English."

"That very thought occurred to me when I read in your letter and learned of Miranda's dying request. Not that I wouldn't help Gilbert in any way I could, it just seemed so peculiar, with me living here in England."

"I know. At first, as much as I hate to admit it, I was very jealous that she hadn't asked Gilbert to bring them to New York permanently to be near me. I loved Miranda so much; I couldn't bear losing her and her children, too. That is, until I realized that it didn't mean Miranda loved you more, or even thought you would raise her children better than me. Which, I know sounds silly. However, I couldn't help myself. Now though, I believe on her deathbed, Miranda was more worried about him." Nodding in the direction of Gilbert. "You know how much she loved him, and knowing how those in New York still hate the Irish, she probably thought you and Benjamin could help him through his grief."

"Funny you say that, because Ben said something very similar when we spoke about it. Do you suppose God kept her alive long enough so that she could have her last request known?"

"Or, Miranda herself wouldn't leave, being as stubborn as she was. As soft-spoken and gentle as she appeared to be on the surface, Miranda had a stronger constitution than me, I think. And that's saying a lot."

Knowing that Elise prided herself on being strong-willed, Felicity smiled. "Well, one thing is for certain, she was right about her choice in men. Since discovering what a truly wretched man Tad was, and knowing what happened with Francois and Lavinia, it does make you wonder if living the life of wealth and privilege had something to do with their obvious lack of character."

"Oh, I don't believe so. No more than being raised a potato farmer means you are incapable of thinking deep thoughts or rising above your lot in life. Just look at Gilbert. I've come to know him well these past few months, and I can tell you, he's a truly remarkable man. Despite him being so withdrawn and sullen most of the time, you should have heard him and

Alfred converse. Why, if you didn't know his background and overlooked his speech, you would have thought he had been educated at Harvard, like Joshua."

"Hmm, is that right? Speaking of Joshua, that was terribly kind of him to make a trip over to Ashwillow this afternoon to see Rupert and Annabelle. They'll be so pleased."

"How are they, by the way?" Elise asked, leaving the window as Mrs. Duncan returned to place the rest of her gowns in the wardrobe.

"Oh quite well, considering Annabelle has been so distraught over Francois and Lavinia," Felicity said, nodding affectionately at the housekeeper. Without trying to appear rude, but wanting her privacy too, she added, "Thank you, Mrs. Duncan. Mrs. Carmidy and I will be in the parlor, if you need us."

"Yes, dear. Thought you might be heading that way, so I've set a tray of tea and biscuits out for you and Mrs. Carmidy."

"How thoughtful of you Mrs. Duncan. Perhaps the children would enjoy a light snack before dinner as well."

"All taken care of, missus." A smile crossed the lips of the elderly housekeeper as she added, "You should 'ave seen the look on Mrs. Carmidy's daughter's face when I asked her if she would like a biscuit. She looked at me like I was maze."

Uncertain what the housekeeper was referring to, but certain Sarah Tess had done something in error, Elise began to apologize for her daughter's actions. "I do hope my daughter wasn't rude to you, Mrs. Duncan."

"Why not at all, Mrs. Carmidy. She was lovely; even though she thought me daft for calling her snack a biscuit. Reminded me of years back, right after you had come from America. Remember, Mrs. Myles?"

"I do indeed." Turning her attention to Elise, to bring her in on the secret they shared, she said, "Here in England they call, 'cookies', 'biscuits'. And if I know my dear housekeeper, she brought the children a plate of sugar cookies to help make them feel more at ease at our home, and to welcome them." Felicity paused to smile warmly over at Mrs. Duncan. "Which is precisely how she made me feel the first day I arrived here in England."

Preening with delight at how her mistress obviously appreciated her, Mrs. Duncan said, "You and your friend go and have yourselves a nice visit and don't be worrying about a thing. Fannie and me have everything under control for the children, and if the baby wakes I'll let you know."

Elise walked over to the crib where Jefferson lay sleeping soundly and glanced over at their nanny. "Girdie, little Jefferson should sleep for another hour or so. If he hasn't woken up by then on his own, go ahead and wake him, so he's not up all night."

"Yes, Mrs. Carmidy."

After Elise patted her six-month-old son on the back lovingly, Felicity led the way to the parlor. As they walked down the stairs to the main level of the Myles's home, Mammy Tess's voice echoed from the ballroom, which had been transformed into the children's eating and play area.

"Why just lookey here. My babes are going to eat like little dukes and duchesses, they are."

Hearing the elderly woman's comment, Felicity turned to Elise. "I'm so pleased that Mammy Tess could make the trip. I've heard so much about her over the years. I noticed she and Montgomery get along quite well."

"Yes, surprisingly enough, they do. As you probably recall, Montgomery was devoted to Miranda and when she passed, there was never any question he would return to New York with Gilbert and the children. I just assumed he would return to work for Alfred; however, that never happened. Montgomery is more like a trusted friend of the O'Flaherty family than a servant, so he steps in and watches over the children mostly. You should see him with them; why, he's like a friendly giant. He even gets on the floor and gives them rides on his back. I can tell you, my boys are going to miss him terribly."

Shaking her head, recalling the first time she had met Montgomery, and how aloof and daunting he had been, Felicity said, "Is that right? And what happened with the other servants, did they also go north?"

"Only Bessie, the poor dear. She's so old and frail these days, and took Miranda's death hard. She's with Mama and Michael. She tries not to complain, bless her heart, but this past winter, the northern cold was very hard on her rheumatoid. You know Chester died a few years back."

"Yes, Miranda wrote me…. My goodness, it's so hard to believe that we've lost so many loved ones. Both here in England and in America."

"I know," Elise said, sadly. "How is Anne? From her letters, she puts on a brave front losing Edward as she did, but I'm worried about her."

"It's hard to say. She's been so withdrawn and distant of late. Now, with her off to Rupert's chateau in France for the season, with Elspeth, I find myself becoming more worried about her as every day passes. I'm certain she feels awkward, especially with the circumstances surrounding his death. Yet to distance herself from me, her cousin…well in truth, it troubles me greatly. Why, it's been months since I've seen Victoria and William." Realizing she was speaking her thoughts aloud, she turned and smiled politely as she poured Elise's tea. "How do you like your tea, Elise?"

"Well actually, I prefer it iced, if that wouldn't be too much of a bother."

Smiling, Felicity said, "Ah, sweetened iced tea; I haven't had that in years. I think I'll join you." Excusing herself, she carried the tray back into the kitchen, as Elise stood and went to the window, watching the children play, carefree. Silently, she shook her head, and thought, *Oh fiddlesticks Anne, you promised to tell Felicity about Victoria before we arrived. Am I to assume then, that you wanted me to break the news to your cousin?*

Hearing Felicity return, she turned and smiled politely at the young boy who was carrying the tray. "Elise, this is Nigel Bartlett, our driver, Jimmy Bartlett's younger brother. Nigel, this is Mrs. Carmidy, our friend from the colonies."

"Pleasure to make yer acquaintance, ma'am," the younger boy, no more than fifteen, mumbled while awkwardly placing the tray down on the table.

Felicity seeing how embarrassed he was, quickly came to his defense at his inexperience. "Nigel has been kind enough to come work for us indoors this summer, rather than assist George in the gardens."

"I see. How very fortunate to have someone so versatile in your employ. I wish we had someone we could rely on like Nigel here, back in New York." Smiling warmly at the younger boy, Elise noted that his face lit up hearing her speak of New York.

"Thank 'ee." Pausing to clear his voice he said more formally, "Excuse me, thank you ma'am." Bowing slightly, he turned to Felicity. "Will you require anything more, Mrs. Myles?"

Felicity, shocked at how suddenly he had changed his speech pattern, foregoing the thick cockney accent to switch to that of one more refined, like their butler Lionel, smiled and said, "No thank you, Nigel." Waiting until he was out of the room and certain they could not be overheard, Felicity leaned closer to Elise. "Well, if I didn't know better, I'd say a certain young employee of ours has visions of leaving England."

"I'd have to agree," Elise whispered. "It makes me wonder if I was that obvious in my youth?"

Felicity, recalling the times she and her family had visited the Browns and had met Elise, smiled over at her. "No, I'd say you had already learned to perfect your craftiness as a child, probably no older than your Sarah Tess is now."

"Oh, believe you me, I know that's true. Every day I am reminded of how I was at her age, and truth be known, it scares me to death. But never mind that for now, you'll know precisely what I mean as time goes by. Tell me about dear Annabelle. How is she really? From her letters I've gathered the news of Francois and Lavinia has taken its toll on her."

"Perceptive as ever, I see," Felicity said, raising her brow and looking at her guest suspiciously, while handing Elise a tall glass of iced tea in the couple's best Waterford crystal.

Noting Felicity's ability to remain cordial to her guest while gauging her sincerity regarding her interest in Annabelle, someone Felicity obviously felt very protective of, Elise smiled. "The years here in the serenity of England's countryside certainly hasn't dulled your senses, I see. If anything, they've improved or I'm getting rusty in my old age," Elise said jokingly, as she sipped on her tea, never allowing her eyes to waver from her formidable opponent.

Feeling less suspicious and ashamed that she had appeared rude, Felicity's tone softened. "Forgive me Elise, if I made you feel uncomfortable."

"Uncomfortable? Why heavens no! You have been the quintessential hostess, opening your home and allowing us to disrupt your life, even seeing to every detail in ensuring our comfort. I should apologize to you, for speaking so brashly. Never being known as discreet, I must have misunderstood that look of concern that I saw in your eyes as I asked about Annabelle, again."

Taking a seat across from Elise, Felicity looked earnestly over at the woman before her, whom she had known for years. And although she had never developed closeness with her, as Miranda and Annabelle had, suddenly she felt as if she could confide in her on any matter. "You were not mistaken Elise, I was suspicious of your motives. You'll have to forgive me; you see, living here in England, socializing with those who are also in contact with Lavinia, apparently has had more of an effect on me than I had realized."

"No harm done. I can't imagine how you and Miranda lived every day of your lives, constantly aware that someone was lurking nearby, ready to strike at the slightest provocation. As it was, poor Miranda's fate was the end result of both of us being too careless I fear."

Puzzled by Elise's comment, Felicity leaned forward. "Pardon me for intruding, and I won't be offended if you don't trust me enough to elaborate on your comment, but surely you don't blame yourself for what happened to dear Miranda."

Suddenly feeling overcome with emotion, allowing her deep-rooted condemnation of herself for not realizing she and Miranda had been overheard that night at the Honeycut's, Elise's eyes welled with tears. "Not for Tad's actions, he was a monster. What he did to Constance is proof of that, but if I had known...."

Stunned at seeing this side of Elise, not realizing how vulnerable she actually was, Felicity moved from her chair to the settee and tenderly took the obviously upset woman's hand in hers. Elise squeezed it, obviously touched by her gesture, and continued. "Last winter, Miranda and Gilbert made a trip up north for the holidays. Perhaps she told you about it?"

"She did. She wrote and said how surprised she was to find that Tad and Constance had arrived the day before."

"Yes, well from all indications, Tad had somehow found about their plans and made sure he and Constance were there as well. Even though Constance was still recuperating from a nasty fall off her horse that had resulted in miscarrying their third child. Well that first night, with Miranda under the assumption that Tad and Constance were at the opera with Mama and Michael, the two of us went down into the basement of the Honeycut's mansion. As it was, we spoke freely to one another, and she confided in me the intimate details of her and Gilbert's history; and how they fell in love. The two of us were completely unaware that Tad had heard every word we said."

Felicity gasped in stunned horror. "Oh no! How can you be so sure?"

"Well for one thing, Constance admitted to me recently that after Tad had returned to Mama's and Michael's home, that very night while his father slept in the room next to theirs, he forced himself on her. What's worse, her account of the incident was very similar to what I heard Miranda speak of in private that night in the basement, without the force, of course. Knowing this, it makes some sense in a twisted way, why after all these years, Tad turned his anger and revenge on Miranda rather than Gilbert. He heard from her own mouth, that it was she who had pursued the relationship with Gilbert, rather than Gilbert tricking her into loving him, as Tad must have deluded himself into believing all these years. Never wanting to admit to himself that he had lost Miranda to a better man, which became abundantly clear after she had discovered what a lack of character Tad possessed."

Elise paused and took a sip of her tea. Wiping her lips with her napkin, she continued. "I know I shouldn't speak ill of the dead, but my deceased stepbrother reminds me of Lavinia in some ways. Two exceptionally good-looking people who had the good fortune to be raised with all the finest life had to offer, yet never could be satisfied, always wanting more. And worse, when discovering they couldn't have it, instead of moving on, they both sought to gain what they felt they were entitled to, at any cost."

Felicity's eyes widened at hearing Elise speak of Lavinia in such a way. It was almost as if she knew of her latest diabolical scheme that had thankfully, failed. Sensing Felicity's reluctance to speak of Edward contracting syphilis from Lavinia, fearing she would be speaking out of turn, Elise eased her hostess's mind.

"Fear not Felicity, I know of Edward and Lavinia's affair."

Shocked, yet relieved, Felicity said, "You do? How? If you don't mind me asking?"

"It's no secret I have a knack at figuring things out on my own, but as it turns out, Anne wrote to me. Explained the whole incident, in hopes of gaining my help."

Confused by her last comment, Felicity pressed Elise for more information. "Anne asked for help? What could you possibly do to help Anne, all the way back in New York?"

Elise, taking in a deep breath, squeezed Felicity's hand tightly. "Felicity, I promise to tell you everything I know, but since it's getting late and I'm certain we'll be interrupted shortly, can we please agree to speak of this later this evening, after the children are in bed? I promise I'm not trying to be mysterious, I just don't want anyone to think I've upset you on our first day."

Judging the seriousness of her tone and the sincerity in her eyes, Felicity nodded. "Suddenly I understand why Miranda thought of you as a sister, Elise. You're not at all as shallow and conniving as you lead people to believe." Then realizing her words were not flattering, she blushed, "Oh I'm so sorry, that didn't come out as I intended."

Chuckling, Elise said, "Oh don't fool yourself, Felicity, I can be just as conniving and ruthless as the next, if pushed." Then wrapping her arm around Felicity's shoulder, she added, "You know what I think? I think my little sis knew somehow I would need a dear friend to help get over my grieving. That's why she insisted I bring her beloved Gilbert and the children to you."

Wrapping her arm around Elise, Felicity nodded her response, feeling closer to the complex and wonderful woman she had known most of her life. Yet until today she had never felt such closeness. Just as Elise had predicted, as they hugged one another, the sound of children's voices rang out from the foyer.

Hearing a soft cry, and recognizing it to be that of Catherine, Elise called out to her. "Catherine sweetie, we're in here, dear. Come tell your Auntie Elise and Auntie Felicity what's wrong." Seeing the auburn-haired girl appear at the doorway with a smudged, muddied and stained dress, Elise surmised what the problem was. Knowing how much she adored that dress in particular, since it was the last one her mother and she had picked out together, she stretched out her arms. "Come here sweetpea and tell your aunties what happened?"

Sarah Tess, standing sheepishly behind Catherine, not attempting to enter the parlor herself, watched Catherine very suspiciously. "I fell down and just look at my dress, it's ruined!" the young girl wailed, taking comfort in Elise's arms.

Elise, nodding over at Felicity as if to say it was all right for her to try to comfort the distraught girl, continued to soothe her by patting her back. Felicity, taking her cue, pulled out a lacy handkerchief leaned toward the little girl, and tenderly began wiping off her tears and mud-splashed cheek.

"Please don't cry, sugar. I'm sure we can get that old, nasty mud off your dress. It's such a pretty dress; did you and your Auntie Elise pick it out special for the trip?"

Looking up at Felicity, she meekly said, "No, my mama bought it for me."

"She did? Well, I can see why it means so much to you then. Did you know that years ago, your mama and I taught other children in New York? And sometimes she helped me buy my dresses, too?"

Fully gaining the young girl's attention, Catherine looked wide-eyed up at her. "Uh huh, Da told me. Not about the dresses...."

"Ah, and did your papa tell you that he met your mama for the first time right there at that school?"

Nodding and pulling slightly away from Elise facing Felicity, Catherine said, "Da said Mama was the most beautiful thing he had ever saw."

Smiling warmly at her, Felicity brought her hand gently around the little girl's waist while speaking softly to her. "Yes, she was. Why, I still remember the day your papa met your mama."

"You do?" Catherine whispered, completely enthralled by Felicity telling her of such an important day, and inched her way closer, as Suzanne entered the room. Felicity paused to let the youngest of Miranda's daughters inch her way closer to her, and placed her hand gently around her waist as well. Suzanne looking innocently up at Felicity, and whispered shyly, "What was my mama doing?"

Lovingly rubbing the younger girl's back, she said, "Well, as I recall, it was the morning after your Auntie Elise and Uncle Joshua's wedding...your mama came to the orphanage very early so we could have a nice long chat. After we shared our special secrets with one another, your mama, being the kind and loving person she was, began to play with the little children so I could get some of my work done. She took several of the little boys and girls over to the play yard and they began to play Maypole. Do you ever play that game with one another?" Seeing both girls nod their head, Felicity said, "Well, maybe tomorrow we could play together, if you like." Suzanne looked over at Catherine, then at Elise to see if it would be all right. She turned back to Felicity, and nodded her head.

Smiling warmly at both girls, she said, "Thank you, I'd like that. Now where was I…oh yes, your mama was singing along with the children, 'Ashes, ashes they all fall down' and clapped her hands when the little ones all fell to the ground. Just then your papa called to your mama, and she went over to speak with him."

Leaning dramatically into the girls, as if telling them a secret she said, "That afternoon, long after your father had left, your mama confided in me that she was still thinking about him. She even told me she couldn't forget his green eyes."

Suzanne's eyes, as green as Gilbert's went as wide-eyed as saucers as she whispered, "What's confided?"

"Confided means when you tell someone your deepest thoughts, or share a secret with someone and you know they will never break your trust."

Catherine, nodding her head said, "I know how to be confided, just like my mama. I never told anyone that Sarah Tess splashed the mud on my dress."

Elise looked over at her daughter, and then back at Felicity, who smiled, trying not to let on that the young girl had just spilled the beans.

"Why, aren't you wonderful? Just as beautiful and precious as your dear mama was."

Realizing that Gilbert was standing in the parlor along with Whitney and Benjamin, Felicity patted little Suzanne's face and said, "Both of you are so beautiful. I could just squeeze you."

Surprisingly, the two girls leapt into Felicity's arms without warning. Kissing them tenderly and cupping her hands around their tiny faces, Felicity said, "My, but you give the best hugs. Now why don't we go up and see what I can do about getting that mud off your dress, Catherine." Seeing a look of disappointment on Suzanne's face, Felicity added, "Would you like to come up with me and your sister? I sure could use some extra help."

Suzanne beamed, and eagerly nodded her head. "Mama always liked me to help her, too."

"Well, having no girls of my own, I can see why." Standing, and offering a hand to each of the girls, Felicity was pleased when they both accepted her offer without hesitation. Leading them past their father,

Felicity nodded as Gilbert mouthed a 'thank you', then noticed Mammy Tess turn and quietly retreat to the ballroom. Pleased to have time alone to bond with the girls, and grateful that the elderly servant realized the importance, Felicity walked slowly up the stairs as both girls began asking her questions.

"How come you don't have any girls, Auntie Felicity?"

"When we change our dresses can we put on some rosewater, like Auntie Elise lets us?"

Smiling down at Miranda's girls, overjoyed at how easy it was for them to accept her, and pleased that they seemed to like her, she merrily said, "Well, I don't know why I never had any girls. But I'm sure glad that you are here to visit me now, though. In answer to your question Catherine, why certainly. It's a young ladies special treat. Don't you agree? Maybe this evening though, you could try a new fragrance. How about trying some of my violet perfume?"

Elise watched the girls interact with Felicity, then looked over at Gilbert, then at Benjamin. As pleased as she was that the girls took to Felicity so readily, a part of her felt left out and without warning Sarah Tess came to sit next to her. "Don't worry, Mama, you still have me." Smiling warmly at her daughter, surprised at how insightful she was at such a tender age, Elise decided not to let on that she knew who had soiled Catherine's dress. She tenderly placed her arm around her daughter instead.

"Why, of course I do, and I wouldn't have it any other way." Kissing her tenderly on the forehead and holding her tightly, Elise looked over at her sons, then at Joey and Lucas, who were engrossed watching Whitney as he patiently tried to show them how to play jacks.

Feeling melancholy, Elise couldn't help but think how much Miranda would have loved being here to see the three families, despite their diversified backgrounds, spend a quiet afternoon together. As if able to read her thoughts, Benjamin smiled knowingly at her, and said, "Yes, this is exactly the way she would have wanted it."

Gilbert, hearing laughter from the second story, and recognizing it to be from his daughters, nodded his head and mumbled, "Aye."

Apparently overcome with emotion, he left the room. Hearing the front door close and knowing he was to blame in part, Benjamin looked over at Elise as if asking permission to leave. Seeing her nod, Benjamin followed Gilbert outdoors, leaving Elise alone with the children and her haunting thoughts. Absentmindedly, she leaned back and rested her head against the back of the settee. Still holding on to Sarah Tess, she slowly began swaying side to side. Closing her eyes to block the stinging tears, she thought, *Little sis, if you are here, please tell me what to do.*

~ Ten ~

Not long after dinner, as the respective parents said goodnight to their children, Felicity giving Benjamin and Whitney time alone to say his prayers, paused briefly outside the Gilbert's adjoining suite. A smile crossed her lips upon hearing voices from within.

"Da, can Auntie Felicity tuck us in tonight?"

"I know she would like to. She only has one child, and has no little girls."

Felicity, waiting to hear Gilbert's response, was touched by how patient he was with them.

"Now girls, your auntie has had a busy day tending to all her guests, you'll see her tomorrow."

Joseph, the youngest son, sat up in his bed and looked innocently up at his father. "Da, does Aunt Felicity only like girls?"

It was Lucas who answered his little brother's question. "No Joey, look how nice she is to Whitney."

Deciding it would not be viewed as interfering, Felicity knocked softly at the door. Hearing soft giggles and rustling bed covers from inside, she peeked her head in.

"Hello children." Turning to Gilbert she nodded respectfully and said, "Forgive the intrusion; I just wanted to check to see if you needed anything."

Gilbert, who had been sitting on the edge of his daughter's bed, stood and obviously not as comfortable around her as he appeared to be with Benjamin, said, "No, we're all set. A wee restless tonight, is all."

"Yes, well that's to be expected I suppose; new surroundings and all. May I?" Felicity, equally uncomfortable, asked permission to enter.

Motioning her to come in, Gilbert stepped away from the beds as Felicity came closer to the children. Smiling warmly down at the girls first, she pulled the quilts up close to their faces then tightly tucked the edges of the quilt under the horsetail and feather-filled mattress before kissing each of their foreheads.

"Goodnight; and thank you for an enjoyable afternoon."

Turning, she walked across the room and smiled down at Lucas. "Since you're such a big boy, Lucas, would it be to your liking if I tucked you in as well?"

Seeing the boy nod, she brushed her fingers through his thick wavy hair and kissed him on the forehead, also. "Goodnight, Lucas."

Turning to Joey, her heart melted seeing him look so small beside his bigger brother. "Well my goodness, how lucky are you, to be able to sleep next to your big brother? Are you comfy?"

Seeing him nod, but looking as if he were worried about something, Felicity leaned closer to him. "What is it, Joey?"

"You didn't wrap me in tight." Chuckling softly she walked around to his side of the bed, and tightly tucked him in before kissing him. "How's that?" she asked softly.

Smiling up at her, he said, "Good, can you sing to me now?"

Unprepared for such a question and not wishing to sing in front of Gilbert, she felt her cheeks turn red. "Well I suppose I can…" Hearing Gilbert clear his throat and hastily excuse himself, Felicity sat at the edge of the bed. Recalling a song she had heard as a child, she began singing, *No End*, while absentmindedly brushing her fingers through Joey's hair. By the end of the chorus, she smiled down at the small child who had fallen fast asleep. Kneeling over him, she kissed his cheek again as he turned to his side, inserting his thumb into his mouth.

Tiptoeing from the bed, turning the kerosene lamp to a soft glow, she went to do the same with the girl's lamp until she saw Catherine staring up at the ceiling with a tear streaming down her cheek. Startled, Felicity immediately knelt beside her and asked, "Sugar, what's wrong. Aren't you well?"

In a strained voice, Lucas answered for his sister. "That's the song Ma sang to us."

"Oh dear…I'm so sorry. I had no idea."

Sitting on the edge of the bed and resting Catherine's head in her lap, she said soothingly, "Catherine, can you ever forgive me? I never would do anything to intentionally upset you, you must believe me."

Biting her lip, she mumbled, "I know."

"Well, what can I do to make it up to you?"

Sheepishly, she looked up at Felicity, and asked, "Will you sing it again?"

Confused by the little girl's request, Felicity looked over at Lucas, and seeing him nod his head, she asked, "Are you sure?"

"It's like Ma's here, too."

Fighting back her own tears, Felicity turned down the lamp and softly began to sing the song again. This time though, when she reached the end of the chorus ,she hummed a few more lines of the melody until she was certain all of the O'Flaherty children were sound asleep. Looking at the four of them, a peacefulness seemed to hover over the room. Gently gliding

Catherine's head back onto her pillow, she tiptoed to the door. Turning one last time, Felicity smiled lovingly at them. "Sleep well, dear ones."

As she stepped out into the darkened hallway, she was surprised to see Gilbert waiting for her. "Oh my, you gave me such a fright," she nervously whispered. "I thought you went downstairs. The children are all fast asleep."

Not certain if he had overheard what had just transpired and suddenly feeling very awkward, aware that he wasn't saying anything, only staring at her, Felicity hastily excused herself.

Pausing briefly before leaving the second floor she turned and saw Gilbert silently entering his children's room. Shaking her head, she thought, *Oh dear, I've upset him.* With a heavy heart, she went in search of her other guests, Elise in particular, interested in finishing their earlier conversation.

Hearing no sounds, Felicity went in search of Benjamin. Entering the library, she was surprised to find him rubbing his hands through his hair, staring up at her and Whitney's portrait hanging over the mantel. Judging by his look, Felicity knew something was troubling him. Feeling her presence, he smiled over at her. "Come sit with me for a spell, you look tired darling."

Sitting on his lap in the fireside chairs as she did every evening, she whispered, "Only for a moment. I'm sure Elise and Joshua will be down soon."

"And Gilbert? Is he having trouble with the children?"

"No. They're fast asleep, though I think he's having trouble with me."

"You? Why ever would you say such a thing?"

As Felicity explained what had happened, she rested her head on Benjamin's shoulder. "Oh Ben, today not once, but twice I bumbled things badly where the children were concerned. Not knowing anything of their lives or their daily routines, I'm so afraid I will say or do something to cause them more pain. You should have seen little Catherine laying there in her bed with tears streaming down her face. I nearly cried for her."

"Yes, but afterwards you soothed her. So it all worked out in the end."

"This time, but you didn't see Gilbert. I know he overhead. What must he be going through or worse, what must he think of me? You don't suppose he thinks I deliberately sang that song just to win the children over, do you?"

"Of course not. Dear Felicity, you worry too much. Gilbert understandably is going through a rough time of it, and from what he said to me this afternoon, I believe he genuinely appreciates the help he's receiving with the children."

"Some help I was. I made his daughter cry, making her miss her mother more than she already does. It makes me wonder even more if Miranda was thinking clearly." Sitting up, facing him, she said, "It is possible you know, that Miranda was in so much pain that she wasn't in her right mind."

"It is possible I suppose, although from what Gilbert said to me after you took the girls up to change, I tend to believe as he does, that Miranda sensed for quite some time, that she was going to die."

Gasping, Felicity jerked with fright as Joshua, entering the room, cleared his throat politely to signify that they were no longer alone. "Forgive the intrusion; did we come down at an inopportune time?"

Felicity, nestled on Benjamin's lap, swiftly stood up, her cheeks blazing with embarrassment. "Why no, not at all. Please come in and join us. We were just talking." Unable to look at her guest, she brushed her skirt nervously with her hand. "Are the children asleep?"

"Yes, bless their pea-pikin' hearts. Even little Jefferson Abraham is out like a log." Glancing shyly over at Felicity as she took a seat, Elise said, "We couldn't help but overhear your comment Benjamin, as we walked in. And without trying to be intrusive, I tend to agree with you both."

Shocked, Felicity sat beside her and said, "You do? What makes you think that?"

As Benjamin offered Joshua a drink, Elise looked at Felicity and said, "You know I'm not one to indulge in the spirits, but this evening I think a sherry might be nice. Care to join me?"

Felicity nodded and said, "Darling, make that two."

Interested in hearing what Elise had to say, he motioned for Mrs. Duncan to leave them as the housekeeper entered the room. "That won't be necessary, Mrs. Duncan, I'll ring if we'll be in need of anything." As an afterthought, he added, "You might want to check in on Mr. O'Flaherty, though."

"Yes, sir."

Waiting until his housekeeper left, Benjamin began serving drinks to his guests as Elise explained why she believed Miranda knew she didn't have long to live.

"It was the last night of their trip last winter. Tad and Constance, along with Mama and Michael, had headed back to Fairfax." Looking over at Joshua for confirmation, she said, "Remember darling, how you took the older children over to spend the night back at our old place, so Miranda and I could have the last night to ourselves?"

"Yes, I do. And as I recall, you two were up half the night reminiscing."

"That's right, but in truth we did more than reminisce. I told her what Mama and I suspected about Tad overhearing us that first night. And that's when she confided in me that she hadn't been sleeping well."

Benjamin, handing Elise her sherry, was confused by her last comment and asked, "Suspected? Did I miss something?"

Quickly, Elise filled Benjamin in about the evening she and Miranda had been overheard by Tad. Exhaling and shaking his head wearily, he sipped at his cognac as he took his seat. "Before you continue Elise, does Gilbert know all of this?"

"Yes, sadly he does."

"No wonder the man has lost his zeal for life. Not only has he lost the woman he loved, but surely he must blame himself for not protecting her from Tad."

"I agree. As much as I hate to admit it, I'd give anything to see him lose his temper—so long as it wasn't directed toward me." Elise nervously giggled.

Felicity, her curiosity aroused by Elise's comment, and recalling the deep sadness she'd seen in Gilbert's eyes after leaving his children's room, asked, "So let me understand, you say that since Miranda's death Gilbert has never shown any anger? How peculiar, considering how volatile he used to be."

"Oh don't misunderstand me. He's been plenty angry all right, but it's a silent, controlled anger. It's almost as he won't allow himself to feel anything, not even anger. It's so eerie, it's almost as if his anger and pain are eating away at his very core, consuming him more as every day passes I fear."

"I'm no expert of course, but since the war, I've met up with a few of those men who served under me, and I can tell you I see the same dullness in their eyes as I see in Gilbert's." Joshua, taking a sip of his drink said, "It makes you wonder just how long they can keep it all in."

"Right, well that doesn't surprise me. In both cases, those poor souls from your unit and Gilbert have lived and seen such horrific things that they are having difficulty coping, I would imagine." Everyone sat and stared at Benjamin, nodding their agreement. "Let us be grateful that Gilbert has chosen to immerse himself in his children rather than another device to numb his tormented mind."

Elise agreeing added, "Yes, which I have come to believe was Miranda's doing. As I said before, I truly think Miranda knew she didn't have long on this earth, and said as much that last night we were together." Pausing to take a sip of her sherry, obviously shaken by the memories of that night, the three of them sat silently waiting for her to continue.

"That evening, Jefferson Abraham was making sounds as he slept, and I made a silly comment about baby dreams. Seeing the strange look on Miranda's face, I asked her in passing if she had been having any dreams. I can tell you honestly, I wasn't prepared for what she told me. And recalling what her nightmares had been, and knowing how similar they were to what I heard happened to her, it shakes me to my very core."

"Really?" Felicity asked, wide-eyed.

"Oh trust me; this is more than a coincidence. Miranda said her dreams were always very similar in content. She would hear her mama crying as she stood in her room at Glenbrook just as she had as a child, then appearing out of nowhere, was Tad, trying to harm her. After a life and death struggle with him, she always saw herself dying at the end."

Quivering, Felicity felt the blood drain from her cheeks. "How dreadful! And how long had that been going on before her death?"

"Well, according to what she told me in January, she had been having them for over six months prior to that. Now if she had them after she left New York, I don't know. Or even if she heard her mama crying that afternoon at Glenbrook, no one will ever know, but she was found in her old room, and she had definitely fought off Tad's attack. So when I say I think Miranda was stubborn enough to hang on just long enough to tell Gilbert precisely what she had planned for him and their children following her death, I mean it."

"Yes, I see why you do...." Felicity's voice trailed off, suddenly unable to control her trembling, she finished the rest of her sherry. Then looking at Benjamin, she meekly said, "Dearest may I please, just this once, break my own rule and indulge in another?"

Elise spoke up and nervously giggled. "Make that two."

Avoiding Joshua's eyes, knowing he would not approve, fearing it would affect her milk, she looked at the portrait of Felicity and Whitney. "My, the artist who painted you was rather good. From the moment I first saw it, I was amazed at how he seemed to capture every detail of you." Realizing she had said more than she had intended, feeling the effects of the sherry, Elise seeing Benjamin come to refill her glass, placed her hand over it. "Come to think on it perhaps I shouldn't, I'll need to feed little Jefferson Abraham later."

"Of course." Looking at Felicity as if to see if she too had reconsidered, and seeing no indication that she had, Benjamin obligingly filled his wife's glass again.

Feeling his eyes on her, she avoided looking at him and turned her attention to her guest. "In all the confusion of settling in this afternoon, I believe I forgot to show you the conservatory?"

Realizing that this was Felicity's discreet way of seeing if she would like some time alone, obviously anxious to continue their earlier conversation, Elise replied politely, "Why yes, I was enjoying myself so much, I've nearly forgotten all about that. A conservatory, you say? Oh, I would love to see it; that is, if it's not too much trouble?"

Glancing over at Joshua, seeing the glimmer in his eye, and realizing she and Felicity were not fooling him, Elise smiled her most alluring smile. "Care to join us, darling?"

"Perish the thought, my pearl," Joshua chuckled, sipping his drink. "I wouldn't dream of it. Not when you have that look in your eyes."

Detecting Joshua's mockery, Felicity casually picked up her drink and walked beside Benjamin. Laying her hand on his shoulder, she softly said, "Dear, I know how much you enjoy smoking your pipe with cognac. Why don't you offer Joshua a cigar while Elise and I have a little chat? You don't mind, do you?"

"No, you and Elise go ahead and abandon us; Joshua and I will muddle through somehow."

Seeing him wink at Joshua, she tapped his shoulder playfully. "Oh, you poor, mistreated husband of mine."

Patting her hand and smiling, he added sincerely, "Go, get reacquainted, while Joshua fills me in on the news of New York. It's been quite some time since I've had a chance to hear the real scoop from someone who knows firsthand."

Hearing a soft cough from the entranceway, Felicity's smile faded as she felt Gilbert's eyes on them. Ashamed that they were enjoying themselves when he was in such pain, she immediately removed her hand from Benjamin's shoulder, and avoided his eyes, looking down at the glass in her hand.

"Ah Gilbert, care to indulge in some cognac?" Benjamin asked cordially as he stood, greeting him by extending his hand. "If not some cognac, perhaps I might entice you with some ale?"

"Would that be English ale or some real stout from Ireland?" Gilbert responded cheerfully.

He was far more chipper than Felicity had seen since his arrival. "Well, if you'll excuse us, we were on our way to the conservatory for a little chat."

Nodding with a refrained smile, Gilbert turned his attention to Benjamin as he responded to Gilbert's earlier comment.

"Well that remark requires a sampling of both by an impartial judge, I'd say. Joshua, I hate to put you on the spot there, old boy, but it's up to you decide this age-old debate about who produces the finer beer."

Joining in on the conversation, Joshua stated boldly, "Well, if I must, then so be it. Count me in."

"Now hold on there Benjamin, I ain't so sure Joshua here is qualified for such a dubious honor. You forget I've had the displeasure of drinking some of that rubbish Americans try and pawn off as beer by calling it lager." Grinning over at the two men, Gilbert waited for either of them to challenge his comment.

Standing, Joshua smiled at Elise. "Dear, you heard the man, not only has he insulted America's brewing capabilities, but my own palate hangs in the balance. So don't be getting that pretty little head of yours all riled up should I need to overindulge in the 'Nectar of the Gods' this evening. After all, a lot's at stake here!"

Shaking her head dramatically as if disgusted, she raised her brow and said, "Well, I can see how much *we'll* be missed. Come along, Felicity." Turning on her heels, unable to pretend any longer that she was angry, Elise turned and winked at Joshua as the women left the library.

Hearing men's laughter echoing through the halls, Elise smiled. "Why, I do believe that's the first time I've seen Gilbert actually smile and mean it, in months. Your Benjamin must be some preacher-man, to have such an effect on him after one afternoon."

"Yes or he's fond of ale."

"Perhaps a little of both. Whatever the reason, it's good to see him smile again."

Sensing Felicity's reservation, Elise wondered if she didn't approve of Gilbert, or if it was her active imagination getting the best of her, feeling the effects of the sherry. Making a mental note to herself to watch their interactions with one another, Elise tucked her hand into Felicity's arm. "My, but this is such a grand, stately home. How fortunate that Whitney can roam around so freely in the country, rather than a congested city."

"Yes, it's quite lovely in the country. Living in New York though, does have its advantages, too. Why, I was just thinking the other day, how much I missed Central Park."

"I suppose after living there so long now I'd miss the lively city life as well. The ideal home to raise a family would be a blend of both; a serene country setting, near an established city, don't you agree?"

"That does sound wonderful. Are you and Joshua thinking of moving out of New York?"

"Oh no, Joshua needs to be close to his work, and with Mama and Michael living so near, I wouldn't want to move. Besides, Grandfather is getting on in age."

"How is Alfred? He must be devastated, him being so close to Miranda and Tad."

"He's actually quite well, considering everything. It's Michael I worry about; despite Mama and Grandfather trying to convince him this wasn't his fault, you can tell Michael blames himself."

"The poor man. I can't image what pain he harbors. To lose your only son, who turned out to be a monster who killed a woman you loved as your own daughter, the pain must be horrendous."

"Yes. Perhaps now with Gilbert and the children away, it won't be a constant reminder to him. Although in truth, following the incident, Michael, Grandfather, and Gilbert seemed to cling to one another."

Shaking her head, they entered the conservatory and she stepped back so Elise could see the entire room. Elise gasped as she walked further into the room, turning around as her eyes took in the sights. "Oh Felicity, how beautiful...." Her voice trailed off as she continued to gaze at the octagon-shaped, glass-enclosed room adorned with tropical plants and statues from Greek mythology. Even the ceiling, a dome with hand-painted ceramic tiles, was of that period. In the center of the room stood a statue of Venus, adorned by foliage at her feet, and lanterns strategically placed around the statue and between curved benches for seating. Nestled against a glass wall amongst more foliage was a demi-desk and chair where one could write and still have the view from inside and outdoors.

"Never have I seen anything so lovely," Elise gushed enviously. "How do you maintain such a room?

"Actually it's similar to that of a greenhouse, and in truth I don't know. Benjamin had it built for me. He and Nigel know the mechanics of its functioning for the benefit of the plants indoors; whereas I look upon it as my sanctuary, which happens to be a wonderful contribution to the home. And since it's been in the Robbins family for generations, I hope others that follow will enjoy it as much as I do.

"When we moved here from New York, the home was in desperate need of repairs after being vacant for several decades. Over time, Benjamin has made sure it was restored to it's original grandeur, updating it whenever possible, but maintaining its architectural design."

"Well, I can't imagine anything more perfect. And you say Nigel knows everything about this room?" Raising her eyebrows and smiling, she added, "Hmm, that young man's worth just multiplied tenfold as far as I'm concerned."

Tucking her arm into Elise's, Felicity led her to a seat, and said, "And we'd like to keep him here with us, so don't you dare try to steal him right from under our noses."

"Now would I do such a thing?" Elise asked innocently.

"Yes!" Felicity proclaimed, laughing but firmly making her point. "If given half a chance I believe you would. Nevertheless, be forewarned, I'm on to you, and tend to be very protective of those I cherish. Which leads me back to our conversation earlier." No longer was Felicity's tone one of merriment. As she took a sip of her sherry, she looked over the rim of her glass, pleased at how she'd maneuvered the conversation back to what was foremost on her mind. "So tell me Elise, what is it that you know of my family that I don't?"

"Before we begin, I must say Felicity, I don't recall you ever being as perceptive and cunning as you are now."

"Ah well, as a child I had little reason to be suspicious of others. Unfortunately, through life's painful lessons, I find myself relying heavily on what my beloved Aunt Gwen taught me, and that was the art of maintaining grace while still managing to acquire precisely what I want."

"You do your aunt proud then, since where I stand, I find myself envious."

"Why Elise Carmidy, I'm but an amateur next to you. But I thank you for such a lovely compliment. Perhaps while you're here this summer, we can share some pointers, which I fear I'll be needing since whatever it is you know must be quite serious considering your reluctance to share it with me."

It was clear by the look in her eyes—Elise enjoyed this cat and mouse toying with such a formidable opponent. "Bravo, Felicity! Again you've managed to get right back on track. I'd toast you if I had something to toast you with."

Felicity reached for a cord near her bench and smiled as she pulled on it. "That can be remedied. Now please, I insist you tell me what it is I should know."

"Where do I begin...." her voice trailed off, noticing Nigel entering the conservatory.

"Yes, Madame?"

"Nigel, please bring us some refreshments." Finishing the last of her sherry, she stretched out her arm for him to take her glass, while looking at Elise as if asking what she wanted.

"I'd love some buttermilk, if you have it."

Turning to her servant, Felicity said, "A pitcher of buttermilk with cheese and crackers would be nice. Will you also see to it that a tray of assorted meats and cheeses are brought in to the library for Mr. Myles?"

"Yes, ma'am. Mr. Robbins has joined the gentlemen."

"Splendid. And Mrs. Robbins, did she accompany him?"

"No ma'am."

Felicity, wondering why Annabelle had not come as well, smiled warmly at her servant as he left the room. As she turned her attention back to Elise, she was grateful for the time alone. As if they had not been disturbed, she responded to Elise's last comment. "Well, as my dear aunt often said, 'At the beginning is always the best', don't you agree?"

Cocking her head, obviously respecting Felicity's ability to remain focused as she maintained her household, Elise began. "Felicity, since it would appear that you require no delicacy from me, I'll be direct if that's all right?"

"I wouldn't expect anything else, Elise. Especially from you."

Taking in a deep breath and a moment to gather her thoughts, Elise said, "Following your sudden departure from New York, having a suspicious nature already, I wasn't fully convinced of the story Vivian and Grandfather told everyone. Especially after witnessing Mr. Sterling sneaking into Grandfather's study that very afternoon after you had set sail. Not that it was easy to recognize him, given the condition of his face. There is no delicate way of saying this other than that he was a mess. Clearly he had suffered a great deal from a nasty brawl."

"Is that a fact? I wouldn't know of such things."

"Well not really thinking much of his arrival, far too preoccupied by your sudden departure and Miranda's, I went to the gardens to sulk. There by accident I assure you, I overheard a rather intense argument between Mr. Sterling and Grandfather, although in truth, Mr. Sterling could barely be heard, his voice was so scratchy. Grandfather did most of the talking or shouting, as it turned out. Never hearing Grandfather rant so, of course I was curious and stepped closer to the open window of his study and that's how I discovered Rupert was the cause of this man's injuries."

Taken by surprise at what Elise was saying, Felicity gasped, but said not a word as Nigel reentered the room with tray in hand. Numbly, she recalled the events of that fateful night where James had attacked her. Vaguely, she remembered that in her shocked state, Rupert and Benjamin had left for a while. Seeing a glass of buttermilk being handed to her by her servant, she managed to find her voice and said, "That will be all, Nigel. Please close the door behind you, and notify the others we don't wish to be disturbed."

As if knowing how disturbed his mistress was despite her efforts to conceal it, he nodded his response as he hastily retreated from the room. Felicity, looking over at Elise in stunned disbelief, asked, "Am I to understand that Mr. Sterling was harmed by Rupert?"

"You didn't know?" Elise asked, obviously surprised by this revelation. "Yes, and quite seriously I might add; he still has a scar just beneath his eye that stretches across his cheekbone. He was lucky not to lose his eye, and his voice, for that matter. As I said, he was so bandaged up, he was barely recognizable; his neck was wrapped and he had bandages around his head that stretched over the side of his cheek. No foolin'. If I hadn't heard Alfred speak his name, yelling that he was never to darken his doorstep again, that all business arrangements the two of them shared were to be dissolved forthwith; I wouldn't have known it was he. As you can well imagine, I was stunned to say the least."

Visibly shaken, Felicity said in a hushed whisper, "How can you be certain it was Rupert who had administered these wounds?"

"From what Alfred yelled. Let me see, as I recall, his exact words were, 'You're damned lucky that Robbins didn't kill you for what you did to his cousin. No man or court in the land would have blamed him if he had, knowing you raped a harmless woman, you depraved bastard!'"

Elise sat silently, letting Felicity process the information she was relaying to her.

"I don't know what to say. I'm stunned."

"Felicity, I warned you I was going to be blunt. I'm sorry if I've hurt you."

"No, no…please go on."

Nodding her head, Elise leaned close. "I give you my word, no one—not even my Joshua knows what I overheard that day. And if it weren't necessary now, I wouldn't have brought it up. You see, part of what I'm about to tell you about Anne, involves James Sterling."

Confused, Felicity gasped, "What? How can that be? Anne would never be associated with James Sterling, especially after what Lavinia tried to do to our family."

"She would, if she were forced to. When pressed, people, and especially a mother, will do whatever it takes to protect their loved ones, especially if it's their child they are trying to protect."

Before Felicity had a chance to interrupt, Elise added, "Please, let me continue, and all of this will make sense, I promise. Now where was I…oh yes, well as I said, I never spoke a word of what I knew to a living soul. And not until Anne asked me to go to James Sterling's home asking for his help, did I realize that James was Whitney's father. You see, the painting that you have over your mantel is exactly the same portrait James has over his!"

The color drained from Felicity's face and she gasped, "What? How can that be?"

"I should imagine from Lavinia, in payment for a substantial cash reward. Everyone knows how desperate she was for money. She had even asked Vivian for some, which Vivian sent to her on a regular basis. However, after her death, I'm sure Lavinia needed a new source of income and went to James. That is, if she had figured out what had happened; which is merely speculation on my part. But given what I already knew, and then seeing the portrait on his wall…I believe honestly, Lavinia being as she is, wouldn't hesitate to gain financially by any means at her disposal."

"Yes, I see what you mean." Felicity's voice was barely above a whisper. She was obviously very shaken, but pressed for Elise to continue.

Hesitating briefly, Elise took a deep breath. "Knowing Lavinia as we do, I think she probably persuaded Francois to help her. And with his association with fellow artists, I'm sure it wasn't difficult finding out from one of his associates who you had commissioned to paint you and your son."

Nodding, Felicity volunteered more information to Elise. "Not difficult at all, considering it was Francois himself who had suggested the artist we hired two years ago when we were on holiday at Rupert's chateau. Francois lives, er…*lived*, close by at his late sister's estate. We had gone there following the revolution."

"Yes, I know of the French revolution. Then I was right. Tell me, by chance was that portrait painted while you were in France?" Seeing Felicity nod her response, Elise continued. "Well then I should imagine it wouldn't be terribly hard for someone to paint two identical paintings at the same time without anyone being the wiser. Did the artist by any chance carry the canvas to and from each sitting?"

"Why yes, as a matter of fact." Seeing where Elise was heading with her questions, she added, "He told us that he feared the children would tamper with his work." Realizing now that this had all been a ruse so a duplicate portrait could be painted, she felt nauseated at how gullible she had been.

Again, Elise respectfully allowed Felicity time to process all the information she had been told.

As if needing more information, Felicity asked, "Elise, I'm still confused as to why Anne sent you to James's home to begin with, though."

"Felicity, what I'm about to tell you is going to be even more shocking than what I've already said. Are you sure that you want to hear it now or wait until tomorrow when you've had time to steady your nerves some?"

Pale and obviously shaken, Felicity mustered up a smile. "How kind of you to even ask…No, tell me everything this evening, please. With the men busy indulging themselves, hopefully, no one will even be the wiser if I'm upset."

"All right, if you wish. But before I go on, I must tell you, Anne promised she would speak of this herself before she left for France and knew if she hadn't, I intended to discuss it with you myself. Obviously, it was too difficult for her to do so, and she left it for me to tend to. I say this to you now only because I want you to know that I am not breaking a confidence."

Nodding her head, Felicity smiled wearily. "Thank you for your candidness, but I had already assumed as much. Please, go on, Elise."

"Apparently, quite some time ago when Victoria was a girl, she made quite a lasting impression on Joseph Pike, when he was in school. A rather negative, lasting impression."

"Yes, as I recall, she was a rather outspoken young girl, and didn't hide the fact that she resented being educated with children from the Union. What does that...." Seeing Elise raise her hand, Felicity allowed her to continue.

"Of course, that was long before anyone found out that Joseph was the illegitimate son of Annabelle's father, correct?

"Correct."

"From what I've gathered, on Joseph's mother's deathbed she admitted who Joseph's father actually was."

"Well, not exactly on *her* deathbed, it was Mr. Pike's deathbed. He had released his wife from keeping the secret of Joseph's true father's identity. Shortly following his death, Mary came forth with the truth. Go on, please."

"According to the letter I received from Anne, Joseph was well taken care of by Rupert once he and Annabelle were notified, and they sent him to a private school in Paris. Is that right?"

Annoyed that Elise seemed to know intimate details of their lives, and aggravated that she was taking so long to get to the point, Felicity said, "Yes. Rupert was very generous to Joseph. In part, to appease Annabelle's conscience and I suppose he didn't want any other shame from what the squire or Lavinia had done, to affect his wife."

"Understandable. Anyway, two summers past, Anne, Victoria and William went to France on a holiday following Edwards's death. Is that right?"

Nodding, Felicity felt her heart begin to pound in her chest, and anticipating the worst, she said, "Yes, just as I said earlier, all of us traveled to Medoc following the revolution, but Anne remained behind."

"Well, during that time it seems Victoria met Joseph, who was on holiday. And from what Anne said, the time spent in Paris was most agreeable for young Joseph. He had developed into quite a handsome man, and now with a formal education, and running with a new set, he evidently had become quite a lady's man. A man, apparently Victoria was quite smitten with, as it turned out. Without Anne being aware of how serious the relationship between Victoria and Joseph had progressed, she and the children returned from France. A few weeks later, much to her horror, she was told by Victoria that she was with child, and the father was Joseph Pike-Bailey-Smythe."

Felicity gasped. "Oh no. Victoria and Joseph...that just can't be. Why, they are just children. "

"Not any longer. Victoria is sixteen, and isn't Joseph a year older? Clearly, they are old enough to conceive a child. Getting back to Anne—not only did she discover Victoria was to have a child out of wedlock; much to her horror, she found out that Joseph had purposely set out to seduce her daughter for the sole purpose of humiliating her. Anne was beside herself, as you can imagine. Especially after living through the shame of Edward's death. Apparently, out of desperation, to avoid any further embarrassment, she went to Rupert and Annabelle demanding that they step in and force young Joseph to marry her daughter before it was obvious to the world that she was soiled. Do you recall a few months after Anne returned, how she, Victoria, and Rupert had returned to France, unexpectedly?"

"I was told that Victoria had been accepted into the art program...and that Rupert needed to tend to his winery. A problem with frost, or some such thing..."

"There was no art program. Victoria went to France so no one would find out about her condition, and to have her child. As the months passed, Anne became frantic. Joseph had disappeared, was last seen in Bordeaux, wherever that may be."

"A rather large port on the west coast of France, off the Bay of Biscay." Felicity answered absentmindedly.

"Yes, well getting back to Anne...Even though she knew in her heart Joseph had no intention of marrying Victoria, Anne continued to search for his whereabouts for Victoria's sake. Evidently, she loves him despite what he did to her. Then last spring, she found out through a private investigator that he had left France and set sail for New York."

Shocked, Felicity repeated Elise's last words. "New York?"

"Yes, New York. That's where James Sterling came in. Anne had pleaded with Rupert to contact James on their family's behalf, to persuade young Joseph to reconsider and do the right thing by Victoria. She was even prepared to set him up in business in the city of his choice as long as Victoria and their son were by his side."

"Victoria has a son?" Felicity whispered. "What's his name?"

"Oh, Felicity please forgive me, this is so awkward for me. I should have told you sooner. His name is Edward Randolph Spencer-Pike. Evidently, Joseph has reverted back to Pike, foregoing Bailey-Smythe."

Not interested in Joseph, only the baby, she asked, "And when was Edward born?"

"Last spring, in late March I believe. From what I have gathered, William has stayed with Victoria throughout most of her pregnancy as well as helping with his little nephew after his birth. He returned to England only when Elspeth or Anne herself could go to be with Victoria and the babe. I'm certain this was to avoid any suspicion from your set."

Her voice barely above a whisper, Felicity continued to ask questions in hopes of fully understanding the grave situation. "So, Rupert and Annabelle know of Victoria's son?"

"Yes, and I'm sure they would have told you if they had not been sworn to secrecy. Have they not kept your confidences?"

As hard as it was for Felicity to accept, even as upset as she was, she had to admit that what Elise said held some validity, but rather than agree, she asked, "So did James help Anne?"

"It wasn't that simple, you see, Rupert would not agree to Anne's proposal. He flatly refused her."

"But you said you went to his home?"

"I did, but not with Rupert's blessings. You see, Rupert would have nothing to do with anything that involved Mr. Sterling. I'm sure out of loyalty to you, so that's why Anne wrote to me. Pleading with me to help her; which of course, I did."

"And James; did he help?"

"Surprisingly enough, he agreed to do whatever he could. Not asking for anything in return either, which in truth, I had been prepared to offer him a substantial amount of money, which Anne had arranged to be withdrawn through Joshua's firm if needed. Which is primarily why Joshua went to see Rupert today. He needed time alone with both Annabelle and Rupert to inform them that James and Joseph had arrived in France safely and according to the telegram we received aboard ship, their trip must have been a success."

Numb, Felicity said, "Is there anything else I should know about, Elise?"

"Nothing, other than you have no idea how much I've agonized over this whole incident, as I'm sure the rest of your family has. When Joshua and I were here after our wedding, I remember how desperately they wanted, no *needed*, to speak of you and know if you were well, yet wouldn't. That is until I pressed Anne. I know that in England you live by a silent code of conduct, which frankly, I won't pretend to understand. Yet, knowing how deeply you have suffered at Mr. Sterling's hands, and not wanting to do anything that could somehow be misconstrued as acting against you, I agreed to help Anne under one condition. And that was, if Anne hadn't told you by the time I had arrived, I would."

No longer able to hold back any longer, tears streamed down Felicity's cheeks. "Oh Elise, I know what an awkward position Anne put you in, and honestly I appreciate your help…it just hurts me so deeply that a member of my own family used me and my son as a payment to get what they needed, as if we were livestock.…"

Unable to complete her sentence, Felicity quietly cried in her hands as Elise hugged her. "Please don't cry, Felicity. Anne loves you. I know she does. I'm sure of it, in fact. Realizing her daughter had been used by Joseph so soon after living through the shame of Edward's death, all she could think of was hiding in France from the rest of the world, to shield Victoria. Not only did she have to console her distraught, unmarried daughter, but also protect her from the slander and ridicule she surely would have experienced if her secret had been discovered."

"But I'm not the rest of the world. I'm her family."

"She probably didn't know how to tell you since so much time had passed. When I told her that I would tell you, I'm sure Anne was relived. Not as the cowardly way out, but in hopes that once you had time to think about it, you would realize that no matter what had happened, you were still blood. Just as she had, when you and Benjamin returned to England. And to her credit, never once did Anne think of trying to get rid of the child as some might have. Instead, she stayed by her daughter's side and did what any half-crazed mother would do, even if it meant swallowing her own pride."

"Ah yes, the English pride. I know of it well."

"As hard as this is to accept, I think your cousin Anne did the only thing she could do under the circumstances, knowing all those silly, cockamamie rules y'all have to follow."

Hearing Elise's last comment, Felicity looked up and smiled through her tears. "Cockamamie? Now that's a term I haven't heard in years."

"Ya well, even though I've been hangin' around with all them Yanks these past several years doesn't mean when I get riled, my southern roots don't come out. Besides, I can't for the life of me think of a better word to describe the foolish demands you here in England put on yourselves, just for the sake of 'Keepin' up with the Jones's'."

"Oh Elise, thank you for helping me to put everything in its proper prospective. No wonder Miranda loved you as she did. You really are so very special. But there is something that doesn't make sense. I never spoke to Anne about Whitney not being Benjamin's son. So how could have she known? You don't suppose Rupert or Annabelle betrayed my confidence, do you?"

"Certainly not. As I said, Rupert would have no part in asking James to help Anne. Did you say you never told Anne? Well, maybe that explains...." Then as if excusing such a thought, shaking her head Elise said instead, "Seems to me if Lavinia managed to figure things out, which clearly she had, given the two portraits, it stands to reason that Anne surmised the truth as well, only she never said anything."

On the verge of hysteria, Felicity said, "And here I thought I had managed to keep my shame hidden from the world when apparently everyone knew all along."

Elise's back stiffened, hearing Felicity claim responsibility for what had happened to her, and angrily replied, "*Your* shame? Why Felicity Myles, I do believe I gave you too much credit before, if you think for one minute what happened to you by the hands of that low-bellied scoundrel is *any* of your fault. I can tell you, I've done things I bear the shame for that will haunt me 'till my dying days, and trust me, there is no comparison to what you are trying to take responsibility for. You were a *victim*, just as Miranda was. No one, not you, nor even poor Miranda, could prevent what those two evil men had in their hearts."

Felicity, shocked at Elise's stern comments smiled wearily, and nodded as if in agreement with her. *If only I could believe you in my heart, Elise*, she thought. Rather than rile her friend any further, Felicity said, "My, remind me never to cross you again."

Seeing her friend calm down, she began asking her more questions and slowly Felicity began to understand more than just Anne's need to keep Victoria's secret from the world. For the past several months she had sensed a strain between her and Anne, and between her and Annabelle as well. All this time she had felt she had done something that had caused her family to distance themselves from her. Yet now, knowing the truth, she realized it had nothing to do with her personally, but they were riddled with guilt for not confiding in her, which ultimately caused the wedge between them. Deciding to rectify this at once, Felicity looked over at Elise. "Did you say that James is on his way to America, and please tell me true, did Rupert know that you were going to speak with me this evening?"

"I'm sure James has left. As I said, we received word that the trip was a success in France. The telegram was short and to the point. It said, 'Thank you for all your help. James is seeing Victoria, her husband, and child back to America.' And in answer to your last question, no. When Joshua went there this afternoon, neither of us knew if you had been told or not. Although, recalling how astute Rupert is, I'm thinkin' he came just in case I did speak with you. Why don't I go check in on my little Jefferson, who's due to be fed soon anyway, and I'll send Rupert out to see you."

"Thank you, Elise...for everything. I'll never forget what you did for me."

Elise smiled warmly at her. "Ya know, as I recall, all the while Miranda was in New York, you befriended her. And if it hadn't been for your help, she and Gilbert might never have had the chance to share what time they had so, don't give it another thought. Besides, that's what friends do, help one another whenever they can. Right?"

"Indeed they do, dear friend."

~ Eleven ~

Late August, 1873

Sitting in the rose garden, Elise read a letter from her mother as Annabelle stared at the invitation to Anne's upcoming weekend extravaganza while Felicity angrily brushed paint onto a canvas.

"I can't paint when I'm so upset...." Felicity's voice trailed off in frustration. Sighing, she put the brush down on the tray of the easel. "I'm telling you, she did this on purpose! The question is, why? Anne knows I detest that man."

Hearing Felicity's comment, Elise and Annabelle glanced at one another, then without saying a word, Elise's eyes trailed back to her letter. Annabelle, realizing Elise was not willing to speak on this particular subject, especially with Felicity obviously so upset, calmly said, "Yes, I'm sure Anne knows, but in all fairness to her, did she have any other choice? After all, you know how much James has done for her. Why, excluding him would be rude."

Wiping her hands on a nearby cloth, Felicity agitated, said, "Rude! Oh Annabelle, please. You know perfectly well, ever since Anne's return she has been cold and distant to me. And it was no coincidence that she misled Elise into thinking he had returned to America, nor forgetting to mention he would be at that luncheon she invited us all to last month. Why, if Whitney hadn't been stung by that bee and had that reaction causing him and I to stay home, I would have been forced to allow that man to see my son."

"Now Felicity, please don't get yourself all worked up about that again. You heard Anne's explanation for not mentioning him; she swears it must have slipped her mind."

"Hogwash! She knew precisely what she was doing; I don't care what she said. You saw that look she gave me when she came by the following day, on the pretense of checking on Whitney. Why she hardly even looked at his swollen jaw, she was far too anxious to question me." Mimicking Anne, Felicity added, "Why Felicity, if I didn't know better I would think you were angry that James Sterling was invited. Surely there's no bad blood between you and he, is there, dear?"

"Try to calm down."

Clenching her hands by her side, Felicity looked at Annabelle. "Oh, she makes me so angry. I don't care what you say, Anne has turned sour against me. And that story about Victoria and Joseph marrying two years ago…honestly, does she think I'm that gullible? It's one thing to tell the rest of her friends that cockamamie story, but to look me straight in the eyes, and not tell me the truth is downright insulting."

Elise smiled, hearing Felicity use the word she had the night she told Felicity about Victoria. Felicity, noting her friend's amusement, snapped, "What? And don't try to say one of your clever comebacks like, 'What's good for the goose is good for the gander', or I swear Elise Carmidy, I'll just scream."

Holding back a laugh, having never seen Felicity so out of sorts, Elise responded, "Why Felicity Myles, I wasn't thinking any such thing. I smiled because you said cockamamie, is all."

Blushing, Felicity shook her head, and took a seat beside Elise. "Can you ever forgive me? I don't know what's come over me. I just assumed you were going to point out, why would Anne tell me the truth when I never felt the need to bring her in on my secret."

Although she had thought of that, Elise opted not to mention it and instead, tenderly patted her troubled friend's hand. "Felicity, you have yourself all worked up, with good reason of course, so don't you give it another thought about snapping at me. What are friends for if not to abuse them from time to time?"

Nervously laughing at Elise's attempt to lighten the gravity of the situation, Felicity looked between her friends. On the verge of tears, she sincerely asked, "How can I possibly be expected to go to such an outing with James there? Why, the mere thought of him makes my skin crawl, and obviously I'm jumpy. Can you imagine what I'll act like when I actually see him? I know I'll never be able to disguise just how much I loathe him."

Annabelle, leaning closer to her, sympathetically said, "Dearest, you can't keep making excuses whenever you know James is going to be there, and especially since the dinner party is a farewell to Elise and Joshua. People will become suspicious. Besides, I'm sure Anne was merely being considerate. After all, she is very fond of them just as we are."

"I know, Annabelle. Benjamin and Rupert said nearly the same thing to me earlier and just as I told them, no matter what I do, I'm trapped. If I don't attend Anne's party again after canceling twice already, I know our set will start speculating. On the other hand, if I go to Anne and explain why I can't bear to see that man, after all these years, I have no guarantee she would comply with my wishes. Why, just out of spite, she might insist I come, to see me squirm. Or make an appropriate excuse saying if I had only told her before she would have never invited James, but now that he's expected, she has little choice in the matter. Besides, even if she did agree to see that he did not attend, which is doubtful, knowing James as I do;

he'd probably make Anne feel beholden to him for helping to restore Victoria's life. Or worse, threaten to expose her lie. So I'm back where I began—trapped and frightened. As it is, too many people know the awful shame I bear. And as careful as we all are, the more people who know, the greater the risk that Whitney might find out. I've worked too hard to protect my son from the awful truth; I won't risk being exposed, not now or ever. Which leaves me feeling hopeless and frightened beyond your wildest imagination."

Sliding closer to her distraught friend, Annabelle said earnestly, "Of course you are, you have every right to be. But Felicity, you must remember you will not have to go through this alone. Those who love you will surround you, and we will make sure that you will never be alone; not even for a second."

Squeezing Annabelle's hand in hers, Felicity took in a deep breath. "I know, but all I keep thinking of is Miranda. You know how fond I am of Gilbert; and I would never say anything against him. Yet as much as he loved her, he couldn't protect her, now could he?"

Elise, seeing Gilbert retrieve a lawn tennis ball that had rolled close by, quickly cleared her throat to alert them of his presence, then motioned toward Gilbert and called out to him. "Gilbert, are you and the children all packed for your trip tomorrow?"

"Aye." Without embellishing further, Gilbert hit the ball with his mallet and walked back toward the men.

Closing her eyes, Felicity fought back her tears. "Oh dear, now look what I have done. Surely he must have heard me." As Felicity stood, intending to make amends, Elise pulled on her arm.

"Felicity, I wouldn't if I were you. If he did overhear you, which is doubtful—but if he did, what possibly could you say to Gilbert that would make either of you feel any better? And if he didn't hear you, then you risk straining your relationship further. Besides, what you said, as sad as it may be, wasn't said in malice."

Watching Gilbert join the other men, and wishing she could take back her words, Felicity shook her head angrily. "See what I mean? I would never do anything to hurt that man, but what if I just did? And people wonder why I'm so frightened...." Unable to finish her sentence, she placed her face into her hands and released her pent up tears.

Both women began comforting her. "Please don't cry Felicity, or we'll all start crying too, and just what will the men think then? As it is, poor Joshua is scared to death I won't actually return to New York. If it wasn't for Joshua's work and Mama, I'm not sure I would."

Annabelle, glancing at Elise, meekly said, "Really? Why, only last night I asked Rupert if there was a way that he could persuade you and Joshua to stay. Surely, Joshua could open a practice in Plymouth and perhaps your mother and Michael could take up residence here and in New York."

Touched that she would be missed, Elise took Annabelle's hand in hers, and squeezed it gently. "How kind of you to say, but I'm sure Mama and Michael would never consider that; especially now with Constance needing them so. Then there is Grandfather to consider; he is in his seventies you know, and despite being as spry as ever, he gets lonely and counts on us. Why, he's waiting for Joshua to return so they can meet up with some security man from Pinkerton, before he'll resume shipping by rail again. I swear, it is almost as if Michael and Alfred thought of Joshua as a partner, rather than their legal advisor. Which is very flattering, mind you, but it does have it's disadvantages too, given the fact that he is already so busy."

"Yes, well, it's no wonder they count on him." Felicity mumbled, pausing to blow her nose into her handkerchief. "From what Ben says, Joshua is well-versed on a number of enterprises. Did you know he was kind enough to look over our holdings and gave Ben some advice on how to diversify? According to Ben, Joshua was very keen on a company making licorice chewing gum.... Oh dear, what was the name of it?"

Shaking her head, knowing the gum, having some in New York, Elise answered, "Black Jack. We had some in New York, and surprisingly, despite its ghastly color, it's quite good."

"Color? I thought it was known for its taste and how it didn't just melt away after chewing it."

"It does both. I just thought the color gray rather peculiar."

"Gray?" Felicity and Annabelle wrinkled up their noses.

"Why, I can't imagine that being very appealing. I wonder if Benjamin knows that?"

"Oh, I'm sure he must have and probably even how they produced it, knowing my husband as I do."

As an afterthought and frowning slightly, Elise asked Felicity, "And you say this is something Joshua feels is a favorable investment? I wonder how chewing gum would make money?" Shaking her head, she added, "Well, if Joshua thinks so, I learned a long while back that he's rarely wrong. Why, before we left New York, he told Grandfather how uneasy he felt about him transporting gold by train out west, and I'll be doggoned if he wasn't right. There was this man named Jessie James who stopped the train by causing some accident and robbed it, and then he and his gang even robbed the passengers."

Annabelle and Felicity gasped, asking simultaneously, "What? Passengers? Surely not women, too?"

Shrugging her shoulders, Elise nodded. "According to Joshua, they didn't much care if it was men or women so long as they had money and jewelry."

"How uncivilized!" Annabelle chortled. "Why would men do such a thing?"

Elise, having seen firsthand how Reconstruction had affected Fairfax, exclaimed, "I blame them politicians in Washington. I swear, they are so busy trying to make the southerners pay for the war, they have forgotten they are men who need to support their families, too. Why, most white folk these days in the south are as poor as church mice, and can't even vote to say what the government can and can't do. They are taxing them to death, while that President Grant is running the government into the ground. You've heard all the scandals that took place in his first term of office, didn't you?"

"My Elise, I wasn't aware you were so well-versed on politics. What does Joshua say about this?"

"Joshua is very supportive of me. In fact, we speak about what's going on in Washington and around the country quite frequently. The way I look at it, as long as women don't understand the fundamentals of how the government runs, what chance do we ever have in gaining the right to vote?"

"Really? After working all day you'd think he'd be too tired to talk about politics."

"Most time he is, so we speak after church on current affairs. I swear, I don't know how he does it, juggling his time between his clients, grandfathers and Michael's holdings and then whatever is leftover, he tries to appease the children and me. Why I'm tellin' ya true, days go by when we barely see him, as he's working from sunup to sundown. Which is why it saddens me that this summer has passed by so quickly. I dread going back to New York and barely seeing him."

"Well, seems to me, you must see one another from time to time and do more than talk about politics...." Annabelle's voice trailed off as she smiled slyly, nodding in the direction of the children.

Knowing precisely what Annabelle was referring to, Elise chuckled. "Why Annabelle Robbins, I do believe associating with me so much these past few months has corrupted the proper English matron of society. Mercy, whatever would your highfalutin friends think if they heard you now?" Pausing to smile at her teasingly, Elise quickly added, "As for your not so subtle innuendo, I never said Joshua worked around the clock, now did I? And for your information, dear Annabelle, although I do find politics a might fascinating, Joshua is far more appealing."

Their laughter echoed softly across the gardens to where the men were finishing a leisurely game of lawn tennis. Hearing the laughter, Rupert smiled at Benjamin. "Well you were right again old boy, her mood seems to have improved."

Nodding his head as he aligned the mallet precisely in the middle of the ball, before striking it, Benjamin said, "Elise is a marvel."

Pausing to watch the ball as it traveled closer to Gilbert's, and seeing he missed it by only inches, he shook his head. Glancing over at Joshua, he added, "You do realize Joshua, we're not letting you and your family leave on Monday."

"Is that right?" Joshua chuckled, keeping his eye on Gilbert as he struck Benjamin's ball, 'poisoning' him and becoming the winner. "Nice shot, Gilbert." Turning his attention back to Benjamin who shook Gilbert's hand, Joshua smiled watching the interchange between the two men who obviously had developed a close bond over the past few months.

"Looks like I'll be practicing up on my skills while you're in Ireland, my friend. Can't be having the master outfoxed by the student, now can I?"

"Ah, even in defeat, I see you English are still full of yerself; claiming such grand titles as master. Well, seems to me a *master* wouldn't be so easily overthrown, now would 'e?"

Turning to Rupert, who seemed distracted, Benjamin said jokingly, "A little help defending our heritage against this Irish bloke would be greatly appreciated, old man."

Wearily smiling, Rupert leaned over to retrieve his ball, then said, "Right, sorry old chap, you're on your own this time."

Sensing Rupert was troubled about something, Benjamin followed Rupert's lead and began clearing the wicket from the grounds so the children wouldn't snag themselves on any wires. "There's a chill in the air this afternoon; I wonder if it will rain this evening."

"It wouldn't surprise me; the trees are already changing color. I suspect an early fall."

Suddenly the levity amongst the four men seemed to disappear as quickly as the winds blew in from the north. Gilbert, sensing Benjamin and Rupert needed time alone, looked over at Joshua. "Say mate, I was wonderin' if ye and Andy might give me and Lucas a hand to gather up all the fishing equipment down by the stream."

"Tell you what, why don't we take all the children and we'll close up the cabin while we're at it. Rupert, can Edwin and Pricilla tag along?"

Nodding his response, Rupert watched as Gilbert and Joshua made their way over to the children. "I hate to see them leave."

"I agree. Having them with us for the summer turned out better than I had thought. We'll have to do this again."

"Right." Nodding, obviously distracted, Benjamin patted Rupert's back.

"What has you so troubled, old friend?"

"Lavinia." Hearing her name, Benjamin's smile faded and he braced himself for what Rupert was about to say.

"Before we left the house today I received a letter from my sister-in-law, or should I say from her doctors. It appears that Lavinia's health is deteriorating at a much higher rate than expected. You may recall me speaking of her bouts of violence and delusions, reliving the past."

"Yes, and in truth, I still feel in part responsible." Seeing Rupert begin to argue, Benjamin quickly added, "Look Rupert, I know you disagree, but Lavinia resented her father and me for arranging our ill-fated marriage. Surely, even you have wondered if that marriage never had taken place, if things might have turned out differently for Lavinia."

"Benjamin, as you know, I've watched Lavinia grow up and I can tell you truthfully, she was on a path of destruction long before you entered her life."

"That may be true, but I was a man of the cloth who allowed himself to be seduced by greed. And if that wasn't bad enough, I gave my heart to another, and she knew it. I'll never forget her words the day she and James left for New York. She purposely needed to see me in pain, to feel vindicated for what her father and I had done. It must have been devastating for her, discovering Felicity and I were married and residing in New York of all places. Such knowledge stripped her of her sense of vindication. Is it any wonder that the hate and anger she had left behind in England, returned?"

"That perhaps is the only thing I'll agree with you on. Seems to me Benjamin, over the years you have forgotten a few of your own sermons. I distinctly recall on several occasions that you preached of forgiveness and God giving each of us free will. Lavinia, as sad as it is for me to say, never learned to take responsibility for her actions let alone the act of forgiveness. It was her choice to plot revenge rather than build a future. And her vengeance was not directed solely at you and Felicity, but poor Annabelle as well. Which is ridiculous since Annabelle was the one who suffered from both her sister and her father's shameful behavior. Perhaps it is time you take heed from your sermons and begin to forgive yourself."

Nodding his head pensively, Benjamin smiled wearily at Rupert. "How good of you to remember, Rupert. I often wonder if anyone was listening, or if my time in the ministry mattered."

"Oh Benjamin, you must know in your heart that even though you are no longer a preacher for the Church of England, your work with the Salvation Army has been beneficial. This leads to me to discuss why I was distracted earlier; it appears Lavinia has requested that I speak to you on her behalf. Apparently my wayward sister-in-law has shown an interest in cleansing her soul, and has requested that only you hear her confession."

"Confession? Why surely you must be mistaken. I'm not a priest, nor is she Catholic. All I can offer her is a way to redemption by accepting Christ as her savior." Having picked up the last wicket and post, he and Rupert headed toward the carriage house to store the lawn tennis game.

Rupert, adjusting the cuff of his shirt under his frock coat, glanced over at Benjamin. "You and I know this, but the doctor was very specific, saying she needed to cleanse her soul and will only confess the sins of her past to Benjamin Myles."

Pausing, still holding on to the cart of mallets, balls, and wickets behind him, Benjamin rubbed his beard as he often did while pondering something troubling to him. Glancing over at Rupert, he said firmly, "Well, then if I am to begin forgiveness for the past, I surely cannot refuse her, especially if she is near the end as you've indicated. I would hate to think of Lavinia meeting her maker without the opportunity of releasing the hatred she held in her heart all these years. And if God has chosen me to be the one to assist her, then I must. Who knows, maybe it will help both of us to bury the past and place the sins that haunt us where they belong—in the past."

"I was afraid you'd say that, and in truth Benjamin, I almost didn't speak to you about this." Sighing as if embarrassed, he added, "From the moment I read the doctor's letter, I've felt uneasy. And as unchristian as it sounds, I've been worried that her request was nothing more than another scheme to cause you and Felicity more pain."

"Don't be too hard on yourself, Rupert. After all, she has orchestrated some rather outrageous schemes in the past, and given the fact we know she purposely tried to infect us all with her disease only a few years ago, I'm sure anyone would question her motives. However, we need to realize that in her current condition and surroundings, there is little Lavinia can do other than hurl insults or cutting words. Having seen firsthand other poor souls with her condition, I tend to believe she knows her time here on earth is limited, and has regrets. Rather than think the worst of her, we must, as good Christians, do all that we can to help a pitiful woman who is in desperate need of salvation if she is ever to experience peace in the hereafter."

"I shall try Benjamin, but do be careful when you go to meet her. I assume you'll want to leave as soon as Elise and Joshua depart."

Nodding, he rubbed his beard again. "Yes, but with James in Devonshire...."

"Forgive me Benjamin, but considering I've had more time to evaluate this, I thought possibly a trip to London might benefit us all. With Felicity worried about James being in town and will no doubt miss the company of your guests, time away would do her good. And then there's Annabelle to consider. If the doctors are correct and Lavinia is at the end, I should imagine she would want to be near her sister."

"Yes, I see what you mean. Yes, let's plan to leave Tuesday, shall we? I'll have Mrs. Duncan pack our trunks and notify the tutor he'll be required to make a trip. How long should I tell him we'll be gone?"

"That's hard to say. Just tell him it's indefinite and that he will be well compensated for his troubles."

Reaching the carriage house, Rupert reached inside the small front pocket of his vest and said, "I hadn't realized how late it is. We had better get back to the woman and see what is needed for tonight if we're to be on time. What time was dinner?"

"The invitation said cocktails from five to seven, so I assume dinner will follow shortly after that."

They walked back to the rose garden to join the others, each lost deep in their own thoughts, and didn't notice that the women were watching them intently.

Elise, taking in a deep breath, looked over at Annabelle anxiously. "My, I had better think of tending to little Jefferson, that way maybe he won't need another feeding until after we eat."

"Annabelle, is it my imagination or have you noticed Jefferson Abraham sure requires a lot of extra feedings whenever his mother tries to avoid something unpleasant?"

Indignantly, Elise planted her fists firmly on her hips, and tried to conceal her merriment at Felicity's observation. "I surely don't know what you two suspicious women are implying. As I recall, only a few minutes ago you thought it perfectly respectable to vanish for a spell after dinner ,using the excuse that the baby needed tending to. Yet now, when I'm certain my dear babe does need his mama, you doubt my intentions and say the most contrary things. Well if that just doesn't hurt me to the quick, I'd like to know what does."

Chuckling, admiring Elise's spirit and ability to keep a straight face while being playful, Annabelle looked apologetically over at her. "Oh Elise, you poor misunderstood thing, will you ever be able to forgive us?"

"Hmm, I'll think on it some." Then winking, she whispered, "By the look on your husbands' faces, I really must be runnin' off. Tell me what's got them so riled up after dinner, hear?" Not waiting for a reply, she scurried off toward the house as Felicity braced herself for yet another announcement that she knew would upset her further.

"Where did Elise run off to?"

"Oh she had to feed Jefferson. Why the gloomy faces?" Annabelle asked, looking between Rupert and Benjamin.

"Dearest, we were just discussing that after the O'Flahertys and Carmidys leave, a trip to London might be enjoyable."

The blood drained from Annabelle's face, knowing from Rupert's tone of voice that he was trying to shield her from something, and fear gripped her heart. "What's wrong Rupert, why the sudden need to go to London? What aren't you telling me about? Lavinia hasn't passed, has she?"

Taking a seat beside his wife, he placed his arm protectively around her. "Now don't get yourself all worked up, dearest. Lavinia has requested to see Benjamin, to make peace with her conscience, and he has graciously accepted to try and give her some comfort in her last days."

Shocked at his comment, Felicity gasped, "*No!* Oh, please tell me you'll reconsider Ben, please. Surely, there must be someone else in London they could call on instead. I need you here with me."

"Darling, I'm not leaving you and Whitney; we're all going to London." Seeing relief spread over Felicity's face, Benjamin added, "Tuesday we shall all travel to London. By the time we return, you can plan for the holidays, and Gilbert and the children's return. We will want to make their first Christmas here in England especially nice, considering this will be the first one without Miranda."

Even as nonchalant as their husbands tried to sound, both Annabelle and Felicity knew they were worried about something, and they discreetly glanced at each other. From a distance, the sound of laughter rang out alerting them that Gilbert and Joshua were on their way back. Rather than continue with their conversation, Felicity smiled at Benjamin. "How thoughtful of you Ben, and you too, Rupert. It looks like you've thought of everything for this unexpected trip."

"Right, then shall I assume you have no objections to leaving on Tuesday?"

Alarmed by the suddenness, Annabelle turned to Rupert. "Well, I suppose, but you do realize the children have school and I'll need to make arrangements to close down Ashwillow."

"Now don't worry about a thing, dearest," Rupert said reassuringly. "Benjamin will get the tutor." as he looked to Benjamin for assistance, Benjamin jumped in.

"As soon as we return to the house I'll send word to Niles Aston that we'll be requiring his services. As for closing down the homes, there really will be no need for that, the servants can keep things up while we're away. So all you two need to think about is where to go shopping when we arrive in London."

Approaching them and hearing Benjamin's comment, Joshua smiled. "Whew, sure glad Elise didn't hear that or I'd never be able to drag her on the boat come Monday."

As Felicity watched Rupert reply to Joshua's comment jokingly, she lovingly stretched out her arms to Catherine and Joey who were anxious to tell her of their adventure down by the stream. Discreetly, she glanced over at Annabelle and judging by the concerned look she saw in her friend's eyes, Felicity knew she was equally worried about this sudden trip. Rather than alert the children, Felicity masked her fears with a smile and answered Joey. "So you found a frog did you, little man. And how big was he?"

Stretching out his little arms, Joey looked up at her, wide-eyed, and said, "This big, Auntie."

Immediately the children tried to correct the size of how big the frog actually was and seeing how aggravated Joey was becoming, soothingly Felicity said, "Well, he must have seemed that big, right Joey?"

"It was, honest, Auntie," he mumbled as he laid his dirty head on her lap. Not caring that her cream skirt was probably being soiled, Felicity patted his head, then looked over at Suzanne who had inched her way in front of the other children. In her hands was a bunch of wild flowers and she held them out to Felicity. Touched by how precious she looked, Felicity smiled and said, "Oh darling, are those for me?"

Smiling proudly, Suzanne shook her head. "For your hair tonight. I'll help you get ready if you want."

"What a thoughtful girl you are, thank you so much. Why don't we go pick out a dress to match them right now, then after you and your brothers and sister change for dinner, both you and Catherine can help me fix my hair. How does that sound?"

Hearing her suggestion, Joey looked up at her, pouting. "How come the girls always help you and me, and Lucas can't?"

Feeling Gilbert's eyes watching her, she looked up at him and was surprised to see anger. Then recalling her earlier comment and knowing he must have overheard her, she blushed and looked away.

"Cause Da needs his boys to help him. Now run along and get all washed up and I'll be up in a wee bit."

Felicity, avoiding Gilbert's piercing eyes, smiled loving at the children as she and Annabelle directed them back to the house. "Pricilla, remember your gown is in Sarah Tess's bedchamber. I'm sure Fannie will have her hands full, so when you finish, please help your little brother."

Turning, Annabelle's oldest child said, "Mother, Edwin is old enough to dress himself. He is five now."

"I know how old he is, little miss. Do what I said and mind your manners."

Seeing the hurt look on his cousin's face, Whitney turned and asked, "Aunt Annabelle, if it would be all right with you, allow me to supervise Edwin this evening, since we're sharing a room."

Glancing from her daughter, who looked lovingly over at her cousin, then at Whitney, Annabelle's expression softened. "Thank you, Whitney."

Immediately hearing her mother's comment, Pricilla leaned closer to Sarah Tess. "See I told you, Whitney always sticks up for me, which proves he likes me more. Wait until he sees my new gown that Father had commissioned especially for me to wear tonight."

Catherine, obviously upset that she didn't have a new gown, lowered her head. Seeing her reaction, Felicity stepped closer and whispered, "Don't be so sad my little darling, guess who else has a new gown waiting for them in their room?"

"Who? Me?"

Nodding her head, Felicity smiled. "All of you do; a gift from Mr. Myles and me, for spending the summer with us. Now run along and see what we picked out for you."

The girls shrieked with delight and ran toward the house while the boys lagged behind with frowns on their faces. Mimicking their scowls, Felicity said, "Well boys, we have no gowns for you, but I have a feeling suits, just like your fathers', with long trousers, are waiting for you. Andy, Caleb and Alfred—you too."

Joey tugged at her skirt, wiping his mud-stained hands as he did. "Even me, Auntie?"

"Yes my little lamb, even you. Now run along and I bet Lucas will help you so you can surprise your papa."

Again he tugged at her skirt, and Felicity asked, "Don't you want to see your big boy suit, Joey?"

"Yes, Auntie."

"Then what's wrong?"

Seeing him motion to her with his index finger, Felicity bent over and was taken off guard when he pulled her face between his hands and kissed her cheek. "Thank you, Auntie!" he exclaimed. Not waiting for a response, he turned on his heels and hollered, "Hey, wait up for me."

Chuckling as she wiped the mud from his hand that now covered her face, she said, "Those little ones are so adorable, I swear, half the time I just want to squeeze them."

Annabelle nodded. "They sure have taken to you, that's for sure."

"Yes, unfortunately their father doesn't share the same enthusiasm. Did you happen to see the angry look he gave me when Suzanne gave me the flowers?"

"Angry look? Why I think you're mistaken, I thought Gilbert looked concerned."

"Concerned? Whatever for?"

"Well despite you trying to conceal it around the children, it was obvious you were upset."

Shaking her head, Felicity brushed off the front of her skirt, and seeing she was only smearing it, commented, "Oh dear, I've just made it worse.... So you think Gilbert wasn't angry? How peculiar. I really thought he was. So tell me, what do you make of our sudden trip to London?"

"Why don't we save our thoughts for later."

Feeling her stomach knot up, Felicity sighed. "Oh how I wish I could think of a way to get out of this dinner party tonight, especially now, after learning Lavinia wants to see Benjamin. Why is it I feel as if my nightmares are suddenly becoming reality?"

"Nightmares? Why, you haven't said anything about nightmares."

Reaching the back door and realizing she had said too much, Felicity absentmindedly smelled the flowers she held in her hand. "Didn't I? Hmm, I thought I had. Well judging by the laughter upstairs, I'd say poor Mrs. Duncan and Fannie could probably use a hand, so we'll have to wait on that, too."

Chuckling nervously, Felicity made her way up the stairs, taking in deep breaths to help steady her nerves, knowing Annabelle would be watching her extra closely now that she had alerted her.

Annabelle lifted her skirts and absentmindedly shook her head as she followed her friend. *Fine Felicity Myles, have it your way for now. Tonight though, Elise and I will worm it out of you, whatever it is that you think you are so cleverly hiding from us.*

~ Twelve ~

Arriving fashionably late, Felicity trembled as she and the others entered the parlor of her aunt's former home, Pixie Halt. Anne, standing near the entrance to greet her guests, nodded politely at Elspeth as she excused herself, gushing loud enough to be overheard. "The guests of honor have arrived at last. I was beginning to wonder what was keeping you."

Elise, stepping forward, politely kissed Anne on both cheeks, and smiled apologetically. "Do forgive us, Anne. It appears little Jefferson Abraham here doesn't have a sense for timing, and kept us all waiting on his lordship as he dined."

Chuckling softly for appearances, Anne replied, "Why certainly, my dear." Exchanging warm greetings with Joshua and then the rest, she stretched out her arms, and said, "Do make yourselves comfortable, I believe you know everyone."

Felicity, holding on to Benjamin's arm, stepped further into the room, keeping her eyes focused on Elspeth, who came to greet them.

"How good it is to see all of you this evening. I was just saying to Anne that I hoped none of the children had fallen ill."

Strategically standing with her back facing the crowd, Felicity said, "Thank you dear, for your concern. However, no need to worry, as they are all as fit as a fiddle. Why at this very minute they are having their own dinner party."

"Are they? How quaint."

Anne, joining in the conversation, added, "Well there's enough of them, isn't there? I'm sure Whitney is a fine host to his guests."

Elise, noting that Anne had deliberately brought Whitney into the conversation, and how it had unnerved Felicity further, took no time in responding to her hostess. "He is indeed! And I can tell you; my Sarah Tess is quite taken with Master Myles. Having Felicity as his mother, favoring her as he does, it's only natural that he's handsome, but what the girls find even more appealing, I do believe, is his personality. There's no denying, his papa has had quite an impact on him." Turning to Benjamin, she smiled sweetly. "Never have I seen a son more devoted to his father than your Whitney is to you, Benjamin. What a fine father you are."

"How kind of you to say, dear Elise. I must say, we do get on rather nicely, the three of us. If I do say so myself."

Before Anne could respond, Felicity leaned closer to Elise as prearranged and asked, "Elise dear, why don't I take the baby for a spell while Anne takes you, Joshua and Gilbert around to greet her guests."

Elise, without hesitation, placed her sleeping child in Felicity's arms. Smiling her most alluring smile, she placed one hand on Joshua's arm, strategically tucking her other arm around her hostess's waist. "Why, that sounds like a wonderful idea." Then leaning closer into Anne, and in an exaggerated whisper, she asked, "Now, who is that distinguished gentleman from India with us this evening, Anne? Or do you have your eye on him, yourself?"

As the four of them started across the crowded room, Gilbert trailing quietly behind, Benjamin took the opportunity to lead Felicity to a fireside chair removed from the guests. Annabelle, escorted by Rupert, latched onto Elspeth's arm. "So tell me, dear friend, do tell why Mr. Freeport is still with us, and not back at his chateau in France, as planned? Why I thought he left a few weeks ago. Could it possibly be that Elise wasn't too far from the truth, explaining his sudden return?"

From the surprised look on Elspeth's face and her hesitation in responding, Annabelle knew the answer to her question, and smiled. "Fear not Elspeth, my lips are sealed; besides, you never said a word, it was Elise who guessed. Doesn't she have the most extraordinary perception?"

"She does! Why it's down right uncanny, if you ask me. How do you think she knew, when Anne and I have not said a word?"

Annabelle, glancing at Felicity, smiled with her eyes while taking a seat. Looking up at Rupert, who stood like a guard dog between Felicity and her, she smiled. "Darling, do be a love and see if Anne has mistakenly put us near the center of the room, near her. With Jefferson Abraham, we really need to be closer to the entrance."

"Yes of course." Looking over at Benjamin, the two men exchanged places in a well-rehearsed maneuver. On cue, as Rupert walked away, Benjamin casually stepped into the position of guarding Felicity.

Feeling less intimidated, knowing she had successfully maneuvered herself from being viewed openly by others, especially James, Felicity leaned into the fireside chair and absentmindedly rocked the sleeping Jefferson in her arms.

"So Elspeth, tell me, just how serious is it between my dear cousin Anne, and Jacque Paul?"

Elspeth's cheeks turned bright red and she nervously patted the front of her skirt to avoid looking at Felicity. "Serious? Why, who said anything about the two of them being serious? From what I've heard they are just good friends. You know how fond he was of Victoria and little Edward."

"Yes, so I've heard from Anne. I must say, I find it rather disconcerting that a complete stranger had a chance to get to know the newest member of my family when I wasn't offered the same opportunity."

"Yes m'lady, I can see how this would be troubling."

Felicity turned her head to see Jacque Paul Freeport standing just to the left of her, James Sterling at his side. Immediately Felicity's smile faded as she and James locked eyes. Feeling the blood rush to her cheeks, she instinctively looked away as her heart raced in her chest. Feeling Benjamin's hand rest on her right shoulder, somehow she managed to find her voice, and she mumbled, "Mr. Freeport, you gave me a fright. I didn't realize you were near."

Not looking up as she spoke, but rather placing her attention on Jefferson, who had suddenly flinched and whimpered softly in her arms, Felicity raised him closer to her and tenderly began patting his back while rocking him softly. "Shh, it's all right, sugar."

"Forgive me, Mrs. Myles for being so brazen as to interrupt you. I could not help but overhear your comment regarding little Edward, though. And if I were in your position, I too would be distressed. Especially noticing how much you obviously love children. You are very good with them, I see. Is your son here by any chance, this evening? I've heard so much about him, and looked forward to meeting him."

Benjamin, clearing his throat, extended his hand to Jacque Paul. "Mr. Freeport, I don't believe we've had the privilege. Let me introduce myself; I'm Benjamin Myles. In answer to your question to my wife, our son Whitney is busy entertaining his own guests this evening."

"Ah, Mr. Myles...." Jacque stepped just in front of Felicity and took Benjamin's hand in his. Shaking it vigorously, he added, "What a pleasure it is to finally meet the man I've heard so much about."

While not leaving Felicity's side, Benjamin graciously nodded his head. "Likewise. Please call me Benjamin."

Glancing between James and Benjamin, and noting the two men only nodded politely, Jacque glanced over at Annabelle, and greeted her. "Good evening Mrs. Robbins, what a pleasure to see you again." Bowing respectfully, he stepped nearer to Annabelle, accepted her hand, and kissed it. "Was I mistaken or didn't I see your husband at your side when you arrived?"

Seeing Rupert approach, Annabelle smiled in his direction. "You did indeed, sir." Glancing at James and giving him a cold nod, she directed her attention back to Jacque. "What a pleasant surprise, Mr. Freeport. I was under the impression you were headed back to France. Since I've never been there, please do tell me all about your homeland."

"My homeland, yes, well I suppose you are right. Being French, but living so long in India, I tend to think of that as my home as well. But in answer to your question, I was intending to return to Medoc, and still shall...." his voice trailed off as he turned and saw Rupert standing between Felicity and James. "Right after I settle a few business matters."

Rather than shake his hand, Jacque leaned forward and hugged Rupert, patting him firmly on the back. There was no mistaking the fact that the two men were very fond of one another.

"Rupert, old boy, how good to see you again. I was just telling your good wife here that I've altered my plans some since we last met. Rather than leave for France from London as planned, I found it necessary to settle a few business matters in Plymouth before setting sail across the channel."

"Right. I hadn't realized you had business here in England, Jacque."

"Well in truth, I didn't until James here convinced me to become partners with him in a new venture."

Glancing over at James, Rupert nodded politely. "Ah, I see. So shall I assume that you'll be staying for awhile?"

As Jacque and Rupert continued to speak, Felicity glanced over at Annabelle who smiled reassuringly then directed her attention back to Elspeth.

"So dear, tell me what your plans are for the holiday season."

"Well, as a matter of fact, Anne and I've decided just this very afternoon to join Jacque Paul at his chateau. Are you, Rupert, and the children planning to go this season as well?"

"Actually, we were thinking of staying here this year. Rupert and I thought it might be nice to open Ashwillow to our friends and have a Twelfth-night ball."

Pouting, Elspeth said frowning, "Really? I was certain you would be traveling south, especially since you haven't been there in a couple of years. I never dreamt you would be having a party. How disappointing, I wish I had known...."

"Known what, dear?" Anne asked, joining them.

"The Robbins' are having Twelfth-night again."

As Anne looked between Annabelle and Elspeth, Elise took the opportunity to edge her way over to Felicity, and strategically sat on the edge of the chair, blocking her friend from James's line of vision. Winking at Felicity, she smiled snidely over at him, then looking at Elspeth she said, "Twelfth-night? Pray tell, what is that?"

As Elspeth explained how Queen Victoria and Prince Albert had restored celebrating Christmas, and the twelve days following—called the Twelfth Epiphany—by reviving the practice of singing carols that had been outlawed by the Puritans in the 1500's, Elise nodded politely. As interesting as it was discovering how Queen Victoria and Prince Albert had trimmed a tree like those in Germany, she was distracted by James and Gilbert's cool exchange.

"Gilbert O'Flaherty, what a small world this is. Who would ever have thought we'd meet again, and in England no less."

"Aye." Gilbert accepted James's hand, shook it vigorously, and said, "It would appear our gracious hostess doesn't mind whom she invites to dine with her, even the likes of us."

Elise noticed that James's grip seemed to tighten around Gilbert's hand and he clenched his jaw hearing his comment. "Well that's a fine how do you do, considering I saved your life once."

"That ye did, and like I told ya in New York, I won't be forgettin' yer kindness. Nor will I forget how me Mandy and Mrs. Myles here nearly had to twist yer arm off to make ya, much like yer doing to me now."

Although both men were smiling, and appeared to be cordial, it was clear that they did not like one another. As James released Gilbert's hand, he jokingly said, "Well so I do." Then changing his tone he hastily added, "So I hear you're returning to Ireland. Should I assume then, that you're intending to remain in your homeland?"

"Home is where your heart leads you, and that would be back to the colonies. Me and the children will probably be heading back there next spring to start anew."

"Oh really, and where might that be, New York or Virginia?" Elise asked, knowing Elspeth wasn't finished with her story, but needing to know Gilbert's answer.

"Oh I don't know, I was giving some thought to Chicago or there about."

Flabbergasted, Felicity leaned forward, avoiding James's eyes, and asked, "Chicago? But why there, of all places?" Realizing she had said too much, by the angered look on Gilbert's face, she hastily added, "I mean, I just assumed you'd stay here for a while or even Ireland."

Always the diplomat, Benjamin hastily interrupted before Gilbert had a chance to respond. "Now dearest, Gilbert has business in Chicago, and from what he has told me of this town, I tend to agree with him, it's a perfect place to raise a family and lay down some roots."

Stunned that Benjamin and Gilbert had discussed him leaving, but never had spoken a word of it to her, she glanced over at Gilbert. "You and the children will be back before Christmas, won't you?"

"Aye."

Sitting back in her seat and suddenly feeling a great loss, Felicity listened as Elspeth, taking the opportunity of getting back to the subject of Christmas, asked, "Oh Gilbert, do tell us how you celebrate the season, in Ireland."

As Felicity sat and listened to Gilbert reminisce how his family had celebrated the season, her mind began to whirl. Never had she dreamt that Gilbert would take the children from her.

Suddenly feeling very protective and maternal toward them, she looked up at Benjamin. *How could you keep something like this from me, Benjamin?* Blocking out such thoughts of betrayal, she leaned further into her chair, still rocking the baby softly as she tried to block out the anger she felt growing inside of her. As her heart continued to race, she barely heard Gilbert speak of the Irish traditions of placing holly on the mantel, doorways, and pictures.

"Holly? Not evergreen?" Felicity heard Elise ask.

"Aye, holly. Folklore has it that the fairy folk would come in out of the cold to find shelter in the holly branches. But me Da said the leaves were like the shining life of Christ, which lives on long after his death; and the berries, his blood."

Hearing blood, his words grew fainter, and Felicity closed her eyes to fight back the stinging tears in her eyes. The stress of the day, knowing she would have to see James, toppled by hearing Gilbert was intending to take the children from her, and knowing Benjamin had kept it from her became too much for her to bear. Without warning, Felicity found herself on the verge of hysteria, desperately needing air. Feeling as if she were about to faint, she opened her eyes, barely hearing Elspeth ask, "A red candle is placed in the window you say? Whatever for?"

"Aye, for Joseph and Mary to find shelter. Then the night of Christmas, a bowl of milk and bread is left on the stoop and the doors are left unlatched...."

As Gilbert continued to speak, Felicity found it more difficult to comprehend and she felt the room begin to spin around her. Leaning slightly forward, her eyes focused momentarily on Gilbert, who seemed distorted to her. From his vantage point, Gilbert noticed that Felicity's head was beginning to bob. Not wanting to draw attention to her, he looked at Elspeth as he discreetly inched in front of Felicity to block her from the vision of others. Having her full attention he boisterously asked, "I bet ya ain't never heard of the 'starvin' wren have ya?"

Certain he had her and the rest of the guest's attention, Gilbert leaned closer to Benjamin, yanked his handkerchief from his lapel pocket while discreetly whispering in his friend's ear, "Get yer Missus outside!"

As if he were a magician, Gilbert stepped back to where he had stood, pulled the fire poker from its stand and while tying the hanky round the tip of the poker, he called on James to assist him. "Sterling, you remember how them young Irish lads straight off the boat go around cupping their hands and follow their mums about as they dance. Why don't you help me demonstrate what they might expect to see in New York at the docks, fer yer friends."

Looking out to the crowd of friends gathered around Anne's parlor, as if needing them to help convince James to partake, and getting applause and cheers as expected, Gilbert snidely smiled at his unreceptive partner. "Be a good lad, and follow my lead and you'll be doin' the jig in no time at all."

Turning back to the crowd, he waved Benjamin's handkerchief in the air. Wringing it between his hands, Gilbert then tied it securely over the tip of the poker stick. "All right, now this 'ere sad pitiful creature is a wren." Looking at it and shaking his head disapprovingly, he said, "Hold on, a few minor adjustments...ye never seen a white wren, have you?" Turning, he rubbed Benjamin's handkerchief in the ash beneath the hearth. Obviously pleased by the soot smeared over the pretend wren, he nodded his head. "That's better."

Dramatically lifting his leg, Gilbert strutted merrily around the circle of friends gathered, turning back and encouraging James to partake. "Step lively, Sterling, or starve as a beggar."

Reluctantly, James followed, clapping his hands while Gilbert raised the fake wren higher in the air, marching and singing merrily around the parlor. Pausing in front of Elspeth who was obviously enjoying the show, Gilbert said, "Won't you be helpin' the poor starvin' wren, m'lady?"

Clapping her hands, Elspeth shook her head and looked pleadingly over at Jacque Paul who casually tossed a coin to James. "Why thank'ee kind sir for helpin' the starvin' wren," spouted Gilbert, as James retrieved it from the carpet. Teasingly, Gilbert shook his head disapprovingly then cupped his hand round his mouth and said to the crowd as if sharing a secret, "Forgive me mate, ee's in need of a wee bit of practice."

Turning to the Hixes, keeping his eye on Benjamin who was now assisting Felicity from the room with Elise at her side, Gilbert merrily said, "Surely the good doctor 'ere, wouldn't want the wren to starve, now would 'ee?"

Getting another donation from Stephen Hix, he worked the room as cheers erupted as James again missed the coins that had been tossed. Then reaching Anne at the far end of the circle, Gilbert bowed dramatically before her. "Thank'ee kindly, fair maiden, for the use of yer parlor to assist me wren and me beggar 'ere. As ya can see we are set fer the winter."

Bowing, Anne smiled politely. "Glad to be of service, Mr. O'Flaherty."

Raising the wren, Gilbert pointed at James, who smiled cordially at the crowd while flipping a coin with his thumb and catching it in his hand. As the two of them took their final bows, Elspeth, clapping her hands, asked, "Oh do tell, why is this done again?"

"Why, for the starvin' wren of course, dear lady, and the lad's empty pockets after the season."

The crowd erupted with laughter and James discreetly whispered to Gilbert, "Think you were clever, don't you O'Flaherty? Well all you proved was, once a beggar always a beggar."

Turning and handing him the pretend wren, Gilbert sarcastically replied, "Is that right, Sterling? Well, in case you hadn't noticed, I wasn't the beggar, you were. And a damn piss poor one at that. Oh by the way, for future reference, I don't give a damn what you think."

Not waiting for a response, Gilbert walked over to Joshua who stood in front of the doorway to the terrace, leaving James standing alone, foolishly holding the wren in one hand and coins in the other.

Jacque Paul, walking over to James as he turned to replace the poker back in the rack, said, "James old boy, I think you and Anne were out-foxed, tonight. Let it go."

Untying the handkerchief from the poker and shaking it off before placing it in his pocket, he glared up at him. "Unlike you Jacque, I'll be damned if I will be denied my son."

Not responding, seeing Anne approach, Jacque directed his attention to his hostess, who said, "Why James, how unlike you to partake in such merriment. I must say, if I had known you and Gilbert were going to put on such a foolish sideshow, I wouldn't have bothered hiring a quartet to play in the gardens following dinner."

"Dear Anne, by now I would have thought you had come to realize that I would do anything to worm my way back into your heart, even making a spectacle of myself for the sake of your cousin."

Confused by his comment, she leaned closer to him, and hissed, "My cousin? What does Felicity have to do with you making a complete and utter fool of yourself before the elite of society? Honestly James, I don't know why I've bothered trying to reintroduce you to my friends when you insist on parading about like some commoner. Surely you know the difference between what is appropriate and what is not, or has living amongst the likes of that Irishman clouded your good judgment?"

Jacque Paul interrupted the two of them. "In case you hadn't noticed, Felicity was on the verge of swooning and your industrious guest, despite his lack of rearing, had the foresight to put on his little dog and pony show, so she could be rescued."

Anne quickly scanned the room and seeing no Felicity, only Elise and Joshua returning from the gardens, turned back toward him. "Ah let me guess, she and Benjamin are in the garden."

"Precisely. I'm surprised you didn't realize something was amiss, especially when that Irish hooligan went over to Benjamin and whispered something to him as he took his handkerchief, rather than using his own," spouted James.

"Oh, you can't be serious, James. Surely you aren't insinuating that both of her lap dogs who've been hovering over her since she arrived, didn't notice our dear Felicity needed tending to, but that ruffian did?"

There was no denying the bitterness in Anne's voice as she spoke, and Jacque, seemingly disgusted, said, "Rather than gloat that your cousin has taken ill Anne, why not find out if she requires assistance? After all ,there is a doctor in attendance."

"Oh Jacque Paul, please don't be annoyed with me, darling. Felicity isn't ill, she's just trying to get a little more attention, and be saved by yet another admirer. It would appear having Benjamin and James here isn't enough, she's now after capturing that pagan Irishman, too."

"Or perhaps she has reached her breaking point, especially having one of her own turn on her," Jacque snarled, not hiding his disgust.

Before Anne had time to respond, she noticed Felicity had returned on Benjamin's arm, smiling sweetly to those she passed, just as she had seen her cousin do countless times before. "See, just as I said, Felicity is fine; a true Phelps through and through." Looking up at him lovingly, Anne added, "Don't look so cross Jacque, we're just having a little tiff and in time we'll kiss and make up. We always do."

Patting Anne's hand, Jacque said hesitantly, "I hope you're right, my dear. For both our sakes."

Noticing her servant Robert motioning that dinner was ready, Anne nodded for him to announce it to her guests. Resting her hand upon Jacque's arm as she passed Felicity, Anne couldn't help but notice how pale she looked. For a brief moment, she found herself weakening, knowing she was the cause of Felicity's distress and almost stopped to give her some reassurance. Just as she did though, the image of Victoria marrying Joseph Pike entered her mind and Anne's back stiffened. Without stopping, she continued walking toward the dining room. *You couldn't leave well enough alone and just forget about your precious Benjamin. No, instead you brought havoc and shame down on me while you remained unscathed. Well, see how you like losing your child, like I've lost mine.*

Anne stood at the head of the table, nodding to her guests as they looked for their seat assignments. She remained poised with Jacque Paul to her left and James Sterling to her right. Seeing the Myles standing near seats at the end of the table across from the Carmidys, Anne realized her seating assignments had been altered, and looked disapprovingly at Rupert. Exchanging cordial nods with one another, she knew whom the culprit was who had taken the liberty of altering her plans. With an insincere smile, Anne took her seat and her guests followed her lead. Again her eyes rested on Rupert as he sat at the carver's chair, and she thought, *How dare you think you can come into my home and manipulate me, you arrogant, pompous ass. You'll pay dearly for this, mark my words.*

Looking out amongst her friends, Anne nodded to her servants and as arranged, a stream of servants entered the room carrying elegant silver trays filled with a variety of the finest dishes, prepared to perfection. As her guests leisurely dined, Anne continued to smile warmly, seemingly enjoying the lively conversation that flowed around the table as freely as did her imported wine. Only those who knew their hostess personally, knew her smile was a façade to cover up the bitterness she carried in her heart, and that her eyes could not conceal as she glanced over to Felicity.

"Dear cousin, with your guests leaving this week, I'm sure your dear Whitney will find it quite lonely at Brookhaven. Perhaps he might enjoy riding with William this week."

William, glancing at his mother, tried to disguise his obvious resentment that she was planning his social activities for him and smiled politely before directing his attention to Felicity. "What a splendid idea. How is the lad, by the way?"

"Quite well. And as much as Whitney would enjoy spending time with you, William, I'm afraid we will have to make it another time."

Not willing to let Felicity's comment rest, Anne said, "And why is that, dear cousin? Why, I can't remember the last time we had the chance to visit with Whitney."

Just then, a servant approached Elise, and hearing their cue that the baby needed tending to, Felicity nodded toward Elise. "Yes it has been awhile, we'll need to remedy that soon." Rising, she nodded politely to her hostess. "If you'll excuse me, young Jefferson requires attention, and I do believe that I'll keep Elise company."

"How thoughtful of you Felicity, but surely dear Elise can manage on her own. Goodness knows she is quite experienced, having so many children." It was evident that Anne resented her leaving, despite her polite words.

"Surely Anne, you wouldn't have me leave our guest of honor alone, especially on her last evening here in England?"

Anne, turning to Annabelle, said, "Should I assume you'll be joining them too, dear Annabelle?"

"Why thank you for your thoughtful suggestion."

The tension between these four women was so noticeable, not a word was said by the other guests, who respectfully kept their heads down as they continued eating, with the exception of James Sterling. Silently he watched as Benjamin helped his wife from her seat; he longed to be close enough just to smell her sweet fragrance that was firmly etched in his memory. *Oh Felicity fair, please look at me once. How can I ever hope to be graced again with your presence if you won't even look at me.*

Much to his surprise, as she turned and bowed to the guests, for a brief moment, their eyes locked. Although she looked away instantly, suddenly his heart raced as if he were a schoolboy and she was royalty. *The years have been good to you; you're even lovelier than before.* So engrossed in watching her as she left the room, admiring how regally, yet delicately she held herself, James didn't realize Anne was trying to get his attention.

Leaning closer to him, so as not to be overheard, she whispered, "You're making a spectacle of yourself. Kindly refrain from openly drooling over your obsession like some love-struck mule."

Seeing the animosity he felt burning in his eyes, Anne matched his look and hastily added, "Restraint. I suggest you follow your own advice."

Nodding with a snide grin, he whispered, "Ah, the student now feels she is the teacher."

Amused, Anne nodded slightly then directed her attention to her guests. "Please join me on the terrace for dessert and cognac." James, standing to help her to her feet, leaned closer and whispered hoarsely, "Felicity fair is not of the same caliber as your son-in-law; she needs to be coaxed and reassured."

Allowing James to escort her to the terrace, Anne nodded to the musicians and at once they began to play softly as the wait staff took their places behind a bar and dessert table. Without glancing at James she said, "As clever as you are James, I doubt even you will ever be able to convince my cousin you mean her no harm."

"Ah, a challenge...care to wager I'll have Felicity fair speak to me by the end of the evening?"

Chuckling she said, "Oh James, and what precisely do you have to offer me that I would be interested in?"

"Why Jacque Paul, of course."

Intrigued, she turned and said, "And if you are able to accomplish such a feat? What is it you require in exchange?"

"A meeting with Rupert."

Saying no more, he left Anne's side to join William and Jacque who chatted quietly as they leisurely walked toward Anne. Nodding politely, noticing the silhouettes of women in Anne's private sitting room, James wasted no time in strategically positioning himself in the shadows beside the French doors of the room, amongst the dense evergreens and lit a cigarette. From where he stood with the door slightly ajar, he listened to the conversation from within.

"She was relentless, I agree. But Felicity dear, rather than getting yourself all riled up about the way your cousin deliberately tried to manipulate the conversation back to Whitney, I'd be asking myself why. The way I see it, Anne has all the makin' of a scorned and bitter woman."

Annabelle, agreeing with Elise's assessment, said, "Elise is right, Felicity. Please reconsider and speak to her regarding James and Whitney."

"No. Never. As I said before, too many people know already and if my suspicions are right, Anne already knows the truth judging by her actions tonight. What purpose would it serve to admit it at this late date? I hadn't trusted her enough to take her into my confidence, years ago."

"Well, all I can say is, you're playing with fire, dear friend. My suggestion to you would be to disarm your opponent where they are the least vulnerable. Take it from someone who knows and is familiar with espionage, don't show your weakness any longer. Anne's using your weakness to get what she wants."

Looking over at Elise, Felicity said, "Want? What do I have that Anne could possibly want? It makes no sense."

"That you'll need to find out, but until you do, I would definitely stop showing her how upset you are. Don't you see? You're feeding right into her hand. Now is the time to be strong, take her off guard, and see how she reacts. Then maybe you will discover what has made Anne so vindictive."

Rising from her chair, Felicity, processing Elise's advice, went to the window and pulled back the lace curtain. Taking in a deep breath, she sighed. "The gardens look almost mystical tonight. There's not a cloud in the sky."

Annabelle looked over at Elise with concern in her eyes and said, "Thank heavens for Gilbert's fast thinking, or I shudder to think what might have happened."

Felicity turned, hearing Annabelle's comment, and asked her, "Gilbert? I thought Benjamin rescued me."

"Oh he did, after Gilbert cleverly alerted him and created a diversion."

"A diversion?" Vaguely Felicity recalled him speaking of the traditions of his homeland.

Anxious to share with Felicity and Elise what they had missed, Annabelle hastily continued. "I must say, he was rather comical. Why, I never dreamt he could be so clever, and flamboyant. And the way he drew James into his little reenactment was brilliant. The more I get to know Gilbert O'Flaherty, the more I like him."

Curious, sitting on the edge of her seat, Elise said, "Oh do tell us everything, Annabelle. I left just as he had taken the handkerchief from Benjamin's pocket. What happened next?"

"Well...."

As Annabelle and Elise chatted, Felicity listened halfheartedly; preoccupied by the brief eye contact she had shared with James. Surprisingly enough she wasn't as shaken up from the encounter as she had feared. She still loathed him from the very depths of her soul for what he had done, but seeing his eyes, Whitney's eyes, looking at her with such adoration was something Felicity had not prepared herself for.

She of course, had always known Whitney had his father's eyes, but seeing them looking back at her tonight from the man who had violated her, caused the memory of that night to wash over her in waves. Especially the words he spoke to her following the attack, no longer capable of blocking them out, as she had done in the past. *'Whether you want to believe me or not, I do love you, Felicity. I am truly sorry that you had to suffer for the sins of your husband. But a man must avenge his wife's honor, even if he doesn't love her. So it had to be like this, me taking you from him, just as Benjamin took Lavinia by force back in England. You do see that, don't you, Felicity?'*

"Don't you agree, Felicity?"

Hearing Elise's voice, Felicity jerked and said, "Agree? I'm sorry. I was distracted. What were you saying?"

"I was just saying that after getting to know Gilbert as we have, I understand why Miranda loved him as she did. Why, he's far more complex than he leads people to believe, with such inner strength and foresight."

"Hmm...is he? My, that is quite a testimonial."

"Are you all right, Felicity, should I go and get Benjamin?" Annabelle asked with concern, noticing that her friend was only going through the motions of conversing.

"No. I'm fine, I was just thinking...." Pausing for a brief second, unable to tell them what she was actually thinking, she said, "Elise, what you said earlier regarding not showing my weaknesses. How would this help in discovering why Anne has obviously turned against me?"

"Well that's where intuition and keen observation takes over. Felicity, I'm sure you will agree that Anne obviously has suffered great pain these past few years. Losing Edward and the circumstances surrounding his death was humiliating to say the least, followed by the calamity of Victoria and Joseph and the necessity of hiding the truth from the world. It all must have taken its toll on her. In her grief and anguish, there's no tellin' how she dealt with such pain. My guess is, based on what I know about your's and Benjamin's past and how Lavinia sought to destroy your lives out of revenge, I'd say in Anne's tormented mind, she blames you in part."

"That's utter nonsense."

"You can't be serious!"

Before Annabelle or Felicity had a chance to question her reasoning further, Elise hastily added, "Don't you see, if you had never returned to America and married Benjamin, Lavinia would not have tried to destroy your lives when hers came crashing down around her. I know it sounds farfetched, but grief and sheer desperation might have warped Anne's sense of reasoning."

"If that's the case, then what can I do to prevent her from continuing?"

Inhaling a deep breath, Elise thought for a moment before answering. "Mama once told me, 'You catch more flies with honey than vinegar'. Well Felicity, my dear friend, you ooze with the gooey, sweet-tasting nectar from bees. If I were you, I'd strike before she gets a chance to get another bee in her bonnet. Send her in hibernation by showering her with kindness, especially to her one weakness."

"And that would be?"

"Why, Victoria and William, of course. They are all she has left that holds any true value to her."

Nodding, Felicity turned and looked out the window again. She knew what Elise said made sense. She also knew she was tired of living in fear, running from her past, and ashamed for not being able to have stopped James from attacking her. She was made of stronger stock than what she had exhibited. Recalling her grandparents' inner strength and how courageous they were, leaving everything they had to start anew with only the love they felt for one another, she thought of her own parents. They had died for what they believed in. Lastly, she thought of her beloved Aunt Gwen, who had willingly gone against the rigid restraints society had imposed on Felicity and Ben Even when faced with her own mortality, Gwendolyn Phelps pressed on courageously. As if a candle had been lit inside her, Felicity felt the courage and strength of those she loved and admired, and her sprits burned brightly within her again.

Taking in a deep breath, Felicity turned to her friend and smiled warmly at her. "Thank you Elise, for reminding me that I come from a long line of strong-willed, often times stubborn, but always courageous lineage. It seems to me, for the past several years I've forgotten. From here out though, I'll be damned if I'm going to allow the likes of James Sterling or Anne intimidate me for even one more second."

From the other side of the building, out of view from the women inside and James, who remained lurking in the shadows, Gilbert smiled, hearing Felicity's comment. *That's the spirit!*

Gilbert never allowed his eyes to stray from the man across the balcony that he despised as much as he had despised Tad. Perhaps more, knowing that unlike Tad, this bastard had succeeded in taking what he felt he was entitled to.

Not long after the Felicity and Elise had retreated to the conservatory, Mammy Tess had come for him, explaining that Joey was crying for his Aunt Felicity. Upon discovering that the mistress of the house had left instructions, not to be disturbed, Gilbert found himself annoyed, blaming her for upsetting Joey to begin with for singing that particular song. Without hesitation, Gilbert went to tend to his distraught child. Finding Joey still calling for his aunt, he protectively carried him to the balcony and slowly rocked him. As the boy lay nestled in his father's arms, still sniffling, the voices of Elise and Felicity carried up to them. Young Joey, hearing his aunts voices, soothing to him, he soon settled down and began sucking his thumb. Only Gilbert, understanding the meaning of the words spoken by the two women was disturbed further.

As he sat continuing to rock his son, to no fault of his own, he discovered the secret that Felicity bore, and without warning, Gilbert found himself fuming. All the pain he had suppressed following his wife's death rose to the surface. By the time he had taken Joey back to bed, he was consumed with rage.

Making his way back down to the study, and after consuming several pints of ale, Benjamin, detecting Gilbert's uneasiness, persuaded his guest to take a walk with him. There in the gardens, after Gilbert confessed what had him so angry, Gilbert listened in silence as Benjamin relived that evening. Never had Benjamin fully explained what he had felt and the months of torment he had experienced following the attack. The two men, harboring the guilt of not being able to protect the one thing in the world they valued most, found solace for their tormented souls, by speaking to each other.

Over the course of the next few months whenever they had private moments together, Benjamin spoke of how he had been able to put the pain behind him and build a new life for himself and his beloved wife. He encouraged Gilbert to do the same for his and Miranda's children. As Benjamin spoke of Felicity and Whitney and how much he loved them both, Gilbert's admiration for him grew, viewing his host as a true man of God. Yet, when Benjamin confessed that he had allowed James to view his son, believing it was the Christian thing to do, Gilbert voiced his disapproval. It was one thing for a man to forgive himself for not protecting his wife, and accept another man's child as his, but quite another to forgive the man who had committed such a heinous act.

Gilbert glanced over at Rupert and Benjamin, who had positioned themselves close enough to the entrance of the terrace to react at a moment's notice. As he watched the two men cordially conversing with others as they mingled amongst the garden, he admired how much restraint they exhibited. His mind wandered to one of several conversations he'd had with Benjamin. Even as he stood feet away from him, he could still hear Benjamin's words ringing in his mind.

"What would you have me do, Gilbert? Go against everything I have been taught and hold dear, by refusing to forgive another man? God didn't say, forgive only if the sin committed against you wasn't too severe. No, he said, forgive. Turn the other cheek. Didn't our Savior, even having been persecuted, beaten, flogged, and ridiculed at the hands of his enemy ask his father, our Lord to forgive them? And forgive is what I must do, if I'm ever to be able to bring happiness to my wife. If I allow hate to remain in my heart, even for James Sterling, then I risk the chance of letting it manifest. Thereby causing more sorrow to my dear Felicity, who has suffered far too much all ready, for loving and believing in me. God has seen fit to bless me with her love, and I will not forget his mercy, forgiving me of my own sins and gracing me to know the peace I have, just sharing a life with this remarkable woman. Therefore, I must do the same, and forgive."

Gilbert turned his head and glared at James, thinking, *I don't care what the good parson said, you deserve to die for what you did. I say an eye for an eye. The world would be better off without the likes of you!*

For a moment, his thoughts were interrupted by Joshua's voice from inside.

"Sweetheart, you really need to step lively. The three of you have been locked away in here far too long."

"Oh, pish-posh darlin'. You're a master of words, think of something convincing to tell that old battle-ax, and I promise we'll be out in just a few more minutes." Gilbert couldn't help but smile, hearing Elise's reply. *Now that's one spirited woman. Pity Felicity didn't have it in her belly to fight like Elise did.*

Over the past few months, he had watched in silence at how Benjamin and Felicity had been able to put their own pain aside and love her son unconditionally. As much as he admired the two of them for this, he couldn't help but worry that by being as genteel as they were, if they were not exposing themselves to greater pain, by being too submissive and trusting. Then this afternoon, hearing the anguish in her voice, he began to realize the depths of her pain. Her words cut him like a knife, and he wondered if Miranda were still alive, if she too, would carry that pain inside her every day, as Felicity did.

Glaring over at James, his rage mounted. In his current state, he imagined what Felicity had gone through, fighting off her attacker. Through his tortured mind and anger, the face of his beloved Miranda melded into Felicity's, and Tad became James. *I might not have been able to stop Tad any more than the parson was able to stop you, but mark my words, you depraved bastard, I'll kill ya with me bare hands if you ever try to hurt Felicity again. And damned the consequences.*

His thoughts were interrupted as the French doors opened further and out walked Felicity. "I just need some fresh air and a few minutes alone. I'll be fine. Go get Joshua, and I'll meet you here in the terrace." Gilbert stood erect, his eyes watching every move she and James made.

Felicity, deep in thought, didn't notice James step from the bushes. Rather than approach her, he whispered, "Felicity, please don't be alarmed. I won't hurt you."

Felicity's back stiffened. Recognizing his voice, she froze with fear. Recalling the vow she had made to herself only moments earlier, not to allow her life to be ruled by fear, she clenched her fists by her side, and whispered, "Have you no decency? Leave. Surely you must know how much I despise you."

"Please Felicity, let me explain."

Turning on her heels, Felicity tried to return inside when James took another step forward. "Please don't leave. I give you my word, I mean you no harm."

"Your word? As if I'd believe anything that came spilling out from the mouth of the devil himself. Let me pass." Her voice, so guttural and filled with hate, that she barely recognized it herself.

As Gilbert watched, he hastily looked between the scene before him, and Benjamin and Rupert who couldn't see James from where they were standing. Turning his attention to Felicity, he heard James say, "I came here tonight only to see you."

"Liar. If that were true, surely the portrait of me hanging over your mantel would have sufficed. How dare you."

"Dare I, you say? Is it not customary to want to view your son, and the woman you love?"

"He is not *your* son, and don't you ever speak my name and love in the same sentence again, you barbarian."

"Felicity, I'm here tonight for one purpose, and that is to tell you personally how sorry I am. I cannot change the man I was, or the things I have done. All I can do now is live with my guilt. Rest assured though, despite how much I want to be a part of your lives, I shall never try to see either of you again, unless you give me the word."

Glancing at him, her fist still clenched at her side, Felicity hissed, "That day will never come. Leave. The sight of you sickens me."

Before James had a chance to respond, Gilbert stepped out from the evergreen and stood glaring at James as he cleared his throat, alerting Felicity to his presence. "Why, the saints are shinin' down on us this evenin'. Never have I seen so many stars twinkle."

He offered his elbow to Felicity, who had turned at the sound of his voice. She took a second to look up at the sky. Inhaling deeply, she placed her trembling hand on his arm. "Why so they are, Gilbert."

Patting her hand, his eyes never wavering from James, he said, "Dear lady, I hope I'm not interrupting. Shall we join yer good husband? I believe he has your dessert and coffee ready."

Just then Elise, Joshua, and Annabelle, coming from the direction of the house, paused seeing James standing near Felicity. Joshua, the first to find his voice, said, "Ah, did I hear coffee? Not that I haven't enjoyed tea, mind you, but freshly brewed coffee sounds mighty tempting."

"Only days before you set sail, the truth comes out." Nervously laughing, Felicity allowed Gilbert to escort her toward Benjamin and Rupert, and away from James who stood smiling politely, his eyes reflecting the hatred he felt in his heart.

"You damn Irish potato farmer, you'll rue the day you spied on me," James hissed, under his breath.

Anne, obviously having seen the entire incident, nodded in his direction, and looked over to Rupert then back at James. Suddenly her smile faded, wondering how she would ever get Rupert to grant James a viewing.

~ Thirteen ~

The ride back to Brookhaven was strained rather than lively as was the case typically when the seven of them were together. As the hostess, Felicity knew she should say something to help lighten the mood, yet in her current state it was all that she could bear even to smile let alone make idle conversation. Glancing over at Benjamin, she realized how sullen he was. Lovingly patting his hand, she glanced out the window of the coach and noticed how clear the sky was. Recalling Gilbert's words as he'd approached her and James, she said. "My, you were right Gilbert, the stars are bright this evening. Why, they look as if they are winking at us."

Politely nodding, rather than comment on Felicity's observation, Annabelle and Elise glanced at each other, wondering when Gilbert had mentioned the stars to her.

"What did you say?" Pausing as if remembering his words, she continued, "The saints are shining down on us. What a pleasant thought."

Rupert cleared his throat and looked over at Gilbert. "Old boy, for someone who is usually so quiet, I must say you were quite lively this evening. Good show."

Everyone knew precisely what Rupert was referring to, and Felicity watched as he and Benjamin exchanged glances. "Aye, if nothin' else, the Irish sure can put on a good show. Why I'll be surprised if I'm not invited for the entertainment to all yer social events when we return."

There was no mistaking the sarcasm in his voice, and Felicity glanced out the window to avoid the awkward moment.

"When precisely do you think that will be, Gilbert?" Benjamin asked, clearing his throat.

"That's hard to say. I promised the children we'd be seeing the sights in County Cork where I grew up before traveling to see me brother and his family in Belfast. Then I had it in mind to spend a few weeks in Dublin, since I've never been."

Surprised, Felicity turned and asked, "My goodness, all that traveling? Why that sounds like it may take quite some time. I was under the impression that traveling can be rather risky this time of the year. How will you be able to get back in time for the holidays?"

Seeing his expression from all her questions and knowing how proud a man he was, she knew she had said too much. "That was rude of me, please forgive me, Gilbert. I was just looking so forward to sharing Christmas with the children...I spoke out of turn."

"Christmas." Elise said, wistfully. "Just thinking of you all sharing the holidays without us, makes me homesick for you already and we've not even left."

Joshua, hearing his wife's comment, placed his arm around her. "Sweetheart, now don't get yourself all upset."

Looking up at him, Elise said sadly, "I'm trying not to darlin' but I can't help it. We've had such a lovely summer...." Her voice cracked and before she could finish her sentence, tears ran down her cheek.

Instantly, Annabelle who was seated across from her, leaned over to pat her friend's hand. "Please don't cry Elise, or you'll have me crying too."

Felicity, sitting next to Annabelle, was suddenly unable to hold back her tears any longer, and nodded, sniffling. "I know how you feel Elise; it has been such a lovely summer, hasn't it?"

There was no holding back the tears after that as the three of them began weeping, Joshua looked over at his host while shaking his head. "I've got a feeling this is going to be the longest goodbye in history. Got any of that ale left?"

"Why, as a matter of fact. I do."

Rupert, tenderly patting his wife's back, looked between Joshua and Benjamin. "I suspected this might happen and took the liberty of bringing along a couple of bottles of brandy. Hope you won't be offended if I pass on the ale and indulge in Armagnac Marcel Trépout 1832 tonight."

Hearing Rupert, Benjamin said, "Ah Rupert, you sly devil. How good of you to bring over such a rare vintage, why I had no idea you still had any Armagnac left."

"Yes, well I've been saving it for a special occasion. Tonight I thought we all might be in need of some soothing; what better method than from the nectar of the grape."

"Spoken as a true connoisseur. I say Rupert, how's your winery doing these days?" Benjamin inquired.

"Evidently better, since I've been away."

Just then, they pulled up in front of Brookhaven and Montgomery stepped out onto the porch. Gilbert, seeing his friend, mumbled under his breath as he opened the door of the coach before it came to a complete halt. "Excuse me. Something must be wrong with the children."

Felicity's heart stopped, and she clutched Elise's hand, both women straining to hear the exchange between Gilbert and Montgomery.

"What's wrong, Montgomery?"

"The children are all fine, but I need to speak with you without them overhearing."

"Yes, what is it?"

"Sir, a woman arrived here about an hour ago. A Miss Kathleen Sullivan."

"Kathleen; that's my brother's wife's sister. Why, what a pleasant surprise. I haven't seen her since she was just a lass." Gilbert smiled brightly and began to go to the house.

"Please, sir, I'm afraid I have some bad news."

Gilbert's smile faded and he stopped. "What is it, Montgomery?"

"Miss Sullivan was quite distraught. You see, there was a riot in Belfast."

"A riot?"

"Yes, sir. According to your guest, your brother and his wife were killed. She fled straight away in search of you as she had nowhere else to go."

"Jake and Mary are dead?" Gilbert's voice trailed off, strained, as he tried to comprehend the news.

Benjamin, hearing what Montgomery had said, spoke up. "Gilbert, I'm so sorry. How can we be of help?"

Gilbert looked at Benjamin with uncertainty. "I don't know." Glancing over at Montgomery, he said, "Where is Kathleen now?"

"Up in a room that Mrs. Duncan made ready for her."

"Why can't she stay with the other children?" Gilbert asked, obviously confused.

"Sir, Miss Sullivan is no child. Mrs. Duncan thought she would be more comfortable in her own room." Pausing to let Gilbert absorb everything, Montgomery said, "Sir, under the circumstances, are we still intending to travel to Belfast if there is rioting going on there? I ask not for my safety, but rather for that of the children."

"Riot? No of course not, the children cannot be exposed to that." Looking to Benjamin, Gilbert asked, "Can I impose on you..."

"You are not imposing, dear friend. Our home is your home. Why not go to your sister-in-law's sister and we'll tend to the children."

Felicity, looking over at Montgomery, asked, "Montgomery, where are the children?"

"Inside, with Fannie and Mammy Tess. They have no idea what's happened."

Without listening to another word, Felicity, having exited the coach, anxiously looked over at Gilbert. "May I please go to them?"

Clearly in shock, he nodded. "Of course. But don't tell them about me brother."

Impulsively, Felicity went to Gilbert's side and kissed him on the cheek. "Of course not. Please know how deeply sorry Benjamin and I are for your loss." Not waiting for a response, Felicity picked up her skirt ran up the stairs. Turning slightly she called out, "Annabelle, please dear, see that our guest is comfortable, and if she has been given a meal." Directing her attention to the stunned Elise, she said, "Coming?"

"Yes, in a moment." Turning back to Gilbert, Elise tenderly hugged him while holding Jefferson Abraham in her arms. "Oh Gilbert, as difficult as this is for you to lose a loved one, I thank heaven you and the children were here in England." Seeing Felicity anxiously waiting for her on the steps, she handed the baby to Joshua. "Mercy, and I thought I was bossy. My goodness."

As they followed Felicity up the stairs, Gilbert looked at Benjamin. "What do I say to her? Hell, I don't even know her. The last time I saw Kathleen she was the age of Peanut. Why I'm surprised that she even remembers me. Why do you suppose she came here of all places?"

"Right. Well you'll find out all the answers soon enough, Gilbert. How long ago was it that you saw her?" Benjamin asked.

Gilbert, removing his hat and passing it to Montgomery, rubbed his chin. "Oh at least twelve, no, thirteen years ago."

"Well that would make Miss Sullivan around seventeen then." Benjamin, transferring his hat and gloves, to Montgomery, assisted Felicity with her shawl. "Gilbert, would you prefer to meet your guest alone?"

Gilbert, looking up the stairs then back at Benjamin, said, "Hell no. I ain't never been one for these sort of things. I could use your help, if'n you don't mind."

Benjamin, turning to his other guests, smiled gratefully hearing Rupert say before having to be asked, "Go. I know the way. I'll have brandy waiting for you both."

Nodding, Benjamin turned and placed his hand on Gilbert's shoulder. "Hold on, I forgot to find out what room."

Just then a red-haired woman in an exquisite green gown that matched her eyes, appeared at the top of the stairs. Seeing Gilbert, she ran to him. "Oh Gilbert, thank heavens you're here."

Elise, who was walking behind Felicity, paused and looked up the staircase. Her eyes grew as big as saucers as she saw the woman clinging to the equally shocked Gilbert. Elise raised her brow noting how his unexpected guest not only didn't look the least bit travel weary, but showed no sign of grief; that was, until she had spotted her prey. Motioning up the staircase, she whispered to Felicity, "Hmm, isn't Miss

Sullivan friendly...ah, to be young again as your lovely guest is, and be able to flaunt it like she does."

Felicity, glancing up at Gilbert and the younger woman, surprised that she still was clinging to a man she had not seen in over a decade, turned her attention back to Elise. "Shame on you. People react differently when they are under such duress."

"Yes, apparently they do." Following Felicity, she hastily added, "And in that dress, looking so alluring, I'm certain she'll be able to console poor Gilbert rather nicely."

"Hush, before they hear you."

Shaking her head, Elise smiled warmly at the children as they ran to greet them.

Kissing Whitney on the cheek, Felicity tenderly greeted all the other children the same, then feeling the front of her skirt being tugged on, she leaned down so Joey could greet her too. Surprised when he showered her with more than one kiss and a tighter hug than usual, she said, "Well my goodness; and what do I owe all this attention too, my little lamb?"

"I knew you would come home early so you could be with me. This is our last night together, ya know."

Before Felicity could respond, Gilbert appeared at the door with his guest by his side. The children, seeing the stranger, rather than run to him as they normally would have, hovered closer to Felicity and Elise. "Children, what if I told ya Da decided you could stay here rather than go to Ireland."

Wide-eyed they looked up at Felicity then back at their father. "Are you going to leave us, Da?" Suzanne asked, meekly.

"Why of course not, Peanut. We're all stayin' on fer a spell with Aunt Felicity and Uncle Benjamin." Not receiving the reception he had expected, Gilbert frowned; then realizing the children were staring at Kathleen, he said, "Children, I have another surprise for you. This is your Aunt Kathleen. She's come all the way from Ireland to meet you."

Never had Felicity seen the children so quiet, and nudging them alongside her, Felicity extended her hand to the young woman. "Hello Miss Sullivan, I'm Felicity Myles. Welcome to our home. I wish we could have met under better circumstances."

"Thank you, Mrs. Myles. You have a lovely home, ma'am. Please call me, Kathleen." Felicity smiled politely, aware that the striking younger woman spoke with no hint of a brogue.

Kathleen, looked down at Suzanne, smiled, then gazed up at Gilbert. "My, but isn't this one the spitting image of her father."

Proudly, Gilbert pointed out his children, calling them by name, at which they cordially bowed respectfully. Looking over at Whitney who stood staring at her, as did the rest of the children, she said, "And who is this strapping young lad?"

Felicity, witnessing her attention directed toward Whitney, said, "This is my son, Whitney Myles."

Whitney, stepping forward, bowed politely and took her hand in his. Kissing it, as he had seen his father do countless times, he said regally, "Pleasure to make your acquaintance, Miss Sullivan."

"My, but aren't we the little gentry."

Smiling politely, Felicity extended her arm to Elise. "Kathleen, I would like to introduce you to my dear friend from America, Mrs. Elise Carmidy."

"Mrs. Carmidy, I had the pleasure of meeting your handsome husband, I believe."

Elise extended her hand to Kathleen, shook it politely, then said, "Yes, well I speak for both of us, when I say how truly sorry I am to learn of your losses." As Elise introduced her to the Robbins children and her own, she noticed Joey, who gingerly tugged at Felicity's skirt again.

"What did she lose, Auntie?" he asked, innocently.

Chuckling softly, and rather than addressing Joey, Kathleen directed her attention to Gilbert and gushed, "Your little one is so charming."

Felicity, noting how the children began to frown, seeing this stranger showing their father so much attention, leaned over and whispered, "Dear ones, why don't you give your papa a kiss good-night and I'll tuck you in tonight. Will that be all right?"

Reluctantly, they did as Felicity had asked then immediately returned to Felicity who smiled warmly at them. "Come along, now." Pausing, she nodded at her guest. "Please make yourself comfortable in my husband's study while we tend to the children. We won't be long."

Seeing Annabelle standing outside the door with one eyebrow arched, Felicity smiled at her. "Why Annabelle, I was wondering where you were. Have you had a chance to meet our houseguest?"

Seeing Kathleen turn toward Annabelle, she said, "No, I don't believe we have."

"Kathleen Sullivan, this is Mrs. Annabelle Robbins."

Apparently recognizing the name, she gushed, "Why, Mrs. Robbins, what a pleasure it is to meet you. I've heard so much about you from a mutual friend of ours, Emma Stern, and her dear father. I'd be honored if you would call me, Kathleen."

"Kathleen, welcome to England. If you'll excuse me, I'll tend to my children and then you can tell me how you and Emma met."

As the three women left the conservatory with the children whispering behind them, Elise looked over at Felicity who shook her head sternly. Obviously, Felicity wanted nothing to be said in front of the children, so Elise glanced at Annabelle who winked merrily at her. Smiling, Elise glanced back to witness Kathleen place her arm on Gilbert's extended arm.

"Oh Gilbert, over the years you've taken such good care of me, why did I doubt you wouldn't now?"

Unable to stop herself from commenting, Elise whispered, "Indeed."

~

Long after Felicity had tucked Whitney and then the O'Flaherty children in, singing to them as she did each night, she stood between their beds and gazed at their faces lovingly. So much had happened to her today; she needed the time to sort it out in her mind. Yet knowing she had an obligation to her guests, she blocked out her earlier conversation with James. Taking in a deep breath, she forced herself to join her guests rather than hide in the children's room.

As she opened the door, she nearly screamed, bumping into Gilbert. Seeing how he had startled her, Gilbert said, "I'm sorry. When you were so long I began to worry."

"No need, they are all fast asleep," she whispered, shutting the door behind her. "Gilbert, I'm glad we had this time alone. I'd like to thank you for coming to my rescue not once, but twice this evening."

Smiling, he said, "Thank you too, for all the care you have given to my children, and for opening your home to Kathleen. It means a lot to me. Kathleen is more than just a relative to Mary. The Sullivan's had three children; Mary, my sister-in-law, Kathleen, and David. Me and David were mates in New York. He was killed trying to protect me, so I owe it to him to watch out for her."

Hearing the name David Sullivan, Felicity's eyes grew wide remembering how at one time Gilbert had been wanted for the murder of a David Sullivan. Recalling how it was Tad's friend Daniel who had actually killed him in the alley after Gilbert and Tad had fought, she meekly said, "That was Kathleen's brother?"

"Aye. Over the years, I've tried to look after her some."

"I see. That was very noble of you."

"Nah, it was the least I could do."

Turning, Gilbert, being a humble man and obviously uncomfortable speaking about the death of his friend or the kindness he had shown another, changed the subject as he descended the stairs. "With you and Benjamin on your way to London in a few days, would you mind if we stay here at Brookhaven, until I secure other living arrangements?"

"Other living arrangements? Why surely you're not intending to leave us Gilbert. Why I thought you enjoyed staying with us?"

"I do, but we can't be living here indefinitely. And with Kathleen here now...."

"Nonsense. You are more than welcome. It's not as if we don't have enough rooms." By now the two of them had entered Benjamin's study. Felicity, looking over at her husband for reinforcement said, "Ben darling, please convince Gilbert he's not an inconvenience to us."

"Inconvenience, why that's absurd. I was just thinking how I might be able to convince you to join us in London."

"London? Why I've recently just left London myself," Kathleen said, obviously accustomed to the finer things in life by the way she twirled the glass in her hand, heating the contents before consuming it. "Such a grand city. Have you ever been there Gilbert?" It was clear that she hoped he would accept Benjamin's invitation.

"Nah, can't say I have. How is it that you were in London, Kathleen? I thought you just arrived from Belfast?"

"I did. The night before the riots broke out, in fact. You see, not long after David passed, a rather wealthy and kind Englishmen traveled through our parts in search of land. He took a fancy to me, even as young as I was, and hired me to tend to his home. As time went by, to my good fortune he arranged with Jake and Mary to accompany him in his travels as a companion and hostess for him. He was very kind to me—hired tutors, coiffeurs, and tailors—and before long, I was transformed from a lowly Irish peasant to that of a respectable hostess, worthy to serve such a man of means. As it turned out, it was quite rewarding for the both of us. I was afforded the opportunity of meeting new people, and my benefactor had a devoted companion. That was until Mr. Strombly passed last July and his daughter Adele no longer required my services. Having no home of my own in London, I traveled back to Belfast, where I arrived the day before the riots took place."

Elise, shocked that the young woman before her would demean herself by speaking of her arrangements so freely, as if she were nothing more than a well paid courtesan, glanced around the room to judge the others' reactions. Seeing not the slightest glimmer of improprieties on any of their faces, Elise chalked it up as yet another English custom she would not begin to understand, and listened as Kathleen continued to speak.

"Fear not though Gilbert, although I no longer choose to speak with a brogue, I gave both Mary and Jake a proper sendoff. Why I even hired keeners, and I tell you true, never have I heard a better keening. And the wake, well they'll not be forgetting that one for some time."

Keening? Wake? What are you babbling about? Elise wondered, not at all impressed with Gilbert's guest.

"That was decent of you. Thank you Kathleen. I can't remember the last time I heard a good moaning at a funeral. Did ya happen to have someone play the pipes before the wake could begin?"

"I did indeed. Why, the sound of the bagpipes echoed over the valley like the sounds of a harp being played by the angels. And as soon as it stopped, the scotch and ale flowed freely."

"Sounds like you gave them a fine and proper sending off. Thank 'ee, kindly. Me brother and his good wife worked long and hard all their life; at least meeting their maker was a celebration."

Waiting for the opportune time to speak, hearing the name Strombly, Rupert cleared his throat and respectfully said, "Excuse me for interrupting, but did I hear you mention the name Strombly. Was that Oscar Strombly, by any chance?"

"Why yes it was, Mr. Robbins."

"Right. A fine man, sorry to hear he's left us."

"Yes, he was," Kathleen replied then hastily added, "As a matter of fact, he was asking an old friend of his about you the day before he passed."

"Is that right? And who might that be?"

"A Mr. Jacque Freeport."

"Hmm, I saw Jacque only this evening. He didn't mention Oscar had passed though."

"Well I'm sure he didn't know. You see, he and his companion, Mr. Sterling, left London for Plymouth following their meeting, or so I was led to understand. Do you know Mr. Sterling as well?"

Hearing James's name brought up in the conversation, Felicity's back stiffened. *Can't I escape him even in my own home?* she asked herself, taking her seat while sipping at the brandy Benjamin had poured for her. Discreetly over the rim of her glass, she glanced at Elise and Annabelle. There was no need for words to be spoken amongst these three women; the bond that they shared was so deep they already knew what the other was thinking.

Elise, the boldest of the three, directed her attention back toward Kathleen, and politely commented, "My, this is a small world isn't it?

Why, we were in the company of both Mr. Freeport and Mr. Sterling this very evening."

"Were you? Now that is a dear man. I must say he made quite an impression on me."

"Yes, I can see that. Mr. Sterling does have that effect on others, doesn't he?" Elise, finding that her brandy had suddenly soured in her mouth, placed her glass on the table before her, no longer able to sip its contents.

Obviously not picking up on the sarcasm in Elise's voice, Kathleen eagerly replied, "Indeed, he does. Normally when a man meets an available woman, he tries to woo her with his charm, but not Mr. Sterling. All he could speak of was his son, and how grand it was to have been reunited with him at last. Such devotion is rare in a man, don't you agree?"

Hearing her comment, Felicity felt the blood drain from her face and she glanced over at Benjamin who avoided her eyes and shifted in his seat. From his actions, she knew he had betrayed her; he had allowed James to meet with Whitney. Unable to hide the resentment she felt in her heart, her mind screamed, *Why?*

Somehow finding her voice, she said, "Well, it's been a long evening and I have a few matters that need attending to. If you'll excuse me."

As Felicity made her way to the doorway, the silence in the room was deafening. Kathleen anxiously looked amongst those in the room, her eyes resting on Gilbert. "Have I said something to offend someone? You'll have to forgive me, but when I'm nervous as I am now, I tend to prattle on."

Answering for Gilbert, Felicity said, "That's completely understandable, Kathleen. You've been through a great ordeal and being with us, virtually strangers, must be extremely difficult." Hearing her voice begin to crack, unable to continue as if there was nothing wrong, she hastily added, "I admire your inner strength and fortitude. If you require anything, please don't hesitate to ring for the housekeeper. Again, welcome to our home."

With that Felicity made a hasty exit and closing the doors behind her, she leaned against the wall, biting her fists to prevent herself from screaming out the agony she carried in her heart.

From inside the study, Elise stood and smiled politely. "Annabelle dear, would you mind terribly if I checked on Jefferson, while you keep Kathleen company? Perhaps you and she would like to get better acquainted in the conservatory, and let our men folk have a few minutes alone to enjoy one of Benjamin's finest cigars."

As Annabelle and Kathleen made small talk, saying polite good-byes to the gentlemen, Elise glanced at Benjamin before retreating from the room. Her heart went out to him, seeing the depth of his pain and anguish. Finding Felicity in the hall, she tenderly tucked her arm around the distraught woman's waist. "Come darlin', Kathleen and Annabelle are on their way to the conservatory."

"How could he?" she mumbled through her tears, no longer able to hold back her grief.

Elise, placing her finger gently over Felicity's mouth said, "Shh, don't let that little wench hear you." Scurrying her off to the cloakroom, she watched as Annabelle escorted Kathleen down the hall in the opposite direction. Once she knew there was no chance of them being seen or heard, Elise guided Felicity up the stairs. Urgently she pleaded with the distraught woman, "Please Felicity, come upstairs with me."

As she continued to escort her friend up the stairs, she prayed silently, *Dear God, just how much can this poor woman bear?*

Somehow managing to get Felicity to her room without alerting the others, Elise gently led her to her bed and allowed her to sob into her pillow, all the while gently rubbing her back. "Have yourself a good cry and get it out. Get it all out."

"How could he betray me like this?" Felicity wailed, glancing up at her friend. "Why? Dear God why? Not my Ben too?" Turning back into her pillow, the room filled with the muffled screams of desperation as her heart continued to break.

Elise knew there was no point in trying to answer her questions now, not until she had released all the pain. As she continued to soothe her friend the best she could under the circumstances, she looked up to heaven and asked, *Someone better help me Lord, 'cause I don't understand myself.*

~

Joshua and Gilbert, sensing Rupert and Benjamin needed time alone, excused themselves, claiming they needed air. Once they'd exited the room through the terrace, Rupert turned and glared at Benjamin, demanding an explanation. "Is it true? Have you allowed that barbarian to set eyes on Whitney?"

Sullen, Benjamin nodded his head, his voice barely above a whisper. "Yes."

"What?" Rupert bellowed, unable to control his rage. "Have you lost your senses? How could you do such a thing, knowing how much it would hurt her? Hasn't she been hurt enough, did she have to be stripped of the only thing she clung to, and that was trusting and loving you?"

"I don't suppose I can ever make you understand Rupert, but I had no choice. It just happened, just as that awful night happened. Do you think I haven't asked myself countless times why I can't protect those I love? I love Felicity. No, I cherish her and Whitney both. Every day I thank God for allowing them to be in my life. Even when I discovered what had happened, I never stopped loving her, nor looked upon her as unclean or soiled. She was my Felicity. Even after I discovered she was with child, I buried any resentment that I harbored for not being able to give her a child from our love. Through God's mercy, I learned to accept how an act of violation to her, that I couldn't stop, had conceived a child. And after many prayers, I began to think of the child she carried in her womb as only hers. And as every day passed, I grew to love that child because it was a part of Felicity. After Whitney was born, I found myself in pure bliss. I had everything. More than any man could ever want or need. A wife I cherished and still do and a perfect son."

"Then why would you allow that foul, depraved bastard...."

"As hard as it was for me to accept then, or even say aloud now, Rupert, that man is Whitney's father. For my son's sake, please, I beg of you—don't defile Whitney by referring to his father with such vile names. James has begged for my forgiveness. He says all he wants is to see the only thing that is good and decent in his life, his son. Who am I to deny him?"

"Why must you always be so damn noble?"

"Noble? I'm sure my beloved Felicity doesn't see me as noble right now. I would suspect she feels I have betrayed her...." Benjamin's voice cracked, and he lowered his head into hands. "How can I love this woman so much, yet continue to hurt her so deeply?"

"Go to her Benjamin, she needs you. Just as you need her. Obviously this is as painful to you as it is for her. We can talk later."

"I can't Rupert. I've let her down through carelessness, and now it's Felicity who has to bear the pain. Since James saw Whitney, I've asked myself countless times if Gilbert is right. Should I forgo my beliefs, and react on instincts, an eye for an eye."

"Stop, Benjamin. Don't you see what you are doing to both of you by second-guessing yourself? End this pain, especially now when you need each other so desperately. Don't allow Felicity to feel betrayed by the man she loves."

Nodding, Benjamin pulled himself from his chair. "Yes, of course you're right. I must go to her."

As Rupert stood watching his friend leave the room, he thought of what Benjamin had said to him, and tried to make some sense of his words. Had he purposely allowed James to see Whitney out of forgiveness?

Recalling that he had mentioned Gilbert, Rupert went out onto the terrace in search of some answers.

"Ah, Gilbert. Just the man I was looking for." Turning his attention to Joshua for a moment, he added, "I would suspect your dear wife is in need of some pampering about now. Please tell her for me how much I appreciate her quick and level head, making a very uncomfortable situation bearable. But mostly, thank her for her generosity for helping my dear cousin at her hour of need."

"I will." Patting Rupert's arm, Joshua stepped inside the study just as Elise arrived. Seeing him, Elise ran to his protective arms and Joshua held her tightly, kissing her head tenderly as she wept in his arms. "Oh darling, I feel so sad for both of them."

Rupert, closing the door to give the Carmidys some privacy, turned, and looked over at Gilbert. "Over the past few months I've watched you with keen interest. And I've discovered Gilbert O'Flaherty is a hard man to gauge. I see in you a pride that far surpasses being an Irishman. Who refrains from showing his own pain as if it's a sign of weakness, yet openly shows great tenderness to his children? You rarely engage in idle chitchat, yet willingly make a spectacle of yourself for the sake of others. Gilbert, despite your gruffness, I believe in you lies a man who can be trusted and is far wiser than you let on. Saying all this, I ask you man to man, hopefully, friend to friend, what do you think I should do to prevent James Sterling from hurting my cousin again?"

Raising his eyebrow, Gilbert smirked as his eyes locked onto Rupert's. "Ya know, I've discovered something about you too. As much as the English annoy me, puttin' on airs, as only you English with yer uppity ways can do, you have a way of discerning even yer most formidable opponents by laying it out on the table. Friends you say? Well hell, why not."

Extending his hand to Rupert, they shook one another's hand heartily. Then looking seriously at him, Gilbert said, "Before I speak to you though regarding Sterling, know this, I won't be goin' against such a good man as Benjamin Myles, not even to his own. So if that is what you had in mind, then yer in fer a mighty big disappointment."

"You know Gilbert, a while back, I used my speech as a means to keep those I didn't trust at bay, and I find myself wondering if you do the same."

"Well, let's just say hearing my brogue reminds me of my Da, and what he stood for, and leave it at that. Now for Sterling...I'm a suspicious cuss by nature, and having lost someone as dear as my wife to another river rat like him, I can tell ya, he's no good through and through. He feeds on those like the good parson up there and his missus, who can't begin to know the depth of his evilness, never having had to live with the likes of him."

"River rat, you say?"

"Aye, lurking in the shadows, ready to pounce on his victim when they least expect it. If given half the chance, that there rat will strike again, and he's using that boy to get what he wants."

Rupert swallowed hard before responding, "Felicity."

"I saw him and the lad together and I can tell ya what, he ain't half as interested in his boy as he is in Whitney's mother. Felicity is like Miranda was, pure and good. He looks at her and thinks he has the right to something as fine as she."

"So you were there when James met Whitney?"

"Aye, we were fishin' down by the cottage and Sterling walked up to us as big as you please. Benjamin was shocked, but he handled it better than I would have, that's for damn sure. He introduced him as an old friend to keep Whitney from becoming alarmed. Soon afterwards I took the lad off with me boys as they talked."

"I'm confused…Why did Benjamin lead me to believe he granted him a chance to see Whitney?"

"Being a true man of God, the good parson has learned to forgive Sterling, even wants to believe his malarkey about repenting. Too bad Benjamin the man, can't be as charitable when it comes to forgiving himself. Unless you live it firsthand, knowing another man harmed your wife and you couldn't prevent it, you can never understand that hellish nightmare."

Rupert said nothing as Gilbert paused and took in a deep breath. Shaking his head, he added, "If that wasn't bad enough, Benjamin has to tell her he failed her again. He's fightin' his own demons, I tell ya. He's taught his boy the difference from right and wrong, goes around saving other souls, all the while hating himself, probably as much as he hates Sterling, or more. He's trapped and that damn river rat knows it. Worse, Sterling enjoys taunting him, probably as much as he enjoys taunting Felicity."

"Not doubting your assessment Gilbert, but if what you say is true, then pray tell, how do we stop that depraved bastard?"

"Short of killing him, I honestly don't know. If I did know, do you think I'd be without me Mandy? Lest you forgot, she had to kill her river rat herself, not being able to count on me to stop him."

~ Fourteen ~

Needing time alone to think, Felicity sat amongst the lush greenery inside her conservatory before sunrise, knowing her guests would still be asleep for a while. Absentmindedly, she rubbed a water spot off the leaf of a philodendron, and thought of Benjamin. She had come to understand his reasons for not being forthright with her, he feeling as if he had not been able to protect her and Whitney from James again. And as much as she had tried to convince him throughout the night that she had forgiven him for not telling her of the incident, as they lay silently in bed, Felicity knew neither of them believed her words fully.

It was if they had returned to that dark period of their marriage following the attack, where both of them grieved in silence. Benjamin blaming himself for not protecting them; and Felicity, trying to cleanse herself from ever having allowed herself to become James's victim to begin with.

Oh Ben, what are we to do…

Her thoughts were interrupted by Elise. "If you're not careful you are going to rub the life right out of that plant. Care if I join you, or would you prefer to be alone?"

Smiling warmly at her friend, Felicity let go of the leaf and patted the seat beside her. "My, but you're up early this morning. Did Jefferson have a bad night?"

"No the little darlin's slept through the entire night. I just was a mite restless and thought I'd find you here."

"Thank you."

"Ya, know Felicity, we don't have to talk. We can just sit here for a spell and watch the sun come up together."

Nodding, Felicity said, "That would be nice, but I could use some advice, and since you're leaving in the morning.…"

Taking Felicity's hand in hers, Elise smiled, patting it tenderly. "I was hoping you would want to confide in me. Did you and your Ben get everything all worked out? Never have I felt so sorry for a man as I did last night. He was so pitiful, my heart bled for him. For you both. I can't stand seeing you both in such misery."

Taking in a deep breath, Felicity agreed, "Neither can I."

"Ya know last night I laid there half the night thinking about you and Benjamin, and that snake. Well never mind him for now, I'll get back to him later. As I lay there, I remembered all of us meeting up in Washington right after the war. Do you remember that?"

Smiling, Felicity nodded her head. "Why yes, I do. I haven't thought of that for years."

"And do you remember, after we found out about poor Old Abe gettin' shot how we fled the city?"

"Yes, as I recall we shared with each other how we had fallen in love with our husbands."

"We sure did. And I recall you tellin' me then how much you yearned for a child. Well darlin' you have a child—it may not be the way you and Benjamin had wanted it, but your prayer was answered, you were given a child. And I'm tellin' ya what; your Whitney is a fine boy. And if that wasn't enough of a blessing, God saw to it that your love could withstand all the pain you both went through, just so you could have that boy. Now, I'm not as religious as your Ben is, but I can tell you this, he probably loved that little boy even before he saw him, didn't he?"

Unable to speak, Felicity just nodded her head.

"I thought so. Now Felicity, I've never asked you to tell me what happened after you returned from England, and how was it that the two of you could build a life after what had happened. I thought it best to let sleeping dogs lie, but I can tell you this, that man loves you. Most men could never have accepted another man's child as your Ben has. Their pride gets in the way. Blaming themselves for not being able to give you a child themselves, or not protecting you. Why, I do believe men care so much about their pride, their minds get all tangled up. I know my Joshua almost allowed his stubborn pride to let him leave Doves Landing without letting me know how much he loved me, just because he thought he was protecting me. The point I'm trying to make here is, Benjamin might be a preacher man with a heart of gold, but he's still a man. I'm thinkin' that there snake probably caught him off guard and that's how he got to see Whitney. And Benjamin just couldn't admit that he had let you down again. Why to a man's way of thinkin' that's like admitting that snake was a better man than he was."

"I agree," Annabelle said, walking into the conservatory. "Please forgive me, for intruding."

"Don't be silly. Come, join us," Felicity said, stretching out her arm to Annabelle.

Taking a seat, Annabelle continued, "Elise is right, Felicity. Rupert and I spoke last night after he had a long talk with Gilbert. Did you know that Gilbert was there the day James appeared by the stream?"

"No, Ben didn't say a word."

"Of course he didn't, Benjamin is too fine a man to make excuses. From what Gilbert said to Rupert, even though he was quite unnerved by James's presence, he never let on so as not to upset Whitney."

"Really?"

"Yes. Even then he thought of what was best for Whitney rather than himself. Since that day though, he's been living in hell believing he's let both of you down. Oh Felicity, I know how much it must hurt you that James saw Whitney, but you just can't be angry with Benjamin over this. He already hates himself for letting you down."

"My poor darling...." Her voice trailed off, looking out the windows onto the gardens just as the sun started to shine over the horizon. Seeing a rabbit hop through her rose garden, she smiled wearily. "How I wish I could be like that little bunny out there and just run away and hide with my Ben and Whitney."

"Well darlin', I'm afraid you can't." Elise patted her hand. "Besides, where would you go? Your troubles would only follow you."

Turning to look at Elise, Felicity said gravely, "I know. What should I do?"

"Well for starters, I definitely wouldn't let that snake come between you and your Ben, that's for damn sure. Why I wouldn't be a bit surprised if he didn't plan this whole thing, knowing eventually you would find out and get angry with Benjamin."

"That's absurd. James Sterling is a master at conniving, but even he couldn't have known that our houseguest would be the one to spill the beans."

"Don't be so sure. Why didn't she tell us herself how she knew him in London? Besides, I don't trust that woman. She's nothing more than a gold-digger hussy, if you ask me. Why she as much as admitted it herself, goin' on about how she was transformed from a peasant to some hostess by that old coot. Where I come from, there's a name for a woman like that."

Coming to Gilbert's guest's defense, Felicity said, "Elise shame on you."

"Felicity, I agree with Elise. Kathleen Sullivan is not someone I trust. I can tell you, the moment I saw her, she reminded me of Lavinia. And after you two left, and I brought her out here, well I can tell you, she is here for one purpose and one purpose only and that's to get her claws into Gilbert."

"See! I told you, I didn't like her." Leaning closer to Annabelle, Elise said, "Come on Annabelle, tell us everything about that little wench before the children wake up."

~

Two stories above the conservatory, in the master bedchamber, Benjamin stared gravely out the window overlooking the grounds. The look of sadness in Felicity's eyes haunted him. Never would he have believed that he would be the one to have put that look there.

Feeling empty inside, he dropped to his knees. "Dear Lord, I have tried to serve you to the best of my abilities, but I fear I have failed you, just as I've failed my beloved wife. Help me please, Lord, to be able to protect her from those who mean her harm. Allow me to be a man deserving of her love, so I can find some peace."

Hearing the door close to their room, Benjamin stood and quickly straightened his jacket and rubbed his hand through his hair. "Ah dearest, I didn't hear you this morning. You must have awoken before the sun came up."

Reaching his side, touched by his prayer that she had overheard, Felicity looked lovingly up at him and smiled. "I did. I went to the conservatory to think." Tenderly brushing a strand of hair off his forehead, her fingers traced his hairline. "As it was, Elise and Annabelle joined me."

"They did? Perhaps we should go down...."

Felicity interrupted him by placing her fingers over his lips. "Darling, will you hold me instead?"

Tenderly Benjamin stretched out his arms and drew his wife nearer to him. Never had she felt him clutch her so tightly as she did now. "Oh Ben, can you ever forgive me?"

"Forgive you? Dearest you've done nothing wrong."

Pulling slightly away from him, her eyes locked on to his. "Yes, I have Ben, I accused you of betrayal when I am guilty of the same. I locked you out of an important part of my life, out of fear." Seeing that he was ready to argue, she looked pleadingly up at him. "Please Darling. Let me speak so we can both find some peace." Nodding his response, Felicity took in a deep breath before continuing. "After the attack, I begged Annabelle not to let you come to me. I was wrong. I was so afraid...."

Pausing, she held tighter onto him to get through this, and slowly spoke again. "I was afraid that after what he had done to me, you wouldn't love me anymore, or think I was soiled. I couldn't forgive myself for becoming so drunk that I didn't realize it was he standing naked beside me as I lay on our bed, and not you, until it was too late."

"Felicity you don't need to do this, it is in the past."

"I do Ben; don't you see the past haunts us even today? Please Ben, let me finish." Again, she took in a deep breath, her eyes locked on to his. "The whole time he took pleasure from me, I struggled, screamed until he placed his hand over my mouth and I feared I was going to die, unable to breathe. I didn't die, and you never stopped loving me. Even when you found out I was carrying his child, your love for me never wavered. Even though I couldn't allow you to come near me, to touch me, feeling so dirty...every time I felt the baby stir in me, it made my skin crawl, I thought of my child as the demon's spawn. And as much as I feared I would never be happy again, you Ben, showed me a way to be happy, to put the pain behind me. And I have been happy Ben, with you and our son. Never once these past few years have you ever asked anything of me, yet I continued to keep that cloud of fear over us. I feared that somehow James or someone else, or Whitney, would find out the truth. Well Ben, James does know the truth. He's even seen Whitney, and suddenly I'm not afraid of him as much as I am of losing what he could never take from me, and that was what we share in our hearts. I love you Ben, more today than when we first met. You have given me so much, I know I am loved, and I have peace because of that love, yet never in all this time have I told you. Can you ever forgive me?" Tears ran down both their faces and they clung to each other.

"I don't deserve...."

Felicity, pulling from him, shook her head. "Yes you do Ben, we both do. We deserve to be happy out of the love that we share. Don't you see Ben, what happened wasn't either of our faults, it just happened. Elise reminded me today that I had yearned for a son. Well darling, God did hear my prayers, he granted me everything I could ever need or want. And even if you didn't conceive Whitney, my son has the father I always wanted for him, and that is you. We are a family, a family that loves one another."

With one seamless motion, Benjamin picked Felicity up in his arms and carried her to their bed, kissing her passionately. Returning his kiss with a passion she hadn't felt in years, hungrily she moaned, "Oh Ben."

Time stood still for them, the years of silent pain they had both been harboring in their hearts had at last been released and replaced with a burning desire to show the other how much they were loved. Releasing his wife on their bed, eagerly they groped at each other's clothing, not caring nor thinking that others were waiting for them; all they thought of was fulfilling their desire for one another. In their haste to undress, a pearl button popped off her blouse, and looking down at the torn material, Felicity just shrugged her shoulders pulling Benjamin closer to her while yanking more firmly at the remaining buttons of his trousers.

Standing naked at last before each other, their clothing tossed around them, Felicity's hand stretched out to Ben, as she lay her head on the pillow. "Darling, come love me."

Needing no further prompting, Benjamin joined his wife. As their bodies intertwined, Felicity no longer was plagued by the horrors of the night James had taken her without permission as it had been every time she and Benjamin had been intimate these past seven years. Now she relished in feeling Benjamin inside her, and matched his urgent thrusts, clutching at his back to assure she had all of him. Caught up in feeling such splendor, she moaned in ecstasy as he continued to bring forth a pleasure she had never known, which only heightened his enjoyment. Reaching a peak of unrivaled rhapsody, they clung together, showering each other with kisses between gasps of air. Felicity began trembling and Benjamin held her closer to him. "I love you Felicity."

"I love you Ben. More than you will ever know." Tenderly cupping his hands around her face, Benjamin gently wiped the tears from her cheeks and smiled down at her. "Perhaps we should think of tending to our guests."

"Elise and Annabelle can handle it for a while longer; right now I'd rather tend to my husband's needs."

"To our needs," Benjamin huskily whispered, tenderly kissing her, arousing a passion again inside them both. The two of them made love a second time, giving themselves freely to the other from hearts that had been bruised for so long, but now were at last healed. No longer the past with silenced doubts or worries of their future plagued them; all that mattered now was the love they shared for one another.

~

Kissing the children after breakfast, Elise glanced over to Whitney who looked concerned that his mother and father had not joined them. "Darlin, please don't fret, your mama and papa will be down shortly. They just have a few things to work out about your trip to London on Tuesday."

"I know, but it's Sunday and we didn't go to church. We've never missed church before. Not ever."

"Well there's a first time for everything. Now run along and watch over the little ones, hear?"

"Yes Auntie," Whitney mumbled, leaving through the front door, calling to Andrew as he did.

Annabelle shook her head. "I sure hope Felicity and Benjamin have worked things out. I hate to see them going through such a hard time again."

Hearing their host and hostess coming down the stairs, Elise, noticing Felicity had changed into another gown, smiled raising her brow. "Well, that's a good sign. I like Felicity's new choice in gowns from earlier this mornin'."

Giggling softly, Annabelle agreed whispering, "Hmm, so do I."

Entering the dining room, Benjamin exclaimed, "Why good morning. What a glorious day it is. Has everyone already eaten?" Kissing Annabelle on the cheek, he turned and walked to where Elise was sitting and bending over slightly, he kissed her too while squeezing her shoulder gently, and whispering in her ear, "Thank you."

Elise patted him on the shoulder and looked over at Felicity as she poured a cup of tea from the buffet table. "Tea, Benjamin?"

"No, I think I'll just snag a roll and head out to find the others." Taking one from a basket, he leaned over and kissed Felicity tenderly on the cheek, then turning Benjamin left the three women in the dining room, while tossing the biscuit in his hand.

Annabelle, her eyes dancing, looked over the rim of her cup as she sipped her tea while Elise, looking out the window watching Benjamin wave to Joshua and Rupert before turning and looking over at Felicity. "I trust you and Benjamin worked things out?"

"Oh yes. Thank you for allowing us the time to talk it out."

"Talk you say?" Elise raising her brows smirked. "Hmm, that must have been some talk, judging by your rosy cheeks and the spring in Benjamin's step. Remind me to have the same little chat with Joshua; perhaps this afternoon during tea might be nice."

"You're shameless!" Felicity chuckled, joining her friends who both giggled merrily.

Annabelle, having difficulty holding back a smile, added in her prim and proper tone, "My sentiments exactly, Elise. This afternoon when Rupert returns to Ashwillow to pick up some wine for you and Joshua to take back with you, perhaps I should go with him so we two can have such a grand chat."

"Why Annabelle Robbins, I can't believe I'm hearing that come out of your mouth. I do believe I've corrupted you."

Glancing out the window, and seeing Gilbert with Kathleen hanging on his arm, Elise's smile faded, and she gestured to Annabelle and Felicity to look also. "Now that's shameless. Just look how that woman hangs on him like honey on a bun." Shaking her head, she turned and sipped her tea. "I declare men are all the same, a woman shows them a little attention and they just lose all their senses."

"Now Elise, are you certain you aren't over reacting simply because Gilbert was married to Miranda?" Felicity asked, her eyes still watching as Gilbert and Kathleen joined Benjamin and the other men.

"No, of course not. I want Gilbert to be happy again, to find love; but not with the likes of her."

Annabelle shook her head. "Maybe Gilbert is only trying to make her feel comfortable. After all, you did say he feels beholden to his friend."

"Oh and don't you think she's not using that to lure him to her, either. Take it from someone who knows a thing or two about turning a man's head to get what you want. And I can tell you that hussy out there sees Gilbert as an opportunity to advance her station in life."

"Well if she is, perhaps it will be good for Gilbert and the children." Felicity paused to butter her biscuit. "Benjamin was telling me that he and Gilbert have had long talks about starting anew. We cannot expect that poor man to live the rest of his life alone, mourning for Miranda. Let me see how Benjamin put it...." Her voice trailed off while taking a bite of her breakfast to gather her thoughts. "Yes, Benjamin said that when two people loved like Miranda and Gilbert did, for him to be able to love again is proof that the love they shared was true. Because it shows how good their love was. Benjamin said it so much better than I'm explaining it, but basically it means he's honoring Miranda's memory by carrying on."

"I agree with you, Felicity, but I know Miranda and she would roll over in her grave if he ended up with the likes of Kathleen *Hussy* Sullivan!"

"Stop that," Felicity snickered. "As for Miss Sullivan, I'm in favor of not letting her—or anyone else, for that matter, spoil our last day together by worry about something none of us has any control over. Now what would you like to do on your last day in England?"

Although Felicity's smile was reassuring, there was no denying she was as apprehensive about Kathleen Sullivan as Elise.

~ Fifteen ~

Arriving in London, Felicity's and Benjamin's playful and lighthearted moods of the past several days became sullen driving past Earlswood Asylum where Lavinia was lodged. The thought of the once vivacious and beautiful woman rotting away from the dreaded disease, in and out of sound mind, was disturbing to them all. Even Kathleen, who knew nothing of Lavinia, was familiar with the hellish nightmare one who contracted syphilis had to endure.

Only the children spoke amongst themselves, Whitney, and Priscilla pointing out landmarks of the crowded and congested city to the O'Flaherty children.

Catherine and Lucas looked around with keen interest as Suzanne, sitting on her father's lap and Joseph on Felicity's, looked intimidated by the sounds and sights of the large city.

"Da, how long do we have to stay here?"

"Only a few days, Peanut."

Felicity, trying to ease the children's minds, said, "If you like, after we're settle in we can go shopping at a wonderful store that has all kinds of toys, made especially for good boys and girls."

Joey, looking up at his aunt, said, "Auntie, am I a good boy?"

Kissing the top of his head through his cap, she smiled. "Yes my little lamb, you're a very good boy."

Saying not a word, only his eyes expressing his pleasure at how at ease Felicity was with his children, Gilbert looked out the window of the coach. Seeing the street merchants clamoring bells to hawk their wares, and street urchins hovering about the streets begging for a pence, he said, "Reminds me of New York, with all the noise."

"New York?" Kathleen wistfully replied, "Oh Gilbert, you must tell me everything of the colonies. I so want to go there someday."

Seeing Gilbert's jaw stiffen at the sight of a small child no older than Suzanne being shoved by a man dressed in a stylish topcoat and hat who refused her any charity, Benjamin spoke up. "Having lived in New York myself, a large city has its advantages and gross disadvantages."

"Aye, two separate worlds amongst themselves; hell or the pearly gates, depending on stature." There was no denying that Gilbert had experienced the worst city life had to offer by the sound of his voice.

Clearing his throat, Rupert said, "Yes well, even those with means, beneath the beautiful garbs and unseen by the naked eye can live in purgatory, tortured in their hearts. Some of their own choosing while others have been thrust there with no recourse. Thank heavens we here today know the value of making every day count."

Gilbert looked over at Rupert, knowing such a comment was not only said because of his wife's sister, or his cousin's current situation; this came from a man who had experienced great inner pain himself. "Aye, I've come to understand that, mate."

As the coach came to a halt in front of the Ruffles Brown near Trafalgar Square, Piccadilly Circus, and Hyde Park, they nodded respectfully; an acknowledgement that they regarded each other as friends and were in agreement with the other's assessment.

A well-groomed coachman approached and Rupert raised his brow and said, "Ah now, we shall be privy to the gentile side of London."

"Children, don't say a word 'til Da says so, hear?" Gilbert said sternly, and the children nodded their heads obediently.

Felicity, glancing between Gilbert and Benjamin said not a word, and held Joey's hand as she was assisted out of the handsome coach.

"Welcome Mrs. Myles, a pleasure to see you again. And who is this handsome young lad?"

Smiling warmly at the coachman, Felicity said, "Thank you, Winston. Good to see you're well. Please see to it that my nieces and nephews from the colonies are well cared for while we are visiting your fine establishment."

Bowing, Winston greeted each of the O'Flaherty children as if they were royalty, and the children responded with smiles and soft muffled giggles amongst themselves.

Not saying a word, Gilbert watched as the party walked with airs into the lobby. Kathleen, leaning over to Gilbert, whispered, "My, Mrs. Myles sure puts on the dogs in public doesn't she? Why you would think she's a Robbins."

"She is, as well as a Phelps." Gilbert hoarsely whispered, "Now hush."

Kathleen's eyes bulged; apparently unaware that Felicity was the heiress of such stately families known throughout all of England.

After being escorted to their suites, Rupert, leaving instructions with the hotel staff and ascertaining the suites were to his liking, waited until they were alone before addressing Gilbert. "Forgive the intrusion but curiosity has got the better of me; was the need for silence because of your brogue? Gilbert, you do realize here in London more than twenty-percent of the population is Irish, don't you?"

"Aye, and I'm sure they've all frequented such an establishment as fine as this. I'll not be having me children experience condemnation from others, simply because of their heritage."

"Point taken. Perhaps in time, with you here in England now, you too will find a happy medium as Felicity has. Being an American in England was not an easy adjustment for her as well. Why when she first arrived here, as I recall, she heard from my illustrious sister-in-law, and others as well I'm sure, that she was nothing more than a commoner from that backwoods country of hers."

"Is that a fact?"

"Indeed. I suppose it is all in how others perceive you, isn't it old chap? Well, enough said. I need to speak with my wife for a few moments. Do make yourself comfortable."

As delicate as Rupert had been, Gilbert knew the point he was trying to make. It was Rupert's opinion that those who viewed the Irish as nothing more than potato farmers, needed to view an educated Irishman with means before that opinion could be altered. Uncertain if he should be angered or grateful for the advice, he headed toward the adjoining room to tend to his children. Hearing soft laughter from inside, he smiled hearing Felicity's voice as she answered all the children's questions with such patience. Behind closed doors, she exhibited the same warmth that he and the children had grown accustomed to, yet while in the presence of others she exhibited a regal quality that demanded respect. *Well perhaps it wouldn't hurt me wee ones to learn from such a woman.*

Entering the room, he saw Felicity kneeling beside Lucas, delicately laying his hair in place after he had removed his hat. "Darlin's don't be upset, Whitney's hair was unmanageable too, until he began using tonic on it. Why not ask your papa if it would be all right if you begin using tonic as well? I believe Whitney has an extra bottle with him."

Seeing that the children were as neat as a pin, Felicity smiled lovingly at them. "My, don't we all look like little duchesses and dukes. Now remember, while in London we must remember to wear our best manners at all time, especially when we're in the presence of others."

"I remember, Auntie," Joey exclaimed eagerly. "Look see, I can bow just like Whitney taught us." Demonstrating, Gilbert watched as his youngest bowed with perfection, extending his hand to her and then said, "Pleasure to make your acquaintance, m'lady."

Curtsying to him, and shaking his hand lightly, Felicity said, "Well thank you, young sir." Noting that Catherine and Suzanne were mimicking her, Felicity did it again in slow motion so the girls could practice with her.

Winking at them, she gave them an approving nod as Joey ran to her and hugged her legs tightly. "See I told you, I could do it."

"So you did my little lamb and so well, too." Then seeing Gilbert leaning in the doorway, Felicity said, "Oh Gilbert, I didn't see you come in." Suddenly feeling awkward, uncertain if Gilbert was angered by taking the liberty of directing his children in this manner, Felicity said, "Well, I should freshen up. If you'll excuse me."

"May I have a word with ya first."

Her heart pounding, realizing she must have offended him, she said, "Yes." Stepping closer to her adjoining room, not intending to be in alone in any man's room, she waited until Gilbert walked across to her. Smiling nervously, she stepped inside her room and noticing that Benjamin had left, probably to speak with Rupert, her heart sank.

As she closed the door to her room immediately Gilbert said, "I see you've been giving my children lessons on proper English manners. And just when did this all take place?"

"I see. No need for you to be angry with me. I just thought...."

"Angry? Did I say I was angry? I just asked when this was decided, m'lady?" The tone of his voice never wavered, but from the look on his face, and the way he said, *m'lady*, Felicity was certain he didn't approve and she felt her cheeks begin to burn.

"Gilbert, I meant no harm, if I've offended you, please...."

"Then you're not going to answer me when all this happened, I take it."

Certain that he was deliberately trying to provoke her, she responded curtly, "I'll answer you, when given the chance. Kindly refrain from cutting me off every time I speak."

Standing before her, his arms crossed and wearing a snide grin, Felicity clenched her fists to her side. "Look Gilbert O'Flaherty, I'm sorry if I offended you by not discussing every detail of the children's and my conversations this past summer...."

Evidently ignoring her first comment, he cut her off again and said, "Ah, so it was this summer then, not yesterday or this morning?"

Becoming flustered by his persistence, she said, "Well not exactly. The other evening when Whitney introduced himself to Miss Sullivan, evidently your children wanted to know how to do the same and asked if I would show them when I tucked them in. Seeing nothing wrong with their request, we've been practicing, with Whitney's help of course."

"Well, m'lady, thank you. That was real nice of you."

Apparently, Felicity's face reflected her surprise, and Gilbert continued to smile as he turned to exit, only pausing when Felicity asked, "Gilbert, if you didn't mind me giving the children guidance then why did you lead me to believe you were angry?"

"Oh I don't know, maybe I like to rile people for fun sometimes. Or perhaps I thought that since you were goin' to be seeing me wee ones so much, it was about time you got to know their Da some too. I don't bite Felicity, so try not to be so standoffish to me."

"I'll keep that in mind, but I'm warning you, when provoked I become cantankerous."

Tilting his head acting to be surprised by her comment, his eyes twinkled merrily at her. "Is that so, why I never would have guessed, m'lady."

Felicity was at a loss for words, and she smiled shaking her head as she closed the adjoining door.

Benjamin stepped back into their room and asked, "What's so amusing, dearest?"

"Gilbert O'Flaherty," Felicity cooed as Benjamin wrapped his arms around his wife's waist. Telling him of the incident, Benjamin chuckled.

"He's right, you know. I've noticed the strain between you two. Perhaps now would be the time to try and get to know one another better?"

"I suppose. I just never know what to expect from him. Half the time when I think he's angry I find out he's not. Most unnerving and not at all easy to figure out."

"Precisely why he acted as he did now, I suspect. I'm sure he was proving a point that you two really don't know one another very well, which is such a shame since you both are going to have such an influence on his and Miranda's children. I'd look beyond the gruff exterior and who he was in New York, and get to know the man he is now. I think you'll find as I have, and apparently Rupert has too, that Gilbert O'Flaherty is a good man. One I admire very much."

"All I can say is, I will try." Then changing the subject she asked, "When are you and Rupert going to the asylum?"

"Tomorrow morning. Rupert is trying to convince Annabelle, as we speak, that she should come as well, in the event Lavinia...." Benjamin's voice trailed off, obviously finding it difficult to say that Lavinia was dying. "Rupert is afraid that if Lavinia should pass, Annabelle might never forgive herself for not seeing her, and making peace with her."

"Oh darling, I'm sure Annabelle wants nothing more than to say her last good-byes. But with so much bad blood between them, and the thought of seeing her in an institution, not knowing the condition she will find her in, must be extremely difficult. If it were me, I'd rather remember Lavinia as she was rather than what she has become by this dreaded disease."

"Annabelle needs to go for both of their sakes. You know her, the guilt of not trying to make peace with her only living relative would haunt her. Not to mention, it's the Christian thing to do, to allow that poor pathetic woman to find some peace before she meets her maker. Dearest, considering we know how vain Lavinia has always been, and witnessing firsthand the effects the disease has had on others, her asking to be viewed in her current state proves Lavinia must have had a change of heart. Her appearance on the outside is not what is important now; we should look at it as a woman who at last wants to be cleansed. Such an act surely must be beautiful in God's eyes."

"Oh Ben, you're such a good man. Do you think it would help if I spoke to Annabelle too?"

"Perhaps, after dinner though. Let's gather everyone together so we can dine. I'm famished."

Not long after dinner as Lucas, Whitney, Benjamin and Gilbert sat in the center of the room playing a game of rummy, Felicity sat quietly reattaching a piece of lace that had come off of Suzanne's dress. With the girl sitting next to her, Felicity, conscious that she was trying to learn from her, rather than repair her dress hastily, she took every stitch very slowly.

Annabelle, sitting near the fire cutting out another outfit for the girls' paper dolls, called to her daughter and Catherine, "Here's another gown for your dolls. I like this one even better than the other." Seeing Kathleen show some interest, Annabelle asked, "Are you sure you wouldn't like to join me cutting the rest out?"

Smiling politely, Kathleen shook her head, fidgeting with her hair. "No thank you, Mrs. Robbins. I really don't have the patience for such tedious work."

Nodding, Annabelle lowered her head and began cutting another article of clothing from the set.

Felicity, sneaking a quick glance at Annabelle, turned her attention to their guest. "Kathleen, if you would prefer to do a little needlepoint, I have a sewing basket inside my room. I could get it for you, if you'd like."

"No thank you, Mrs. Myles. Sewing of any kind isn't something I look upon as recreational. I swore I'd never take up another needle and thread when I left Belfast."

Responding with a nod, Felicity continued pushing the needle through the velvet and lace, making certain the stitches were small so as not to be too noticeable.

"Mrs. Myles, why not send that out? I'm sure the management of such a fine establishment as this must have a seamstress readily available to accommodate their guests," Kathleen exclaimed, obviously bored just sitting inside the room.

"Oh I don't mind, besides Suzanne seems eager to learn. Reminds me of when my grandmother taught me."

Rupert, raising his head smiled. "Is that so, I didn't know Aunt Elizabeth enjoyed sewing."

"Hmm, she did indeed. Why she was always puttering about making something for one of the slaves or a needy family in town."

Glancing over at Gilbert's youngest daughter, smiling she said, "Sweet pea, would you like to try now?"

Catherine, who was busy playing with Pricilla at their feet, looked up briefly and said, "She's too little, Auntie. She'll ruin it, just like she almost cut off my doll's head."

Seeing Suzanne's shoulders slump forward, Felicity said, "Nonsense, Suzanne's the perfect age to sew." Placing the dress in the girl's lap, Felicity wrapped her arm around her shoulders and instructed her how to hold the needle. Then guiding her fingers through the lace and velvet material, showing her how to come back through the material and pull gently on the thread, Suzanne completed her first stitch. "See, you did it wonderfully. Why in no time you'll be as good as me."

Beaming up at her aunt, Suzanne suddenly frowned as if thinking of something. "Auntie, are you really my aunt?"

"Well, there are all kinds of aunts, dear. Some that are related by blood and then there are others who become your aunt from love."

"See, I told you, Suzanne," Catherine spouted. "Mama didn't have any brothers or sisters."

Suzanne still pouted and Felicity whispered softly to her, "What wrong, sugar?"

"I wanted you to be real."

"Sweet pea, I am real. In my heart, where it really matters, is a place for all of you."

"Papa too?"

Trying not to show Suzanne how unnerving her question was, Felicity smiled warmly at her. "Why of course, darling. Not as his aunt though, but as a friend."

Guiding her fingers through to the next stitch, Felicity felt her cheeks flush and discreetly glanced over at the table where they were still playing cards. Although Gilbert was not watching her, by his smirk, she knew he had overheard them.

"Da, it's your turn," Lucas anxiously called to his father.

"Hold on there lad, give me time to think."

Sighing, Lucas stared at his father who was looking at Whitney. "Hmm. Ya know, I think I'll be picking up the whole pile. Yes these here cards will do me nicely." Glancing over at Whitney and grinning, he pulled out the ten of diamonds and waved it slightly before placing it in his hand. "Can't be lettin' Master Whitney get this one, now can I?"

Whitney shrugged his shoulders as his jaw dropped. "How did you know I needed that, I didn't say a word."

"Lad you're a smart one, just like your Da, able to figure things out quick, but you got your Ma's eyes and they gave ya away."

Glancing between his father and Gilbert, looking confused, he said, "Mum's eyes?"

"When your Da laid that card down, them blue eyes of yours lit up like it was gold. Remember lad, the eyes are the mirror to your soul, ya can't be letting people read you through your eyes."

Agreeing, Benjamin nodded his head, "Son, there's more to playing cards than just matching cards up; you have to watch your opponents and what's been laid. Unfortunately, your father doesn't have the same skills as Gilbert here, despite his kind words, otherwise I wouldn't have laid the ten down to begin with."

"Ah, don't be too hard on yerself there mate, I had me lots of practice in New York. When you're playing for food money, ya tend to take it a bit serious."

"Excuse me Uncle Gilbert, did you say you played cards for food money? Wouldn't it have been more prudent not to chance it playing cards?"

Benjamin obviously embarrassed by his son's question, scolded him, "Son, certain things we don't ask."

"The lad meant no harm. He's curious is all. I said he was as quick as you." Looking over at Whitney, Gilbert added, "Young Master Myles, back when I was a lad like yerself, I did me a lot of stupid things, not havin' a father like you do to guide me. And yer right, playing cards fer food wasn't the wisest thing I ever did. Back then I had to prove something, and didn't think things through like you've been taught to. If I knew what you do, my life would have been a lot easier. But tell ya what...." Gilbert, laying the cards down in front of him that played in his hand, smiled at Whitney, saying, "It sure did teach me how to play the game, though." Discarding the ten of diamonds, he winked at Whitney. "Out."

Leaning his head back, Whitney groaned and Benjamin patted his son's shoulder. "Don't give up son, you've got the knowledge to win next time."

"I do?"

"Absolutely, your opponent just gave you his secret for success, he watched you."

"Right, my eyes...." Nodding his head, Whitney eagerly picked up the deck of cards and began shuffling. "Ready for another round, Uncle Gilbert?"

"Ah, a might too eager lad. Never let your opponent know what you're thinking, keep 'em guessing." Seeing Whitney nod his head as if remembering what he was being told, Gilbert chuckled and stood, stretching his back. "Why don't you and Lucas practice some, why me and yer da get some air."

Benjamin glancing over at Rupert, said, "Care to join us, old man?"

Lifting his head to look over at Benjamin, Rupert said, "You go ahead. Interesting article here...I'll save it for you Gilbert, it's about that company you were telling me about in Chicago that's transporting perishables by rail using ice...ingenious. What will they think of next."

Not needing to reply, both men went to the terrace and Benjamin, waiting until Gilbert had closed the door to the terrace, said soberly, "I'm glad we have this time alone. There is something I need to discuss with you."

"From the tone of your voice, it sounds serious."

Taking out his pipe, Benjamin pensively nodded his head while searching for the appropriate words. "Before you arrived, I must tell you Gilbert, I feared that you would not allow me to help you through your grief, recalling the last time we had seen the other."

"Aye, you wed me and Mandy."

"Right. There was no mistaking the resentment you held in your heart for the English, yet you freely yielded your feelings that day for her. And quite frankly, what I walked away with after your wedding, was the depth—no fieriness of your love for her. So was it any wonder I had reservations at how I would be able to help a man through his grieving, knowing how passionate you were."

"Beggin' yer pardon Benjamin, but I didn't ask for yer help, now did I? I'm not some charity case."

Benjamin, looking over at his friend, seeing the restraint it took for him not to lose his temper, said, "No you didn't. But as a man of the cloth, I felt God had sent you here to us for more than Felicity to watch over your children. In my mind, I viewed Miranda's last request as not only a way for her to assure the children would be well cared for, but when faced with her own mortality, it was you she worried about. And this was her way of caring for you after she was gone."

"Where is this leading, Benjamin?"

"Right, well as I was saying, when I heard Miranda requested Felicity here in England affirmed my suspicion. Especially with Elise so readily available and knowing how close they were. I took it as a sign that Miranda was asking me to help you. And frankly, I was prepared to do whatever it took to reach you, not so much for your sake, but for hers." Benjamin paused for a moment and inhaled a few puffs from his pipe. "What I didn't realize at the time though, was that you were sent here to help me, as well. Gilbert, you and I have shared a great deal with one another, having gone through similar fates. Thanks to you in part, I no longer carry with me the guilt that was silently eating away at me."

"Nah, you're me mate."

"Indeed. Having you here with us, knowing you will help me to protect Felicity and Whitney, means the world to me. At Anne's party Rupert and I were at her side, yet it was you who saw her nearly swoon and then later on the terrace.... The point I'm making here is, I thank God he sent you here."

"Look, I appreciate your words, but they ain't necessary. I look upon helpin' you and your missus as helping my Mandy girl, so enough said."

Knowing it made Gilbert uncomfortable to be praised, Benjamin changed the subject. "So after we go to the asylum tomorrow why don't we all take in the sights of London?"

As the two men stood talking, Felicity couldn't help but notice how at ease they were with one another and she smiled. *Ben's right, I should try harder where Gilbert's concerned.*

~

Following the morning meal, Rupert and Benjamin escorted their wives to the carriage. By the sullen expressions the four of them exhibited, there was no denying this was not an outing any of them viewed as pleasurable. Even Felicity, who had agreed to tag along at the last moment to support Annabelle, felt an uneasiness that she couldn't explain. Hearing Annabelle ask Rupert if he was certain that there wasn't going to be any trouble with the two women arriving unannounced, she sat listening to Rupert's response.

"After all the money I've donated to that institute, I assure you my dear, Dr. Mercer wouldn't dare turn me down. I sent word to him yesterday upon our arrival that if Lavinia was up for a visit, we intended to visit there this morning, and I requested privacy. Not that I'm opposed to seeing the rest of those wretched poor souls, mind you, but I see no need to add to the unpleasantness of such an already grave visit."

"Thank you Rupert, darling. Did Dr. Mercer happen to mention in his note this morning how Lavinia was today? What I mean to say is, do you suppose she'll even know we are there?"

Nodding he said, "Yes dearest, although her condition appears to be worsening, having difficulties in breathing, he said she was alert and understood we were intending to visit and seemed to perk up some."

Felicity, seeing the pain in Annabelle's eyes, reached over and tenderly patted her friend's hand and then glanced at Benjamin, who had barely spoken a word all morning. As sad as she was for her friend, she knew how troubling this was for Benjamin. Meeting Lavinia today, he would have to come to terms with a woman he had once been wed to, and at last put to rest the demons that plagued him from their volatile past.

Since learning that he had agreed to see Lavinia, as hard as it was for Felicity to accept, and rather than voice her concerns further, she kept reminding herself that this was who he was, a man of the cloth.

Riding to the asylum now though, her heart began to race. No longer could Felicity block out the nightmares that had plagued her over the past several months, and she stirred in her seat. Her anxiousness turned to a feeling of impending doom, able to see her dream vividly in her mind now. She, Benjamin, and Whitney were running from Lavinia and James until a gunshot rang out. Then suddenly she was left alone weeping, slumped over a male figure in her dream; then without warning she found herself suddenly transported to a cliff, fog enclosing her. Frightened, she would cry out, but her words were lost and hollow.

At that precise moment, a merchant, banged on a drum, the sound echoing through the crowded streets, and Felicity jerked, startled.

"Are you all right, dearest?' Benjamin asked.

Smiling wearily at him, she nodded. "Yes, a little jumpy is all."

Placing his hand over her knee, Felicity lovingly looked up at him. *Should I tell him how frightened this makes me?* she wondered. Then recalling his words yesterday regarding Lavinia, she knew that they were not only said for the benefit of Annabelle, but it was Benjamin's way of explaining how he felt as well. Placing her hand over his, she gazed out the window, trying to push her tormented thoughts behind her.

When the coach came to a halt, those inside said not a word. Taking in a deep breath, Felicity reminded herself before stepping from the coach; *It's only a dream. Be a good wife; this is his calling.*

Entering the lobby of Earlswood proved more unnerving than she, Rupert and Annabelle had anticipated, judging by the look on their faces upon hearing the muffled sounds of shrill screams echoing from the upper rooms of the brick building. To help ease the situation, while waiting for someone to escort them, Benjamin softly whispered, "Mercer's office is this way."

Holding tightly onto his arm, Felicity watched as Benjamin nodded respectfully to a nurse who was on her way down the stairs from another floor. Seeing the familiarity both exhibited to the other, Felicity surmised it must be someone he recognized from previous visits to the institution. "Don't trouble yourself Julia, I know the way. Dr. Mercer is expecting us."

"Yes, Parson."

As they followed him, the tormented screams of those locked away inside, continued and Felicity glanced over at Benjamin with great admiration. *Oh Ben, all this time coming here, never have you explained just how awful it is, only saying what comfort it gave you to help these poor wretched souls.*

Entering a wooden door after a soft knock, Benjamin smiled to a small frail woman and said, "Mrs. Hastings, would you please notify Dr. Mercer that the Robbins's and I have arrived?"

"Yes, Parson."

After the woman scurried to an adjoining office and announced them, a man in his sixties, his hair askew as he tightened the rims of his glasses around his ears, appeared at the door. "Ah, Mr. Robbins, Benjamin, please come in. I wasn't aware you were bringing along other guests this morning."

Rupert, taking the lead, curtly said, "This is Lavinia's sister, my wife, Annabelle Robbins and my cousin, Benjamin's wife, Felicity Myles." Not waiting for the doctor to extend a greeting to them, Rupert pressed on. "I thought if Lavinia was up to it, perhaps she and her sister might have some time together following Reverend Myles's visit."

Obviously uncomfortable with Rupert's suggestion, after stretching out his hand for them to take a seat, he said, "Of course Mr. Robbins. However as I've indicated in my letters to you, your sister-in-law is prone to acts of violence and is easily agitated. After the parson's visit, I'll be able to determine if that will be wise."

"Certainly." Glancing over at Benjamin and seeing that Benjamin agreed with the doctor's comments, Rupert directed his attention back to the director. "Reverend Myles, having been here on several occasions before, knows precisely what to expect, while I and my wife on the other hand, need clarification as to what the effects of the disease has had on Lavinia specifically. In other words, please paint us a picture now, in the event we do see her so we can prepare ourselves. I'm sure you will agree that to be taken off guard and show surprise at seeing her condition would ultimately agitate Lavinia."

Hesitating briefly, rubbing his forehead, it was clear the doctor was trying to be as delicate as possible as he directed his attention solely to Annabelle. "Mrs. Robbins, your sister has suffered greatly by this unforgiving disease. As I've mentioned earlier, not only has it affected her mind, unfortunately she has suffered other side effects as well, including a loss of most of her hair; her face and other areas of her body have been left discolored, and her teeth are rapidly decaying. For today's visit, she has been permitted a veil to cover her face. However, I must warn you, she does have difficulty keeping it in place from her persistent cough. With nothing to secure it to her head, it does slip quite readily, so be prepared. I must warn you though, under no circumstances should you offer your sister assistance. Miss Bailey-Smythe does not allow anyone to touch her, so if it does slide from her head, kindly speak to her in a slow, even tone, and suggest she replace it. Otherwise, she will become quite agitated and will have to be removed bodily from the room. This will be unfortunate, but necessary for both of your safety."

On the verge of tears, Annabelle nodded her head gravely. "I understand."

"Mrs. Robbins, as difficult as it is hearing this, please, if you should be permitted in seeing your sister today, I must insist you show no emotion as you are now. In Lavinia's current condition, such actions may appear to her as pity, which will only induce rage. We have sedated her lightly, but I assure you even though she is calm at the present, that can and has changed on a moment's notice."

Annabelle, stiffening her back hastily, wiped a tear that had dropped to her cheek. "Yes, of course, forgive me for becoming emotional."

Benjamin standing said, "Well, if there isn't anything else I should be aware of, I'll go to her now. I assume she's in the room across the hall with Rudy."

"Yes," the doctor said, nodding his head while standing. "Shall I accompany you?"

"No, thank you. If Lavinia is as easily agitated as you say, I think it best I see her alone."

"Of course, but Rudy will have to remain. And Reverend Myles, do see to it the door remains locked, one can't be too careful."

Hearing his comment, Felicity's eyes widened as she looked over at Benjamin. Such precautions she'd never dreamed necessary. Benjamin, sensing his wife's uneasiness, smiled reassuringly at her. "Fear not dearest, whenever I've met with a patient the doors have always been locked. I'll be back in a few minutes."

Suddenly fear gripped at her heart and seeing him exit the room, she called to him, "Benjamin...." Aware they were not alone, and not wanting to add to his burden further she meekly said, "God be with you."

Nodding knowingly at her, he smiled lovingly and said, "He is, my dearest."

Exiting the second door of the office, which led him to a hall facing the room reserved for family viewing of patients, Benjamin took in a deep cleansing breath before knocking on the closed wooden door. From inside, he heard a metal latch, turn opening a small window. Seeing Rudy's face appear through the small opening, Benjamin smiled at the male attendant and waited for him to unlock the door from inside.

"Well Revered Myles, been a long time. Miss Bailey-Smythe has been waitin' on ya like a good girl. Ain't ya, missy?"

Benjamin's eyes trailed to the frail figure sitting in a chair, dressed in a black gown, sizes too large for her, her head slumped, unable to see her face through the black lace that draped to her shoulders. "Hello Lavinia," he said solemnly, waiting until he approached her as Rudy walked to the back of the room.

From under the veil, he heard raspy breathing, and although he could barely hear the woman underneath the black shroud, he recognized the voice to be that of Lavinia. "I was afraid...you wouldn't...make it in time."

"I'm here, Lavinia. God provided you the time needed."

Not responding to his comment, she raised her arm slightly, motioning him closer. From the loose-fitting garment, Benjamin noticed the dark spots trailing up her arm, but never let on, and obligingly walked closer to her, taking a seat directly across from her. Waiting for her to stop coughing, he placed his hat on his lap.

"You look well." she finally managed to say. "Your coat is wool—what time of the year is it?"

"It's autumn, the leaves are just beginning to turn and the air has a crispness to it."

"Ah..." she paused, gasping for air. "The same time...when we met."

Benjamin, not saying a word, allowed her to speak at her own pace.

"It was at the Hix's party. You came looking like a true gentry, so handsome."

Benjamin, was stunned by her comment. Vividly recalling he had thought there had been attraction between them, yet afterwards when he had met with her to discuss her father's proposal, Lavinia had flatly denied ever being the slightest bit interested in him. Claiming the sight of him was detestable. *Was it possible Lavinia hated him because he hadn't pursued her?*

"Father saw my interest in you." Again, she paused, coughing fiercely into her hand. Once able to continue, she said, "That was until I was sold, like livestock." Even between her gasps of air, there was no denying the pain in her voice as she spoke to him.

Sensing she was becoming distraught by the pitch of her voice, he said earnestly in a soothing tone, "Forgive me Lavinia, for the pain I have caused you. I have no excuse for my actions, only the deepest sorrow for accepting the squire's offer, causing us both such misery."

Her tone again leveled off as she struggled for breath. "Noble...to the end, Benjamin...." her voice trailed off as she struggled from the guttural coughing and brought her hand underneath her veil.

Allowing her some privacy, Benjamin turned to Rudy as if asking if there was something that could be done to help her. Seeing the man shake his head, he returned his attention back to Lavinia and froze, seeing a small pistol grasped in her hands pointing directly at him. "Well die noble too! Just as noble as you lusted after that tart."

Wasting not a second, Lavinia pulled the trigger and instantly Benjamin cried out as the bullet entered just above his abdomen.

In slow motion, he heard Rudy call out, "Sweet Jesus."

Expecting her to shoot again, Benjamin reached for the gun in her hand and grabbing it. Somehow he managed to drop it in his pocket as he slumped to the floor clutching at his midriff.

The piercing burning in his stomach matched the piercing catcall of Lavinia's screams of joy.

With Rudy between her and Benjamin, full of rage at not being able to witness his suffering, Lavinia began to kick and scratch at both men. Rudy, trying to aid Benjamin, pushed her frail body aside, causing her to lose balance and topple to the floor, sliding between Benjamin and the door. Her veil no longer concealing her face allowed the grotesque creature she had become to be revealed. In between choking for air, and witnessing Lavinia scratching at the floor, her piercing laughter echoing throughout the room, Benjamin heard pounding at the door.

"What the blazes has happened? Open this door at once!"

By the time that Rudy stood to answer, Dr. Mercer, having unlocked the door himself, stormed into the room. Seeing Benjamin on the floor in a pool of blood, he gasped, "My God, Benjamin you've been shot!"

Hearing the doctor's comment, Felicity rushed past Rupert and ran to her husband's side, and screamed in horror, "No. Dear God, no!" Reaching his side, falling to her knees, weeping, she asked, "Ben, darling can you hear me?"

Lavinia, seeing Felicity's reaction, became even more vocal, screaming and thrashing about, trying to stand. "Watch your Ben die. The man you stole from me, you tart!" she screamed uncontrollably, coughing between hysterical shrill laughter and gasps of air.

Numbly Annabelle, still in the entrance, watched as the doctor and Rupert helped Benjamin up, guiding him out of the room. As they approached her, seeing the front of Benjamin's suit becoming soaked in his own blood, she heard a shriek she was certain came from her. Stepping aside so they could pass, Annabelle hardly heard the attendant as he called to her.

"Move, m'lady, I need to lock this here door behind us."

Annabelle nodded, and watched as the creature Lavinia had become continued to scratch at the floor like a rabid animal, gasping for air all the while wailing, "Not even your precious God, can save you now. Die, in front of your tart. Die...."

Annabelle's body jerked as the door slammed, echoing through the dimly lit corridor. No longer able to see her sister, the sounds from the room haunted her as she stood frozen in place. In a daze, she watched the orderly and other staff rush into the director's office with medical supplies, as Felicity knelt beside her husband holding his hand. Seeing Benjamin's blood now on Felicity's gloves, Annabelle hardly felt Rupert's hands wrap around her shoulders. Numbly she looked up at Rupert, a loud ringing in her ears and just before everything went blank, she whispered, "What has that monster done?"

Lifting his wife in his arms, Rupert called to the doctor, "I need smelling salts, my wife has swooned."

Felicity, in shock herself, continued to weep softly at her husband's side. Grasping at her gloves, she hastily discarded them and gently began wiping traces of blood from his lips. Looking anxiously at the doctor who was assessing his wounds, she leaned closer to Benjamin. "Darling are you in much pain?"

"No. Please don't cry, dearest." Raising his hand, he tenderly wiped her tears, and in doing so he inadvertently smeared blood on Felicity's cheek. "I'm sorry...." his voice trailed off and Benjamin winced as the doctor rolled him over slightly to see if the bullet had exited through his back.

Believing Benjamin was apologizing to her for what Lavinia had done to him, Felicity whispered, "Shh, you have nothing to be sorry for. I love you, Ben."

Smiling wearily at her, he said, "I love you, dearest, but I've bloodied your face. Reminds me of the mud that was smeared on your cheek the day

I fell in love with you, when we lost our footing on the path. Do you remember?"

Before she could respond, the doctor announced, "Mrs. Myles. The wound is deep, and the bullet appears to be lodged inside him. We have no way to remove the bullet. I'm sorry. The best I can do is try to minimize your husband's bleeding and give him something for the pain."

"No," Benjamin whispered, "I want to be coherent. Bandage me up as best you can so I can be taken to our son. When I meet my maker, I want to be with my family, not here."

Hearing Benjamin's words, Felicity bit her lip and looked at the doctor, and said bravely, "You heard my husband, make him ready so I can take him to our son."

Seeing him wince as the doctor began bandaging him, she leaned closer to Benjamin and kissed his cheek, "Darling, look into my eyes so you don't feel the pain, only my love. The doctor will be finished soon."

Stroking her hair, he whispered, "My beloved Felicity, how I love you." Frowning slightly at her blood and tear-stained face, he whispered, "Please darling, don't let Whitney see his mother covered in his father's blood. He'll be frightened enough."

Looking up at a nurse pleadingly, she smiled gratefully at her seeing she had already brought a wet cloth.

"Thank you," she whispered. Without hesitation, she rubbed the blood from Benjamin's hands then receiving another cloth, she removed the blood from her cheek as well. "Is that better, darling?"

Benjamin nodded faintly, rubbing her lips with his fingertips and they smiled knowingly at one another, recalling how she had kissed his thumb that day in front of the vicarage as he had removed the mud from her face. Slowly she kissed his thumb now, and whispered, "Please darling, stay with me. I love you so."

Regaining consciousness, Annabelle began softly weeping. "Is he...?" her voice cracked, unable to finish her question.

"Dearest, we may not have much time. Benjamin wants to be with Whitney."

Understanding her husband's comment, Annabelle nodded. "Then we must leave now. Make the arrangements, Rupert, please."

Motioning to Dr. Mercer's elderly secretary, he ordered, "Don't leave my wife's side. I'll be right back." With that, Rupert ran from the door, everyone understanding that he was making the coach ready for Benjamin.

"Mrs. Myles, please listen to me carefully. I have managed to place enough pressure on the wound to help minimize the bleeding; but I must warn you, any sudden jerks will result in opening up the wound again."

"How long…. When should I change the bandage?"

"I'll tend to a few things here and follow you; that is unless you prefer someone else to tend to your husband."

"Doctor Mercer could anyone else help him further?" It was understood she did not doubt his competence, but was only asking for medical advice.

"Mrs. Myles, in my opinion, trying to remove the bullet is not an option. Surgically removing the bullet will only speed up the inevitable; we in the medical profession simply do not have the training in these cases. Personally, I would have rather seen the bullet exit his body. Not seeing the gun, I can only assume it was of a small caliber, considering the size of the wound. From my experience, not knowing what organs have been damaged, if any, I would recommend you make him as comfortable as possible."

The startling reality that Benjamin was dying hit Felicity just as brutally as if someone had slapped her repeatedly. Trying desperately to hold back her tears for her beloved Ben's sake, Felicity solemnly responded, "Is there anything we can do to make him comfortable?"

"There is little we can do, but come to understand and accept that your husband is in the care of God's hands now, my dear. I assume you are staying here in London?"

"Yes, the Brown Hotel."

"Once he has been transported there and is situated, with his permission of course, I can offer morphine to lessen his discomfort."

"Surely there must be something I can do?"

Tenderly he said, "My advice to you now would be to spend whatever time remains, together. I've seen others with similar wounds hang on for several days, even weeks, while others leave us rather quickly. As I said before, Benjamin really is in God's hands now." Glancing down at Benjamin, he said, "The gun, how did Miss Bailey-Smythe get it?"

"I have no idea…I turned to look at Rudy, then when I turned back, she had it in her hand. It was so sudden, I didn't have time to react, she just shot me."

"Well, don't worry about that now, you just lay still with your missus while I get more orderlies to help move you."

As the doctor barked orders for a stretcher, he called upon Rudy to get his cab from the livery stable. Rupert, having returned and hearing the doctor's request, said, "That won't be necessary, I took the liberty of having your man bring the cab around when my driver removed the seats from our coach."

"Good thinking." Directing his attention to Jimmy he said, "Mr. Myles has been stabilized—do make sure he's not jerked around. Take it nice and easy. The slightest jostling could cause him to hemorrhage."

Glancing at Jimmy Bartlett, Rupert, seeing the driver nod in understanding, said, "Assist Mrs. Myles, I'll tend to my wife."

"Yes, sir." Stepping closer to where his employer lay on the couch, he said gravely, "Come along me beauty and let Jimmy 'ere get the vicar to his boy."

Benjamin looked up at the man who was obviously shaken and softly said, "Thank you, Jim. I knew I could count on you."

As Benjamin was carried to the rig on a wooden slab, Felicity walked beside him, solemnly holding her husband's hand, while Jimmy Bartlett held tightly to her other arm. "Mrs. Myles, you let 'em get the reverend in first now, and let me help you in the rig later 'ere. Ain't no seats so you'll be needin' to be on the floor for a spell."

"Don't worry about me Jimmy, just please be careful."

"Yes, ma'am, you can be countin' on old Jimmy."

As if this was his mission, Jimmy barked orders to the staff of the hospital as they placed Benjamin securely inside the coach. Rupert tried to console his distraught wife as Rudy, who had been directed to attend to Lavinia, came up to the doctor and whispered something in his ear. Pausing to listen to his employee, the doctor nodded gravely then approached Rupert. "Mr. Robbins, a moment of your time, alone please."

Obviously annoyed, Rupert snapped, "Surely this can wait."

Interrupting him, Dr. Mercer firmly said, "No, sir. It can not."

Escorting Annabelle to Jimmy, Rupert turned and glared at the doctor. "Well what could be more serious?"

"Sir, I'm sorry to say that your wife's sister has passed."

The blood drained from Rupert's face, and he turned his back to ensure Annabelle could not see him. "What? How can that be, we just witnessed her.,,"

"When Rudy went to take Miss Bailey-Smythe back to her ward, he found her dead. I can only assume she choked, she was quite excited, as you saw for yourself."

Taking in a deep breath, Rupert curtly responded, "Send for the undertaker, make her ready to be buried. Once Benjamin is situated, we can deal with her later. I'll require a competent nurse and orderly to accompany *you* to the Brown, immediately."

Realizing this was not a request but rather an order, Doctor Mercer directed two of his staff to accompany him. Within moments both coaches were headed toward the Brown Hotel, with Rupert sitting on the buckboard alongside Jimmy. Giving the driver last minute instructions on what to do upon arriving, he then slumped in his seat. *Dear God, what's to become of poor Felicity now?*

~ Sixteen ~

After arriving at the Brown, taking the necessary precautions to bring the mortally wounded guest through the delivery entrance so as not to alarm other guests, Felicity, with the help of the staff from Earlswood, made Benjamin comfortable. Gilbert, learning of the shooting, had Montgomery take his children, along with the Robbinses sightseeing with the aid of Kathleen, while Rupert escorted the distraught Annabelle to her room. Whitney, realizing there was a reason why he was not permitted to attend with the other children, sat quietly in his room, fearing the worst.

"Has something happened to Mother?" he asked Rupert and Gilbert as they entered his room, seeing the grave look on their faces.

"Son, it's your father. He's been wounded and it's quite serious."

"Father…." He gasped, "How?" As Whitney listened to the details, he glanced over at Gilbert. "Is Father going to die?"

"Lad, your da is a good man. He must have work to do in heaven, otherwise God wouldn't be sendin' fer him now."

Understanding what Gilbert was saying, Whitney bravely asked, "Can I see him?"

Nodding, Rupert patted him on the back. "The doctor and your mother are making him comfortable. As soon as they're finished, I'll take you in to see him Whitney. But before I do, you must promise not to hug him around his waist; it could cause him a lot of pain."

"I promise," he replied meekly.

Just then, the door opened to the adjoining suite and the doctor nodded to Rupert. "He's asking for his son. I'll take him; they want some time alone."

"Yes, of course. While they are visiting, will you please check in on my wife? She's quite distraught."

"Of course."

The doctor, obviously accustomed to working with those in need of comforting, kneeled beside the frightened boy and spoke calmly. "Master Myles, may I call you Whitney? I feel I already know you after the fine things your father has told me of you over the years."

Acknowledging Whitney's nod, Dr. Mercer continued, "Whitney, your father and mother are very sad, as I know you are too. What I'm about to ask you many men twice your age would not be able to do, but your father has assured me that you are very brave. Can you be brave enough to say good-bye to your papa? Can you do that?"

It was clear that Whitney resented being spoken to as if he was a child, but respectfully asked, "Can Father speak?"

"Yes, but don't be alarmed if you see traces of blood on his lips. Think of it as he bit his lip, alright?"

Nodding his response again, the doctor rose and escorted Whitney into the room. Gilbert, obviously taking the news of Benjamin's shooting harder than what Rupert had anticipated, looked shocked as Gilbert hissed, his voice just above a whisper, "What are you intending to do about this? And don't be tellin' me you're goin' to let her get away with this just because she's rich and you don't want to soil her good name. 'Cause I'm warning ya, if it takes every dime I own I will see her hang from a noose for harming my friend."

"Gilbert, there will be no need, Lavinia is dead. She died shortly after shooting Benjamin. She was mad, I tell ya. Apparently she became so excited at what she had done, in a fit of sorts, she began clawing at the floor, cackling like a crow and drowned in her own fluids. And dear Annabelle witnessed it all."

"Sweet Jesus, forgive me for spoutin' off like I did. I just lost me temper, remembering me own sorrow and hatin' to see someone as good as the parson to be taken away like this."

"I know...." Rupert's voice trailed off when the doctor returned. "How is he?"

Shaking his head, Mercer replied, "Not well. He's bleeding from his mouth at an alarming rate, although the wound itself has lessened, which means he's bleeding internally. I don't give him much time. Let's take a look at your missus so I can get back inside with the Myles' if they need me."

Escorting the doctor to Annabelle's room, Gilbert leaned his head in his palms, and recalling vividly Miranda's death, he fell to his knees and called out in a hoarse whisper, "Why take him too? Can't we poor bastards have any of the good ones down here with us?"

Hearing the door open, and seeing Felicity, he hastily raised himself from the floor. "The doctor's in with Annabelle, should I get him?"

"No. Benjamin wishes to see you," she mumbled, her voice devoid of emotion, hollow and frail.

"Aye." Following her into the room and seeing Benjamin, chalky white, lying in the center of his bed and whispering softly to his son, Gilbert stood silently and listened. "Son, I know you'll take good care of your mum for me, just remember to take care of yourself too. You won't be able to see me anymore, or hear my voice, but know this son; I'll be watching you from heaven. If you need some help figuring things out, go to Cousin Rupert or Mr. O'Flaherty, they'll help you. "

"Yes, Father. Can I kiss you?"

"Of course you can." Lifting his hand slightly to draw him near, Benjamin held his son's head close to his. "Remember always, how proud I am of you. Now go on out and sit with Cousin Rupert while I speak to Gilbert. Can you do that for me, my beloved son?"

"Father, I don't want to say good-bye."

Smiling wearily, Benjamin said, "You don't have too son. I'll never be far. I love you and your mother too much to leave you alone. You will remember that won't you?"

Kissing his father again, Whitney turned with a quivering lip then ran from the room. Felicity looked over at Benjamin, and seeing him motion for her to go to him, Gilbert approached the bed. As if sensing Gilbert didn't know what to say, Benjamin said, "Friend, I know how hard this is for you, but I need a favor."

"Anything."

"The gun...get it from my coat pocket."

"You have the gun? How?" Gilbert said stunned.

"I took it from her...before she could shoot it again." Benjamin watched as Gilbert, not wasting a second, went to the valet and searched his blood-soaked suit jacket.

Holding the double-barreled 5-inch handgun in his palm, he gravely looked over at Benjamin. "This here gun was custom made. Pearl handles—the jewels look real."

"Find out who gave it to her."

"Aye, I give you me word. Is there anything else, friend?"

Benjamin's breathing become more shallow and he nodded his head. "Look after my family. You are a good father. Take Whitney under your wing...Felicity will need your help too...." Benjamin paused, wincing just as Felicity came back into the room. Gilbert, seeing her, inconspicuously tucked the derringer into his pocket and said, "I won't let you down."

Allowing them whatever time he had left alone, Gilbert left the room and Felicity leaned over the bed, gently caressing her husband's forehead. "Darling, are you certain you don't want the doctor to give you something for the pain?"

"No. Come lay beside me."

Gingerly, Felicity edged herself onto the bed, and Benjamin said, "Please...closer...just as you did...on our wedding night."

"You remember...." Tenderly helping him to lift his arm, she leaned her head on his shoulder, feeling his arm wrap around her slightly. "Darling, am I hurting you?" she whispered.

"No. Do you remember...when I met with your aunt alone...the day I asked for your hand?"

Understanding what he meant, even though his words were broken up, she said, "Yes, I was so frightened when I came into the room. The two of you looked so sullen."

Nodding his head slightly, Benjamin spoke just above a whisper, "I asked her...what had changed her mind...about letting us see each another. She told me...after the ball...you suffered in silence. She loved you too much...to let you live the rest of your life alone...with only memories of the past. Dearest, I love you too much...for that too."

Hearing it was becoming more difficult for him to breathe, softly she whispered, "Please, darling let's not speak of this now."

"We must, dearest. You...have given me...such joy...more happiness...than I deserved. I can't bear the thought of you...being alone...without love."

Lifting her head slightly, their eyes locking, she fought back her tears. "I only want you, please don't leave me, Ben."

"This is God's will...not mine." Kissing her head, he added, "Did I ever tell you...that every day...since we wed...I wake up...and thank God. For my sake...please be happy, my beloved Felicity. I...promised your aunt...to make you happy."

Wiping blood from the corner of his mouth, she looked at him, "Oh Ben, you must believe me, you did make me happy. More than you will ever know."

Smiling faintly, he whispered, "I love you. I always will. Lay beside me...let me hold you, before I go."

Wanting desperately to grant the man she loved with all her heart his last request, she laid her head back into the hollow of his shoulder. Within seconds, she felt his arm fall from her shoulder sliding along her back. No longer able to hear his heart beating, or the raspy sounds of him gasping for air, she knew her Ben had left her, yet she couldn't bring herself to leave him. Whispering through her tears, she said, "Go in peace, my darling Ben, and know, I shall always love you too."

~ Seventeen ~

Hearing his name being called out amongst the passengers on deck, Joshua raised his arm and hailed the ship's porter. "Over here."

"A telegram for you, sir."

Elise raised her brow and shook her head in disgust. "It's already happening, and we've not even arrived in New York yet. Honestly darling and you wonder why I'm dreading getting back home. Your father has already written you twice. Who's this one from, Grandfather or Michael? "

Reaching inside his pocket to retrieve a coin to tip the porter, Joshua looked down at the telegram. "Hmm, neither. It's from Rupert."

"Rupert? How peculiar...I would have thought they would be having far too much fun in London to write us." Elise's attention was diverted for a moment, seeing Nigel tuck the quilt back around Mammy Tess's ankles as she sat in a deck chair with Caleb and Albert nearby. "Look how attentive Nigel is with Mammy Tess. Why you would think they've known each other for years?" Seeing the distressed look in Joshua's eyes, Elise said, "What is it darling?"

Tucking the paper into his pocket, he motioned for Nigel. "Keep a close eye on the children for a while Nigel, while Mrs. Carmidy and I go below."

"Yes, sir," Nigel Bartlett, Felicity's former employee said. "Beggin' yer pardon, sir, how much longer do you think it'll be before we see land?"

Joshua, looking over the horizon, rubbed his brow. "Shouldn't be much longer." Directing his attention to his daughter who was standing near him, he said, "Sweet Pea, you stay here and tend to Mammy Tess, and help out with the younger boys. You can do that for me, now can't you?"

"Yes, Papa," Sarah Tess answered adoringly. Hesitating for a second, her father bent down to give her a pat on the head. Receiving it, Sarah Tess promptly took her leave from her father's side to stand by Tess who sensed Joshua's sudden mood change and smiled up at him. "Don't be frettin' none about us, Massa Joshua, me and my little girl here, we'll be just fine. You and Miz Elise go on now."

"What's wrong Joshua? Something has happened, hasn't it? Is Felicity all right? Dear God, tell me Gilbert and the children haven't taken ill?"

Pasting a smile to his lips, Joshua tried to sound convincing. "Don't be getting yourself all worked up, my pearl. Let's you and I go to our cabin, and we can have a chat there." Directing his attention to his eldest son, he added hastily, "Andy, come take Jefferson Abraham from your mama. Be real careful now, son."

"I will Father," Andy said, dutifully taking his youngest brother in his arms. It was clear that the eight year old was quite comfortable carrying toddlers, and he smiled as the nine month old reached for his brother's hat with one hand while sucking his fist with his other.

Being led away from her family by Joshua, Elise asked urgently, "What's wrong Joshua? Don't try to tell me there isn't anything either because I can tell by the look in your eyes."

Tenderly holding Elise at her waist, he said, soothingly, "Sweetheart, I should know better than to hide anything from you. As soon as we're alone I'll tell you everything."

Realizing the news must be extremely bad if he wanted them to be alone, gravely she nodded her head as fear gripped her heart.

"Don't you want to see the harbor when we arrive in New York?" asked a woman Elise had become acquainted with while abroad the ship.

"No, I'll see it another time," she mumbled softly while continuing down the congested stairway as other passengers anxiously went toward the upper deck.

Once safely inside their cabin, Joshua, still holding Elise's waist, said, "Darling, brace yourself. The news is far worse than you can imagine. Benjamin has been shot."

"Shot?" Elise gasped. "How? He'll be all right though, won't he?"

Seeing Joshua shake his head slightly, Elise immediately became hysterical. "No. Dear God no!" Through her tears she whispered, "Benjamin's dead? That can't be. Who would do such a thing?" Pulling away from Joshua, her eyes widened. "Don't tell me, James?"

"No, darling. Rupert's telegram said Lavinia shot Benjamin before dying herself."

"What?" Elise gasped. "Lavinia is dead too? How?" Pleadingly she added before he could respond, "We have to go back. Joshua please, we need to go to Felicity. She needs me."

Pulling his wife closer to him, he said, "Sweetheart, we can't."

Feeling her struggle, Joshua held her tightly as he spoke soothingly to her. "We don't even know when the next ship will sail. And have you forgotten what Michael said in his telegram yesterday? Alfred isn't well, and your mother can't tend to both him and Constance. Besides Gilbert, Rupert and Annabelle will be there to help Felicity through her grieving."

"Oh Joshua...." she looked up at him with tears rolling down her cheeks. "I can't believe he's gone. What is Felicity going to do?"

A roaring cheer onboard alerted them that the ship was approaching New York Harbor, but neither of them made any attempt to leave the other's arms. "I can't imagine what she must be going through. First Edward, then Miranda and now Benjamin...." Elise's voice trailed off and her grasp tightened around Joshua's shoulders. "Promise me Joshua, you'll never leave me."

Hoarsely he whispered, "Who knows what the future holds. All I do know is, from here out, I'm spending as much time as I can at home with those I love."

~

Within minutes of arriving at the Honeycut mansion, even before Elise had time to freshen up, Alfred sent word through his nurse that he wanted to see his granddaughter at once, and if she didn't comply, he would come to her. Obliging him, Elise sat next to the man she had grown to think of as her grandfather, and scolded him lovingly. "Grandfather, shame on you for making such a fuss. What will your nurse think?"

Waving his hand in disgust, clearly not the least concerned with what the nurse thought, Alfred motioned Elise to draw nearer. "I'm sorry to hear about Benjamin," he whispered hoarsely. "Fine man...far too young to go like that."

"I agree," Elise sadly said. "I still can't believe he's gone. How do you suppose Lavinia was able to get a gun, locked away in that asylum for so long?"

"Heaven knows, but it proves one thing, and that is, when it's your time to go, He comes for you."

Fearing her grandfather was concerned by his own mortality, she said, "You do know that doesn't mean you can just give up and leave us too, don't you Grandfather?"

"Me?" Alfred chuckled softly to avoid coughing. "Heavens no. I'm not going anywhere just yet. Although hearing of Reverend Myles's death has got me to think some about you and your Joshua."

"Us? For goodness sakes, why?"

"Dear Elise, I think you already know how much I admire your husband's keen mind, and look upon him as my advisor. Well if it's agreeable with you, I want to turn all my holdings over to him to run as the sole chief executive from here on out."

"Agreeable with me? Surely, my opinion does not matter in yours and Joshua's business dealings."

"On the contrary, my dear. Your husband has been able to accomplish what only some men dare to imagine; he has maintained harmony between family and his work, and rather successfully in both arenas I might add. To his credit, this was accomplished by having you as his wife. It's clear to me that your Joshua will do nothing that will put the love you both share in jeopardy. So it stands to reason, before I approach Joshua, I must be certain this is in agreement with you as well. Loving you as I do, I would be amiss if I proposed something to your husband that would cause you unnecessary worry, especially knowing what has taken place with Benjamin and Felicity. I can only imagine the pain and suffering she must be going through now without the man she loved so deeply."

"Grandfather, when we were notified of Benjamin's passing, both Joshua and I were badly shaken, perhaps even more than when we lost Miranda. When she left us so suddenly it was painful, and we grieved deeply, all of us, you included, yet we had Gilbert and the children to tend to, and it helped to ease our grief. Yet now, learning of Benjamin's death, unable to do anything to help Felicity, I think the reality of how fragile we truly are has sunken in. Suddenly I find myself not wanting to waste a single second God has granted me with those I love, especially my Joshua. You have no idea how much I agonized over him being away in the war, and missed him. For three long years, I didn't know if he was alive or dead, if he even loved me still, it was all I could do just to keep going. It was hard, perhaps the hardest thing I've had to endure, but I kept going because of Joshua. And I mean it Grandfather, I cannot nor will not, live like that again. I'm not like Gilbert and Felicity, I will not be able to live without seeing Joshua on a regular basis, he's a part of me. I'm far too selfish to carry on in his memory. The person I am today is because of Joshua. I need him, more than you know.

"I understand, dear girl."

"What I'm about to say may sound as if I'm being ungrateful, or a woman just rambling on who doesn't fully appreciate what it is you are offering us. Please don't misunderstand, I am truly grateful for your generosity and know the financial security it will bring us for our future and our children. Yet, if given the choice of giving up financial security for time with my husband, there is no contest, it's Joshua I value. No amount of money will bring Miranda or Benjamin back, and I will not waste a second ever again with my loved one. So if this proposal you intend to extend to Joshua means I will see less of him, I'm going to be truthful Grandfather, I would rather you didn't offer it then. Even if it entails forfeiting financial security. We can manage nicely on what Joshua brings home from his law practice."

Nodding knowingly he said, "Enough of such talk, tell me how Gilbert and the children are."

As Elise filled Albert in on their visit including how Gilbert and Benjamin had hit it off, Albert nodded, asking questions from time to time. Elise held nothing back from her grandfather, knowing he knew the intimate details of what had transpired between James and Felicity following Miranda's and Gilbert's escape. As she relived the night of Anne's party to Albert, Elise noted the twinkle in her grandfather's eyes.

"So Gilbert had James parading around as a beggar did he?" Chuckling loudly, Albert sat up in his bed, and as Elise continued speaking of how Gilbert had been watching James in the shadows as he spied on Felicity, Albert was so enthralled, he asked for assistance to sit up.

Obligingly, she propped more pillows behind his back. "Grandfather, I can tell you true, never have I been more surprised by anything as I was seeing the effect England had on Gilbert. I swear, by the end of the summer he wasn't the same broken man who left here. It was as if he transformed right before my very eyes. And I mean it, the look in his eyes as he glared at James was more than unsettling, it was downright frightening. Why it was as if all the hatred he had harbored in his heart for Tad came to life and was aimed at James Sterling. "

"Is that right?Hand me my bed-jacket, dear. I want to stretch my back some and take a seat by the fire."

Assisting Albert to a nearby fireside chair, Elise listened as Albert spoke how it made sense to him. The two of them were so engrossed in conversing, neither realized that over an hour had passed until his nurse, Miss Simpson, entered the room.

Shaking her head disapprovingly, she said in an authoritative voice, "Mrs. Carmidy, I agreed to this visit against my better judgment with the understanding it would not be long. Not only have you two been chatting well over an hour, but I see you have moved my patient, who was ordered to complete bed rest by his doctor, from his bed."

Elise, suddenly alarmed that she had done something that would be harmful to her grandfather's health, stood and began to apologize when Albert interrupted her.

"Lest you've forgotten young woman, I am the one who pays your salary and I determine how long I visit with my guests. In the future, I suggest you remember that if you intend to keep your position. As for bed rest, I was resting, that was until you so rudely interrupted, so leave us at once. And send for Mr. Carmidy and the children. When I'm tired, I will ring for you and not a moment sooner. Is that clear?"

"Yes, sir." Mrs. Simpson, obviously embarrassed, bent her head as she left the room.

"Damn uppity woman, coming into my home and presuming she knows what's better for me than I."

"Grandfather, I'm sure Miss Simpson has only your best interest at heart. Perhaps she's right, we have been chatting for quite some time.

"So we have; and I haven't felt this good in weeks! So dear Elise, kindly respect my wishes as I have regarding you and your Joshua."

Just then Joshua and the children entered the room, and hearing his name being spoken, Joshua said, "Hmm, have I caught you two plotting against me again?"

Seeing Joshua, Alfred began to rise from his chair, but sat back down seeing the disapproving look from Miss Simpson from the doorway. Instead he raised his hand and shook it heartily, "Joshua, how good to see you."

"Why Alfred you old fraud, and to think I was worried hearing of your illness."

"Illness, hmm, I'm just old and obviously in need of a long visit with my granddaughter. She's good medicine, you know."

Smiling over at his wife, he nodded, "Yes, she is."

The children anxiously looked on, and smiled with delight as Alfred motioned for them to come closer. "Come over here, and let me see how much you've grown." Kissing each of them on the cheek, he stretched his arms out for Jefferson Abraham. "My goodness, this strapping young boy can't be my little Abe."

Sarah Tess glanced over at her mother. Seeing she was not correcting Alfred for shortening her youngest brother's name, boldly said, "Grandfather, aren't you going to ask me how I liked England?"

Chuckling, he said, "Why my little princess, I don't need to, I see England must have agreed with you rather well, or perhaps you enjoyed the company of a certain young man." Seeing her eyes widen he said, "Hmm, could it be that you enjoyed Master Robbins' company?"

"Edwin? Oh no Grandfather, he's far too young for me. Besides, Catherine fancied him. I on the other hand, found Whitney's company ever so pleasurable."

Trying to conceal his amusement at how matter of factually Sarah Tess spoke, he said, "Is that so, and I trust Master Myles was equally impressed with your attributes as well, my dear?"

"He was. As a matter of fact, he's promised to ask Father for my hand in marriage, once we're old enough."

Elise, hearing her daughter's comment gasped then joined Albert as he roared with laughter. Not finding their reaction to her announcement at all amusing, Sarah Tess looked up at Joshua and tapped her foot firmly on the carpet. "Father, please don't let Mother and Grandfather laugh at me. Whitney and I love one another, just like you and Mother, and we will be wed!"

Joshua looked over at Elise, and knowingly they smiled at one another recalling a similar confrontation Sarah and she had when Joshua had returned from the war. Looking at Sarah Tess now, Elise couldn't help but notice the similarities between her daughter and herself.

"Dear Sarah Tess, I wasn't laughing at you. I was laughing at how you reminded me of myself. You see, when your father came home from the war, I told your grandmother I was returning to New York with him, with or without her consent. And seeing you speak with such determination was like looking in the mirror is all."

Hesitantly she looked over at Elise. "Honest, Mother?"

Stretching her hands to her willful daughter, she cooed, "Truth. Now come and give me a hug."

"So you approve of Whitney then?"

Joshua, clearing his throat, answered for the both of them. "Sweet Pea, Whitney Myles is a fine young man and in ten or fifteen years, if you still feel the same, I'll consider allowing my little girl to be courted by him."

Alfred, still smiling, said, "Well, I hope to be around long enough to see how this budding romance ends up. At any rate, I do believe this will be the longest betrothal in history." Seeing Sarah Tess frown with uncertainty, Alfred added. "Sarah Tess, after your father and I've had a chance to discuss business and I've taken a rest, perhaps you would consider visiting me for awhile after dinner and you can tell me how you won Master Myles's heart."

"Yes, Grandfather, I'll even tell you who Andy's sweet on."

Glancing over at her eldest son, Elise saw the tips of her son's ears turn scarlet red. To avoid his mother's eyes, he stretched out his hands to his younger siblings. "Come along Caleb and Albert, let's play some marbles."

As Elise leaned over to kiss her grandfather, she overheard Andy say, "I knew you couldn't be trusted."

"I can so. You never said I couldn't tell Grandfather."

"Hush up, you knew what you were doin'."

As the Carmidy children made their way toward the door, Elise heard Caleb whisper, "Sarah Tess, you promised. I'm tellin' Papa you kissed Whitney."

"Me too," chimed in Albert.

"Hush, Mama's behind us."

Shaking her head, vowing to spend more time with her children now that there were only the five of them to watch again, Elise smiled graciously at the nurse, noting how attractive she was. Surmising she was a few years her senior, she paused to address her. And although Elise's tone was cordial, there was no denying she was conveying the message to her grandfather's nurse that she was the mistress. "I'm sorry to disrupt your schedule, Miss Simpson; surely you must agree though, visiting with his family is quite agreeable with my grandfather. This evening, following the children's bedtime, I trust you will find the time to enlighten me as to his condition."

"Yes, Ma'am."

Maintaining an air of authority, Elise said, "Excellent. Nine o'clock this evening, in my boudoir suite, if you'd please."

As Elise walked down the two flights of stairs, she knew the nurse's eyes were transfixed on her; feeling the hairs on her neck rise, she made a mental note not to trust Miss Simpson. Hearing the sounds of children's laughter coming from inside the parlor, Elise, still holding on to Jefferson, turned to close the door and glanced up the flight of stairs. Seeing the nurse now perched outside Albert's bedchamber sitting in a chair, Elise matched the woman's cold stare and raised her brow. *Hmm...Do I detect resentment, Miss Simpson? Why is that?*

~

As Joshua discussed business with Albert, Elise and the children visited quietly with Sarah and Michael in the parlor. Nodding politely, Elise listened as Sarah spoke of Constance's condition and the news from Fairfax. Momentarily, she glanced over at Michael and smiled, seeing him lying on his side next to the boys as they shot a boulder into the circle of marbles on the carpet.

"This is the castle, Grandfather," Caleb explained, tracing the circle of marbleize. Placing a larger glass marble just in front of his tucked thumb that was under his curled index finger, he exclaimed, "I'm going to try and knock the king from his castle."

"Ah...." Michael said, nodding at his grandson.

Sarah, seeing Elise was not paying attention, scolded her. "Why daughter, I swear you haven't heard a word I've said."

"I'm sorry Mama, I just keep thinking about Felicity."

"Do you want to talk about it?"

"No." Elise shook her head. "There's nothing more to say. Tell me about Grandfather and where you found his nurse."

"Clare? We were lucky to find her. Mary suggested we call upon her after going through several nurses. Seems your grandfather is not the most cooperative patient, and ran them off."

Smiling at her mother insincerely, Elise said, "Ah Mother Carmidy, you say?"

Elise glanced over at Tess, who was chuckling at Sarah Tess as she cut out a new set of doll clothes for her paper dolls, holding her tongue out slightly and moving it in the direction she directed the scissors. "That there tongue of yer's is goin' to get bitten off if ya not careful there, Missy."

Sarah, motioning over at Elise said, "Tess looks good. I could have surely used her this summer though. Between Albert being so difficult and with poor Constance having such a bad pregnancy, all I can say is thank heavens for Clare. She's been a godsend."

"Again you refer to Miss Simpson as Clare. I take it that you and she have become rather friendly?"

"Why, I suppose we have. She is Margaret's friend you know, and with us knowing so many of the same people, it just seemed the thing to do."

"How nice. So tell me Mother all about your new friend, Clare Simpson. And how is my dear sister-in-law?"

Frowning, detecting Elise's sarcasm, Sarah said, "Why Elise Carmidy, you don't even know her and I can tell by the tone of your voice you've taken a dislike to her. Just because you and Margaret have never gotten along, doesn't mean you can't be friends with Clare."

"Why, I don't know what you're referring to Mother. Margaret and I get along just fine."

Sighing, Sarah took a sip of her tea. "Yes, of course you do. When was the last time you invited your sister-in-law over just for a visit?"

"Considering I've been away for the summer, I can't recall, Mother. Is there a point you're trying to make?"

Not hiding her displeasure at her daughter's insolent tone, Sarah said, "Shame on you, Elise. Seems to me, you've taken a dislike to Clare Simpson because she is Margaret's friend; or did Alfred tell you that she and Joshua courted for several years before the war?"

Elise's back stiffened hearing her mother's last comment and Sarah knew she had said too much. Deciding it best not to say anything, Sarah took another sip of tea, waiting for Elise's retaliation.

Glaring at her mother, her voice elevated slightly, Elise spouted, "Shame on *me*? Well Mother, in less than a minute you've managed to supply me ample reason not to cozy up to Clare Simpson. First, I couldn't imagine why a complete stranger, an employee no less, would have the audacity to give me such an icy glare as she just did. Yet now finding out what I have, it makes perfect sense. Not only is she a friend of that pious, self-righteous, sister-in-law of mine, but now I find out she was romantically involved with my husband too." Hastily standing with clenched fists by her side, Elise snapped, "Well shame on you Mother, for befriending a woman I obviously would be offended by having in my home!"

Joshua, opening the door to the parlor at that precise moment, overhearing Elise's comment, looked at his wife and grinned. Although his question was directed toward Sarah, his eyes never left Elise's. "Mother Honeycut, would you mind terribly if I take my beloved wife for a breath of fresh air?"

"Yes, that would be quite acceptable, son." Judging by Sarah's tone, she was relieved for a few minutes alone.

Feeling Joshua's hand in the small of her back, Elise took in a deep breath saying not a word until they were well out of range of being overhead. "Is it true Joshua, were you and that woman lovers? Why didn't you tell me you knew her when we first arrived home? And how long did you court one another?"

Pulling his wife nearer to him, not responding with words, he leaned over and his mouth came crushing down on hers. Hungrily his tongue parted her lips and Elise moaned, returning the intensity of his kiss. Pulling slightly away from her, his eyes locked onto hers and Joshua huskily whispered, "Do I detect a hint of jealousy?"

"Oh you detect more than a hint, Joshua Carmidy. As lovely as your diversion was, I still want my question answered."

Chuckling, he kissed her forehead, pausing briefly between each answer, he said, "No. There wasn't any time. The truth is, for five years we would attend family functions."

Frowning, realizing he had answered all her questions at once, she matched the answers to the questions and smiled sheepishly up at him realizing he had not responded to Clare and he being lovers.

Wrapping her arms around his neck, she cooed, "Why is it that we've been in New York for over seven years and I'm just now finding out about this woman who obviously meant a great deal to you, if you courted her for five years?"

"Darling, you're jumping to conclusions. When I had a break from Harvard and there was a family function or a party, on occasion I escorted Clare. Nothing more."

"Are you sure, Joshua? Mama's exact words were that you and she courted for several years."

"Clare and I were friendly, yes; her being friends with my sister, it was inevitable, but sweetheart, I never actively courted her. Margaret wanted me to, but with Clare and I attending different colleges in different states, it never worked out. Besides, I was never really attracted to Clare. Have you forgotten, I always said, I preferred a woman with fire...."

Interrupting him, she pouted, "You said spirit, Joshua. Have you already forgotten."

Tracing her lips with his fingers, he cupped his hand around her face. "Sweetheart, from the night I set eyes on you in your mother's parlor, there has never been another woman in my thoughts or in my heart; only you. You must believe me, Elise, I never loved until you, and will never love again."

Seeing the depth of his love in his eyes, she whispered, "Oh Darlin', I love you so much it hurts sometime. Please forgive me for doubting you, I just get a little over sensitive from time to time."

A wide grin spread over Joshua's face, and he asked, "Are you trying to tell me something, sweetheart?"

Sheepishly she nodded her head and said cautiously, that she hoped Joshua would be happy that they were going to have another child. "I was waiting for the perfect time to tell you."

Lifting her off the ground, he twirled Elise in the air and shouted, "Halleluiah!" Then bringing his wife closer to him, showering her with kisses, he huskily whispered, "This is the perfect time."

Hearing laughter from the gardens, Sarah Tess mumbled under her breath, "What in the world is Mama and Papa doin' out there?"

Sarah glanced at Michael then smiled at her granddaughter. "Well if I'm not mistaken, your mama just told your papa that you were goin' to have another brother or sister."

Shaking her head, she announced firmly, "A brother. I don't want a sister!"

~ Eighteen ~

A few weeks following Joshua and Elise's return, the couple waited anxiously in Michael's parlor as Constance was to give birth to her and Tad's child.

"Bet this seems a might peculiar for you, Elise, waiting in anticipation for the birth of a babe rather than delivering new life," Michael said, clearly making small talk to help pass the time. "When do you expect my grandchild will be making his grand entrance?"

"*His?*" Elise lifted her head from her knitting to look over at Michael. "Who say's I'm having a boy? It could be a girl this time you know."

"Why yes it could, but your mother says you're having another boy by the glow on your face."

"Oh pish posh, what glow? Well, if this babe is a boy, Joshua promised I can call him Zachary."

"Yes. and if we're blessed with another daughter, she'll be named Emma Rose."

Repeating the name, Michael said, "Emma Rose Carmidy has a nice ring to it. Here's hoping you get your little girl, Joshua."

"Now who said I was hoping for a little girl?" Joshua chuckled, then glancing over at his wife and seeing a frown on her brow, his smile faded. "Sweetheart are you all right?"

"Fine darlin', I was just thinking about Felicity and how peculiar it is that after all these years we would meet up with her brother Erasmus, in our own home of all places. I wonder why he goes by C. W. Phelps now rather than his Christian name? No wonder he could never be found after the first battle of Manassas. And to think you saw him just before the war ended and didn't even know he was Felicity's brother. Hmm, what a small world this is."

"That it is, as far as him going by C.W., hell I'm sure he has his reasons. Whatever they are, it's his business and I'll respect his privacy. But I don't think I'll ever forget the look on his face when you walked in here this afternoon and called out his name. He looked as if he had seen a ghost."

"I know. And to think if Constance hadn't gone into labor I might never have met him again."

"Oh you would have met him, I'm sure," Michael interjected. "Especially now that Joshua is taking over all of Father's holdings."

"*We're* taking over the holdings. Partners, remember?" Joshua corrected Michael, raising his finger.

Looking at his son-in-law over the rim of his glasses, Michael said, "For the next year, but then you have the controlling share according to our agreement. Which by the way, how is Charles handling the transition of your clients to his workload? He must be overloaded since he received the lion's share of Tad's clients as well."

"Actually, he's doing rather well; no complaints so far. With him starting his own family, I'm sure the extra income is helpful."

Just then the sound of a baby crying echoed through Michael and Sarah's home. Michael stood and rushed over to the foot of the stairs anxiously awaiting the news of his grandchild. Seeing Sarah step from the room carrying a child wrapped tightly in a swaddling cloth and smiling, Michael breathed a sigh of relief.

"You have another grandson, Michael," Sarah said. "And he and his mother are doing just fine."

Taking the steps three at a time, Michel reached for him and gasped seeing how much he looked like Tad. "Oh my goodness, just look at you little man. Why, you're the spiting image of your father."

"Yes, a bit unsettling for Constance I'm afraid, dearest. She's asked for the nurse to care for little Thaddeus John for the time being."

"The nurse?" Michael asked. "Surely Sarah, you can't be serious."

"Michael dear, Constance has been through so much, give her time to adjust."

"Adjust? Lest you've forgotten this is her child too!"

~

For the next several weeks, Constance saw her son only when it was absolutely necessary, and never alone. She made it clear the child made her feel uncomfortable. It came as no surprise when she proclaimed that her milk had dried up and that other means to feed the child would have to be made.

Everyone knew of course, this was not the truth, but rather than force Constance to feed a child she clearly felt no love toward, goat's milk was provided for the nourishment of the Honeycut heir. Days passed without Constance looking in on her child. When she announced that she would be returning to her own home alone, (Michael's old home) and that young Tad would be better off with Sarah and the nurse, no one spoke a word or intimated that she was abandoning her child. Instead, Michael and Sarah kept hoping that in time she would eventually feel maternal toward the child, and come to think of him as hers rather than the son of Tad.

That hope soon dissipated when Constance came to see Sarah the first Friday of the new year.

"Why Constance dear, what a pleasant surprise. Come in. Have you come to see the baby?"

"No, Mother Honeycut. I would rather not. I come here today only to ask a favor. One I have no right to ask, but I fear that if I don't, I shall end up in an asylum."

"Oh Constance, surely you exaggerate. You are just overwrought. Tell me what it is you need, and if it's in our power, you know Michael and I will do everything we can to help you, dear."

"Mother Honeycut, I will come directly to the point. When I asked to leave here after the birth of, that child, it wasn't because I preferred to be alone, rather than with you and Father Honeycut."

Sarah noted how Constance still referred to young Tad as "that child" or something less impersonal, rather than by his own name. Saying not a word, Sarah listened as Constance continued.

"I'm sure you must have heard me cry out at night. The nightmares were constant. I thought if I left here, the place where Tad raped me…where that child of his was conceived, somehow, I'd feel some peace, but I haven't. And now I fear, I never will."

Sarah said not a word, allowing Constance the chance to speak her mind freely.

"You have no idea what it was like to live with him. He was the devil, Mother Honeycut, I honestly believe that. He killed three children of his own, raped and beat me repeatedly, tried to kill me, tried to rape, Miranda. And we all know how she died trying to defend herself. Don't you see, I'm afraid that he'll still hurt me somehow through, that child. Which of course is ridiculous, but I'm so tired, I can't think straight. And every time I close my eyes, I see him, ready to attack me through that baby."

"Constance, that doesn't make sense, you know Tad is dead. He can never hurt you or anyone again, and that sweet little boy upstairs is just that, an innocent baby. You just need time. Perhaps a holiday away from New York, Virginia, and all the memories that haunt you would be helpful."

"That was what I came here today to ask of you. Please, Mother Honeycut, I don't want a holiday. I need a new start. A place where I'm not haunted by the past. A place where I can forget the woman, I've become. You can't imagine what it feels like to look at the child you gave birth to and see the man you despise. I can't help it. God knows I've tried, but every time I see that child, it makes my skin crawl. I loathe him."

Breaking down and sobbing into her palms, Sarah gingerly placed her arms around Constance and rocked her tenderly as tears ran down her own cheeks. *Even from the grave, Tad's evilness still causes such heartache.* Hearing Constance's words, somehow Sarah accepted that nothing she could say or do would ever change Constance's feeling for her and Tad's child. The thought of any mother hating her own child cut Sarah like a knife, yet she held no animosity for this poor girl who had been through so much. Leaning her head back on the sofa, rocking the distraught woman in her arms.

"Don't cry Constance, I'll speak to Michael. Perhaps San Francisco would be a good place to rebuild your life, dear."

Although Sarah had not spoken her thoughts, she knew Michael saw the uncanny similarities of his grandson beginning's and his son's. Like Michael, she wondered how history repeating itself would prevent the same fate from falling on this innocent child.

A poor innocent child was being abandoned by its mother simply because he resembled his dead father, just as Michael had abandoned Tad because he resembled Emily. Unable to imagine the pain that Michael and Constance were feeling over the loss of their child, Sarah whispered a prayer. "The sins of Tad were of his own choosing, Lord. Please don't let his wickedness continue to destroy the lives of these fine and decent people whom I love. I beg of you, for all of our sakes, help us Lord to restore peace in our hearts."

Michael, who had been in his study and had overheard Sarah's and Constance's conversation, including Sarah's prayer, inhaled a deep breath and released some of the anguish he had carried in his heart for so long. Nodding his head he thought, *Sarah's right, Tad wasn't taught to hate or be cruel. That was of his own choosing.* As if a candle had been lit inside him, Michael finally was able to accept in his heart what his mind had been trying to tell him since Tad's death. *Son, I'm sorry if I failed you, but you were loved, you were taught the difference between right and wrong, somewhere along the way, you just chose a path so dark you couldn't find your way back home. I hope at last, that you have found the light.* Finishing his prayer to his dead son, he walked across the hall and stood at the entrance of the parlor staring at his wife and daughter-in-law.

Dear Sarah, what would I do without you. Your love already has guided me to peace a long time ago. Clearing his throat, Sarah and Constance jerked and hastily dried their eyes. Sarah, seeing the tenderness in her husband's eyes as he gazed at her, returned his smile. In that instant, Sarah knew that as difficult as it might be to raise a toddler as his own, at last her husband's heart was healed.

"Constance dear, as sad as my heart is to see you go, I will help you begin a new life. Please remember though, I shall always think of you as my daughter, and if you should ever decide you want back into your son's life or ours, the door is always open."

True to his word, Michael called upon the help of the only man he knew and trusted from San Francisco; C.W. Phelps. With the aid of this mysterious man who spoke very little, but for some reason had taken a liking to Michael, by spring, all the necessary arrangements for his daughter-in-law to begin a new life were complete. A home was purchased and lavishly furnished, money had been placed in a trust with an established attorney in the area, and to ensure the solicitor would remain honest, Michael hired C.W. Phelps to oversee Constance's estate.

Over the next few months, Michael came to look upon C.W. as more than a business associate, but also as a trusted friend. Before sending Constance off to her new life, Michael confided in this gruff man, confessing the sins of his past and those of his son's.

Not as a means to gain sympathy from him or even to explain how a mother could leave her child. But rather as an assurance that this man realized Constance had been a victim, just as Michael was certain that C.W. still viewed himself. Michael held nothing back, knowing this was his only chance for C. W. to fully understand the depth of pain that had been caused at the hands of a man who had never learned to forgive or love.

As he finished his story, Michael pointed out how ironic it was that he and his sister, a thousand miles apart from each other, had both been called upon to help victims that had suffered at the hands of an evil man. Felicity, to help Gilbert and Miranda's children, while he was being asked to help Tad's wife. Both agreed to do whatever they could, unselfishly, despite their own inner pain and grief.

For an instant, Michael was certain he detected a hint of tenderness in the man's cold dark eyes, yet when C.W. did not comment, Michael respected his wishes, and did not elaborate further.

Today though, on this unseasonably warm April morning, as Michael waved his final goodbye to his new friend C.W. and to Constance Hildebrandt-Honeycut, he couldn't help find amusement in how serendipitous life was at times. There was Constance, a woman running from her past, who sat next to a man who had ran from his past years before. Both had vast fortunes at their disposal. One would use it as a means to mask the pain in her heart, while the other would refuse to claim his inheritance out of bitterness and misguided foolish pride. Michael was certain that in his tormented mind, C.W. believed that by accepting his inheritance, he was sending a message of forgiveness. And that was something he wasn't prepared to do.

As the train pulled away, Michael looked at the hopeful faces of those that passed by him. He began to wonder how many of them were like that of Constance and C.W., who were on their way to the "Land of Opportunity" out of necessity; closing the door to a life of disappointments and regrets to begin anew. A smile crossed his lips as a thought entered his mind. *Wouldn't it be something if Constance and C.W. could heal one another's hearts?*

~ Nineteen ~

Devon, England
May, 1874

Sitting in the conservatory, gazing out the window and seeing Whitney approach looking downhearted, Felicity sighed. She knew the cause of his sullen expression in part was witnessing his mother so withdrawn since Benjamin's death. Yet despite knowing this, Felicity just couldn't bring herself to feel any emotion again. It wasn't as if she had forced herself to stop feeling joy or sorrow, it had just happened, without her even being aware.

Last fall, as Rupert pulled her from Benjamin's lifeless body, a part of her died too, and no matter how she tried, Felicity just couldn't fill the gaping void in her heart without Ben in her life. She went through each day doing precisely the same things as the day before, preoccupying her time, doing what was expected of her.

"Mother, I'm home," Whitney called out while climbing the stairs to his room. "Uncle Gilbert is stopping by later."

Glancing down at the letter from Elise, she sighed. *Last year, we were preparing for your arrival....* Realizing she had broken her own rule and allowed herself to think of the past, Felicity scolded herself. *This will serve no purpose other than to upset you.* Lifting the seal from the cover, she began to read.

Dearest friend,

Well I guess Mama was half right, again! I did have a glow, which explains my darling son, Zachary Thomas, but not even Mama can explain the glow Joshua has these days, holding his newest daughter, Emma Rose. Can you believe it? I had twins! Again!

Hearing a chuckle and realizing the unfamiliar sound was coming from her, Felicity laid Elise's letter on her lap and slowly traced her lips realizing she was smiling and it wasn't forced.

Her smile soon faded though when Gilbert stepped away from the door leading outside.

"Why Gilbert, I didn't hear you come in. How long have you been here?"

Oh, a spell. Long before your lad returned."

"Is that right? Why on earth didn't you let me know you were here?"

"I don't know, m'lady. I was curious if you acted like a statue even when you were alone."

"Excuse me? A statue? What a terribly cruel thing to say Gilbert. Have you come here today to deliberately antagonize me?"

Shrugging his shoulders walking closer to Felicity he added, "Why is it m'lady, that I seen ya smile last night at that river rat, and again just now when yer all alone. But when yer with yer boy you hardly even speak? And if my ears weren't deceiving me, I do believe that was a chuckle comin' from ya too. So I guess it's just yer son and those that love you, you've been savin' that sour face for."

"What did you just say to me? How dare you judge me, when I don't see you laughing and making merry, and Miranda's been gone far longer than my Ben has."

"That may be so lass, but I ain't been feeling sorry for myself, locked away in this damn prison for better than nine months either, now have I? Why, truth be known I wish this damned room was never built."

Detecting a hint of liquor on his breath, she tucked Elise's letter in her pocket and stood up, leaned away from him as far as she could without stepping into a potted plant. "You've been drinking haven't you? Otherwise, you would never speak to me in this fashion—"

Before Felicity could finish her comment, Gilbert blurted, "Aye and probably will be havin' me another pint or two before the night's through."

Firmly she said, "Go home Gilbert, and leave me be." Seeing him not yielding, she stepped to his right to walk past him, and her eyes widened seeing that he matched her step. "Stop this. What has gotten into you today?" she scolded.

"Oh I don't know…This mornin' I woke up and got to thinkin', Gilbert old boy, it's been nine months since yer mate has passed and his widow still walks around like we buried him just yesterday. Doesn't care a lick that her boy is hurtin'. Have ya even noticed that those who love ya are worried sick about ya? But ya let that low life back into your life and entertain him like he's a duke or some such. And it rubbed me the wrong way, so I decided to do something about it, is all."

"Is that right, well mind your own business and leave me be." Felicity again tried to step away from Gilbert, but he matched her step. "Stop this Gilbert. I mean it, let me pass."

"Can't do that. Not 'til I understand why you let that river rat come to this house again last evenin' with that there cousin of yers."

"I owe you no explanations." Felicity again tried to step out of Gilbert's way. "Stop it I say Gilbert. You have no right…you're drunk."

"Yer husband gave me the right, the day he made me promise to look after you and his boy. And havin' the likes of that man in this house, walking' around as big as you please like he belongs here, gives me plenty of right to find out what he's doin here. And for your information, I'm not drunk. Yet! I had me a drink or two—"

Before he could finish, Felicity snapped sarcastically, this time inching her way past him, "A drink or two?"

Gilbert, not willing to let her walk away from him, grasped her arm and swung her back around to face her. "Oh no ya don't, m'lady, not until you be answerin' my question."

"How dare you! Unhand me at once, Gilbert."

"Ah, so m'lady can raise her voice, if'n she needs to defend her actions regarding that low life." Changing his tone suddenly, he asked sincerely, "All I want to know is why do you let that man come here, Felicity? Don't ya see he's just usin' yer weakness to get closer to ya?"

Not caring that he was genuinely concerned, angered that he held her against her will, she clenched her fists by her side. "Unhand me I say. You don't understand."

Again the fierceness in his eyes glared at her and he snapped, "Ya think I can't understand the complexities of grieving and how that river rat is worming his way back into yer life to get back into yer bed?"

Felicity gasped, hearing his comment, and angrily jerked her arm free from his hold to slap him across the face. Shocked by what she had done in her rage, she gasped again then started to flee.

Gilbert gripped her arm and said calmly, "I had that comin' m'lady. I'm sorry. I just don't understand how you can be afraid of that man before your husband died, and now welcome his visits. Surely you must know his kind never changes, no matter what he says."

Felicity began trembling, struggling to be free from his grip. "There are things you don't understand, I tell you. It's complex."

Again, Gilbert glared at her as he spat indignantly. "Too complex for a simpleton like me, m'lady?"

Felicity, still struggling, finding herself becoming more agitated, raised her voice as she continued to free herself from his grip. "Stop it Gilbert, I never said that. There are things about my son, I will not discuss with you. Why are you doing this, and why must you keep calling me m'lady?"

Undaunted by her questions, Gilbert continued to hold her one arm as she struggled to be free, pushing away from him with her other hand. "Ah, so would you have me believe that river rat is here for the boy's sake? Is that what he's been fillin' that pretty head of yers with? I ain't no fool, but maybe you are? Did it spark yer heart hearin' a man say he loved ya again? Was that why you were smilin' a few minutes ago?"

Felicity's eyes widened and she struck him again. "How dare you speak to me in this manner!"

Just as before when she struck him, Gilbert just stood there not defending himself, only staring at her. "How dare I? M'lady, I haven't comprised my convictions, the question is, have you?"

Enraged at his implication, Felicity struck her fist into his chest and yelled, "I don't care what Benjamin made you promise...." she wailed between her tears, "You have no right to say such things to me. I hate you. I hate you Gilbert O'Flaherty."

Realizing Gilbert no longer had a hold of her arm, Felicity now hysterical, turned and began to run from him, but was detained as Gilbert slipped his arm around her waist from behind. Feeling her begin to struggle, he tenderly crossed her arms in front of her chest then holding her firmly up against him, he whispered hoarsely in her ear, "Let it out Felicity. Let it all out. You been holding all that pain for far too long."

As if a dam had opened, Felicity screamed between her tears. A gut-wrenching cry came from the depth of her soul, and immediately Gilbert turned her to face him, and comforted her as she continued to cry out, "Ben...Ben...help me...I need you."

Seeing Whitney race into the conservatory along with Jimmy Bartlett and Fannie, Gilbert waved them off. He knew what Felicity needed now more than anything was to be able to feel again, even if what she felt was pain.

Sobbing she asked, "Why did you do this to me Gilbert. Why?" She continued to scream through her tears. "I can't bear the pain. I miss him. I miss my Ben."

Jimmy, taking Whitney by his shoulder and seeing the young boy well up with tears, hugged him and wiped a tear from his own eye. "I'm thinkin' yer mum there could be usin' a good cry. How 'bouts you and me go 'round to Ashwillow and see if'n Mrs. Annabelle could come by fer a visit tonight?"

Turning to look back at his mother who still was crying in Gilbert's arms, Whitney nodded his head. "Yes, let's hurry."

Seeing them leave, Gilbert whispered, "Oh m'lady, I'm sorry to get ya all riled today, but ya weren't thinkin clearly."

"Then you were deliberately trying to antagonize me, but why?" Felicity asked through her tears.

"When I came here last year after losing my Mandy girl, the parson made me talk out my feelings. It helped me, but you ain't let a soul into your private hell, not even Whitney. When I heard from Whitney that Anne and that river rat came by here last night, well, it got me so riled, I could hardly contain my rage. So I had me a few shots of whiskey to get me courage up and came over here to get you all stirred up too."

"Why? That was so cruel of you."

Gilbert, handing her his handkerchief, said softly, "Felicity, if you want that sort in your house, then so be it. But I'll be damned if they are going to waltz in here and take advantage of you when you're not thinkin' straight."

Wiping her tears, she looked sheepishly at Gilbert. "You know don't you? About James, I mean."

"Let's just say, m'lady, I know lots of things and leave it at that. Some things just don't need to be said, now do they?"

"I'm sorry I slapped you, Gilbert. You know, I don't really hate you. Don't you?"

"Shh, another thing best left unsaid. As for the slappin', hell it 'twas more like a beatin' I'd say." Rubbing his cheek that was still red, he winked causing a faint smile to spread across Felicity's lips.

Seeing her reaction, his eyes danced merrily, and with a thick Irish brogue he added, "Think nothin' of it m'lady. We both needed to be stirred up some I reckon. And I can tell ya what, that slap of yer's woke me up good and proper. Remind me never to get you fired up again."

Felicity's smile broadened and Gilbert placed his arm in the small of her back. "Tell ya what, it's a lovely afternoon, why don't you and me take a walk out back until Annabelle comes by."

"Annabelle is coming here?" Felicity asked, brushing away the last remaining tears.

"Aye." Leading her into the gardens, he moved his arm around her shoulders. Glancing at him from time to time, she felt protected and found herself calming down as they walked in silence. She may not agree with Gilbert's methods, but he had accomplished what no one else had and that was to force Felicity from the safe cocoon she had been hibernating in.

Leaning her head on his shoulder as if it were the most natural thing to do, she allowed herself to remember the memories she had blocked from her mind for so long. Especially the last day they had with one another and the promise she had made to her Ben.

Casually she asked, "Gilbert, do you still miss, Miranda?"

"Everyday. 'Till the day I die, I'll miss her. Yet, I know she would want me to carry on for her, so in memory of our love, I force myself to be the man I know she would want me to be. The parson taught me this, and as hard as it is for you to lose him, you must try to be happy. Once you decide to carry on for his sake, it does get easier. You'll never forget him, nor stop loving him, he lives in your heart, but by picking up the pieces of your shattered life, it's like giving him a gift. A gift so precious that only you two can share, and ain't no one taking that away from ya, lass."

"A gift...." Felicity's voice trailed off and again they walked in silence.

~

From the second story of Brookhaven, Kathleen glared out from her bedchamber widow at Gilbert and Felicity walking arm in arm. "That will be enough of that Gilbert O'Flaherty. I'll not be letting you and that lovely fortune of yers slip through me fingers without so much as a fair-thee-well," she hissed. "Anne was right again, she said you had more on your mind than fulfilling an obligation to the prim and proper Mrs. Myles's late husband."

Feeling her blood begin to boil, she stomped away from the window and paced about her room. "Now what the hell am I'm supposed to do? James only wants a mistress while he waits for his precious Felicity, and Gilbert's too worried about protecting the devoted, distraught widow to even notice I'm alive."

Glancing in the mirror at her reflection, she whispered to herself, "Well we'll just have to change that, now won't we?" Glancing back at Gilbert and Felicity as they continued to walk the gardens, she arched her brow and hissed, "I've been patient long enough, Gilbert O'Flaherty! As of tonight your mournin' days are over! Rather than sit around and watch those brats of yours, or the grieving widow needlepoint, 'tis about time you started feelin' like a man again. And this here lass intends to bring out the virile Irishman in ya again, before that prissy widow does, or my name ain't Kathleen Sullivan!"

A devious smile crossed her lips as a plan formed in her mind. "Now to keep the grieving widow occupied while I arouse the widower." Hastily, she rushed to her writing desk and scribbled a quick note. Then wasting not a second, she rang for the housekeeper.

Within minutes Mrs. Duncan knocked at her door and entered. "You needed something, Miss Sullivan." The housekeeper did nothing to mask her annoyance at the guest when everyone in the house was worried about the mistress.

"Not I, Mrs. Duncan, with Mrs. Myles so distraught I thought it would be helpful if she was surrounded by her loved ones at a time like this. Will you please have this note delivered right away to her cousin, Anne Spencer?"

"Jimmy and Master Whitney are on their way to Ashwillow for Mrs. Robbins, so that won't be necessary, miss."

Kathleen's back stiffened at the housekeeper's insolence, yet she showed no offense. From the time she had arrived, Kathleen was aware that Mrs. Duncan looked upon her the same way as her own sister and Gilbert's brother Jake did. Beneath the fancy gowns and perfumed skin, they only saw a peasant who had turned into a high-paying prostitute. Inhaling a deep breath and pasting a smile to her lips, she looked Mrs. Duncan in the eyes and forced her voice to remain as refined as she had been taught.

"Mrs. Duncan, I know you don't like me much and think of me as only a tart. But surely even you wouldn't deny your mistress the benefit of someone who also has grieved over losing a husband, just because it was my suggestion?"

Neither denying nor confirming Kathleen's opinion of her, Mrs. Duncan cheeks turned scarlet and her eyes faltered as she accepted the note from Kathleen's hand. "I'll have Jimmy rush this over to Mrs. Spencer the moment he returns."

"Thank you," Kathleen responded politely to the housekeeper who meekly shut the door behind her. Whispering under her breath, Kathleen hissed, "Think what you want of me ya old biddy, but I'll be respectable when I get Gilbert to marry me and you'll still be nothin' but some servant washin' asses when told."

From her balcony window, she watched indiscreetly as Annabelle and Rupert arrived. Kathleen rolled her eyes and shook her head in disgust, seeing Annabelle rush to Felicity's side. *Ah the devoted boring heiress has arrived*, she thought as she continued watching the two women walking arm in arm. *Run for the shelter of the conservatory and pour your hearts out to one another.* Glancing over at Rupert and Gilbert, she knew from the direction that they were headed that the men would converse over a few drinks in the library. No doubt to take the edge off having to endure the monotonous whining of such dull women who acted more like grandmothers than women in their thirties.

Her thoughts were distracted at seeing Jimmy Bartlett drive off in the coach toward town. She knew he was delivering her note to Anne and a smile crossed her lips. *Well tonight things are going to be a bit livelier around here. Especially if that devilishly handsome man James comes along with Anne. How he excites me...* She wistfully thought, then stopping herself from fantasizing what it would like to be with such a man as she had countless times over the winter just to endure her boredom, she scolded herself. "Don't be wastin' your charms on that one, he's far too clever for you to snag. Gilbert on the other hand, well that shouldn't be too hard at all. If I've learned anything this past year, Gilbert needs to feel that he's protecting a woman. And I'm thinking those big strappin' arms of his could protect me rather nicely."

Dreamily, she recalled how she had watched him the other day as he chopped wood near his cabin by the stream. His chest and arms glistened as he continued to split the wood with the ax. "Oh how I pray you are as passionate with a woman as you were chopping that wood."

Kathleen caressed the cleavage of her breasts in her low-cut gown. "It won't be long now," she sighed. Recalling how taut his abdomen and broad chest were, she found herself becoming aroused. "Oh yes, Gilbert O'Flaherty, I will make you mine come hook or crook."

Seeing that her cheeks had a glow to them at thinking what it might be like at experiencing a younger man, she snickered. "Mustn't look like a mare in heat Kathleen; Gilbert prefers the demure lady-like types." Adjusting her breasts so just enough of them were showing to entice a man, but not revealing too much so that it would be perceived as vulgar, she continued to primp in front of the mirror. Then looking at her reflection she whispered, "Yes, this is sure to capture a man's attention. Now go make certain the poor distraught widow leaves the widower to someone who wants to stir the passion inside him."

Leaving her room, she headed straight to the conservatory. Glancing at the black wreath and taffeta hanging from the baluster, she thought, *I won't be missing these gloomy things hanging about, that's for sure.* Then the thought occurred to her; *What if Anne isn't successful in convincing Felicity her time of mourning is over? A smile crossed her lips, Anne Spencer not getting her way, perish the thought!*

As she entered the conservatory, just as she had suspected, nested on a bench were Felicity and Annabelle. Before they had seen her, she overheard Annabelle say, "As I said before, I may not agree with Gilbert's methods, but I must say watching you these past nine months so non-responsive has had us so worried. I shall always be indebted to Gilbert, who obviously must care about you as much as Rupert and I do. With this breakthrough, maybe now you can try, dear Felicity, to put your life back together."

"How? Benjamin was my life."

"As hard as this is for me to say, and for you to hear, dear Benjamin was not your life. He shared a part of your life, just as my Rupert does mine. He even added a sweetness to your life, and although it has hurt you that God chose to take him from you as he did, in time we will come to understand just as Benjamin often said...."

Before Annabelle had a chance to finish, Felicity softly said, "All in God's time."

Clearing her throat to make her presence known, Kathleen approached the two of them. "I hope I'm not disturbing you. I was worried about you Mrs. Myles."

"No need to apologize Kathleen, nor worry either, I'm fine. I do wish though, that you would call me Felicity."

Smiling politely at her hostess, she said, "Oh I don't think that would be possible, Mrs. Myles. You see, as much as I've tried to rise above my humble beginnings, I suppose some things just remain embedded, and that's to show respect to your elders."

As subtle as Kathleen's comment was, it was clear that she viewed the two of them as women she had no intention of befriending.

Not responding, both women smiled insincerely waiting to see what it was that she had interrupted them for. "Mrs. Robbins I couldn't help but overhear what you said about Gilbert just a few moments ago. And I find myself in complete agreement with you. Gilbert is such a wonderful man, not only kind, but so wise, too."

Realizing Kathleen must have been deliberately trying to eavesdrop on them since it had been several minutes since either of them had spoken Gilbert's name, she raised her eyebrow, much like she did with Pricilla and Edwin when she disapproved of their actions. "Kathleen, I notice you don't find it disrespectful calling Mr. O'Flaherty by his first name." Pausing to get her point across, she continued, "Putting that aside for the time being; you'll need to refresh my memory, what exactly was said regarding Gilbert since we were discussing other private matters long after discussing him."

Ignoring Annabelle's attempts at correcting her for intruding on their privacy, only commenting on what she chose too, Kathleen said, "Feeling the way I do for Gilbert, I forget he's closer to your age than mine, I suppose. But then again I guess it's because he reminds me of a man half his age, keeping himself so active by riding, fishing, woodcarving, just to name a few of his attributes. What amazes me most though is he's such a man of contradictions, one moment he's cutting his own firewood then the next playing the flute, and rather well, too."

"My, it does appear you've taken quite an interest in Gilbert. Why I had no idea he had such a full life here at Brookhaven. Plays the flute, you say?" Felicity's voice trailed off, stunned that this young woman knew more about her houseguest than she did.

"Oh yes, and he's been teaching Whitney and Lucas too. Although I think Whitney only plays the flute so he can spend more time with Gilbert."

"Is that so." Overcome with guilt, realizing she hadn't paid much attention to her son since the death of Benjamin, Felicity closed her eyes to block the stinging tears welling up in her eyes. *Gilbert was right; I have shut out my beloved son, along with everyone else who cared for me, from my life for so long...*

Her attention was diverted hearing Annabelle's question to Kathleen.

"So tell me, Miss Sullivan, should we assume that by you coming forth with so much information regarding Gilbert's habits this evening, it's also a declaration of your feelings for him as well?"

Smiling shyly, Kathleen purred, "Am I really that obvious, Mrs. Robbins or is it that you are so perceptive?"

"You flatter me, Kathleen, which I'm sure was your intent. Just as I'm sure you must have seen Felicity and Gilbert walking arm in arm in the gardens this afternoon. And obviously, this must have troubled you. Am I right so far, Kathleen?"

Kathleen was visibly unnerved by Annabelle's abruptness, speaking so frankly and she sputtered her answer, "Why Mrs. Robbins, I don't know what to say. You certainly have taken me back by your candidness. And keeping on the same note, I will respond with a firm yes. It's no secret I owe Gilbert a great deal and over the past several months, I find I've grown very fond of him. Yet, I didn't react to my feelings wanting to give him time to grieve the loss of his wife. Then as you've said, seeing him consoling Mrs. Myles this afternoon did arouse my curiosity. In fact, I came here now to find out if Mrs. Myles was interested in him romantically, although I wasn't intending to be so blunt about it."

Glancing over at Felicity, she hastily added, "Mrs. Myles, despite my feelings for Gilbert, if you are interested in him romantically, it goes without saying I will step aside."

Annabelle raised her brow, and scoffed, "How terribly gallant and noble of you, Kathleen."

Hearing the sarcasm in Annabelle's tone, Felicity gave her friend a disapproving glance then directed her attention back to Kathleen.

"I assure you, Kathleen, there is nothing between Gilbert and myself other than two friends helping one another through a terribly difficult time. I shall not stand in your way or any other woman for that matter, who may find Gilbert happiness."

Nodding, she smiled at Felicity, and said politely, "Thank you. And just so I am clear on this, despite my anxiousness, seeing you and Gilbert walking arm in arm, I was terribly sorry you were so overcome with emotion today."

"Thank you." Felicity's attention was diverted hearing the sound of the knocker at the front door. "Who could that be?"

Sheepishly, Kathleen answered, "Begging your pardon Mrs. Myles, after seeing how distraught you were, I took the liberty of sending word to your cousin, Mrs. Spencer."

Annabelle's back stiffened again, and she responded coldly, "How terribly kind of you and I'm sure having Mr. Sterling and Jacque Freeport as guests this evening explains your lovely gown."

Ignoring her friend's comment, Felicity stood and walked to greet her guests.

Immediately entering Brookhaven, Anne Spencer wasted no time in directing orders to Felicity's staff. Rupert hearing her, stepped out of Benjamin's study, and said sternly, "I hardly think you are in a position Anne, to determine when Felicity wants to end her period of mourning. If it comforts her to continue showing respect to her late husband, then so be it."

Not the least flustered by Rupert's tone or words, Anne responded abruptly, "Our dear cousin would continue to openly grieve her loss until she was old and gray if given the chance, but it's clearly not helping her, Rupert. And today's outburst is proof of that. You have never lost a spouse so do not presume to understand how imperative it is for anyone who has. If Felicity is ever to find peace in her heart again, she must let go of the past."

Turning to Mrs. Duncan she sternly said, "I mean it, take down all this dreadful black at once. It is nothing more than a constant reminder to my cousin that she has lost someone very dear to her and I will not abide by her living her life in memory of the dead one moment longer."

Rupert's scarlet face looked between Anne and her guests. "Is there a reason why you had to come with Mr. Sterling and Jacque? Surely with Felicity already upset it stands to reason she would prefer solitude."

"Well as I recall, the night of our dear cousin's coming out dance, after that dreadful scene Randolph committed, wasn't it at your father's and my aunt's insistence that Felicity continue? Now you tell me, if they were alive today do you think either of them would abide her hiding away and dwelling on the past? Why of course not, they would tell you the same as I am now, Felicity comes from a fine lineage. She's a Robbins and a Phelps and it's about time she was reminded of that."

Felicity, followed by Annabelle and Kathleen, entered the foyer and hearing her cousin's comment said, wearily, "Anne dear, I'm perfectly aware of my heritage. How good of you to remember as well. Thank you for dropping everything this evening and coming to my rescue, but as you can see, I am perfectly fine."

Glancing at her servant, she said, "Mrs. Duncan please tell cook to expect another three for dinner."

"Yes, Mrs. Myles." Waiting until her servant had scurried away, she nodded politely to her other guests. "Good evening, Mr. Freeport, Mr. Sterling, perhaps you would care to join Rupert and Gilbert and my other guests out in the garden for a drink before dinner."

Turning to Anne, she added, "That is of course, if my dear cousin has no objections to my suggestion." From the cold stare she gave Anne, there was no denying Felicity resented her earlier comment.

Turning in time to witness Anne's reaction, Felicity paused and directed her attention to Rupert. "Would you be a dear and act as host for a few minutes, Rupert? I would like a few minutes alone with Gilbert." Turning to him, she said with pleading eyes, "That is, if you don't mind?"

"Of course, as you wish, m'lady." Seeing the merriment in his eyes as he added his pet name for her, she smiled warmly at him and waited until Rupert led the rest of her guests out to the garden. Extending her arm for Gilbert to escort her to Benjamin's study, she turned and said, "I see you still insist on calling me, m'lady."

"I see no need to change that just because of a few tears shed."

"I wouldn't expect anything less from you, Gilbert." Reaching inside her skirt pocket, she pulled out the letter she had begun to read earlier that had caused her to smile, and handed it to him.

"Not that I owe you an explanation for my earlier smiling, that you obviously took offense to, but I thought you might find this interesting as well. It's from Elise. If you please, I'd prefer you didn't read the first page, since it's personal."

Accepting the letter from her, Gilbert began reading and coming to the part where Elise mentioned that she had given birth to twins, he smiled. "Well saints be praised, they got themselves another set of twins. Now that is good news. Emma Rose and Zachary Thomas, fine names, for a fine couple."

Taking back her letter, she raised her brow. "What; no apologies for jumping to the wrong conclusion; no words of regrets for saying such unkind words to me earlier?"

"M'lady, I might have misjudged yer smile earlier, but from where I stand nothin' has changed—that there river rat is still lurkin' about now, ain't he?"

"Yes Gilbert, he is a guest in my home, not at my request, I assure you, and certainly not for the reasons that you accused me of earlier. I'm fully aware of the type of man James is, and for the record, I do not hold any stock in a word he says."

"Then why?"

"Because, I can't protect myself from the unknown, anymore than Benjamin could prevent Lavinia from pulling a gun from under her dress and shooting him. Don't you see Gilbert? I can't keep living in fear. I'm far better off knowing what my enemy is doing, and try to keep him in my good graces rather than provoke further rage from him. I realize I am putting myself at risk, but with dear friends such as you, Rupert and Annabelle, perhaps I'll be able to outwit him this time rather then he get the best of me as he did in New York. Besides, he is Whitney's father and although he will never be able to claim him as his own, surely you as a father can understand how he needs to see his son on occasion. Even if it's only as a friend of the family."

"Thank you, Felicity, for telling me why you're letting the likes of that man back into your life, but surely this line of thinkin' isn't one of a clear mind. Mark my words, that man will never be satisfied until he has you and that boy."

Wearily, she smiled at him. "Oh Gilbert, I know you don't approve, and who knows, maybe I am making yet another mistake. But you must believe me when I say to you, I've not made this decision based on any other reasons than what I I've shared with you this evening. So please, I'm asking you as a friend, don't make things harder for me."

"All right m'lady, I'll not be sayin' another word regarding the likes of him for your sake, but mark my words, that man ever hurts ya again, I won't be responsible for my actions."

"Well hopefully, it will never get to that." As she began walking to the garden to join the others, suddenly she thought of what Kathleen had said earlier, and she paused. "Gilbert, is it true that you've been teaching Whitney to play the flute?"

Nodding his head, he frowned apprehensively and said, "Aye, he and Lucas seemed interested in it, so I thought I'd give it a whirl."

"That's nice. Maybe someday you might let me hear you play."

Shaking his head, he glanced at her and said, "I like to play some of the folk tunes from back home, nothin' fancy. The wee ones seem to like it, but I'd feel self-conscious if anyone else heard me play."

"I see." Feeling discouraged that her attempts at becoming involved in Whitney's life weren't going to be as easy as she had hoped, she suggested, "Well perhaps, I might be able to join you and the children the next time you go horseback riding?"

"You, m'lady? Now that's a sight, I'd be paying money to see."

"Why, Gilbert O'Flaherty, I'll have you know I'm an accomplished equestrian. You seem to forget I was raised in Virginia, off the Chesapeake

Bay. As a girl, my brother and I would take the boat out and do a little fishing, as well. So perhaps you wouldn't mind if I tagged along with you and the children from time to time. I'm not trying to horn in on your time with them, honest Gilbert. It's just Whitney spends so much time with you and I'm afraid I've neglected him...."

Interrupting her, to help ease the burden of her trying to explain, he said in a cheerfully mocking tone, "Tell ya what, I promised the children we'd be takin' a ride come sunrise. Nothin' fancy mind ya, Miss Equestrian, so you might not be able to show off all them skills you claim to have, but if you're so inclined you're free to join us."

Chuckling, she walked out the French doors leading to the gardens and said, "You don't believe me, do you?"

"Sure I do, m'lady, and the next thing I'll be hearin' is how you caught yourself a fish this long once." He stretched out his arms a little over twelve inches and smiled at her.

Felicity, shaking her head while grinning, placed her hand over one of his and stretched it out further, then proudly, raised her brow. "This would be more accurate, Mr. O'Flaherty. And one day, we'll go to Plymouth and fish off the Bay and I'll prove it, too. Lest you have forgotten, I am a Virginian, born and raised near the Chesapeake."

"Aye, I had heard that a time or two—well let's be making that soon m'lady, before that fish story of yers grows some more."

As they joined Annabelle and Rupert, laughing amongst themselves, Gilbert slapped Rupert's back. "Mate, this here cousin of yers must have kissed the blarney stone 'cause she's got the gift of gab, if ever a lass did. Why she's just challenged me to see who could catch the biggest fish in Plymouth. You and yer missus care to witness this historic event?"

"Right. A day fishing on the Bay sounds very pleasurable."

Looking over at Annabelle and seeing she was in favor of a trip, Rupert said, "Yes, how about next week and we could venture up the coast for a few day and take in the sights if you like?"

"That sounds good to me!" Gilbert eagerly answered and turning to Felicity, merrily said, "Well lass, are you and Whitney up for a little adventure? Or are you trying to squirm your way out of proving what a great angler you are already?"

"A trip you say?" As she looked up at Gilbert, instinctively she knew he understood her hesitation. By her venturing away from the sanctuary of her home, it was as if she symbolically had agreed to go on with her life.

Gilbert smiled warmly at her and said, "It's time, m'lady."

Taking in a deep breath, Felicity nodded her head and said, "Yes, that sounds lovely. Is there anything I will need to do to prepare for our little holiday?"

"Just pack yerself a frock that will be suitable to go fishing in and let me and Montgomery worry about the rest, Felicity."

Nodding her response, Gilbert, obviously pleased, smiled and turned to look out amongst the others in attendance. His smile faded as his eyes drifted to James, approaching Kathleen where she stood on the other side of the garden.

"Restless, Kathleen? I was just thinking that a woman like you could never be satisfied in the confines of the country. I see it in your eyes how you crave the excitement of the city."

"Mr. Sterling, I'm sure I don't know what you are implying. Is it so hard for you to believe that both lifestyles I find enjoyable? Why, have you forgotten I was raised in the country?"

"Ah indeed. Although when we met in London, how ingenious of you to fail to speak of your humble beginnings. Could it be that you were preoccupied trying to latch onto another wealthy benefactor to hostess his affairs, since your benefactor was on his death bed?"

Kathleen's smile remained planted firmly on her lips even though his words were cutting. "Judging by your lack of social graces that you've just demonstrated, one might wonder if all this wholesome country air is to your liking Mr. Sterling as you so emphatically pointed out to our fair hostess last evening. Perhaps the strain of concealing your inner desires to obtain a greater prize is getting the better of you. Might I remind you that by hurling insults at me may only cause you to falter in winning the heart of a certain widow? However, it may improve my chances at winning Gilbert's heart considerably, since we both know how protective he is."

Chuckling, he said, "Why Miss Sullivan, aren't we rather bold this evening, discussing such improprieties openly."

"Bold? One can never be too bold with their friends, can they Mr. Sterling? And considering I delivered such a convincing performance the night of my arrival of your devotion to your son, I assumed we were friends."

"And we are, my dear lady. Yet, I must say, this business agreement does appear to be rather beneficial to only you, Miss Sullivan. Rescuing you from the streets of London, where Emma Strombly would surely have thrown you out onto the streets had she discovered what really had killed her father. Now don't you agree, a few convincing words from you on my behalf does seem rather trite compared to what I did for you, my dear? Perhaps we should renegotiate our terms again?"

"Hmm, and what would I have that possibly would interest you, Mr. Sterling?" Pausing, Kathleen slowly caressed her bare neck and chest with the tips of her fingers and smiled alluringly at him. "I do find it amusing how you recall every detail of rescuing me in my hour of need, but fail to mention why you agreed to help me in the first place. As I see it, Mr. Strombly having a heart attack at such a delicate time was yet a string of good fortune that has been bestowed on you Mr. Sterling. After all, a trip and lodging to Devon in exchange for my silence of you leaving a gun with your ex-wife in hopes she would kill herself did seem fair to you at the time. As I recall, my little comment to our hostess was not a part of our bargain, but rather a thank you for arranging my sister's and Gilbert's brother's wake following us learning of the riots in Belfast. This is primarily the reason why I've continued with my silence, even after discovering you rid yourself of your demented ex-wife, but you were freed of Mr. Myles as well. So perhaps it is I who should be renegotiating our little arrangement." Sighing as she stroked a strand of her hair, she asked, "I find myself wondering though, just what you could possibly have that I would be interested in."

Chuckling, James leaned closer to her. "My dear Miss Sullivan, we both know what you desire most, and as I've stated before, I am only too happy to accommodate you."

"Ah yes, your generous offer to set me up in a lovely little cottage to be your mistress, all while you pursue the affections of the lowly distraught widow. Now why is it again, Mr. Sterling, this would be appealing to me? Especially when I can have everything I want without your help. Or have you forgotten what I will be obtaining, once I become Mrs. O'Flaherty? Respectability, wealth and the gratification of a man who is mine for the taking."

James, being very careful not to be overheard, leaned closer to Kathleen. "Come now, Miss Sullivan, we both know that potato farmer will never satisfy all your desires. You'll become bored with him before the bloom is off the bud, that is, if you even get him to the altar. So again I ask you, why would a tempting morsel such as you, waste yourself on man too old and dull to ever appreciate you, as I would?"

"Mr. Sterling, how kind of you to be concerned about my welfare. And in truth, what you say does hold great merit, except for one point you bring up that does confuse me some. Perhaps you would be good enough to enlighten me?"

"Why certainly, my dear."

"I was under the impression you and Gilbert were close in age? That being the case, why is it that he would be too old to satisfy my urges, when you keep telling me how well you could?"

There was no denying that James enjoyed their sparring, by the way his eyes danced as he gazed at her, and Kathleen knew he craved her more now, than ever before. Her breathing increased, signaling to him that he was not alone in his desires.

Blackmailing each other was not only exciting to them both; it was the aphrodisiac that kept the undercurrent of wanton passion for each other mounting. To further entice him, Kathleen leaned closer, and once certain his eyes had trailed to her firm breasts that pressed against the bodice of her gown, she whispered seductively, "Do be careful Mr. Sterling. I would hate to see all the plans you painstakingly have orchestrated to try to convince a certain widow of your devotion to her, be lost in a fleeting second. Especially if she saw you now, gazing down the front of my gown. As exhilarating and flattering as I find it, I'm certain our prim and proper hostess would not." Then straightening her back and smiling at him, she added, "Although judging by the jealousy in Gilbert's eyes as he sees us conversing so long, perhaps I do owe you a favor after all. Maybe one day we will need to settle up, before we forget who owes each other what."

Without waiting for his response, she stepped past him nonchalantly and smiled at Anne and Jacque, engaging her ally in conversation. "Ah Mrs. Spencer, how good of you to invite me to go shopping with you in Plymouth next week. You can't imagine how much I appreciate this."

"Nonsense dear, after all you have done for me, it's the least I could do."

Annabelle, taking Felicity's arm, said, "Come dear, I wouldn't dream of keeping you from your other guests."

Felicity, smiling politely at Gilbert and Rupert followed Annabelle, and once away from them, whispered sternly at her friend, "What in the world has gotten into you tonight? First that rather shocking encounter in the conservatory and now you practically are dragging me across the lawn to speak with Anne."

"Yes, well that little tart, Kathleen, reminds me far too much of my late sister. And let's just say this time, I'm going to stop her kind, cold in her tracks before she has a chance to contaminate those of good breeding."

Felicity just looked mystified at Annabelle and realized the death of Benjamin and Lavinia had also changed her dear friend as well.

~ Twenty ~

Long before the sun came up, Felicity, dressed in riding attire and sat anxiously waiting in the foyer for Whitney. *Perhaps this isn't a good idea,* she wondered while fidgeting with the old leather gloves she hadn't worn in nearly a decade. *What if Whitney is shocked by my sudden behavior, or worse would rather I didn't tag along with him and Gilbert?* Not having told her son that she was intending to come with them this morning, she knew all she had to do was return to her room and he wouldn't be the wiser. Pushing away her urges to run back into her room and hide from the world, she scolded herself, "No. Gilbert is right, it's time."

Her mind wandered to Gilbert and the events of the previous day. Accepting what he had said in her mind, Felicity wished her heart would do the same. Despite his words, she still felt that she was betraying Benjamin in some way, even though his last words were asking her not to live a life of loneliness. The feelings of betrayal were intensified by her dream last night, which was in part why she had wakened so early this morning, and why now she was so anxious.

The dream began as she was standing on a cliff looking out to sea. Just as it had before Benjamin's death, she felt a deep sadness, but now after his death, the feelings intensified and the fog was so thick she felt overcome by darkness. She cried out, but no one could hear her. However, unlike those dreams in the past, she suddenly saw a glimmer of light in the distance. As the light grew brighter through the thick fog, she was able to see a man approach in the distance. As he continued to draw nearer, she felt her heart beat stronger in anticipation. The thick fog engulfed her like a heavy blanket and she struggled to see who this mysterious man was, his face blocked, yet she felt his presence. Suddenly without warning, he pulled her close to him and feeling his arms around her, his breath on her face, her heart raced. Then she felt his mouth on hers, the tenderness of his lips sending a wave of desire through her like none other she had ever known. As abruptly as the kiss had begun, the man released her from their moment of passion; and Felicity awoke with a start, seeing the mysterious man in her dreams to be Gilbert.

Recalling Gilbert's lips on hers from her dream, Felicity jerked, hearing her son call to her.

"Mother? What are you doing here?" Whitney asked and Felicity tried to block out the dream, and smiled at him.

"Why I've been invited to ride with you today, that is if you don't mind my company."

"Mind? On the contrary, Mother, I think that would be grand. You just surprised me is all." Looking curiously at her, he asked, "Where did you get those clothes and gloves, Mother? I've never seen them before."

Wrapping her arm around her son's shoulder, noticing how tall he was getting, she said, "That's because I haven't worn them since I came to England. As a matter of fact, I had to drag them from my old trunk. Why do you ask Whitney, don't you like them?"

Squishing his nose up, he said hesitantly, "Not really Mother. They look so...so...." It was clear he was looking for the appropriate words to describe them without sounding offensive.

"Old and outdated?" Felicity asked.

"Yes, not to mention the coat is red! I don't ever recall you dressed in red before."

"Why, Whitney Myles, I'll have you know, my wedding dress was red. Your father actually picked it out for me."

"Father picked out a red wedding dress? How peculiar."

Realizing her son was heading toward the door, she paused. "Dearest, aren't any of the other children going too? And what about breakfast? Aren't we going to get a bite to eat before we go riding?"

"Yes, Mother. Uncle Gilbert always prepares breakfast for us at his cottage. And Lucas is already there, he spent the night with his father."

Shocked by her son's comment, she followed him through the door and mumbled, "Lucas stays at the cottage? And did you say *Gilbert* cooks you breakfast? Is it any good?"

Chuckling, Whitney said, "Yes, Mother. Of course it is. And every night one of the children spend the night at the cottage with their father. He calls it their special time together."

"Really? Why wasn't I aware of this?"

Shrugging his shoulders, Whitney kicked at a twig on the ground. "You've been a little sad lately, I suppose."

Hearing the pain in her son's voice, she hugged his shoulders tightly. "Oh Whitney, I'm so sorry."

"Mother, don't worry, Uncle Gilbert has explained everything to me."

"He has? Well did he also tell you how very much I love you?"

Smiling up at her, Whitney slipped his arms around his mother's waist and hugged her back. "I love you too, Mother. I'm really glad you're up to riding with us today, even if you are wearing that dreadful outfit."

Kissing his cheek, Felicity sighed in relief, grateful that her son did not hold any ill feelings toward her for abandoning him all these months.

"So tell me true, does Gilbert really know how to cook? Because I'm starving."

Nodding his head emphatically, he said, "He does, indeed. I do hope he made us Boxty on the griddle."

Hearing this unfamiliar dish, Felicity shook her head while smiling. "Well I hope it tastes better than it sounds."

By now the two of them had crossed the creek and were approaching the cottage. Noticing smoke coming from the chimney, Felicity glanced over at the stack of firewood and thought of what Kathleen had said about Gilbert cutting his own wood. The faint smell of something cooking filled her nostrils and she raised her brow. "Mmm, something sure smells good."

Just then Gilbert opened the door to the cottage and greeted them wearing an apron and a wide grin. "Fàilte madainn mhath!"

Whitney eagerly climbed the steps of the cabin and cheerfully responded by saying, "Good morning to you too, Uncle Gilbert."

Rubbing the top of Whitney's head after the boy removed his hat, Gilbert said, "Ah lad, you were supposed to respond in Gaelic."

Glancing at Felicity, he added, "Welcome m'lady, to my humble abode or should I say your second home." Directing his attention back to Whitney, he called out, "Hang up yer coat in the wardrobe and wash yer hands, we got company today. And don't be getting into the Boxty until we say grace."

Hearing Whitney respond, Felicity smiled. "My, it appears you have quite a routine. I hope I'm not intruding."

"Now why would you be intrudin' in yer own place, m'lady?" Stretching his arm and noticing the apron around his waist, he quickly removed it and stepped closer to the doorframe allowing Felicity to pass. "I made a few changes since I moved in here last autumn; hope you approve."

As soon as Felicity walked through the door, she was awestruck at the woodwork that adorned the three-room cottage. "Gilbert, where did you find such lovely furnishings?"

"He made them, Mother."

"Da let us help. I carved this claw myself, Aunt Felicity."

Smiling at Lucas who was standing near a game table next to a window, she walked across the immaculate room and kissed the top of his head.

"Good morning, dear Lucas."

Directing her attention to the pedestal, three-prong legs of the table and the claw in particular that he was pointing to, Felicity knelt down and rubbed the wood with her hand.

"Oh my, this is beautiful. And you did this, Lucas?"

"Yes. Da showed me how."

"Well my goodness, never have I seen such fine craftsmanship by someone so young. Perhaps for my birthday, you would make me something."

Not to be outdone, Whitney walked across the room and pointed to a curved top boxed-chest that lay nestled on a table between two fireside chairs. "You'll never guess what this is, Mother."

"I have no idea, son." Proudly, he opened the lid and inside laid a hand-carved wooden chess set. Instinctively her hands went to touch one of the pawns and she gasped, "Oh my." Turning she looked at Gilbert, "Did you?"

"No. Whitney carved each and every one of them himself—all thirty–two pieces."

Dumbfounded, with tear-filled eyes, she said, "Oh Whitney, they are beautiful. This must have taken you forever."

"And look Mother, they have felt on the bottom of every one so they won't scratch the table that Uncle Gilbert has made."

"I see that, I don't know what to say...." Hugging her son tightly, she whispered, "I'm so proud of you, Whitney."

"Thank you, Mother. Can we eat now? Boxty is my favorite."

Chuckling she nodded her head. "So you've said."

Whitney and Lucas scrambled to the table and sat on the bench near the wall, while Gilbert took her hat and gloves as she removed her riding coat.

"The water pitchers full and there are fresh linens on the dry sink. I'll be right with ya," Gilbert called out, walking over to a hallstand. Felicity watched mystified as he knelt over and placed her belongings inside a drawer on the base of the stand. Realizing she was staring, she turned and searched for the dry sink. After he had taken her coat, Felicity walked across the small but orderly kitchen area and peeked at the pan on the woodburning stove. "Smells good! I take it this is Boxty?"

"Aye," Gilbert said, standing beside her.

Moving so that he too could wash his hands before the meal, she said, "Here, now there's plenty of room for you too, that is if you'd like."

"Mother, it's bad luck for a man and a woman to wash their hands in the same sink."

"What?" Confused by his comment, she smiled. "Oh Whitney, that's silly. Who ever told you such a thing?"

The boy looked cautiously at Gilbert, who responded, "I did, m'lady." Turning to Whitney, Felicity noticed that his cheeks were suddenly rosy, and he added hastily, "Lad, that's only if they are courting, betrothed, or it's their wedding day."

"Courting? Isn't that the same as betrothed?"

Lucas shook his head, correcting Whitney. "No. Courting is when the man falls in love and tries to win the fair maiden's heart. Betrothed is when he already has it and that's when his troubles begin."

Hearing the explanation, Felicity couldn't help but snicker under her breath. "My I've never heard the affairs of the heart explained quite like that before." Looking at Gilbert, she raised her brow, trying to mask her amusement. "Are we a bit superstitious, Gilbert?"

"Me? Nah." Hastily he dipped his hands in the basin, and brushed them dry with a towel. "Let's eat."

Escorting her to a chair, he poured her a cup of coffee. "Today, it'll be coffee. Forgot you preferred tea, otherwise I'd have got some from Mrs. Duncan last night."

Smiling at how ironic it was for her to be served by him, she politely replied, "Actually, I prefer coffee, I just got in the habit of drinking tea with Benjamin...." Her voice trailed off and her smile faded feeling a slight pang of guilt again, and she looked down at her napkin. "Coffee sounds wonderful, I hope it's strong."

"Is there any other way," he said, but judging by his eyes Felicity knew Gilbert knew how uneasy she had suddenly become. "How do you take it?"

"If you have cream and some sugar that would be lovely."

"Got it right here. So happens that's how I take it too." Glancing at the boys who were trying to wait patiently, he chuckled. "Look at the two of ya, yer tongues are a waggin' like a dog." Placing the sugar in the center of the table he added, "Now don't be forgettin' yer manners; lady before you gents."

Frowning slightly, not understanding what Gilbert meant by his comment, Whitney said, "You sprinkle the sugar over the Boxty, Mother."

"Ah, I see."

Just then, Gilbert served what appeared to be a thick pancake in the center of her plate and said, "Dab a little butter on it first, then sprinkle the sugar over it." Watching to make sure she did as he instructed, he waited until she took her first bite.

"Mmm, it's a potato pancake."

Shaking his head, serving the boys theirs, he replied, "Nah, a potato pancake is thinner and it's served with a thick whiskey sauce."

"Not where I come from, it's not," she said, chuckling.

Lucas eagerly put a bite of food in his mouth and Gilbert scolded him, "Did ya forget somethin' there lad?"

"Grace," he mumbled quickly chewing his food. "I forgot Da, since Aunt Felicity took a bite."

"No harm done, son." Then bowing his head, Felicity followed suit and glanced over at Whitney whose head was already lowered as he peeked anxiously over at Gilbert. "Go ahead lad, it's your turn."

Smiling proudly, Whitney began. "May the blessing of the five loaves and two fishes, which God divided amongst five thousand men be ours; and may the King who made the division put luck back in our food and in our portion. Amen."

"Amen," Felicity muttered, amazed that Whitney said the words of this unfamiliar prayer as if he had spoke them thousands of time before. Surmising it must be an Irish prayer; she smiled realizing what a diversified upbringing her son was experiencing—English, American, and now Irish, as well. Taking a sip of her coffee, she listened to Gilbert and the two boys decide where they were venturing out today on their ride, and she was awestruck at their ease with one another. Glancing at Gilbert as she took another bite of her Boxty, she suddenly understood the depth of why he felt he had a right to speak to her as he did the day before. These past nine months as Felicity had been grieving her loss, Gilbert had been honoring his obligation to Benjamin. He had taken Whitney under his wing as if he was his own. Suddenly overcome with gratitude for this wonderful man who sat across from her, she nearly didn't hear Gilbert when he asked, "Something wrong?"

"No, everything is perfect. Thank you, Gilbert."

For a brief moment, their eyes locked and he smiled knowingly at her. There was no need for the words to be spoken; Felicity knew that Gilbert understood her words of gratitude were more than thanking him for the meal he had prepared for them.

~

Within the hour, the four of them were riding through the moors of Dartmouth, with Felicity riding astride and Gilbert pulling back riding next to her rather than with the boys.

"Gilbert, you can ride ahead if you like, I'm quite content just trotting along and taking in the scenery."

"I will after you and Girt get better acquainted. That mare can be a bit cantankerous from time to time; spooks real easy. I would have preferred you on this gelding, but with that saddle of yers, his back wasn't long enough."

"I'm impressed, you know a lot about horses. As a matter of fact, I've discovered you're very knowledgeable in a number of subjects—

carpentry, woodcarving, cooking, and apparently a master in explaining the affairs of the heart to young men."

There was no denying she was poking fun at him and she added with a grin, "Oh and I forgot—superstitious. Not that I see where that will be beneficial, mind you."

"Yeah well, ya never can be too careful. No sense in borrowing trouble and angering the fairies and saints, now is there?"

Tilting her head inquisitively, her eyes dancing merrily, she said, "Why Gilbert O'Flaherty, you are superstitious! And just how many fairies have you seen today?"

Clearly Gilbert was not amused and in a fatherly tone, said, "Now don't be mocking what you can't see lass, they don't take kindly to that sort of thing."

Trying to keep a straight face, she said, "Is that right? I didn't know that." Glancing over at him, looking as serious as she could, she asked, "So tell me, just in case I should ever come across one, just what do these fairies look like? Are they little people with cute wings, flying from flower to flower?" Pointing to her left, she gasped, "Look, over there, near the hedge, could that be one?" Then shaking her head sadly, Felicity sighed, "How sad, it's only a butterfly."

"Laugh all ya want there, lass. You'll not be hearin' me mock the little people.'"

"Ah, so they are little people, are they? And do they have wings…and can they fly?"

Not waiting for a response, Felicity kicked the mare's side with her left heel and stirrup and instantly Girt took off to a full gallop. Not expecting such a jolt, she frantically began pulling on the reins to slow the horse down. Without warning the horse jerked to a stop causing Felicity to lose her balance and shift forward then immediately be tossed from her saddle as Girt lifted her front legs. With her left foot still locked in place in the stirrups, Felicity was dragged alongside the horse like a rag doll, knocked unconscious as soon as her head hit the ground. Gilbert, witnessing the incident, yelled out "Whoa," while grabbing the reins of the mare until it came to a full stop.

Whitney and Lucas, hearing Gilbert yell and seeing Felicity dangling from the horse, raced to them as Gilbert slid from his horse and gingerly removed Felicity's foot from the stirrup.

"Felicity, can you hear me?" he frantically whispered, kneeling beside her. Seeing blood running down the side of her head, he placed his hand under her jaw and feeling a pulse he sighed, "Jesus, Mary, and Joseph, don't let her die."

By then Whitney, seeing his mother lying on the ground, jumped from his horse and screamed out "Mother!" Falling to his knees beside her, shaken, looking pleadingly at Gilbert he asked, "Is she dead?"

"No. Listen to me son, your mother is not going to die. I won't let her."

Becoming more frightened, the young boy began sobbing. "Mother wake up, don't leave me. Please, don't leave me." Seeing blood appear on her petticoat from beneath her skirt which had hiked up, he gasped, "She's bleeding bad, Uncle Gilbert, help her."

Gripping the boy's shoulders, and forcing him to look at him rather than at Felicity, he said, "Listen to me Whitney, your mother is not going to die, but I need your help." Looking up at his son who had now joined them, he said, "Lucas, tie up the horse then you and Whitney ride to Brookhaven and fetch me a doctor. Have Montgomery send over plenty of sheets and have Fanny and him meet me at the cabin."

Whitney, becoming hysterical said, "No, I want to stay with Mother."

"Son please, do what I ask. I need to tend to your mother. Can you do this for me?"

Seeing him nod, he said, "Good, now hurry up." Helping the young boy to his feet, he turned and directed his attention back to Felicity. Lifting her skirt farther he saw that her right leg had been badly scraped, probably from a rock or tree branch as she was being dragged. Lifting the torn garment and seeing how deep the cut was, he hissed, "Sweet Jesus." Reacting on instinct, Gilbert stood and yanked at his belt until it was free from his trousers, then began wrapping it around her leg just above the cut, pulling tightly on the strap as Felicity moaned. Seeing Whitney and Lucas still standing dumbfounded nearby, he called out over his shoulder, "Go on, you're wasting time. I need bandages."

Not moving from his spot, tears running down his cheeks, Whitney said, "Uncle Gilbert, you will be gentle, please don't hurt her."

"Son, I will treat your mother as if she were an angel. Now go on, get some help."

Tearing at his shirtsleeve, seeing the boys doing as he instructed, he knelt beside her and gingerly placed the cotton material against the open wound then applied some pressure. Felicity moaned and moved her head slightly, and he hoarsely whispered, "Sorry M'lady, but I have to stop the bleeding."

Softly she whispered his name, "Gilbert...." Then her head rolled to the side and Gilbert knew she had passed out again. Wasting no time, he tore at his other sleeve and wrapped it around her calf. Examining her right temple and seeing it was only a surface cut, he gingerly slid his arm under her neck. Lifting her in his arms, he began carrying her toward the cabin.

Gazing down at her limp body, he prayed, "Sweet Jesus, I'm beggin ya, don't take her from me too."

Despite the distance and the burning pain in his arms and back, Gilbert continued to press on in almost a run. As he reached the cabin, perspiration dripping down his face, out of breath, he kicked at the front door and it swung open. Hearing the banging sound, Felicity stirred slightly in his arms and he hoarsely whispered, "It's all right, Felicity, I've got ya."

"Gilbert…it hurts…Gil…." Again she drifted out of consciousness and he gingerly lay her on his bed. Noticing a tear running along her right sleeve and blood dripping down her wrist he hissed, "Christ almighty, where's all this blood coming from?" Not wasting a moment, he yanked at her gloves, pulled on the sleeve of her coat and winced, seeing a bone protruding from her forearm. Noticing the front of his shirt was covered in blood, he began carefully undressing her all the while whispering, "Don't die on me Felicity. Please God don't let her die."

Having removed all her clothing except for her pantaloons and corset, he rolled up her petticoat and gingerly placed it beneath her arm then frantically he looked about the room for something to use as bandages. Running to the wardrobe, grabbing a sheet, he began tearing it into long strips as he raced to the dry sink for water. With the basin still filled with soapy water from the morning, Gilbert hastily dropped the sheet on the table. Carefully carrying the filled basin to the opened door, he flung the water out onto the porch, and then turned to retrieve the pitcher. Filling it with fresh water from a wooden barrel at the side of the cabin, Gilbert went back inside the cabin placing the pitcher and basin on the floor near his bed. Returning to the sheet he quickly finished tearing it until he had ample rolls. Then opening a drawer from the chest, he pulled a tin of ointment from it and placed that beside the basin of water then knelt beside Felicity.

"Felicity, I'm sorry but this is gonna hurt." Taking her limp hand in his, taking in a deep breath, he pressed the bone back into place and immediately Felicity yelped in pain. Cupping his hand around the open tear in her flesh to help stop the bleeding, he gazed at her and noticed she again had passed out. "That's right, sleep M'lady. Let me care for you."

Lifting his hand away, he immediately tended to her wound, and once her arm was fully wrapped, he removed her corset. Lifting her head, he placed her broken bandaged arm against her bare chest, then with the rolls of cotton he made a sling to support her arm next to her chest.

Cleaning all signs of blood from her chest and arm, he stood and removed a clean bed-shirt of his from the chest of drawers and placed it over her head. Propping her up, he pulled it down to her waist then lay her head back onto the pillow and pulled her left arm through the sleeve of the shirt.

Directing his attention to the cut on her right leg, Gilbert untied the belt then gingerly removed her pantaloons. Cleaning the gash of dirt mixed with blood from her leg, he than bandaged that wound as well. Once finished he pulled the nightshirt down to cover her naked lower torso. Guiding his hands under her, he covered her with the quilt before tenderly washing the cut on her forehead just below the hairline.

Felicity moaned and tried to open her eyes but kept falling out of consciousness. Removing the combs from her hair, he tenderly lifted her head to brush her long brown hair with his hands to her left shoulder. Carefully removing a strand of hair from the corner of her mouth, he tenderly cupped her face in his hands. Felicity moaned softly in her sleep and he responded by lowering his head, and gently placing his mouth over hers.

Hoarsely he whispered, "Shh M'lady, it's all over now. Just rest, me bueddy."

Gazing at her, he tenderly traced her lips with this rough thumb, watching her every movement until he heard the sound of horses approaching.

Gilbert was surprised to see that Stephen Hix, visiting from London, was the doctor called in to tend to Felicity. Stephen, seeing Gilbert, gasped, "Dear God, what the hell has happened? Gilbert, you look like you've bathed in blood."

Numbly, Gilbert looked down at his shirt and trousers. "Aye, Felicity's. She broke her right arm, the bone went clean through the skin and there's a cut on her leg, real deep, Stephen."

Entering the small bedroom, he closed the door behind him and said, "Well step aside and let me have a look at her." Lifting the quilt, and seeing she was cleaned and wearing a man's bed-shirt, her wounds already bandaged, he glanced over at Gilbert before unbuttoning the white, cotton garment. Placing his hand inside the bed shirt, he gently lifted Felicity's arm.

Hearing her moan, Gilbert said, "Careful, she's real sensitive there."

"Right, I can see that. You say the bone ripped the flesh?"

"Aye, I had to set it back in place; then I placed this balm over it and wrapped it." Bending over he picked up the tin and handed it to Doctor Hix.

"Hmm, what is in the ointment?"

Shrugging his shoulders, Gilbert said, "Mainly bees wax and the oils of some herbs and roots. It's a recipe from my grandda and I use it for when I cut my hands whittling."

Nodding and returning the tin to Gilbert after smelling it, he said, "Well, the bleeding has stopped, so there's no point in aggravating her wounds again. The best I can do for her now, is give her something for the pain, and come back tomorrow to change the bandages to make sure no infection sets in. If she comes down with a fever, send someone out to get me. But other than that there's nothing I can do for her that you already haven't done. Make sure she gets plenty of rest. Why don't you have Montgomery bring round a wagon and you can transport her to Brookhaven."

"No. She's resting now. Why move her? I'll stay here with her tonight along with Fannie." Glancing down at her with concern, he said, "Are you certain there isn't anything else she'll be needin'?"

Bending over and pulling out a syringe, the doctor pulled out a glass bottle and looked over at Gilbert who was running his hands through his hair. "She'll be fine, Gilbert. The morphine might make her a little lightheaded and nauseous, so I would avoid any heavy meals for as long as she's on the medication." Bending over, he injected Felicity with a dose of morphine and she moaned, and Gilbert went to her side.

"Is that hurting her?"

"Burns some when it goes through her veins, she'll be fine in a few minutes. She'll be out for probably the better part of the night, so get yourself cleaned up, you look like the devil." Turning, he went to the door then said, "Tomorrow you'll have to tell me what's in that ointment of yours."

"Sure thing, and thanks Stephen." Shaking his head, he stepped out of the bedchamber and said, "She's been well cared for, so not foreseeing any complications I'd say she'll be up and around in no time. Her arm's been broke and she has a nasty gash on her leg, but by morning she should be able to sit up for a while."

"Doctor Hix, may I see my mother?"

"Son, your mother is sleeping, and I'd rather you didn't."

Hearing Whitney, Gilbert called out, "It's all right Stephen. Let the boy see his mother."

"Fine; but just for a few minutes."

Whitney crept inside the room and seeing Gilbert covered with blood, he gasped. "Don't be frightened son, it's just a wee bit o'blood is all. The important thing is your mum here, is going to be as good as new."

"Really, Uncle Gilbert? Are you sure?"

"Sure as the sun is going to set and come up again tomorrow. Now come closer and give her a kiss, lad, before you go back to the house with Montgomery."

"I want to stay."

"Boy, I'm going to have my hands full takin' care of your mum here and I need you to be lookin' after my wee ones for me. Will ya do that for me, Whitney? It would be a great help to me."

"All right, Uncle Gilbert. But can I come back tomorrow morning?"

"Make it tomorrow afternoon, lad. Your mum here needs plenty of rest, and we don't want to be disturbin' her none. All right?"

Nodding, he leaned over and tenderly kissed his mother's cheek, then said, "Mother has your bed shirt on, Uncle Gilbert."

"Aye. Her clothes were all torn and bloody so I had to get her into something clean. That's all I had. Tomorrow, when you come by, you can bring her some of her own things so she feels more comfortable. Now run along and be a good lad. I'll see you tomorrow."

Nodding, Whitney walked solemnly to the door then turned. "I will see her tomorrow, won't I, Uncle Gilbert? I mean, she's not going to die like Father did, is she?"

"No, lad. I promise. You'll see her again tomorrow. Whitney, send someone round to get your cousin Rupert and Annabelle."

"I already did, sir."

"That a boy, good thinking." Turning his attention back to Felicity, he said as an after thought, "Send Fannie in here, would ya?"

"Yes, sir." Pausing to look at his mother one last time before he left, he said, "Don't worry Uncle Gilbert, Mother won't be angry that you dressed her in your clothes. She'll be glad that you took such good care of her."

Smiling faintly, Gilbert began gathering all her bloody clothing and seeing Fannie enter the room, he said, "Stay right by her side while I go to the stream and clean up. If she wakes up or moves, yell for me. Understand?"

Looking gravely down at Felicity, she said, "Yes, sir."

Not waiting for a response, Gilbert rushed around the three-room cottage, discarding her clothing and tending to caring for his patient. Once he had emptied the basin, he dragged the dry sink from the kitchen and placed it by his bed, then returned with a kitchen chair. Before going to the stream, he started the wood stove, and placed a kettle of hot water on it to boil. Returning to his bedroom, he opened the chest of drawers, pulled out a fresh change of clothing then turned to look at the servant. "I mean it now, yell loud enough for me to hear."

"Yes, sir." Taking a seat by her mistress, Fannie glanced out the window and saw Gilbert running to the stream. "Well Mrs. Myles, less my eyes are deceivin' me, I'd say you got yerselfs a real nice man lookin after ya, who sure is actin' like ee's in love, or I ain't never seen a man in love before."

~ Twenty - One ~

Just after daybreak, Annabelle, having fallen asleep in the high back chair, awoke with a stiff neck. Stretching her neck, she glanced about the dimly lit room, hearing only the sounds of a clock ticking and Gilbert rocking back and forth in a chair by Felicity's bedside, and she sighed. *Poor man, he hasn't slept a wink. Surely, he doesn't blame himself for this accident.*

Recalling the promise he had made to Benjamin, she shook her head. *Well if you are anything Gilbert O'Flaherty, you are definitely a man of your word. No one could have taken better care of Felicity and Whitney since Benjamin's death.* Standing and stretching her back, she walked to the doorway and looked in at Felicity. "Any change?"

"No. I was thinking that I should fetch Doctor Hix. He said she'd sleep a good while, but surely he didn't mean over fifteen hours?"

Entering the room and watching the pattern of her breathing, she said, "I'm sure she's fine Gilbert. Why don't you let me sit with her awhile and you get some rest."

Shaking his head, he said, "Nah, I couldn't sleep, but I could stretch me legs some. If she wakes though...."

Anticipating his question, she nodded her head. "I promise Gilbert, if there is any change I will have Fannie come and find you."

"Thank you." Leaning over the sleeping Felicity, he gently placed the back of his hand against her brow. Feeling no change, he stepped around the bed and waited until Annabelle had taken her seat before taking his leave.

"Gilbert, I won't leave her. Go. Take a walk."

Smiling, he nodded his head. "Forgive me. I must be more tired than I thought."

Watching him leave and waiting until she heard the front door close, she leaned closer to the bed and gently patted Felicity's arm. "You've been though so much this past year, dear friend, but you can't sleep your life away. Please wake up soon, before that man makes us both have a breakdown. He's like a mother hen."

Having no reaction from Felicity, Annabelle stood and walked over to the dry sink. Noticing the stack of clean linen, she smiled. "My goodness, he's thought of everything."

After drying the restless sleep from her face, she heard Felicity say in a groggy voice, "What time is it?"

Turning, she smiled, and said, "Well, good morning, sleeping beauty. How do you feel?"

"Sore...and thirsty. Did you say morning?"

Pouring her a drink of water and lifting her head slightly, she said, "Drink it slow Felicity. You've had a nasty fall and were given morphine for the pain."

After just a sip of the water, she looked up at Annabelle, "Where is Whitney? He must be so frightened."

"He was. But in truth, his sprits were high after he was permitted to see you. When we arrived, he told me that his Uncle Gilbert had kept his word, he didn't let you die and he cared for you like you were an angel. And believe me that isn't far from the truth."

"Did he? I must thank him.... How long have I been sleeping?"

"You've slept the day and night away, dearest."

Groaning after trying to raise herself up in the bed and seeing she was no longer in her riding clothes, she said, "Did Gilbert tend to my wounds after I fell from my horse?"

"Yes. That's what I was just saying. Even Stephen Hix commented on what excellent care you received. Why, he told Rupert and I that he could not have cared for you better himself. Why do you ask?"

"I thought I was dreaming he was here," Felicity said, sleepily.

"Who? Stephen or Gilbert?"

"Gilbert. I don't recall anything about Stephen Hix being here."

"Maybe you were unconscious when Stephen arrived, but Gilbert was here all right. As a matter of fact, he's never left your side since the accident."

Pausing, she called for Fannie. After a few moments the tired servant appeared in the doorway. "Yes, Miss?"

"Please find Mr. O'Flaherty and tell him that Mrs. Myles is awake." Directing her attention back to Felicity, she added, "I promised Gilbert that I would send for him if there was any change. He's going to be so disappointed that he wasn't here to see you wake up. At my insistence, he left here only a few minuets ago to stretch his legs."

Taking her seat beside Felicity, she asked, "Do you remember the accident?"

Lifting her hand to rub her head, she said wearily, "Yes. I was teasing Gilbert about being superstitious and I rode ahead. The mare must have gotten spooked and I was thrown. I remember falling...Then him saying something about me not dying. Actually, I think it was a prayer."

Felicity rubbed her temple to try and recall his exact words, able to see other images flash in her mind as well, she continued, "Then I think he did something to my leg. All I remember is feeling his hand on my leg and that it hurt so badly. I cried out I think, or I did in my dream anyway."

Annabelle listened intently, and seeing her friend pause, said, "Go on dear, you're doing quite well."

Smiling wearily, Felicity closed her eyes for a moment as if trying to get her thoughts clear, then said, "The next thing I remember is a loud crashing sound, and I felt him carrying me. I was either dreaming or I heard him say something about me bleeding so much. Yes. I'm sure he said it, because he had blood all over him. But he had no sleeves on his shirt. Does that make sense?"

"I don't know. I didn't arrive until much later. Perhaps you could ask Gilbert."

Agreeing with her, she said, "Yes." Feeling a sharp pain in her arm, she rubbed it beneath her covers, and winced. "My arm, is it broken?"

"Yes, dear. I'm afraid it is."

"I thought so. I vaguely recall Gilbert putting a sling around my neck and feeling my arm resting on my bare skin." Looking at her clothing, she realized she had been naked, and she turned to look over at her friend sheepishly.

"Annabelle, so many things are rushing through my mind, but they are all mixed up. I know I kept having the same dream I had the night before, but then I remember other things too. It's so blurry, I recall hearing Gilbert tell me he was sorry, that this was going to hurt and then I felt his hand on my arm. And he was right, the pain was so strong, I couldn't bear it. Then I was back on this cliff, looking at the fog. I remember feeling his hands removing my combs from my hair. I remember that clearly because the bun in the back of my neck was causing my head to hurt more and it felt so good when he brushed my hair to the side…and feeling his hands on my face…."

Felicity's voice trailed off as she recalled his mouth on hers, tenderly kissing her. She began to wonder if it had really happened or was just a dream. With her free arm she absentmindedly traced her lips with her fingertips, almost positive that he had done the same just before whispering, "Shh M'lady, it's all over now. Just rest, my bueddy."

"Felicity, are you all right?"

Opening her eyes and smiling wearily over at her friend, she whispered, "Fine, just trying to make sense of what was a dream and what really happened."

Gilbert, who had been standing in the doorway overhearing their conversation, cleared his throat. "Aye, I was just wondering the same. Are you really awake or am I just dreaming it? How do you feel? Do you need something?"

"Hello Gilbert. I'm fine." She smiled, lifting her head slightly, adding, "Sore and starved."

Annabelle, shocked that he was there, not having heard him come back in, asked, "When did you return?"

Looking puzzled, but still watching Felicity, he replied, "Return? I never left. I stepped outside for a second to get fresh water so I could brew up some coffee."

"Coffee? Mmm, that sounds lovely."

Gilbert smiled warmly at her, and stepped outside the room leaning over to pick up a tray that he had placed on a table just outside the room. Then entering, Annabelle noticed that on the wooden tray he was carrying was a cup of coffee, a bowl of beef broth that he had made earlier yesterday afternoon, and slice of bread.

"Here ya go, M'lady. Nothin' fancy mind ya, but the doctor said you should only have something light."

Annabelle, suddenly feeling awkward as if she were intruding on them, stood up. "Coffee does sound good. I think I'll venture into the kitchen and pour myself a cup as well."

"I'm sorry. I should have thought to pour you a cup, too."

"Think nothing of it, Gilbert. Obviously you had other pressing matters on your mind." Smiling, realizing the look she saw in Gilbert's eyes as he looked at Felicity wasn't that of a man only fulfilling an obligation. "If you'll excuse me, I'm sure you two have lots to discuss."

Reaching the door and hesitating just a moment to watch as Gilbert tenderly raised Felicity's head and helped steady her hand as she sipped the coffee, Annabelle's smile broadened. *Ah Felicity, how lucky you are to be loved again.*

~ Twenty-Two ~

From the porch of the cabin, Rupert exclaimed, "For gods sake Gilbert, be reasonable, Felicity would be much more comfortable in her own bed. It's not as if you've never stayed at Brookhaven before."

"Lest you haven't noticed, I ain't since we returned from London and buried Benjamin. It's not fittin'. Besides, I sure the hell ain't going to sit by her bedside now!"

Inhaling a deep breath and looking at the man he had grown so close to, Rupert said, "Right. I guess that would seem a bit awkward, since the woman you love shared that same bed with your friend."

Gilbert's eyes widened and he looked at Rupert, amused by his friend's observation. "Who the hell said anything about me being in love with Felicity?"

"You did. Perhaps not in words, but your eyes gave you away, old chap."

Expecting Rupert to have an objection at how he felt toward his cousin, Gilbert squared off his shoulders and said, "And?"

Rubbing his chin, all the while gazing at Gilbert, Rupert said, "And, I think you and Felicity would be good for one another. God knows the two of you deserve some happiness after the heartache you both have suffered. Putting that all aside though, old chap, I'm afraid you are in for more heartache. I know my cousin, and I'm uncertain if she'll ever allow herself to be loved again, even if she feels love for another in her own heart. She is fiercely loyal, and if I know Felicity, she will think loving again is a betrayal to her first love and in your case a dear friend as well. Underneath her genteel and soft exterior lies a stubborn woman when she has her mind set on something. So, I wish you all the luck in the world and hope you are not an impatient man, because I'm warning you, to change her mind you'll need the persuasiveness and diplomacy of ten men."

Gilbert chuckled, and said "Haven't you heard that we Irish wrote the book on diplomacy? Why I was taught that diplomacy is the ability to tell a man to go to hell so that he looks forward to making the trip. And although I'm not promising that by her choosing to open her heart to a man who truly loves her, will guarantee a lifetime of bliss, it sure the hell is a far cry better than the hell she's sentenced herself to live in now."

"Here, here! Well as I said before Gilbert, I wish you all the luck in the world. As for her returning to Brookhaven, let's make a compromise. We were intending to take a holiday to Plymouth at the end of the week, why not forgo Plymouth all together, and allow her to convalesce at a friend's estate in Glastonbury for a fortnight? The change of scenery will do us all some good."

"Glastonbury...Hmm, the Isle of Avalon...aye, and hopefully with that luck you so generously have bestowed upon me, Gwyn ap Nudd will send down a few of his fairies in my bidding."

"Right, well I'm sure on the ride there, you will fill us all on what you just meant." Glancing over to Fannie who had stepped onto the porch, he said, "Yes, what is it Fannie?"

"Mrs. Myles has been bathed and has asked to see Mr. O'Flaherty, sir."

"Fine. Fannie, go up to the house and have a few things of Mrs. Myles' brought to Mr. O'Flaherty's cabin. You and Mrs. Myles will be staying here until the end of the week. And do have your good husband come round for a chat, would you please?"

Gilbert interrupting said, "Rupert, rather than Fannie bring some of her things here, why not have Whitney stay with Felicity? The two of them could use the time alone together, and me and the lad could tend to his mother. That is if you'd be good enough to take my wee ones to stay at Ashwillow until we leave."

Shaking his head, Rupert chuckled. "Why is it I get the feeling you had this all planned out before I even arrived here today."

Grinning deviously, he jokingly said, "Why Rupert my good fellow, are you accusing yer mate of being conniving?"

"Cunning perhaps, but never conniving." Glancing at Fannie, he added, "You heard Mr. O'Flaherty, bring a few things of Whitney's over instead, Fannie."

"Yes, sir."

Obviously pleased by the smirk on his face, Gilbert excused himself. "Well if you'll excuse me, M'lady has beckoned her lowly servant." Noticing Annabelle at the door, he nodded his head politely as he passed her on his way back into his bedroom, and she smiled noticing his triumphant grin.

"Well, dear husband of mine, I'll give Gilbert his due, he sure must be a master in persuasion if he got you to change your mind so easily."

"You might want to hold those accolades, my dear, he's still has to convince Felicity, and that may prove to be his downfall."

From inside the small bedroom, Gilbert, closing the door behind him smiled at Felicity who was propped up and sitting in the bed wearing a pale blue dressing gown. "Well don't you look lovely this afternoon. Your bath must have agreed with you. Although I must say, I'll miss seeing you in my dressing gown."

Embarrassed by his comment, her cheeks turned rosy and she glanced down at the flower coverlet, and brushed it softly with her fingertips. "Gilbert, this is rather awkward to ask, especially after the wonderful care that you've given me, but when am I to return to my home?"

His smile faded slightly and he said, "Felicity, if we try to move you now there is a risk of jarring your arm or bumping your leg. Why not stay here for a few days? After all Felicity, this is your home too."

"No, this cabin is yours Gilbert; you have made it a warm and cozy home. When I arrived here yesterday morning...." Her voice trailed off for a moment, and sheepishly asked, "It was yesterday wasn't it?"

Grinning at her, he nodded his head and said, "There' abouts. A lot has happened since then, hasn't it?"

"Indeed it has. Where was I? Oh yes, regarding me returning home. I've inconvenienced you long enough and I really must insist I return to Brookhaven. Stephen Hix said my leg is healing remarkably well and I could get up tomorrow and walk around on it a bit, so Gilbert there really is no need for you to feel you must look after me any longer."

"First you are not inconveniencing me, Felicity, and second, you act as if caring for you has been an obligation. It's been my privilege. Why move you when you have everything you need right here?"

"That's very kind of you to say, but I can't stay Gilbert. Look around, your lovely tidy home is now littered with my belongings, not to mention, where are you intending to sleep? Surely, you must agree this is foolish when there are so many vacant rooms at Brookhaven. It seems far more practical if you are so inclined that is to continue looking after me, you could return to your old room there."

"Felicity, don't be frettin' yer pretty head about where I'm goin' to sleep, just think about getting better and let me be worrin' about the rest."

"How can I rest when I know I've disrupted your life? Please Gilbert make the arrangements to take me home."

"Ya know, I'm thinkin' that this is one of those times in life where a compromise is in order. Has it occurred to you that there are other matters to take into consideration other than the lack of space here at *our* cabin?"

Felicity smiled and nodded her head at his referencing the cabin as theirs.

"For one, has it occurred to you that while you're here, no one can be disturbin' ya like that cousin Anne of yers, and her friend the river rat? Then there is Whitney to consider; not that I'm pointing the blame, mind you, but you and he have drifted apart since his father's death. Can you think of a better way to mend that distance and help your son's feelings of hopelessness by caring for his mother? Besides Felicity, I enjoy taking care of you. So why would you want to return to Brookhaven when you're comfortable here?

"Gilbert all your points are valid, yet you still haven't addressed the issue of space."

"There's plenty of space and I'm not asking you stay for weeks, just a few days until we take the trip up the coast."

"The trip? Why I assumed that we would have to cancel since my accident."

"Well fishing might be out of the question, but there's no reason why we can't have you convalesce overlooking the Glastonbury Tor, now is there?"

Tilting her head, unfamiliar with the name, she said, "Glastonbury Tor?"

"Aye, a mystical isle which isn't an island at all, but has a rich history that has fascinated people over the ages with the mysterious lights that sparkle around the Tor at night."

"Mysterious lights around the Tor?"

"Aye, on the way there I'll explain the fables, including how centuries ago it's said that the adventures of King Arthur and the Knights of the round table took place there too. In fact, legend has it that he and Guinevere were wed at the abbey. So you see M'lady, this is perfect for convalescing."

"It sounds lovely, but taking a holiday doesn't resolve my inconveniencing you."

"Shh, I wasn't finished with my compromise, Felicity. You realize of course, you make it extremely difficult to negotiate when you're being so stubborn."

"Stubborn? Why Gilbert O'Flaherty what an unkind remark to say. Seems to me I'm not the one being stubborn here. We both know it makes perfect sense for me to return to Brookhaven. And I don't see why Anne would feel the need to bring her friends over to visit. Surely they wouldn't intrude when I'm incapacitated."

Casually he walked to his chest of drawers, opening the top drawer and removing the stack of clothing inside it as Felicity voiced her objections to his comment. Her voice trailed off seeing Gilbert continue moving clothing about in his drawers, and she said, "Have you heard a single word I've said, Gilbert?"

"Aye, every word M'lady." Pausing, he looked up at her. "You just said Anne wouldn't bring her friends over to intrude when you were incapacitated. Go on," he casually said, while setting her clothing inside the drawer he had just cleared.

"Well it's rather distracting when you're fussing about. What are you doing anyway? I thought we were negotiating?"

Nodding his head, he glanced in her direction and raised his brow. "Aye lass, we are. I was merely giving you time to spout off at me for pointing out how stubborn you're acting and move your things to the chest of drawers to tidy up a bit."

Flabbergasted, Felicity's mouth dropped, and she chuckled. "And you call me stubborn? Gilbert in case you haven't noticed, I haven't agreed to stay. So you might as well just remove my clothes and personal items right now."

Placing the last items of hers in the chest, he calmly shut the door and turned toward her with a smirk. "My, I wasn't aware you had such a nasty disposition when you get riled. And so easily, too." Shaking his head, he walked toward her and added, "Tell me M'lady, what else should I look forward to discovering these next few days?"

Again she laughed, shaking her head. "Oh no you don't. I may be incapacitated, but I know what you're up to and this is not my idea of a compromise."

Innocently, he asked, "What? I was merely pointing out that you are not an inconvenience to me. Look for yourself, there's plenty of room for your belongings and mine, and with a few minor adjustments with the furniture there will be room for your chaise that Montgomery is bringing over."

"Chaise?" Shaking her head, she looked seriously at him. "Gilbert, as much as I appreciate everything you are doing for me, this is foolish. There's no room for a chaise. Why you can barely move around in here as it is with all the furniture you keep bringing in to accommodate me. And you still haven't addressed where you're to sleep if I'm in your bed. As much as I love being here, this will never work."

All the while she was talking, Gilbert calmly moved furniture to the other side of the room then noting that she was finished, he said, "Brace yourself M'lady, you're going for a wee ride."

"What? Gilbert please don't do this, I haven't agreed to stay."

Pulling the foot of the bed toward the window, he walked toward her, leaned over, and placed his fingers over her lips. "Enough. It's settled. You said you loved being here, and since I love having you and I'm making room, there's nothing more to discuss. The negotiations are over."

"Over? When did they begin? Correct me if I'm mistaken but compromise means a concession, to my way of thinking no comprise has been made on your end."

"Surely you jest, I made room for your belongings and am in the process of moving the furniture. Does that not show my willingness to come to terms with you?"

Before Felicity could respond Gilbert placed his index finger on her lips. Feeling his touch she recalled her dream — their eyes locked, and her heart began beating faster feeling his breath on her cheek. Nodding her head slowly, she muttered, 'Fine."

Gilbert slowly lowered his hand and huskily whispered, "Thank you." Then standing again, he continued gliding the bed from its current location to angle it overlooking the window outside. "With that settled, what would you and Whitney like for dinner?"

~

From the fireside chairs in the lounge, Rupert looked over at Annabelle and said, "What the devil is going on in there? Why it sounds like he's moving furniture."

Annabelle just nodded her head, smiling. Her eyes focused outdoors watching Montgomery and Jimmy approaching, carrying Felicity's chaise. Turning toward her husband she said, "Well, it would appear that not only has Gilbert managed to convince Felicity that she is staying, he's making room for her furniture as well."

Shaking his head while returning to reading his newspaper, he chuckled under his breath. "Irish diplomacy at work."

"What?" Annabelle asked, while opening the door for Montgomery and Jimmy.

"I'll tell ya later, my dear." Seeing along with the men, that Anne, Whitney, Jacque, and James were following closely behind, Rupert stood, and shook his head wearily. "Well let's hope it applies for the English as well." Lifting his finger for the men to wait, he walked across the room and knocked at the door of Gilbert's bedroom. Peeking his head in and seeing that the furniture was completely rearranged, he motioned for Gilbert. "Old chap, can I see you for a moment?"

Frowning slightly, Gilbert approached the door, and whispered, "What is it?"

"Felicity has guests."

Judging by Rupert's look, Gilbert knew who he was referring to as guests, and immediately Gilbert's jaw clenched firmly. "I'll not be having the likes of him in my home."

"I'll take care of it Gilbert, not to worry. You stay in here with Felicity. What shall I do about Anne?"

"Have her wait until Whitney has time to visit with his mother. The lad comes first."

"Right. The chaise has arrived by the way."

"Good, have Montgomery bring it in."

Opening the door wider, Rupert motioned for the men to come forth. Once they had passed, Whitney, inching his way by the others still gathering outside the door and seeing Gilbert, called out enthusiastically, "Uncle Gilbert, are Mother and I staying with you for a few days?"

Escorting Montgomery and Jimmy Bartlett back out of the room after they had placed the chaise where directed, Gilbert ,rubbing the eager boy's head while shutting the door, said, "Aye lad. Thought it would be nice if you and me took care of your mum for awhile. How does that sound?"

Glancing between Gilbert and Felicity, he smiled. "Splendid." Inching his way closer to Felicity, he asked with concern, "Are you still in pain, Mother?"

"Hardly at all, dear." Smiling warmly at her son, Felicity stretched out her right arm. "Now come and give me a hug and kiss. I've missed you."

Gilbert leaned against the wall giving the two of them some privacy while listening to the conversation taking place outdoors. Listening to Rupert's comments, his eyes danced merrily.

"Ah, Jacque and James. What good fortune you arrived today. Perhaps you would be good enough to assist me in getting the O'Flaherty children settled in at Ashwillow? Since Felicity and Whitney are going to be spending some time with Gilbert, Annabelle and I will be tending to the children."

Anne, hearing Rupert's comment, huffed, "Surely you can't be seriously entertaining the notion of Felicity convalescing in this…this shabby little cottage when she has such a beautiful home of her own. Rupert, these arrangements are utterly preposterous! I demand you take my cousin to Brookhaven, where she can receive the proper care she needs."

"Anne, might I remind you, you are hardly in the position to demand anything. This is Felicity's decision, and I happen to agree with her wholeheartedly. And as far as the cottage goes, why I find it rather charming and warm, nestled amongst the trees with the babbling brook nearby lends itself to the serenity that dear Felicity needs after such a harrowing accident."

"Be that as you may, I hardly think *that man* is qualified to care for Felicity properly."

Shaking his head as that of a father correcting a child, Rupert said, "Regretfully Anne, again I must differ with you. Not only did Gilbert save Felicity's life with his quick thinking, stopping her from bleeding to death after her dreadful fall, 'that man' as you so eloquently have just called him, carried her over two miles to safety. Whereupon, he set her arm that had broken through her flesh and was bleeding profusely, he tended to her other wounds, and since has given her exemplary care. So, I would say none of us should be worried about Felicity's welfare while she is under Gilbert's excellent care."

Pasting an insincere smile to her lips that did nothing to conceal the resentment she held for Rupert, she ardently replied, "How enlightening. Pity none of you saw fit to notify me of Felicity's condition until this afternoon. Perhaps then I too could have been privy to the heroic efforts of Gilbert rescuing Felicity at her hour of need."

"There were more pressing concerns my dear, than notifying you and your entourage. Besides, Felicity only awoke early this morning and since she was no longer in a life and death situation, it hardly seemed necessary to cause you undue stress."

"How thoughtful of you, Rupert. Now, if you'll let *us* pass we wish to see Felicity."

Still standing at the entrance of the cabin, Rupert politely said, "That won't be possible as Whitney is in with his mother at the moment. And as you so graciously pointed out earlier Anne, Gilbert's home is rather small so I'm afraid there won't be room for everyone, only family." Directing his comment to Jacque and James, but still addressing Anne he said, "I'm sure these fine gentlemen won't mind waiting to visit with Felicity when she returns to Brookhaven."

Jacque cleared his throat, clearly amused by the situation, nodded his head politely and said, "Rupert, speaking for James and myself, please send our fondest regards to dear Felicity. As I recall, you mentioned something about needing our assistance, old friend. How can we help?"

Gilbert, hearing all he needed to, stepped away from the wall smiling, and hearing Felicity bring up Glastonbury and not receiving the reaction she had hoped for from her son, she looked over to Gilbert for assistance.

Leaning over to Whitney with sparkling eyes, he said, "Known by some still as Avalon Isle, lad."

Whitney's eyes glistened with excitement, and he whispered excitedly, "Avalon...Really! Oh Mother, that's where King Arthur and the knights of the round table held Camelot."

Smiling she said, glancing at Gilbert, "So I've been told."

"Did you know Mother that Arthur was born out of wedlock and was raised by Merlin the great wizard? When all of England was in search of the rightful heir to the throne, he as a boy, pulled a sword from a stone." Whitney paused, theatrically mimicking pulling out an imaginary sword from the floor. Then raising his arm high over his head, he boisterously said, "Excalibur!"

Amused by her son's excitement but puzzled asked, "Excalibur?"

"Aye lass, the powerful and mystical sword of King Arthur."

Oh Mother, I can't believe we're going to Avalon...I've never been to anywhere that we've read about in a book before."

"Ah, so this is a story from a book, but not real then?"

"Oh no Mother, it's real alright." Looking for Gilbert to back him up, he said, "Uncle Gilbert, tell her? Read to her Le Morte D'Arthur."

"Lad, your mother doesn't want to hear of King Arthur and Lady Guinevere; perhaps I could read another book that would be more to her liking."

Seeing the disappointment on Whitney's face, Felicity said, "I would love to read this book."

"No Mother, Uncle Gilbert reads it for us."

Smiling at him, seeing his face light up again, Felicity glanced over at Gilbert. "If it's not too much trouble, will you read to me about King Arthur? And perhaps this next week you would enlighten me on your fairies as well, Gilbert. Seems there's a lot I need to know before our great adventure to Avalon."

Smiling, he bowed as addressing royalty. "I'm at your disposal M'lady. But first, let me move you over in your bed so Whitney can snuggle close."

Whitney, moving from the side of the bed, watched as Gilbert leaned onto the bed and gingerly placed Felicity on the far left side so that her arm and leg were protected. Again as he held her close their eyes locked, and Felicity felt her cheeks turn crimson. Replacing the coverlet snugly around her, noticing her rosy cheeks, concerned that she had come down with a fever, he asked while instinctively placing the back of his hand over her forehead, "Are you feeling all right, Felicity?"

Feeling her heart beating faster, she looked away, whispering, "Fine. Just a little flushed is all." Glancing at Whitney and patting the pillow beside her, she watched indiscreetly as Gilbert went to the small bookshelf beside his chest of drawers to retrieve the book. Finding the one he was searching for he glanced at Felicity again and said, "Lad, only a few chapters this afternoon. Your mother needs her rest."

~

Anne, who had been waiting for over an hour, began nervously tapping her fingers on the top of the chair's arm and huffed, "Honestly, what could she possibly have to say for this long? And to a boy, no less? Besides, it's only his voice I hear, not Felicity's and Whitney's."

Annabelle looking annoyingly at Anne's hand, said, "If I'm not mistaken, Gilbert is reading to them. And keep your voice down, the walls are thin."

Groaning, Anne rolled her eyes and spat under her breath, "How quaint." Crossing her arms over her chest she mockingly whispered, "He rescued her, he cooks for her, tends to her every need and now he even reads to her? Perhaps it's not wise for me to take Kathleen after all this evening, perhaps she should stay and chaperone." Seeing Annabelle's disapproving look she added, "Oh honestly, not even you, the mistress of goodness, is going to say you don't see what's going on around here, right beneath your very nose."

Ignoring her obviously negative innuendo, Annabelle smiled at her and said innocently, in a low voice, "I do indeed, I was just wondering how I might get Rupert to indulge me with such pampering."

Angrily shaking her head, she snarled, "I would expect such a comment from you. Honestly, I don't know why I bother sometimes."

Taking everything she had not to laugh aloud, Annabelle whispered softly almost mockingly, "Now Anne, should I be offended by that comment? Or would you have the lowly mistress of goodness, now try to prove that I am worthy of your friendship?"

Anne's mouth dropped and she glared at her. "Well how very cunning of you Annabelle, I see some of your sister's nasty disposition rubbed off on you."

Shifting in her chair, feeling her blood begin to boil at being compared to Lavinia, Annabelle remained composed on the surface. "How amusing you should try to compare me to my sister when you are the one who has shamefully been plotting against one of your own family members. From where I sit, I'd say that it would appear that you have been greatly influenced by Lavinia, you being friends with her for so many years."

"Plot? Whatever do you mean? I've done nothing of the sort."

Annabelle, not wavering from her opponent's glare chortled, "Come now Anne, you seem to forget whom I'm married to. Rupert and I have a very close relationship; we share everything. Do you honestly think I don't know that you've made a deal with James Sterling in exchange for his help in securing the marriage between Victoria and my half-brother?"

It was Anne who shifted in her chair this time. "My but don't we have a suspicious mind Annabelle? First accusing me of plotting, and now I've supposedly made deals as well? What an active imagination you Bailey-Smythe's have. I'd be careful my dear, or you might end up in an asylum like your sister."

Not the least provoked by her comment, she said softly, "Anne, we both know what sent Lavinia to that asylum and it wasn't due to any mental illness,. She had a disease. Shall we discuss the disease my sister had, which if memory serves me right, Edward contracted from her?"

Anne shot up from her chair and spat in a hushed voice so not to be overheard, "How dare you! I will not tolerate another second of this!"

"How dare I? How dare you! What audacity you have to walk in here and continue hurling innuendoes that there are improprieties going on between Gilbert and Felicity. Now either you sit down this instant, or so help me God, I'll do more than hint around to improprieties of you and your family. I give you my word that I shall openly share a laundry list for all to hear."

Anne shook with rage and took her seat, glaring at Annabelle. "Seems I've underestimated you, Annabelle, but I assure you, it won't happen again."

Smiling ruefully at her opponent, she whispered calmly, "Anne, there is no need for either of us to threaten one another, nor be enemies, for that matter, especially over Gilbert caring for Felicity."

Taking in a deep cleansing breath and changing her tone, she leaned over and put her hand on Anne's knee as a sign of sincerity. "Anne, since his arrival, that man has proven time and time again what a kindhearted and genuinely devoted father and friend he is. Prior to Benjamin's death, he gave his word to him that he would take care of Whitney and Felicity, and for the last nine months that is precisely what Gilbert has done. Every day he took Whitney along with his children on walks, riding with him, whittling, reading to him, all the while poor Felicity was completely withdrawn, grieving in her own private hell. It was Gilbert who snapped her out of such sorrowful depths, so it's only natural for him to tend to her now. Anne, from the bottom of my heart, I'm truly sorry that you didn't have someone to help you through your grieving. But we did try, that's why we helped you keep Victoria's pregnancy and later her having a child out of wedlock, a secret. Surely, you must know it wasn't to protect the name of another Bailey-Smythe. That name was tarnished years ago by Father and Lavinia. And truth be known, I was pleased the name ended with Father's death. Until of course, we discovered that Joseph was Father's son and he too followed in Father's footsteps, fathering an illegitimate son himself."

"What purpose does it serve anyone to bring up all these painful memories, Annabelle?"

Having to correct Anne again for speaking in a regular voice, she whispered, "Please Anne, keep your voice down."

Anne responded with an indignant wave of the hand and Annabelle continued. "I've watched you turn from a dear and kind woman to one filled with bitterness and resentment. When there is no need. You have a wonderful man who loves you, and has been waiting patiently for you to be rid of all the pain and hate that you carry in your heart. Please, I'm begging you for your sake, and Felicity's, don't continue to try to have her suffer just because you did. It will only destroy you in the end. Just look what hate did to Lavinia."

Anne, tears welling up in her eyes, looked over at Annabelle. "You can't begin to understand the pain I feel, you have a husband who loves you. He didn't disgrace you and betray your love with a woman you thought of as a friend. Did you know that I had helped support Lavinia for years when you and Rupert shunned her? Only to be repaid for my kindness by having her seduce my husband and try to infect us all with her disease, just so she could get back at Felicity and Benjamin. Why should I suffer because Felicity loved a man who was obviously weak enough to be seduced by power and greed?"

Gasping, Annabelle said in a hushed voice, "Anne, how can you speak ill of the dead like this? Benjamin was a good man who made mistakes yes, but he more than made up for them following his ill-fated marriage to my sister, which she had annulled so she could go run off and marry James Sterling. Who in my opinion is despicable."

"Despicable? Why whatever do you mean? Wasn't it James Sterling who came to my aid when no one else would; namely you and Rupert? You knew how desperate I was for that low-life, half-brother of yours to take responsibility for his actions and marry Victoria, yet neither of you would help me."

Furious, Annabelle glared at her and in a harsh whisper, said, "Is that how you see it, Anne? Who hid you and your daughter away in their chateau, and lied to your friends saying Victoria was enrolled in art school? It sure wasn't that man; it was Rupert and me. And not because we cared a damn about Joseph's reputation either, it was for you. You, Anne! Because we couldn't bear for you to suffer."

Shaking her head in denial, she murmured, "If that were true then why wouldn't you help me when I found Joseph, and make him return?"

"You know the reason Anne. You've known since the day Whitney was born."

"Ah so now I'm to be included in dear Felicity's tragic secret?" Anne snidely whispered.

Hearing her sound so flippant, Annabelle shook with rage and hissed, "Don't you ever, and I mean ever again, treat that horrific incident with such indifference. Did you find her in her bed, curled up in a ball whimpering in shock after that beast nearly choked her to death as he maliciously raped her? No! I did. That's why I knew of it. Not because she trusted me more, or loved me best, but because I was the one who found her after what he had done to her. As God is my witness, every day since, I wished to hell Rupert had killed him for what he did, rather than merely scar him."

Anne quivered and closed her eyes, tears running down her face. "I swear I didn't realize the depth of her pain."

Gilbert, who had mistakenly overheard the last part of the conversation, entering the room to inform them that both Felicity and Whitney had fallen asleep, cleared his throat, and hoarsely whispered, "Excuse me. Perhaps this conversation would be best taken far from here. Might I remind you both, that Felicity has just been through a harrowing experience, not just falling from a horse, but losing her husband as well? The last thing she needs right now is to be reminded of the hell she has lived through, or worse, let her beloved son find out what his precious mother had to endure at the hands of a monster. Thank heavens the two of them are fast asleep so they did not overhear this conversation. Annabelle, I know you love Felicity and you were trying to help her, but please—not here."

"Of course, I'm so ashamed."

Nodding to Annabelle, he then directed his attention at Anne and said coldly, "As for you, Anne, all I can say is, be careful when you are playing with the devil, because you will get burned." Then addressing them both, Gilbert finished by saying, "Now I am going back and try to forget what I just heard. But before I go, I'm begging you, please, let that poor woman inside that room heal. God knows she deserves that much."

With that he closed the door and both Annabelle and Anne cried in silence as Gilbert tried desperately to erase the images that Annabelle had described so vividly. Checking to see that Whitney was sound asleep, he walked over to Felicity's side of the bed. Seeing tears streaming down her closed eyes, without saying a word, he leaned over and gingerly picked her up from her bed. Felicity didn't struggle, only rested her head on his shoulder. "I'm so ashamed, no one was ever to hear of that dreadful night."

Carrying her to the chaise, Gilbert gently rocked Felicity in his lap and whispered, "Shh, don't cry anymore M'lady, it doesn't matter. They did me a favor, least now I can put my mind to rest rather than conjure up my own notions. So let's you and me just think of it as a bad nightmare from the past. Let the fairies come and take away the pain, so it won't be hurtin' ya anymore, lass."

Lifting her head, she whispered, "Is there really such a fairy that could do that?"

Smiling lovingly at her, he said, "Aye. There are wee ones that can do all your bidding, even mend the pain you harbor in your heart."

Sighing, she whispered, "Even if there aren't fairies, it's comforting to think there are." Suddenly feeling awkward, knowing she shouldn't be sitting in the arms of a man, particularly a man who looked at her with such tenderness, she said, "Gilbert, I'm very tired. Will you please take me back to *your*...the bed now."

Nodding, he did as she asked, and once she was resting on her pillow, he whispered softly, "Sleep lass, and let yourself start to believe in sunny days ahead. Anything is possible, if you have the heart for it."

Closing her eyes, Felicity thought of his words to Annabelle and Anne, then what he had just said to her. *Oh Gilbert, I wish there really were fairies who could mend my broken heart.*

~ Twenty-Three ~

Carrying Kathleen's packages, watching her nod alluringly at the male guests taken by her beauty, James smiled. It had been quite some time since men had looked at him enviously, being with such a desirable woman, and he drank in the feeling of superiority.

Reaching her room and looking for the key in her beaded drawstring purse, Kathleen said, "I must say James, I can't recall the last time that I've enjoyed a gentleman's company as much as I have yours." Finding her key, she placed it in his free hand and smiled suggestively. "Now why is it though, I have the distinct impression that shopping with a young woman all afternoon was not exactly stimulating for you?"

James grinned at her choice of words as he opened the door, whereupon Kathleen cocked her head and sashayed into the room, completely undaunted at the prospect of entertaining a male companion alone. "If you would just put my lovely purchases in the drawing room, I'll sort through them later. I'd offer you refreshments, but water is all I have." Her voice carried as she stepped into a separate room of the suite. Returning with her hat, gloves, and matching suit coat removed, she smiled, noticing that James had pulled out a silver flask from the breast pocket of his suit and was extending it toward her.

"Fear not Kathleen, a man in my position comes prepared. Care to join me in the nectar of the gods?"

Walking over to where he stood, she raised her brow suggestively while taking the flask from his hand. Then extending her head back far enough for him to gaze down at the top of her firm breasts pressing against the bodice of her cream-colored chiffon blouse, she purred, "And what position would that be, James?"

His eyes never wavered from her as she drank from his flask. "I can assure you, not in the position I would like to be right now," he growled huskily.

Smiling seductively, returning his flask and slowly caressing her fingers against his hand, she cooed provocatively, "Yes, I would imagine you would feel that way under the circumstances." Pausing long enough to be certain that she had his undivided attention, her tenor changed from that of sexual innuendo to a mocking tone.

"Especially, since the lady fair who you've pined after for so many years has slipped right through your fingers. Even as we speak, I'm sure Gilbert, with his big strapping arms and broad chest...." Her voice trailed off before finishing her sentence and she calculatingly began brushing her fingers along his jacket to further antagonize him. "Where was I...Oh yes, Gilbert surely must be tending to the vulnerable widow's every need. I almost envy Felicity. I know what I would do with such a virile man."

James, not amused by Kathleen's attempts at trying to provoke jealousy in him, hastily took a long swig from his flask. Feeling the warmth of the aged brandy glide down his throat, he responded snidely, "Need I remind you, my dear, that your meal ticket is being yanked right from under your nose?"

"Is it? Not if I've already moved on to someone else who can afford me even a greater level of respectability and financial security than Gilbert O'Flaherty had to offer."

Judging by the glimmer in his eyes, Kathleen knew that James had assumed she was referring to him, just as she had hoped.

"Ah, so then should I assume that you are now looking to open up negotiations, Kathleen? Although, I must say if that was your intent, we could have forgone wasting so much time shopping today."

Smiling ruefully at him, she cooed, "And miss out on being adorned with such exquisite care by a man obviously accustomed in making a woman feel appreciated? Now pray tell, James, why would I have been so foolish as to do that? Especially when I've already completed quite a rather lucrative arrangement with my dear friend, Mrs. Freeport?"

Starting to become annoyed by her toying with him, he hastily corrected her. "Mrs. Freeport? You mean Mr. Freeport, don't you, Kathleen?"

Shaking her head cunningly, hearing the edge in his voice, she continued to stroke his arm with her fingertips, and said, "No. I mean Mrs. Anne Freeport. They were married in a lovely garden ceremony just this past Thursday, midst the quaint surroundings near Gilbert's cabin, so that Felicity could witness the joyous occasion. Although I must say, I was surprised to see that you weren't on the rather exclusive guest list."

Any amusement that James had felt from their little tit-for-tat- faded and he grasped her arms, and spat, "What are you rambling about Kathleen?"

Glancing at her arm, she said firmly, "Unhand me at once, James! You're hurting me."

James, complying with her demand, released her arm and spat indignantly, "That's preposterous! Jacque would never have married Anne without inviting me; not to mention we've been in each other's company since Friday and neither of them have said a word."

"Yes well, I would imagine that's because Mr. Sterling, you are not one of their favorite people right now and they had other pressing matters on their minds; like helping Joseph Pike steal your company right from under your nose."

"Rubbish, Jacque would never do such an unscrupulous thing as that!"

Her face becoming very serous, she said, "Oh I assure you what I say is true. It appears that Anne, after hearing from Annabelle how maliciously you attacked her cousin back in New York, and overcome with grief and remorse for consorting with the devil, went to Jacque. Who was extremely sympathetic to poor Anne. And he offered to assist his new stepson—who is unscrupulous and rather knowledgeable of all your business affairs—to begin his own import and export business. Which as it turned out, wasn't very difficult since you gave him a free hand to oversee your dealings while you foolishly remained in England in hopes of winning the heart of a woman who despises you." Shaking her head remorsefully, she added, "Clearly James, it appears that it is not I who is need of renegotiating, but rather, you. Especially now that Joseph and Victoria are well established and are in no need of your help. Now that Anne has revoked your invitation to be reintroduced back into her circle of friends, just how do you intend to see your precious Felicity?"

Outraged by Kathleen's comments, James started for the door, but stopped in his tracks at Kathleen's next snide remark.

"If you're intending to discuss this with the blushing bride and groom, I'm sorry to inform you that they are on their way to meet up with the Robbins, O'Flahertys and Myles family. A multi-celebration of sorts; to welcome the newest member, rekindle the unity they once all shared, and a well needed holiday for Felicity to recuperate from her harrowing experience. In fact, I would say the festivities should well be underway, since they left this morning long before we went shopping. Just think James, while you were showering me with all your divine attention in hopes to bed me, no doubt, Gilbert, I'm sure was further establishing an even deeper relationship with his precious, 'M'lady'. And judging by the way those two look at one another these days, I should imagine it won't be long before he makes her his own freely, without force."

"You're lying!" he turned, raising his voice.

"Oh James, such bad form is so beneath you." Glancing in the direction of the closed door to the bedchamber, she called, "Oh Matilda...."

Kathleen glanced over at James victoriously, who did little to mask his surprise, obviously believing they were alone as his eyes trailed to Anne's personal maid as she opened the door.

"Yes, miss?"

"When did Mr. and Mrs. Freeport say they would be returning from their holiday?"

"They didn't give a specific date miss, just said in a fortnight."

"Thank you, Matilda. Would you please run out and purchase some refreshments for Mr. Sterling." Turning her attention to the stunned James, she said, "What do you prefer? We have so much to discuss this evening that I doubt your little flask will be sufficient."

As James gave instructions to Matilda, Kathleen shrewdly took a seat in the center of couch in hopes that he would join her there, rather than in the chair across from her. Seeing him turn toward her, she gently patted the seat beside her. "Come, James. I promise not to be cruel to you any longer. Surely you must have several unanswered questions, and I assure you, I am at your disposal for the rest of the evening."

He glanced at her, then motioned at his jacket as if requesting if requesting permission to remove it, whereupon she responded agreeably, "Please, by all means, make yourself comfortable."

Her heart began beating faster as she watched him remove his jacket and loosen his neck scarf, knowing that tonight at last, she would finally have her fantasies fulfilled on her terms. Anticipating thoughts of such a fierce and handsome man ravishing her sent waves of excitement through her and she thought, *You won't have to force yourself on me, James. I gladly want all of you and not just dessert.*

After answering all of James's questions and still detecting the cutting sarcasm in his voice, she said, "James, you don't need to continue to be so defensive, haven't I just answered all your questions direct and truthfully?"

"Ah, so now should I believe that you no longer enjoy seeing me squirm, when today you clearly enjoyed plotting against me?"

"I did, very much in fact." Noticing that Matilda had returned, she added, "Matilda, that will be all for tonight. I'll see you first thing in the morning. And do be prompt."

"Yes, miss," the servant responded, letting herself out.

Standing, Kathleen smiled at James, and cooed, "Let me serve you, James." Pouring both of them a glass of brandy, she glided slowly and seductively back to where he sat sulking and obviously still angered by knowing he had been duped. Kathleen knew he was searching his mind, trying to figure a way back into Anne's good graces and so she began speaking softly where she had left off prior to Matilda's return.

Leaning over the coffee table so he could view her pert breasts, she smiled at him. "As I was saying James, I did rather enjoy toying with you. And although Anne made me promise I would not allow you to know until we had returned, the way I chose to tell you was strictly of my own doing. You see, since the first time I met you at old man Strombly's, you have taken great pleasure in watching the effect you had on me. From the beginning, it was clear I desired you, yet you placed conditions on both of us enjoying each other's company. Which was very unkind of you; so I decided to see just how much I could arouse you. Especially today in particular, when we no longer had anything the other needed or wanted to barter for except the craving of each other's body."

Taking his drink, James gulped it back and said, "Go on Kathleen, you definitely have my undivided attention."

Kathleen lowered her eyes, sipped slowly at her drink, enjoying the full warming effects of the brandy. Raising her eyes to his, sensually wetting her lips with the tip of her tongue, certain he was taking in her every move; she returned to her seat and offered her remaining brandy to him. "Would you care for this James or dessert?"

Intrigued by her comment, he huskily said, "Dessert?"

Placing the brandy on the table between herself and James, she said, "Dessert was a term that Mr. Strombly used for a particular pleasure we indulged in. Now you can either have dessert or the brandy, but not both."

"Hmm, do tell me Kathleen, what did Strombly find so enjoyable, that I would choose it over the nectar of the gods?"

Gliding from the couch like a Persian cat, she knelt before him and slowly began to unbutton her blouse as she spoke softly, her eyes fixed on his. "After my father and mother sold me at the age of eight to be Strombly's servant for a few shillings a week, he took me to his home in London."

Tugging gently at her now unfastened blouse, Kathleen slowly slid the sheer garment over her shoulders before continuing. "That evening before I could have dinner, he took me into his bedchamber, whereupon he locked me in, removed his trousers and glided my hand over his enlarged manhood. Cupping his hand over mine, he continued to push my hand more and more quickly up and down until he was gratified. Then looking down at me he said sternly, 'Girl, before you are to eat tomorrow, I shall have my dessert.'"

Stopping long enough to untie the drawstrings of her corset, slowly and deliberately, she released the strings from the loops. Seeing his breathing becoming deeper, exposing more of herself for him to gaze upon, she said, "For days following that first evening, when he came for me and asked for dessert I would tell him I wasn't hungry. Until finally starved, I gave him his dessert eagerly so that I could eat. For a while this was enough for him, until he forced me to gratify him not with my hand, but my mouth."

James, understanding what she meant, inhaled deeply. Between her removing her corset fully, exposing her full rounded breasts to him, and the effects of the brandy, James slid further into his seat. "What happened then?" he asked eagerly.

Unfastening the buttons of her skirt, she said, "Then old man Strombly declared on my eleventh birthday—knowing I had become a woman—that as a present from him, he was going to give *me* dessert. There I lay on his bed with my skirt hiked up to my neck, frightened and scared as he stroked me with one hand and himself with the other, until he cried out." Kathleen's voice trailed off as she slid her unfastened skirt, hooped slip, and pantaloons over her taut stomach and James gazed at her, paralyzed where he sat, anticipating all of her. Briefly standing to let her clothing fall around her feet, and seeing his appreciation for her nakedness, her long delicate fingers began caressing her shapely figure. Kneeling back in front of him, with his eyes transfixed on her, she moaned softly, brushing her hand slowly below her stomach.

In a slow, hushed whisper, matching the movement of her trailing hand she spoke again.

"For months this continued, and slowly I began enjoying the sensations he brought to me, stirring beneath his touch. Then one night, he lowered his head between my legs; and that evening I knew why he had groaned with such pleasure. I screamed out, wanting more, and he gratified himself by rocking up against the side of my bed like a wild dog as he drank in the sweet nectar of my desire."

Kathleen paused and looked at James, seeing he had begun stirring in his seat, his manhood bulging between his legs. "After that night, if I wanted something special—a new dress, shoes, tutoring—I would offer him dessert rather than him having to ask for it in the confines of his locked room. My reward for such actions was that my gifts became larger. Strombly, obviously pleased, viewed himself as godlike for having made me long for dessert, a child, begging this old wrinkled man to be aroused. Over time, my yearning to have the same gifts bestowed on me that his daughter was given freely, became foremost on my mind. I discovered how easily I could entice him, especially as he aged. I became his obsession. He would want dessert served in his office, in the coach as we drove to church, or even as he made an excuse to leave dinner guests waiting so that he could be satisfied."

James, fully engorged by the vivid picture that Kathleen had painted for him, whispered hoarsely, "And when did Strombly decide he wanted to experience all of you?"

"He never did, always telling me that he would open my package on a very special occasion. The evening that you came to his home with Jacque, he was evidently upset at how I had been taken by your charms. Don't you recall him saying that he needed my help finding imported cigars for you and Jacque? When I had refused to accommodate him, telling him where they were instead, he became outraged. Fearful that I would give to you what he had been saving all those years, he came to my room after you retired. He demanded that my special package be opened that night, saying he hadn't saved his prize to lose it to the likes of you. As he came up on my bed, me begging for dessert instead, understanding fully that this was all that I had that was truly mine, he pushed me into the pillow. Frantically I tried to keep him from forcefully taking me. In his struggle to take what he thought was his, he began grabbing at his chest, groaning in pain. I scurried off the bed and watched as he kept gasping for air, clinging to his chest with one hand while trying to reach for me with the other. His last living words, were that my package belonged to him. When he collapsed, I was frightened, knowing that he couldn't be found dead in my room or I'd be thrown out onto the streets, so I came in search of you to help get him back to his own room. Strombly had told me all about your past indiscretions, so I knew I could make you help me."

Oblivious to the fact that from the first moment he had met her she had been negotiating for services rendered, just as she had been taught to do by Oscar Strombly; fascinated by her story and interested only in satisfying his own lustful greed, he asked, "So, are you telling me Kathleen, that your *special package* is still unbroken?"

"I suppose some might say that, since I've never been with a man fully."

"My God." he hissed. "Why did you tell me all of this?"

"Because from the moment I saw you, I knew it was you I wanted to give myself to. For months I have yearned for you, imagined what it would be like to feel you open my package. Yet all you wanted was to taunt me, or make arrangements. Now you have nothing to bargain with James; so again I ask you, would you care for dessert or for that brandy? You can have one or the other, but not both." Looking at him, seeing him lusting for her body, Kathleen felt empowered and no longer like a victim. Now she was setting the terms.

As Kathleen had anticipated, he chose her, leaning forward, eagerly panting, he growled, "Dessert."

Triumphantly, she guided him back on the couch, and skillfully began unfastening his trousers as he yanked to remove the rest of his clothing.

Pleased by his eagerness, she proceeded to describe her terms. "James, I will give you dessert willingly, as long as I, too, get my dessert. And then, I want you to open my package, knowing I give you this freely, too. All I ask in return is for you to make this a special occasion. One that I have waited for and dreamed about all these years. And please James, above all else; make me scream out as I did that first night I came to know the pleasure of being aroused. Loud enough to drown out the memories of that bastard ever having brought me pleasure. I want to remember it as you who quenched my hunger and desire. Can you do that?"

Feeling her delicate hand on his manhood, he gasped, "Yes, you lustful wench, I'll gladly satisfy what Strombly never could."

After Kathleen had skillfully sent his body into gratifying spasms, she gingerly began caressing her inner thighs and watched as she aroused him again by stirring a longing within her body by her own hand. Never had he witnessed a woman touching herself in such a way, which ignited such a hunger in him that eagerly he wanted to fulfill her desires as she had done for him. Lowering himself from the couch onto the floor, he glided his broad shoulders between her raised knees becoming even further aroused at how freely she expressed the pleasure she felt by her touch, moaning slightly. Lowering his head between her legs, his tongue penetrated her, and Kathleen's moaning became louder and more frequent, intensifying his longing to please her. Becoming more aroused, her pelvis began matching his thrusting tongue until she was moaning, "Yes.... More James...please, more."

Squirming at his touch, she raised her head slightly and wrapped her hands around his head , crying out softly as her hips rocked feverishly up and down against his face. Then collapsing, spent, she released her grip from his head and breathlessly gasped as he inched his tongue up her taut stomach and his hand cupped her breasts. Lowering himself over her body, feeling his bare skin against hers, she again gasped, "Oh, my God!"

James felt empowered by her expressions of pleasure at feeling his skin touching hers. Waves of raw desire rushed through his veins; he had to please her. To further excite her, he sucked her nipple, gently at first, but as her excitement increased, so did his hunger until he was biting her hard nipple. Completely aroused again, Kathleen responded by arching her back and groaning, begging for more. As he deliberately pressed his manhood near her inner thigh to further entice her, rocking closer to the mound of hair between her legs, she raised herself up to him, gasping, "Oh James, please; now...I saved myself for you...please!" she cried out.

Never had he felt such raw desire. Beneath him was a woman who had just given him such erotic pleasure, unmatched by anything he had ever known, and now she begged for him to take something that only he would have for the first time. Raising her arms above her head, propping himself up so that he could watch as he entered her, he groaned as she raised her hips to take all of him. "Yes." she groaned, immediately matching his rhythm until she buried her head in his shoulder to help muffle her screams of ecstasy. Knowing that he had satisfied her, James feverishly released his desire in her. As he came crashing down on her, Kathleen, panting breathlessly, whispered, "That was perfect. Now will you please take me to dinner?"

Raising himself slightly, he smiled and nodded. "Only if you promise, I can have dessert afterwards." Closing her eyes, she sighed in euphoric splendor; she had at last gotten what she wanted and needed all these years, and Kathleen purred, "Only if you beg."

~

After spending a night repeatedly bringing each other to sexual heights neither of them had ever experienced before; James leaned over the side of the bed and huskily said, "After I have time to rest, we need to talk. Anne may think she has out maneuvered me for the time being, but I always get what I want. And what I want now, after experiencing such pleasures with you my lustful little wench, is for you to return with me to London. There I'll shower you with all that your heart desires, for your dessert."

Realizing that he still believed she could be bartered with, when he no longer had anything to offer her, she did not respond and waited until he closed the door; then Kathleen released her tears. *I'll not be yours or anyone's mistress again, James Sterling. I'll find me a man to love me, even if he's still a boy.* Pulling herself from the bed, and seeing the lateness of the hour, knowing that William Spencer would be punctual, she quickly began to wash away the night of sated passions from her fatigued and satisfied body.

Gazing at her reflection in the mirror above the dry sink, she hastily dried her eyes. "There'll be none of that, Kathleen Sullivan. No man is worth shedding tears over. You got what you wanted from him, so don't be getting yourself all misty eyed." Recalling how masterfully he was able to bring her satisfaction time and again, she whispered under her breath, "Old man Strombly, ain't it befittin' that James Sterling did open my package after all, you old miserable bastard. I hope to God you are either rollin' over in your grave or rottin' in hell, precisely where you belong for making me your sex slave."

Blocking out the memories of her innocence that had been robbed from her by Oscar Strombly, she took great satisfaction in knowing what she valued as her only treasure was given freely without force, and on her terms. Recalling how James had not only fulfilled her expectations of what it would be like to fully experience a man, he had exceeded her expectations by begging for more. "Saints be praised, I didn't allow some inexperienced rambunctious boy to have such honors. I had me a man who appreciated what a prize he'd just won, even if he was too stupid to realize I'd just enslaved him."

Hearing Matilda letting herself in after knocking, and seeing she was an hour early, Kathleen called out to the maid, "I'm running behind Matilda. Please get my belongings gathered up; we still have much to do before Mr. Spencer arrives this afternoon. He won't be taking kindly to have to wait on the likes of me."

Rushing around her room, choosing a yellow gown from her trunk, suitable for attracting a young heir of distinction, she hastily began brushing her hair. Not hearing a response from the maid, and becoming annoyed, Kathleen stepped out into the parlor and froze seeing William Spencer standing before her, gazing adoringly. "Oh my, William, you're here hours before I planned. Where is Matilda?" she asked, her eyes darting around the room as her heart pounded in her chest. Lowering the hairbrush from her auburn hair which cascaded over her shoulder, she nervously said, "I'm sorry, I thought you were."

"Matilda." Anne Spencer's youngest child, a tall and lanky young man, with a baby face for eighteen, stood smiling at her. "I gathered as much. And fear not, dear Kathleen, I don't mind waiting for someone as lovely as you. Especially when you glow, as you do so early in the morning."

Lowering her head to mask her embarrassment at being caught off guard, she hastily looked about the room to be certain there was no evidence of what had happed only hours before between she and James. Seeing only their two glasses, one empty and hers still half full, she panicked. Realizing he had already seen them, she took in a deep breath. "Glow, you say? Why William, what you see is a woman embarrassed. If you'll excuse me, I need to finish getting ready."

"Of course. Take as long as you need."

Returning back to her room, hastily Kathleen began picking up her gown from last evening lying next to the bed, and spotting James's neck scarf in the pile of discarded clothing she sighed, *Thank heavens he never saw that.* Folding it, she placed it in her trunk along with her other belongings. *What the devil is he doing here at the crack of dawn?* Looking around the room to see if she had missed anything else, her heart stopped, hearing him speak to her through the door. "Was James Sterling here last evening?"

"Why yes, he was. Why do you ask?" Closing her eyes, fearful that her chance at respectability had been ruined before it had even begun; she froze where she stood.

"I thought so. I see a bottle of his favorite brand of brandy. He must not have stayed very long though, since it's been hardly touched."

Sighing, she said, "Aren't you the observant one."

"How did he take the news about Mother's and Jacques wedding?" Hearing his question, Kathleen knew he didn't suspect anything and hastily made up her bed. "Actually, he didn't say much about it." Rushing to the vanity, she bent over and twisted her long hair to the ends, then wrapped it in a loose bun onto the top of her head. Placing a few combs to keep it in place, she headed to the door. Seeing him twirl her half-empty glass of brandy in his hands, she began walking toward him. William, not aware she was behind him, called out to her.

"No? I'm surprised, you know Kathleen, this was really very generous of you. Mother shouldn't have left it to you, to tell James. I had wanted to be the one."

"William, I offered," she said softly. He jerked around and noticing his surprise that she was back in the parlor, she smiled and stretched out her hand for the glass.

He handed it to her and she continued. "Your mother has been very kind to me since I arrived, it was the least I could do for her. Besides, I can understand why your mother doesn't want her son to be involved in this."

Obviously angered by her comment he said, "Mother still thinks I'm a child and apparently, so do you. Kathleen, how old are you?"

"Me? Why, I'm seventeen. Why do you ask?"

"My point exactly. You're a year younger than me and a woman, yet Mother trusts this to you to take care of rather than her son who she refuses to treat as a man."

"I see your point. And I'm not taking side's mind you William, but being primarily raised in London, I have lived a life that has afforded me the opportunity to see both sides of human nature. Whereas, you living primarily here in the country, perhaps she thought I would be better equipped to handle someone as unscrupulous as James Sterling. Not to mention, who else better to disarm him, but taking a woman on a shopping spree? As it was, everything turned out better than even I had hoped for."

"If this is your idea of making me feel better, I can assure you Kathleen, you are failing miserably. James Sterling is not only unscrupulous, but a man who attacks women. And you had no business being left alone with him." Seeing the surprised look on Kathleen's face he added, "Mother thinks I don't know what he did to cousin Felicity, but I know a lot more than she thinks. Which is why as soon as I received her telegram to escort you back to Pixie Halt, since she and Jacque were on their way to meet up with the others, I left immediately and drove through the night."

"You did? Why, for goodness sake?"

"Isn't it obvious, Kathleen? You're a defenseless woman who has no business being alone with a man like that. Despite being left with Mother's maid, who was useless as far as I'm concerned, considering I just walked in. Why, by the way, would you leave your door unlocked?"

Realizing that James must have left it unlocked when he left earlier, she said, "I must have forgotten to lock it." Changing the subject, suddenly feeling bombarded by so many questions, she said, "This was very gallant of you, William. Thank you. If you're not too tired, we could leave now. All I have to do is get my hat and fetch Matilda."

Just then, the maid entered the room and seeing William, said, "Mr. Spencer, you're early."

Hastily, Kathleen spoke so that William, obviously upset about the door being unlocked, wouldn't question Matilda. She had no desire to try and explain her actions as to why she would excuse Matilda when James was still in her room. "Yes, we've already established that. Matilda, will you please see to it the driver comes and retrieves my trunks and other packages while Mr. Spencer and I go for some breakfast?"

Tucking her arm inside William's, she said smiling up at him, "I don't know about you, but I'm famished."

As the two of them left the room, she glanced at James room, and said a silent prayer. *Please God, don't let him come out and spoil everything.* Then a sudden thought of him going for breakfast and finding them in the hotel restaurant sent her heart beating faster still. "William, would you mind terribly if we venture away from the hotel for breakfast? I had hoped to see more of Plymouth; as a matter of fact, Matilda and I were intending to go shopping before you arrived unexpectedly..."

Patting her hand still nestled on his arm, he said, "Say not another word, I have the perfect place in mind. Kathleen, I do have a request to make, though. Since we're going to be spending so much time together these next two weeks perhaps you wouldn't mind calling me what my friends do—Will?"

"I would be honored, Will."

Leaving the hotel, a smile crossed Kathleen's lips and she began feeling lighthearted, almost giddy. She had accomplished what she'd set out to do, and being with a man her own age, not expecting anything from her other than her company, she found quite pleasant. As they leisurely strolled the streets of Plymouth, she found herself enjoying the conversation as he spoke of the town's origin and notable historic facts. Fascinated that he knew so much about the town, Kathleen was surprised to learn how he and his father had come there quite frequently so that Edward could escape Anne. As mesmerized as Kathleen was to know the details, she was mindful not to ask too many question, so as not to be offensive.

Returning to the hotel, Will dropped off a letter that Kathleen said she had forgotten to give to James from Anne, with the front desk staff before they headed back to Pixie Halt. On the journey back to Devon, Will spoke freely to Kathleen about his life, and of his family's history. Kathleen learned about Felicity coming from America and the turbulent marriage between Benjamin and Lavinia. Will helped her to understand the complicated intertwining of the Robbinses and Phelpses, ending with his sister and Joseph Pike. Interested in the role that James played in assisting Anne, Kathleen found it particularly fascinating how Will had primarily been the one who stayed with Victoria as she remained hidden away at Rupert's chateau with her child, born out of wedlock. Listening to him speak of his sister and nephew, she came to understand he had a great depth of compassion for others and was fiercely loyal to those he loved.

As they approached Devon, seeing children in a nearby field, she motioned to Will. "Look at them. How wonderful it must be for them to just run about and play as they do. It almost makes me want to be a child again."

Frowning slightly, detecting a hint of remorsefulness in her voice he asked, "All this while, I've rambled on about my ill-begotten youth, yet you've never said a word of yours. Tell me dear Kathleen, all there is to know about you, so when we arrive at Pixie Halt, it will be as if we have known one another all our lives. That way, the next two weeks we will be more like old friends getting reacquainted rather than strangers trying to determine if we can trust each other."

Kathleen, turning back toward him, hearing him refer to his childhood as ill-begotten, tried to mask her sadness at the memories of the childhood that had been stolen from her. "Will, your childhood wasn't ill-begotten. You were with your mother and father and even though they had problems between them, you and your sister had each other; and from the sounds of it, you both always knew you were loved. A feeling that I …well, let's just say it sounds lovely to me." Trying desperately to prevent herself from shedding the tears she felt stinging her eyes, she pasted a smile on her lips. "And I already think of you as a friend, so why is there any need for us to discuss my sordid past in order for you to think of me as your friend, too?"

Seeing the tears in her eyes, and realizing Kathleen had painful memories of her past, he said, "Forgive me Kathleen, that was rude of me. Of course I think of you as a friend. A very dear friend." Then looking out the window to give her time to compose herself, and seeing a boy with a blindfold over his eyes peeking from under it, then dashing toward a little girl, Will said, "Ah the rogue, no fair." Motioning to them, he chuckled and said, "He cheated just to catch his lady fair."

Kathleen, needing a distraction, watched and said, "Now why would you think he wanted only to catch that particular girl, couldn't he just have wanted to win the game?"

"There are no winners or losers in that game Kathleen, the little rascal passed two other girls just to tag that one in particular. No, take it from me, that lad was after his lady fair alright, and judging by how the little girl didn't make any attempts to run too far from him, she wanted to be caught."

Watching the two children as the coach drove past, and seeing the boy place the blindfold over the girl's head then steal a kiss before running off, she chuckled. "Ah well, it appears you were right. Very astute of you Will, I shall take heed and will guard against keeping my secrets locked away securely while in the presence of such a master sleuth."

Becoming very serious, he gazed adoringly into her eyes and said, "No need, fair lady, you see, I already know all I need to know."

Hearing him refer to her as a fair lady, touched by the sincerity in his voice and how tenderly he gazed at her, Kathleen looked out the window. *Oh if only I were a fair lady*, she thought. Then taking a deep cleansing breath to rid herself of the feelings of melancholy that were clouding her mind, she scolded herself, "*Don't be doing this to yourself Kathleen, capture his heart while he's vulnerable.* Instead though, she said, "How much longer do you think it will be until we arrive at Pixie Halt?"

"Not long, why do you ask?"

"No reason other than that suddenly I find I'm fatigued, and a little hungry."

"Right, well I have just the remedy for all that ails you. A leisurely picnic amongst the fields of lavender and goldenrod will surely raise your spirits."

Kathleen, never hearing the term of picnic before, asked, "Picnic, you say?"

Will, noting that she didn't understand him and wondering if it could be possible that she had never been on one before, decided not to question her since the past obviously upset her. "Yes, I'll have cook pack up a luncheon for us while you change into something more suitable to frolic through the meadows in."

Understanding that he wanted to luncheon in the meadow, she nodded her head and smiled, all the while admonishing herself for not seizing the opportunity and trying to entice him with her sexuality. Deciding that she was just tired, not having slept the night before, she vowed that during their picnic she would begin the seduction of the eligible William Spencer.

~

That afternoon and the days that followed it was Will who began to capture Kathleen's heart, despite her denial of looking forward to sharing time with him. Every day she experienced new ways of having fun—riding horses, playing checkers, reading to one another by the fireside at night and above all others, feeling his gentle touch on the rare occasion their hands grazed each other. As the fortnight rushed past Kathleen, she suddenly found herself feeling panic in her heart; she had not accomplished what she had set out to do. Deciding that this afternoon while on their picnic she would make Will desire her as a woman, she was very selective of her outfit, taking more time than normal to do her hair, and as she looked into the reflection of the mirror she was surprised by what she saw. Before her was the image of a young, attractive girl instead of the overdressed voluptuous beauty she had seen in the past. *What has happened to you Kathleen Sullivan? Have you lost all your senses, how can you get a man to desire you looking like a strumpet?*

Hearing a knock at the door, knowing it was Will coming to collect her, Kathleen's heart raced and she called out while looking at how she could improve her appearance, rather than change from the mint green summer frock. Lowering the puckered gathered sleeves further down her shoulders to reveal more of her breasts, she glanced back into the mirror. Viewing how alluring she looked, she smiled pushing her firm breasts higher in her corset so that more cleavage showed, and she whispered under her breath, "Yes, this will do nicely. If he doesn't notice me today there is something wrong with him."

As she opened the door, getting the reaction she had hoped for—his eyes trailing down her face to her revealing neckline, and seeing his cheeks turn crimson, she asked, "Is there something wrong, Will?"

Hardly able to keep his eyes off her, he mumbled, "No, not at all. You just startled me is all; I thought you would still be awhile."

Giving Will, her most alluring smile while tucking her arm through his and noticing he was carrying a basket, she said seductively, "Mmm something smells delicious, I'm so hungry I could eat you."

Noticing that he cleared his throat in reaction to her carefully planned words, again affecting him just as she had hoped, Kathleen looked innocently at him waiting for his reply.

"Right, well if I'm not mistaken lady fair, we have all your favorites; some chicken, Brie, grapes and ah yes, I've selected a rather nice Bordeaux to accompany such a grand buffet."

Taking the opportunity of snuggling closer to him without it appearing too obvious, she cooed, "Mmm, wine. And pray tell, what do we owe such an honor to Will, this fine and glorious afternoon?"

Will's smile faded slightly and he said, "Well, I don't know if it's a celebration as such, but I received a wire from Mother. She and Jacque will be returning the day after tomorrow."

Taking in a deep breath, no longer feeling as lighthearted as she had only seconds earlier, she said, "I see." Trying to force a smile to her lips while walking down the stairs, she added, "Well at least now you'll be rid of the burden of entertaining me all the time. Not to mention I'm sure you've missed your mother, dreadfully."

Shifting the basket in his hands, to open the door, he said, "It was no burden, dear Kathleen. As a matter of fact, I can't remember when I've had a better time in all my life."

Touched by his comment and the sincerity in his eyes, she whispered, "Neither have I."

Finding a perfect location with the moors in the background and heather and goldenrod abundant, he spread out a blanket for her to sit, and Kathleen said, "Oh Will, this place is lovely. Why I can't imagine a more perfect location to have a picnic."

Taking her hand to help her take a seat, he whispered, "Nothing compares to your beauty Kathleen. Thank you for looking so beautiful today."

Taken aback by his comment, she found herself suddenly embarrassed—feeling she had never felt before when a man had paid her a compliment. Her eyes shyly locked onto his and she whispered, "Thank you, Will. Not just for bringing me here today, but for the past two weeks. It truly has been like that out of a fairytale for me. I shall always treasure this time with you."

Slowly Will lowered his head and as his lips touched hers, Kathleen felt a tingling rush through her veins she had never known before, never having been kissed before by a man as a show affection. Then as he lifted his head from her, Kathleen out of instinct, never feeling such sweetness from a man before, brought her fingers to her lips. Suddenly realizing that over the years, she had been shown how to excite a man and be excited in return but had never known that a kiss could stir such emotion.

Will, tenderly brushing her cheek, whispered, "Forgive me for not asking permission for taking such liberties, but I have wanted to do that for so long. I couldn't help myself."

Lowering her hand, Kathleen did not know how to respond. Was it possible that he was apologizing for allowing her to experience such tenderness?

Gazing at her lovingly, he asked, "May I please kiss you again, Kathleen?" Nodding her head, her heart pounded in her chest feeling his arm wrap around her. As his head lowered, anticipating his mouth on hers, she felt a tingling again. As Will's mouth came crushing down on her, feeling his tongue part her lips, Kathleen, enjoying such a sensation found herself hungrily responding, matching his urgency and grasped him around the neck. Slowly William pulled from their passionate embrace leaving Kathleen breathless.

"We need to stop."

Uncertain as to why, she nodded her head again not knowing what to say or do, never experiencing anything like this before.

Will, misunderstanding her silence as she being inexperienced in sexual encounters, took her hand and said, "Let's have a bite to eat, shall we?"

Trying desperately to understand what was happening to her, why a kiss could stir such feelings, Kathleen said, "Shall I serve?"

"No, let me." Smiling warmly at her, he opened the basket then smiled, recalling the day they had returned from Plymouth. Taking the linen napkin and folding it diagonally, he lightheartedly said, "Instead, how about a game of blind man's bluff?"

"Blind man's bluff?" she asked, her lip curling upward, his smile contagious.

"The game the children were playing when the boy stole the kiss from that little red-haired girl?"

"Oh yes, I didn't know the name of the game they were playing."

"Why Miss Sullivan, you're trying to test my astuteness, aren't you? Surely, dozens of boys have stolen a kiss from you while playing blind man's bluff?"

Fearful he didn't believe her, she said, "No, never. In fact, a boy has never stolen a kiss from me either. You forget Will, I was very young when I left Ireland to become a servant girl. There was no time to play such games."

Detecting a hint of sadness in her eyes, he said merrily, lifting her to her feet, "Well then it's high time you played."

Shaking her head, she said, "No, this is silly."

"Silly?" Will raised the linen to his eyes and said, before tying it, "You had better get a move on Kathleen or I'll have to tickle you." Waving his hands before him, he jokingly said, "That's what happens to those who don't participate you know."

Seeing his eyes dance, Kathleen said, "Is that really true?"

Pulling the cloth over one eye he said, "Well, that's my rule. And I can tell ya, I'm relentless. I had poor Victoria many a times laughing so hard, she'd cry."

Hesitantly, she backed away and as he lunged for her, looking ridiculous, she giggled, only causing him to lunge at her again. Squealing, she began to dodge him laughing more all the while he chased her. Running to a nearby tree, not making a sound and seeing him call to her, then spinning around as he stretched his arms out before him, she couldn't help but laugh. Hearing her, he pulled up the blindfold to peek, then ran and caught her. Giggling in delight, leaning against the tree to catch her breath, she said, "No fair, you cheated."

Pulling her to him, letting the blindfold fall around his neck, feeling her breath on his face, he looked lovingly at her and whispered hoarsely, "I had to or I'd be too tired to steal that kiss, my lady fair."

Their eyes locked, and she whispered, "You don't have to steal it Will, I will gladly give it to you."

Again pulling her into his arms, he hungrily kissed her. Feeling her respond so readily, Will's hands began to move over her body, causing her to moan. Pulling away from her, he huskily whispered, "I love you, Kathleen."

"Oh Will..." Overcome by emotion, she showered him with more kisses. Tenderly he guided her to the ground, all the while kissing each other. As their passions mounted, they began groping at each other's clothing until at last they were joined as one. Erupting in a fiery explosion, they clung to each other breathlessly, and Kathleen, flooded with unfamiliar emotions, closed her eyes and clung to him as tears ran down her cheek. Softly he whispered in her ear, "I meant what I said, Kathleen. I do love you."

Hearing his declaration of love, feeling undeserving of such words from a man as kind and loving as he, she whispered through her tears, "I know..."

He lifted himself, and seeing tears running down her cheek, he quickly pulled himself off her and said apologetically, "Oh God, I hurt you. Can you forgive me?"

Shaking her head, hearing him ask for her forgiveness, fearing he had caused her pain, Kathleen became more tearful. *Could it be possible that a man could be so tender?* Fighting the feelings welling in her heart for him, she pulled him closer to her. "You didn't hurt me, Will."

Obviously he was confused and hearing her still crying, said, "I'm sorry the first time we made love wasn't more special for you..."

"No. It was very special."

Lifting his head again, his eyes showing his bewilderment, he asked patiently, "Then why are you crying?"

Lovingly gazing up at him, she cried, "Because, I love you too."

Smiling, he brushed her tears away and took her in her arms, hugging her tightly. "I don't understand why loving me would make you cry? Love isn't supposed to make you sad, Kathleen, it's a thing of joy. Especially, when two hearts share the same feelings."

Unable to explain what she felt in her heart, wishing it had been him, she had saved herself for, Kathleen just said, "Please Will, just hold me so I believe this is really happening."

"My lady fair, you can believe in my love." Tenderly he held Kathleen in his arms and for the first time in her life, Kathleen knew real security in the arms of a man that only two weeks before she had thought of as just a boy.

~ Twenty-Four ~

On the return ride from Glastonbury, Felicity listened to the others merrily speak of their great adventures. The children, enthralled by the tales of King Arthur, spoke of their hero and the Knights of the Round Table as if they personally had known them all while Rupert, Annabelle, Anne, and Jacque, finding the legends of Joseph and rumor's of the Holy Grail being buried there, far more intriguing. Every night after the children were settled in, the four of them would continue their debate about whether the story of a sacred vessel from the Celts had been somehow intertwined with the chalice used by Jesus at the Last Supper. Each presented their ideas based on new information they had received from their daily outings.

On several evenings, Felicity and Gilbert ventured out to visit the Glastonbury Tor so that he could prove to her that the little people, who he had spoke of often while she convalesced, were not just Irish Folklore. At the Tor, mysterious colored globes of lights had been reported to be seen over the centuries and he was determined that Felicity see them as well, proving that this was indeed the home of Gwyn ap Nudd, King of the fairies.

Closing her eyes, she recalled the previous night in particular and how she had witnessed something unusual. She and Gilbert, spending their last evening at the base of the Tor, sat inside the coach side by side, with the doors opened, gazing out at the rocky hill with a stone tower at its peak. Suddenly Gilbert, seeing something, stretched his arms around her shoulders and guiding her arm with his, pointed out what appeared to be dark mauve-colored balls of light descending from the Tor. Fascinated by what she was witnessing, she didn't pull from his touch, but rather, leaned into his shoulder, his arms wrapped around her as they excitedly watched the spectrum of lights continue for at least three to five minutes. Immediately following, she turned to him. "I saw them, you were right!" Burning with excitement, her heart raced faster realizing he was holding her in his arms and how natural it felt, as if she belonged there. Their eyes locked and slowly he leaned in and their lips found each other. As they continued to kiss, neither of them pulled away, but came closer, expressing the pent-up longings that they had been shying away from since her accident. As the kiss ended, Felicity laid her head on his shoulder allowing herself to enjoy the comfort of his protective arms around her.

Their silence was broken when Gilbert whispered, "This magical moment was given to us by the fairies. Accept their gift M'lady, just as I accepted long ago that loving you was the right thing to do."

Hearing his words again now in her mind, Felicity glanced at Gilbert as he merrily spoke to the children. As she watched him, she could not deny it was indeed a magical moment, one she would cherish in her heart forever. But now in the light of day, miles from the mystical land of fairies and fantasies, Felicity vowed she would never allow herself to block her memories of the life she had shared with her beloved Ben as she had last night.

Knowing the pain this would cause Gilbert, a man she had grown to admire and trust, whom she owed so much, she turned her head and gazed out the window numbly. It broke her heart to have to repay the kindness that he had given so freely, to now tell him that she would never allow herself to love him.

From the moment he had brought her home from their magical drive, she felt a great sadness in her heart. The spell had been broken and she had spent the night analyzing why this had gone so far and sorting out her feelings. She concluded that the attraction they both felt for one another had nothing to do with love, but rather, with fulfilling a void in both of their lives. She needed to feel alive again, and he was so eager to protect a woman, especially since he had not been able to protect Miranda. Of course, it was only natural for them to turn to each other for comfort, but this was not love. And for her to continue to lead him on, letting him believe that loving her was right, was only selfish; not to mention that the guilt she felt betraying not only her friend, but her beloved Ben, was more than she could bear.

Then early this morning, recalling how this had begun and how he had pulled her from the despair of sadness, her thoughts trailed to Kathleen's conversation with her. So Felicity, to help ease her own burden of guilt, decided that she must help Gilbert find love again, and that Kathleen already showing an interest in him was the best for all concerned. She just could not let such a wonderful man, who had such a great capacity to love, waste another moment believing he was in love with her.

"You alright, M'lady? You look like you were lost in a fog."

Hearing Gilbert, she turned and said, "I'm fine, in fact I've just found my way out."

Lost in her own thoughts, Felicity hadn't noticed the look exchanged between Rupert and Gilbert. Then, after a few moments of silence, Gilbert speaking to everyone said, "Did I ever tell ya about the tale of the Merrows?"

"Merrows? I don't believe so," Rupert said halfheartedly, obviously concerned with Felicity's sullenness, glancing briefly at her with a slight frown. "Seems to me some of that Irish diplomacy is in order about now Gilbert, to help brighten our spirits from the long journey."

"Aye, mate. Well the Merrows are sea maids who are quite beautiful and have a particular fondness for humans. They are known to wear feathery hats or in the northern waters were it is cold, they wear a cloak made of seal skins. From time to time when they see a lowly fisherman, they will come ashore and discard their cap and cloak and appear as a human. Only a wee webbing between their fingers and their flat feet can be seen different between them and mortal women. Now if the fisherman finds he fancies her despite them being different; and if he is fortunate, he'll find her cap and cloak and hide it from her and take her as his bride."

Annabelle, engrossed in the story said, "And are they happy?"

"Aye, very happy. As I said, the Merrows fancy humans and leave the past behind, finding happiness living with her new husband. They can live a happy life, filled with laughter and joy, especially since she brings with her the great treasures she has acquired from lost ships at sea."

"Ah how lovely, and she lives with her new husband never missing what she was or the life she had before?"

"Never lass, the memories of the sea stay in her heart but she finds new happiness with her husband. For years they can share a life with one another, a good life and raise a family, until the sea-maid finds her cap or cloak. Then the urges in her to go back to the sea cloud her mind, until she forgets how happy she had just been and eventually returns to the sea, abandoning the new life she made for herself. Leaving her poor husband, their children, everything behind just so she can return to the sea, to live alone."

Annabelle frowned. "How very sad for her and the fisherman."

"Aye, it 'tis indeed."

"So wouldn't it have been best if the fisherman never took on the Merrow as a wife?" Felicity asked. "Surely, it was never meant to be."

"I suppose some could see it that way. But the way I see it M'lady, if it wasn't meant to be for the sea maid to find happiness in a new life, she wouldn't have been in search for the fisherman in the first place, now would she?"

Felicity knew Gilbert speaking of the Merrows now, was no coincidence. He was trying to persuade her not to return to the life that she had locked herself into following Benjamin's death. Ignoring the others nodding their heads in agreement with Gilbert, Felicity persisted. "Yes, but what if the fisherman took her off guard, and she didn't really want to find a new life? What if when he had found her, she was just taking time from the sea to rest?"

"Ah M'lady, even if that were the case, why would she abandon a new life, filled with happiness, simply to go back to the sea to live alone, when there are those who love her on shore? It makes no sense for all of them to be so sad."

Angered that he would discuss such a thing in the presence of others, Felicity stubbornly said, "It does to me! Especially if her heart still belonged to her first love. Some things are meant to be and the fisherman should have known not to try and make the Merrow live as a human just because he wanted her to be. Surely, there were other humans that he could have built a life with? As I see it, the two of them were foolish to begin with, to even try to begin a new life, which was doomed from the start. They would have been better off to never have met to begin with."

Turning, Rupert looked at Gilbert and shook his head as if signaling his friend not to press the subject any further. Inhaling a deep breath, Gilbert leaned his head back, and for the remainder of the trip, only small talk from time to time was shared amongst the weary travelers. It was as if they all knew Felicity had decided to close her heart off and return to her life, mourning the loss of her Ben.

Anne, noticing that they were approaching Devon, said, smiling warmly at her new husband, "Well, looks like our honeymoon is over dear Jacque; how I will miss the mystical sights of Glastonbury."

Jacque replied warmly, "Fear not lovely lady, we shall find a way of keeping its memory burning brightly in our hearts forever. It took both of us too long to start life over again; we will not be foolish enough to let it slip from our fingers simply because we left that mystical place."

Hearing his words, Felicity was stunned. Could it be this man felt he had the right because he was her cousin's husband, to try and interfere with her life? Turning her head, she listened as Jacque continued.

"It's no secret to any of you that I fled my homeland in search of a new life. For sixteen years, I searched in vain for my lost love and the child that had come from our ill-fated love affair, to no avail. All those years in India, away from my own kind, a part of me longed to return back to where I thought I belonged. And after I had returned following the death of my sister, leaving the life I had built, I foolishly believed that the reason I had returned to France was because it was the right thing to do." Turning to Anne, he continued, "Then I met you. And over time I came to understand that the reason I had not been truly happy in India all those years wasn't because I didn't belong there, but rather, I never allowed myself to open my heart. And ironically again, I find myself residing in a land foreign to me, but this time, I will not be foolish enough to close my heart to what matters most, and that's love."

Then looking amongst the other adults, he smiled warmly. "Which is why I propose that you all come and dine with Anne and I tonight. It took a long time for all of you to reconcile the hurt from your past and become a family again. Let us spend this first night back in Devon, amongst the memories of the past, with one another. So that the mystical forces of Glastonbury and what we found there helps to heal the wounds still lingering, before the mystic powers of our trip fade from our memories, shall we?"

Rupert, clearing his throat, said, "Here, here, I couldn't have said it better. But then you French have always been a master in the words of love."

"Why of course, it is in our blood."

Realizing there was no way to exclude herself without appearing rude, Felicity said, "That sounds lovely, but surely we all need time to get settled, perhaps tomorrow would be more suitable? Besides, I had hoped to have a chat with Gilbert this evening."

Anne, smiling at her said, "Well how long could that take? Dinner together tonight sounds perfect, and I won't take no for an answer. We all have to eat, and besides you need to fetch Kathleen, not that she would be in the way, mind you. Let's give ourselves a couple of hours, shall we? That will give us all plenty of time to change for dinner and take care of anything we need to."

Nodding, feeling her cheeks turn crimson at being pushed into something she did not want to do, Felicity cordially smiled. "I'll see you then in two hours."

Jacque, turning to Gilbert said, "And you Gilbert, it wouldn't be the same without you joining us."

Briefly glancing over at Felicity, Gilbert said, "Aye. I'll be there all right; wild horses couldn't keep me away."

Turning her head, detecting stubbornness in his tone, Felicity thought, silently mimicking his Irish brogue, *Be as stubborn as you like Gilbert O'Flaherty, but I'll not be changing me mind. And not even all the fairies in the world are going to change that!*

Rupert, signaling for Montgomery to pull over, instructed Jimmy and Fannie and his servants to join them in their coach while Anne and Jacque continued on to Pixie Halt, back in their own coach.

With a brief goodbye, Felicity, arm still in the sling and having no alternative but to accept Gilbert's assistance from the coach, hastily looked away as their eyes briefly met. For an instant, seeing him look at her as he did, she began to wonder if what Jacque said held any merit. Then looking at Brookhaven, recalling the life she had shared with Ben, she stood firmly on her own and said in control, "Thank you, Gilbert. Would you please take a few moments to speak with me before returning to your cabin?"

"Are ya sure lass, this can't be awaitin' until you had some time to rest? Fatigue can make ya a wee bit confused at times."

Turning, she stubbornly said, "No. I've never been clearer in my thoughts than right now."

Taking a deep breath and shaking his head, after sending the children off to play, he followed Felicity up the stairs into Brookhaven. Entering Benjamin's library, the scent of him still lingering in the air, he ignored it, and forced himself to sound merry. "M'lady beckons her humble servant?"

Trying not to sound as cross as she felt, Felicity said, "First off, you are not my servant Gilbert; and secondly, I am not now or ever will be, your lady." Seeing his smile fade and readying himself to try to plead his case, she hastily added, "Since my accident, I have found myself becoming more dependent on you. Even though a part of me kept trying to push you away, I needed so desperately to feel the comfort you so generously gave to me, that I let this situation continue for too long. I shall always be grateful for what you have done for me Gilbert…"

"Felicity, what we share together is not a situation, or an obligation, or even trying to console one another from a broken heart. And surely you must know in your heart that what I did to care for you was because I wanted to."

Her eyes softened and she said, "Gilbert I have come to understand why Miranda loved you as she did. Beneath your rough exterior is a warm and caring man, who I admire greatly." Taking a deep breath to gather the courage to go on, she said, "But Gilbert, I will not allow myself to let either of us betray the love we had for Benjamin and Miranda as we did last night. It is wrong for us to forget that they were and always will be, the loves of our life."

"Loving one another Felicity, isn't disgracing or betraying their love, it's an extension of their love."

"Stop!" she demanded with tear-filled eyes. "*Yes it is!*" she yelled. "To me it is. We've been deluding ourselves that what we feel is love. Don't you see Gilbert; we both were in need of friendship and consoling? And now that our hearts are healed, we need to go on with our lives. I'm not like you, Gilbert. I can't just fill the void in my heart by loving another. We are two very different people, from different worlds."

"Ah, so this is what it comes down to, the grand lady doesn't want to be givin' her heart to that of a man who is not as lofty as she is used to.

Well your lips last night didn't seem to think less of me. Why, as I recall they were as hungry for me as I was for you."

Outraged, she clenched her fists at her side, and said, gritting her teeth, "Don't you ever speak to me in that manner again." Feeling herself quiver with rage, she added, "Such a remark only proves Gilbert, that you don't know anything about me. Last night was special. We both were under a magical spell, but now that spell is broken. Today though, I've come to my senses, nothing more. Why must you tarnish the memory that two dear friends shared?"

"Friends? That wasn't friends kissing, Felicity. Not like that! And you want me to believe you've come to your senses?" he ranted. "Is that what that pretty little head of yours thinks? Well Felicity, as I see it, thinkin' the way you are, proves you have *lost* all your senses. Why, you're actin' like the Merrow."

With a fist clenched to her hip, she yelled, "And that's another thing; how dare you think you had the right to bring up some silly Irish folktale, just to try to convince me that you loving me is right? It's not right, Gilbert. It never will be right. I don't want you to love me, I don't want you to look at me like you do, and I sure don't ever want you to discuss our affairs in front of my family again!"

"Is that right! Well don't be actin' so high and mighty with me Felicity, I seen plenty of times you lookin' at me with love in your eyes. And don't try to deny it, 'cause I saw it. Even when you tried to hide it; and obviously not just from me, but from yerself too, lass."

Taking in a deep breath to calm herself, she said sadly, "Oh Gilbert, you're wrong. What you mistake as love was gratitude. Please Gilbert, find someone else worthy of your love. Kathleen has said she is fond of you, go to her; show her the attention you have shown me…"

Not giving her a chance to finish, he yelled, "What? You think you can rid yourself of me by pawning me off to another, like my love don't mean nothin'? Givin' it away like it was the air you breathe? Is that the kind of man you take me for?"

Felicity began to weep, realizing she had offended him, and said, "No, Gilbert, you misunderstand me. I was only suggesting that if you could show Kathleen the attention that you have shown me, perhaps she could return the love you so greatly deserve."

"Fine lass, I'll shower Kathleen with all the attention she can handle, if that will make ya happy. 'Cause God knows that's all I've been tryin' to do. But you might be askin' yerself this—why would ya let a man who loves ya, slip through yer fingers because yer being too stubborn to admit what's' in yer heart?"

"I know what's in my heart, Gilbert. I still love my Ben." Unable to carry on any further, Felicity ran from the room as Gilbert stormed through the front doors and out of Brookhaven.

Hearing the door slam, Whitney turned and said, "Is everything all right with Mother, Uncle Gilbert?"

"Yer mother is fine lad. Tell her I'll come fetch her for dinner at the Freeport's in an hour. And be tellin' her too, if she ain't ready I'll be carryin' her stubborn arse if she be likin' it or not."

Not waiting for a response, Gilbert stomped off in the direction of the cabin as Whitney looked sheepishly over at Lucas and said, "Did I just hear your father say, 'ass'?"

Catherine's eyes got as wide as saucers, and she answered for her brother, "Da must really love your mum plenty, if she made him that mad."

Little Joseph looked up at his older sister and said, "Da didn't act like he loved Auntie Felicity, he looked real mad."

Consoling her youngest brother, Suzanne said, "That's how boys and girls show their love sometimes, Joey." As if proving her point, she added, "Just look at how Lucas and Sarah Tess fought."

Lucas pushed his sister and said, "Oh yeah, well look at you and Edwin. Besides, Sarah Tess didn't kiss me, now did she..." Looking angrily over at Whitney, he said, "She preferred *Whitney*."

Hearing the sarcasm in Lucas's voice, just as it had been following the Myles's departure, Whitney waved his hand in disgust, mimicking Gilbert as he had seen him do countless times in the past when annoyed. "Ah, not this again. Ta hell with ya. I'm checking to see how Mother is."

"Awe, I'm tellin' Da you swore," Joey said, innocently.

"Go ahead. He ain't my father!" Whitney snapped.

"Isn't."

Whitney, looking as if he would explode, turned and darted towards the house.

Lucas, clearly angered himself, scolded his sister and pushed her again. "Now see what you did."

Suzanne angrily pushed him back and then ran away. Lucas promptly chased after her. Gilbert, hearing the squeals, thinking that they were playing, shook his head angrily, and huffed under his breath, "Well at least some of us still have the magic left in our hearts."

~

By the time Felicity and Gilbert arrived at Pixie Halt, it was clear that they weren't the only ones who had been fighting. From the coolness between William, Anne, and Kathleen, it was clear they were merely being polite to keep up appearances. From time to time, Felicity noted how Will looked pleadingly at her, and she responded by turning her head. By the end of the meal, with no one able to think of any more small talk, everyone exhausted from trying to appear jovial, Gilbert turned to Kathleen. "Lass, recently it was brought to my attention that I've been neglectful in showing you the attention you deserve, you being a guest of mine." Pausing to glare at Felicity, he added, "So let me make amends to you tonight. What would you say to a nice evening ride to gaze at the stars, just the two of us?"

Kathleen hestitated. Feeling Will's eyes on her and wanting to hurt him as much as he had just hurt her, she said, "Why Gilbert, I would love to go riding with you. Why, with the moon shining so brightly, any girl would be foolish to turn down such an offer from such an appealing man as yourself."

Turning to Rupert, Gilbert said, "Mate, you won't mind taking Felicity back to Brookhaven, will you?" Directing his attention to Felicity he said, "You don't have any objections to this arrangements, do you Felicity?"

Her heart pounding in her chest, feeling suddenly warm, Felicity looked at him coldly. "Why no, not at all. I'll leave the door open for you, Kathleen."

Gilbert rising, taking Kathleen's arm, paused hearing Will say, "Must you leave so soon, why, Kathleen hasn't even had dessert. It's your favorite, clotted cream."

Clearing her throat, nearly choking on his choice of words, she turned and looked at Will with hurt-filled eyes. "Well as it is, suddenly I find clotted cream too rich for my blood. I'll stick to something a little more to my liking, Will*iam*."

Turning to Anne, she said coolly, "Thank you for dinner and your kind hospitality, Mrs. Freeport."

"Yes, well all good things do come to an end, sooner or later. Don't they, my dear?"

Annabelle, hearing the edge spoken between the women, turned and looked over at Felicity who was indiscreetly watching Gilbert glide his arm around Kathleen, placing his hand in the small of her back to escort her out. Unable to watch any longer, Felicity's eyes dropped to her lap, and she closed them for a moment while taking in a deep breath. Annabelle, seeing her displeasure, frowned sadly and looked over at Rupert, who shook his head slightly, as if signaling his wife not to discuss it with his cousin yet.

Anne, seeing Will stand, said firmly to her son, "Sit down, William." Then directing her attention back to the others, she pasted a smile on her lips and said warmly, "We still have dessert."

William, glaring at his mother and throwing his napkin on the table, said,"I suddenly find I have no appetite." Bowing politely, he said, "If you'll excuse me."

Anne watched in horror as William defiantly left the room and called out to Kathleen. Glancing over at Jacque, she smiled warmly hearing him say, "Fear not dear, William is a good lad, he'll never do anything to break his mother's heart."

From the foyer of Pixie Halt, hearing Will call to her, Kathleen paused and whispered to Gilbert, "If you wouldn't mind giving me a moment of privacy. This won't take long."

Seeing how upset she was, Gilbert respectfully nodded his head and went to the door. Turning, he called to her loud enough for Will to hear. "I'll be right outside waitin' if ya need me."

Smiling, uncertain why after all this time he should suddenly be so kind to her, Kathleen watched silently as Gilbert closed the door behind him, then she turned and said, "What do you want, Will? Did your mummy give you permission to say goodbye to me?"

Trying to reach for her hand and seeing her jerk away from him, he paused. "Kathleen, it's not what you think. She was just surprised finding us like that. Given time, she will change her mind and I'll be able to make her see that it's you I love."

"Love?" she asked her voice higher than she had intended. "Will, you already proved how much you loved me this afternoon by letting her say those things about me. And to think I believed you when you said love brings people joy. Well you lied to me Will, because what I feel is no joy. Only more pain, and I'm tired of feeling pain. I'm tired of being ashamed of who I am. And I'm damned tired of you. So leave me be, William, while I start having me some of that joy and fun that you keep talkin' about. Isn't that what this last couple of weeks has been for you, having some fun, proving you're a man to get the poor peasant girl to love ya? Then watch as you tear her heart from her? Well, you got what ya wanted, now I'm going to get me a real man, who's old enough to stop doing everything his mother tells him to!"

Turning, she rushed from Pixie Halt, crying, and pleadingly whispered, "Please Gilbert, get me out of here."

Pulling her protectively into his arms, he escorted her to the coach, and motioning Jimmy to drive, he sat and waited as Kathleen cried the tears he wished he could shed. Reaching inside his coat pocket, he passed her his handkerchief and looked up at the stars. "I could use me some help down here Lord."

Through her tears she said, "He ain't goin' to be helpin' the likes of us, Gilbert. He's got better things to do with his time than to be mendin' a couple of Irish peasants' hearts, trying to raise themselves from the dirt."

"Ah, so that's what ya shedding all them tears for lass, young William has broken yer heart, has 'e?"

Nodding she said, "He told me he loved me and I believed him...but not enough to stand up to his mother when she said I wasn't good enough for him."

"Well what did ya think she was goin' to do lass, you parading around here like some floozy since you arrived? Ya think she was goin' to make ya a cake and let ya steal her only boy?"

"You're a fine one to talk about me making a spectacle of myself when all I've been seeing you do is make a damned fool over the prim and proper Mrs. Myles. Like she's Queen Victoria in the flesh. What's wrong, did she get tired of wiping her boots on ya, is that why you got time for me all of a sudden?"

Grasping her arms, he shook her, and yelled, "Don't you ever speak of her like that in my presence again, or so help me God..."

"What Gilbert? Do ya think you can hurt me any more than I haven't already been hurt by other men, or by myself? Go ahead; hit me if that makes ya feel better, but let's face it—we just ain't good enough for their kind."

Releasing her, he scoffed, "You don't know what yer talkin' about. Felicity ain't like that and William Spencer isn't either. He's a good lad with a tender heart. If he said he loved ya then he does."

"Really? Then why..."

"Ya think I got any answers, girl? Hell, I can't figure out me own problems! How am I to be helpin' you?"

A smile came to Kathleen's lips. "Well Mr. O'Flaherty, I just got me a plan that could be helpin' the both of us. What do ya say if we get some of these blue bloods somethin' to get their hearts a-pumping?"

His eyes danced merrily, and he said, "What did ya have in mind, Miss Sullivan?"

For the remaining drive around the back roads of Devon, the two of them spoke not in anger but rather, how they could assist each other. As they arrived back at Brookhaven, Gilbert, spotting Felicity glancing out the second story window from the children's room, said, "Ah well, partner it looks like the lovely widow is a bit restless this evenin'. Damn, it don't seem loving someone should be so hard."

"Ya tried showering her with your love, so now let's see what she'll do if she thinks she's losing it to another."

"Well, I can tell ya from a man's stand point, young Will won't be taking losin' his lady fair, especially after he worked so hard to win your heart. Now don't be givin' into sweet nothin's. Make him wed ya girl, and don't be givin' anything away for free again until he does."

Kathleen's eyes open wide, and she whispered, "How did you know…?"

Smiling, he opened the door to the coach and helped her out. Knowing Felicity was still watching, he said, "Cause lass, the way he looked when I placed my arms around your back to escort you out, was that of a man protecting his property from an intruder."

Leaning up to kiss his cheek, she whispered, "That wasn't just to make the widow jealous Gilbert; that was also to thank you for not judging me."

"Think nothin' of it, and I mean that. Don't be getting' your heart all confused and think I'll be changin' my mind on changing horses in mid-stream. Felicity is all I want. Now do what I say from here on out. Don't be flauntin' about wearing your fancy gowns like your some cat on the prowl. You'll win him by bein' a lady."

"I remember. I'll see you tomorrow for our picnic luncheon with the children."

"Aye. Tomorrow."

The two of them entered Brookhaven and seeing Felicity walking down the stairs, greeted their hostess cordially. "Hope we didn't disturb you, Mrs. Myles."

"No, not at all." Glancing at Gilbert she said, "Catherine is a little under the weather this evening and I was waiting up to tell you."

Hearing her comment, Gilbert darted up the stairs and into his children's room, and Felicity turned back toward Kathleen. "I hope you found your drive pleasant? It certainly was a lovely evening for it, the stars were plentiful."

"Were they? I hadn't noticed. I was too enthralled by Gilbert's company I suppose. Now if you'll excuse me Mrs. Myles, I find I'm suddenly very tired."

Surprised by her comment, seeing her climb the stairs and turning toward her bedchamber, Felicity asked, "Aren't you going to wait until Gilbert returns to see how Catherine is?"

Turning back at her hostess, raising a brow curiously, she said, "Whatever for? They are not my children, now are they Mrs. Myles? And I can assure you, I'm certainly not trying to impress their father by being the dutiful caregiver."

Felicity stood half way down the landing frozen in shock, repelled by Kathleen's comment. *What's that supposed to mean? Is that what you think I've been doing?*

Outraged, Felicity went into the study and began pacing. Not willing to admit why she was so angry, she went to the liquor tray and pouring herself a sherry, she sipped at it watching the stairway to see when Gilbert would be returning. Hearing a door open, she took a deep breath and put on a smile, and called to him, "I trust she's fine now?"

Pausing, Gilbert said with no emotion, "Sleeping like a log." Then he walked out the front door, leaving Felicity standing in the middle of the room so angry she could scream. Looking at her glass, seeing her hand trembling, she threw the glass in the fire and screamed into her clenched fist. *Damn you, Gilbert O'Flaherty!*

Gilbert, standing outside the door, heard the glass crashing from inside the study, and smiled as he took the steps two at a time. *Ah M'lady, that's a girl...get mad enough to fight for me.*

~

New York, N.Y.
July, 1874

Entering the children's nursery and seeing Elise gently bouncing their four-month-old daughter Emma, on one knee while reading aloud a letter with her free hand, Joshua shook his head and smiled.

"Just look at you. Every time I see you with our children, I fall in love with you all over again."

Smiling and stretching her arm for him to come and kiss her, she cooed seductively just as they became eye level with each other. "That would imply that you fell out of love with me, which had better not be the case, dear husband of mine."

Kissing her tenderly, he pulled away slightly and said, "You were always far too clever for me, my pearl. What I meant to say was, I fall in love with you even more."

"Much better," she cooed gently, caressing the nape of his neck as he leaned down to take his daughter in his arms. "Where are all the other children? It's so quiet in here I thought I had entered the wrong house by mistake."

"Mother and Michael wanted to take the two boys for a walk in the park, and Nigel and Mammy Tess took the older children out back to play in the doll house."

"It's good of Michael to always include Zack in all their activities with little Tad."

"It is, but I've tried to reassure them time and again it's not necessary every time they do something special with Tad, to include Zachary. He's far too young to notice and I know we won't be offended."

"I think Michael has reasons other than not showing partiality to one grandson over the other. I believe he's trying to make sure little Tad is brought up experiencing a large family, rather than isolation, as his son was raised."

"I'm sure you're right, one thing is for sure, that little one sure gets a lot of attention. He wants for nothing between Mother, Michael and Claire."

Chuckling he said, "You should see how your nose squints up every time you mention her name."

"It does not! You're just trying to get my goat, knowing how much I don't like her."

"You don't?" Joshua gasped teasingly. "Why darling, what a surprise."

Playfully slapping his leg, she said, "Joshua Carmidy, I mean it, quit teasing me, I'm in no mood. She may not be after you anymore, but that doesn't mean I trust her. Coming around on her days off and visiting with Grandfather. Honestly, does she think I can't see through her sudden devotion to him? She's after Alfred's money, just as sure as Kathleen is after Gilbert's. And no one can tell me differently, I tell you true, I know it as sure as I know my name is Elise Carmidy!"

"Well Elise Carmidy, come and dine with your starving husband. And you can tell me all about your letter from Annabelle, and how Kathleen is trying to snag herself a rich husband, which has obviously put you in such a suspicious mood."

Her eyes widened and she said, "How did you know?"

Helping her to her feet, he lovingly teased, "Because I know everything there is to know about you, my pet."

Indignantly she huffed, "Hmm, is that so."

"Why certainly, I've made it my number one priority in life, lest you've forgotten."

Smiling warmly at him, she cooed, "I haven't forgotten, darlin." Placing her hand on the side of his face, she whispered, "Have I told you today how much I love you, Joshua?"

"Not today." Lowering his head to kiss her, he huskily whispered, "Perhaps you could show me though, since the children are all off enjoying themselves this afternoon."

Not hesitating, she called for the nanny, Beatrice, and then leaned closer to him, smiling seductively. "Nothing would please me more."

With Beatrice entering the nursery, Joshua handed his daughter over to the middle-aged nurse. "Emma has been fed and should be ready for her nap. If the other children return, please tell them Mrs. Carmidy and I had a few private matters to take care of and we'll be down shortly."

"Yes, sir."

Tucking his arm around his wife's waist, Elise whispered as they left the room, "Couldn't you think of anything original darlin', we're always havin' matters to discuss in private."

Raising his brow suggestively, he responded, "And we have the children to prove it, too." No sooner had they closed the door of the nursery, than he bent down and in one seamless motion picked her up in his arms. Wrapping her arms tightly around his neck, Elise cooed, "Oh darlin', it's been nearly ten years since we wed, and you excite me today just as you did then."

Just as they reached their bedroom door, a piercing scream echoed from the back of the house and immediately Joshua placed Elise on her feet and ran down the flight of stairs three at a time. Seeing little Alfred in Nigel's arms, screaming out in pain, Joshua yelled, "What is it, Nigel? What the hell happened to my boy?"

"He fell out of a tree, sir. I tried to catch him…"

"Send for the doctor at once!" Joshua demanded, taking his son in his arms. "Let me see, Alfred."

Alfred, letting loose of his arm, cried out, "Papa it hurts. It hurts real bad."

Joshua, looking at the arm, knew at once it had been broken; the lower half of the forearm between the elbow and the wrist dangled outward and was turning blue. "Elise," he called out to his wife, then realizing she was already beside him, lowered his voice as he said, "Have Beatrice get plenty of ice and a large bowl, we have to pack it to stop the swelling."

Nodding, knowing that this was serious, recalling all those soldiers she had tended to during the war, fear gripped at Elise's heart as she ran screaming for the maid. Joshua, holding Alfred in his arms, soothingly tried to console his five-year-old son. "Why, you're a wounded little soldier just like your papa once was. Do you remember me telling you how I got shot in the war and how much it hurt?"

Through his tears, he nodded his head. "Papa, it burns inside."

"I know, Alfred. Try to be brave now son, and let your mama and papa take care of you until the doctor comes."

~

Well past midnight a week later, from the second story of the Honeycut mansion, an oil lamp burned brightly as Elise sat weeping next to her son's bedside, after hearing the grave news the doctor had just delivered to her and Joshua.

"Are you sure there's nothing else that can be done?" she asked pleadingly. "Boys break their arms all the time and they heal just fine. Why, my friend in England broke hers this past May and she didn't have to have her arm amputated."

"I know this is hard to accept, but you can see his hand is black. The blood isn't flowing to it anymore and infection has set in. If we don't remove his hand now he could lose his whole arm, or worse, we could lose him all together."

Clinging to Joshua, who knelt by her side, she cried, "Oh Joshua, I can't bear it. This can't be happening…"

Gingerly trying to help his wife to her feet, he said solemnly, "Come sweetheart, you sit with your grandfather while the doctor does what he has to do to save our boy's life."

Shaking her head adamantly, Elise pulled away from him. "No! Please don't make me leave, Joshua, please. I want to stay with Alfred."

"Sweetheart, this is going to be gruesome, are you sure you can withstand it?"

Pleading her case, she rambled, "I've seen gruesome sights before. Don't you remember during the war? Why, I even saw you with a bullet hole clean through you. Don't make me leave our boy, Joshua; please, I need to be here with him."

"All right sweetheart. But you have to move away from the bed so that the doctor can perform the surgery."

Standing on her own, trying to regain her composure, she nodded her head and let Joshua lead her to the end of the bed. She watched in horror as the doctor placed drops of ether in a cloth and laid the cloth over Alfred's nose again to be certain he was still asleep. Ascertaining that Alfred was fully unconscious, the doctor then reached inside his black bag and pulled out what looked to Elise like a small saw. Holding her breath as she saw him extend her son's disfigured tiny hand toward him, she clenched her fist and bit down on it as a portion of Alfred's arm was removed. As the doctor lay the limb beside him while stitching up the exposed area, she leaned her head into Joshua's protective arms and cried silently. "What's to become of our little boy now, without his hand?"

"Why sweetheart, little Alfred is going to learn that life isn't measured by what you have lost but by what you have."

Wearily Elise smiled at Joshua, amazed that even at a time like this, he knew precisely what to say to ease her troubled heart. "Oh Joshua, thank God you taught me that lesson so long ago. I can't imagine what my life would have been like if I had lost you."

Pulling his wife closer in his arms, he tenderly kissed her head, their eyes resting on the doctor as he continued stitching the skin around Alfred's severed bones. "My pet, I was just thanking God that you taught me that lesson, so now we can now pass it on to our son."

~

August 1874
Devon, England

For several weeks, it had been a battle of wills between the three of them. Gilbert's moods ranged from anger, to being sullen and withdrawn, to deliberately avoiding being around Felicity altogether. While Kathleen continued antagonizing Felicity every chance she could by commenting on how much fun she was having being in the company of such a wonderful man, which only infuriated Felicity more. At first she Kathleen for being so willing to share time with him, when she was supposed to love Will; then radically placing the blame on Gilbert for being so willing to give his attentions to another, and even though she had suggested it, she resented him for doing it so eagerly and willingly. Now Felicity felt melancholy, succumbing to the fact that it was too late for her to sort out what she was feeling in her heart; Gilbert had moved on.

Although Felicity had never witnessed the slightest improprieties between them, with the exception of Kathleen kissing Gilbert's cheek that first night, it was clear they were becoming closer as every day passed. She had noticed how the two of them, when they thought she wasn't noticing, would speak softly to each other as if they had secrets, and Felicity would look away not saying a word, telling herself this was best for all concerned.

On occasion, Will would drop by unannounced, saying he thought he'd take Whitney for a ride, but all the while looking for Kathleen. Finding out that she and Gilbert where out somewhere together, he would leave shortly afterwards sadder than when he'd arrived. Felicity knew the hurt he felt, afraid that he had lost Kathleen to another, but knowing also how Anne opposed any relationship between Kathleen and her son, she tried to remain neutral. As every day passed though, Felicity began hating herself for suggesting that Gilbert see Kathleen. Why hadn't she just left well enough alone, since now Will and she were both miserable.

Tonight, having dressed to go to the village dance, she looked in the mirror and found herself almost in tears. *I can't keep pretending it doesn't matter. It does. Please God, help me to stop caring what he does.*

Having always looked forward to the dances in the past, ever since Benjamin had taken her there so many years ago, Felicity now found that tonight she dreaded going. How could she be expected to put on a happy face, watching Gilbert dance the night away with Kathleen? As if that wasn't bad enough, the three of them were riding over together.

Taking in a deep breath, looking down at her arm which no longer needed to be bandaged, fully healed, she gazed at the scar. Closing her eyes, she recalled the care Gilbert had given her, his tenderness, the touch of his lips on hers. "Stop this!" she whispered. "It's too late Felicity, now let him go, so he can be happy."

Taking in a deep breath for courage, she silently opened her bedroom door and saw Gilbert standing outside the children's door, lost in thought. Closing the door to only a crack, she silently watched him, and found it curious that he looked so forlorn. *Could it be he's not happy with Kathleen?* she wondered. Suddenly he smiled as Kathleen approached from the end of the hall saying, "Ready for a grand night?"

"Aye lass. Don't you look lovely tonight." His words cut Felicity like a knife; her fears were true, he now looked at Kathleen with adoring eyes instead of her. Unable to bear seeing any more, Felicity closed her eyes and shut the door, tears running down her cheeks.

Hearing a knock at her door, she knew they were letting her know they were ready and she called out to them in the steadiest voice she could manage. "I'll be down in a minute."

Immediately brushing the tears away, she ran to the mirror and seeing her face was becoming blotchy, showing she had been crying, she began waving her hand before her face. Realizing she had been partially right after all, what Gilbert had felt for her wasn't love after all. *So you're not that sort of man who gives your heart so easily away, Gilbert? What malarkey!*

Numbly, she walked down the stairs and seeing the two of them speaking in hushed voices, Felicity cleared her throat. "Sorry to have kept you waiting."

Kathleen, turning in her direction, smiled cordially at her. "Is that a new gown, Mrs. Myles? I don't recall you wearing it before."

"Yes, I bought it while on holiday in Glastonbury."

"Ah, Gilbert has spoken so much about your trip. It sounds like an enchanting place."

"It was indeed," Felicity said, glancing briefly at Gilbert who stared back at her with a cold, blank stare. She hadn't expected him to comment on her dress, or the fact they had picked it out together, but she thought he might make a comment about her arm not being bandaged. Getting no reaction, she numbly walked closer to the door and waited as Gilbert opened it. Bravely, she walked down the steps of Brookhaven, noticing the silhouette of the two of them behind her, Kathleen's arm resting on Gilbert's; and she tried to block out her pain. *They have to leave. I can't bear it another day.*

The entire ride over, Felicity sat silently looking out the window, closing her eyes and praying the nightmare would end. As the coach pulled up, and hearing the lively music already playing, Gilbert stepped out and tenderly taking Felicity's arm in his, he said, "I'm glad that your arm healed so well. Are you certain it's wise for you to leave it exposed like this with so many people going to be in attendance?"

Surprised by the concern in his voice, she looked up at him and for a moment as their eyes met, she felt a hint of warmth gazing back at her from his green eyes. "Stephen said I'm completely healed, and I should be fine," she said softly, her heart racing in her chest.

"Are ya now, lass?"

As she stepped from the carriage, glancing to the ground to gauge her footing, she realized that his hand still lingered tenderly on her arm. Not pulling from him as she had in the past, she slowly raised her eyes, inhaled deeply, seeing that he was still looking lovingly at her, expecting an answer to his question, which she had believed to have been rhetorical.

"Only my arm, Gilbert." Time stood still for her, no longer were they staring coldly at each other, but without him saying a word, she knew by the look in his eyes that he still loved her. "Oh Gilbert, I'm sorry. I was wr..." She paused, hearing her name being called by a tall man in the shadows. As he emerged, her heart raced faster, and recognizing him at once she gasped, "Is that you?"

Nodding his head, he continued to approach and hoarsely whispered, "It's me, Felicity. I've come to ask if you can forgive me?"

Running past Gilbert, Felicity squealed as the stranger scooped her up in his arms as she showered him with kisses, crying his name, "Erasmus!" Then suddenly she whispered shyly, "I'm sorry," and timidly correcting herself, she said, "Casper."

He smiled lovingly at her and said, "Actually, these days I go by C.W. but you can call me, whatever you like."

Gilbert, who had inched his way closer to see who this man was who had earned such a response from Felicity, stood frozen as she showered him with kisses again, all the while crying and clinging to him.

Gilbert politely cleared his throat.

Turning her head, smiling through her tears, she eagerly stretched out her arm to Gilbert as Erasmus set her back to the ground. Gilbert noted how she cupped her arm around his waist with one hand while letting her other hand linger on the stranger's chest. "Oh Gilbert, this is my brother. C.W. Phelps."

Judging by the surprised look on Gilbert's face, it was obvious he didn't even know Felicity had a brother. *Brother*? His glare turned to one of relief as C.W. stretched out his arm, Felicity still clinging to him around the waist and beaming at both men.

"Well, it a pleasure to meet ya. I'm Gilbert O'Flaherty."

"Pleasure to make your acquaintance, O'Flaherty. I've heard a lot about you from my missus and Joshua."

Felicity, hearing her brother's comment, squealed again with excitement. "Erasmus, you have a wife? Joshua? Do you mean Joshua Carmidy? How do you know, Joshua? Where is your wife, I want to meet her?"

Erasmus Phelps, shaking his head and smiling, said, "I swear sis, you'll never change. Still firing questions before I get the chance to answer the first." Turning to a woman who was still hidden from plain view, he said, "Constance, sugar, this here is Felicity, and I think you already know Gilbert, here." Turning back toward Gilbert he said, "Beggin' yer pardon, O'Flaherty for the informalities, but I've heard so much about you, it's like we're old buds."

"Gilbert is just fine with me, C.W." Turning to look at the woman who was approaching, Gilbert's smile faded, and Felicity frowned, glancing at the woman who had caused such a reaction.

"Hello, Gilbert." Then smiling warmly over at Felicity, Constance said, "I don't suppose you remember me, Felicity?"

Looking closer, she removed her arm from C.W.'s waist and brought her hand to her mouth. "Oh my goodness, Constance Hildebrandt." Eagerly she rushed to her and laughed, hugging her warmly, hearing her brother correct her.

"Phelps, Mrs. Constance Phelps now, sis."

"Why, I can't believe this," she excitedly exclaimed, glancing between her brother and Constance. "How did you meet?" Then noticing Gilbert's drawn expression she suddenly remembered, Constance had been married to Tad.

Before anyone had a chance to answer, Felicity, seeing Rupert and Annabelle's coach pulling into the dirt path leading to the barn, excitedly bounced up and down and gripped her brother's hand. "Come and meet your cousin, Erasmus—Rupert Robbins and his dear wife, Annabelle."

Dragging him closer to where the coach had parked, she excitedly threw her arms around his neck, looking up at him in disbelief. "I still can't believe you're here."

Rupert stepped out from the coach and seeing how excited she was, her excitement contagious, chortled, "Well my goodness Felicity, what a pleasant surprise to see you so chipper." Then glancing at her companion, he said, "I take it sir, you're the reason for my dear cousin's sudden outburst of enthusiasm."

Before either men had a chance to speak, Felicity, overcome with tears again, said, "Rupert this is Erasmus."

Hearing her speak, Rupert, never one to show much emotion, lowered his jaw and his eyes widened. "Erasmus Phelps?" he asked in stunned disbelief.

Extending his hand to his cousin, Erasmus said in a thick southern drawl, "I go by C.W. these days, but it's me, in the flesh. Pleasure to meet ya, Rupert; at last."

Eagerly, Felicity peeked inside the coach at Annabelle as the two men greeted one another, practically dragging her out from inside. "Annabelle, come quick; it's my brother, he's come to England to find me. Can you believe it; he came to find me! He isn't angry with me any more…If only Auntie Gwen could be here."

Nodding politely to the stranger, who had disappeared back in '65, she said, "What a pleasure to meet you at last, sir." Instinctively, she began hugging Felicity who was overcome with emotion, weeping again. "I'm so happy for you, Felicity."

All the pent up tears Felicity had locked away for years following the death of her parents, came crashing down on her in waves of uncontrollable tears. Realizing they were drawing a crowd of onlookers, Rupert said, "Well it would appear we all have a lot to catch up on. Might I suggest we take this reunion where we can have some privacy?" Looking over at Gilbert, who was quietly chatting with Constance about Fairfax, he said, "Old chap, help me gather Felicity, we're all heading back to Brookhaven."

Nodding politely to Constance before excusing himself, Gilbert went to Felicity's side and protectively placed his arm around her shoulders. Glancing over at Annabelle, as if asking why she was crying so hard, Annabelle said softly, "Having her brother's forgiveness has just caused our dearest Felicity to break down the dam she has built around her heart. She needs to cry it out, but more than that, she needs you, Gilbert."

Knowingly, he nodded at Annabelle, smiling warmly at her while tightening his grip around Felicity's shoulders and guiding her back to the coach as she clung to him, trying to speak through her tears. "I do need you. Oh Gilbert, I'm so sorry, you were right, please forgive me."

"There's nothing to forgive, M'lady."

Hearing him refer to her by his pet name again, the name she had admonished him for using, but had desperately missed, she smiled through her tears and lovingly looked up at him and whispered, "You called me M'lady...oh Gilbert."

Again her tears flowed, and he tenderly tried to console her, whispering, "Yes, M'lady."

C.W., seeing his sister in such a state, looked anxiously over at Rupert, and hoarsely whispered, "Sweet Jesus, what have I done?"

Smiling wearily, patting his cousin on the back, Rupert said gratefully, "I'd say you've just unlocked the demons she's been carrying around in her heart for over a decade. Thank heavens you're here; maybe now she can find peace at last."

Gilbert, getting Felicity back inside the carriage, whispered, "Stay here, lass. I'll get Kathleen."

As if remembering Kathleen, she said whimpering, "I'm sorry that you and she will miss the dance."

"There'll be other dances, lass. Don't be worryin' your pretty head over that now, too. Stay here, I'll be right back."

Stepping out of the coach, Gilbert started looking about and Rupert, who had been joined by Anne and Jacque and had just finished the introductions, called over to him, "What the devil is wrong now, Gilbert?"

Not recalling even escorting her from the coach, Gilbert scratched his head and said, "I seemed to have misplaced Kathleen."

C.W., politely excusing himself from his other cousin, jovially said, "O'Flaherty, if Kathleen was that young woman you and sis were with, she just took off with some young fella a while ago. I heard her calling him Will, I believe."

Gilbert smiled, shaking his head and mumbled under his breath. "Good fer you, lass."

Anne, hearing the news, gasped and looked anxiously between the men, demanding action. "Do something! I won't stand for this!" Then glaring at Gilbert, she hissed, "This is your fault! If you hadn't brought her here, none of this would have happened."

Jacque, trying to soothe Anne, said, "Calm down, you're becoming hysterical, dearest. You go along with Annabelle and Rupert, and Gilbert and I will find them. They can't be too far ahead of us."

Hearing Jacque include him in the equation, Gilbert glanced between them and Felicity. Swearing under his breath, he hastily peeked back inside the coach and said, "A slight change of plans, Felicity. I've got to go and find Kathleen, before Anne sends out a lynch mob."

Felicity's heart sank, but bravely she nodded her head and said, "Of course..."

Anne frantically hailed them. "Hurry up Gilbert, before they get away." He leaned in the coach further, and said, "I'm sorry, M'lady, I'll be back as soon as I can."

Believing he wanted to prevent Kathleen from running off with Will because he wanted her for himself, Felicity said sadly,, "I understand, Gilbert. It's fine..."

As he dashed from the coach, he called to Annabelle, "Stay with her until I return."

Annabelle, glancing between Constance and Anne said, "Why don't we women take Felicity's coach and you and your cousin take our coach, Rupert darling?"

"Right. Where is your carriage, C.W.?"

"Don't be worryin' about me none. I'll have him follow."

"Good show."

As Erasmus ran to where his driver stood beside the rented coach, Rupert took Gilbert aside and whispered, "My guess is they're heading to London, since you've just purchased Lavinia's townhouse for Kathleen."

"Aye, I was just thinkin' the same thing." Anxiously looking over at Jacque who again was calling for him, Gilbert added, "Take care of Felicity for me, Rupert."

"I will, and you take care that Will doesn't do anything rash. I mean it Gilbert, running off with that woman will kill Anne."

Within minutes the three carriages were on their way and Felicity, seeing Gilbert leave with Jacque, closed her eyes allowing herself to cry for the man she had lost to another. *Goodbye Gilbert, I hope you find her, for your sake.*

~

Hours had passed as the Robbins's and Phelps's waited for the return of Will and Kathleen. Huddled in the study in Brookhaven, they described the events of their lives that had occurred while Felicity and her brother had been apart. Felicity held onto C.W.'s hand, stroking it gently from time to time, still not fully believing that he was there with her. She was so immensely grateful that they were at last reunited, it never occurred to her to ask why he had abandoned her when she needed him most, or why he had kept his whereabouts from her all these years. His reasons were completely insignificant to her now; all she cared about was that she and Erasmus had made amends.

Glancing at Constance, she smiled warmly at her, knowing in part that the love they shared was the reason Erasmus's heart had healed from the anger and pain he had held onto for all these years. Then hearing of how he had contributed to Constance's healing after her devastating marriage to Tad, Felicity was surprised that Joshua and Erasmus had seen each other often since their return, yet no one had informed her.

"Sis, don't be angry with your friends. I made them promise to keep it from you until I was ready to accept some of the responsibility for the past."

"Oh, Erasmus, let's make a pact with one another just as we did as children. Do you remember?"

"I remember." Lifting his pinky and hugging her, he added, "The infamous, pinky swear."

Felicity smiled, then nodding and lifting her pinky, eagerly said, "Let's pinky swear, Erasmus, that we will leave all the pain and suffering we caused one another in the past, where it belongs."

Locking fingers, they hugged and Rupert smiled. "Well, it's late. I'm sure you and your dear wife are tired, C.W. Why don't I ring for Mrs. Duncan to show you to your room, while Annabelle takes Felicity to hers?"

"No Rupert, I can."

Raising his arm, he said tenderly, "Felicity quit being so stubborn. You're tired and I'm sure Annabelle and you want a few minutes alone, just as I need a few minutes with Anne."

"Not that I'll admit to being stubborn Rupert, but I am tired, and rather than trouble Mrs. Duncan, I'll show Erasmus and Constance to their rooms, only if you promise to send for me when Kathleen and Gilbert return." Seeing her cousin agree, she rose and hugged her brother, and then turning to Constance, she whispered while hugging her, "Thank you so much for bringing my brother to me. I shall always love you for this."

"Thank you, Felicity, for never having stopped loving my wonderful husband."

After tending to her guests behind closed doors with her dear friend, Felicity said, "Isn't it ironic how life is sometimes? Tonight, being reunited with Erasmus reminded me of how much joy I had when Ben and I were finally reunited after so much sorrow and heartache, only to lose my beloved aunt within seconds."

Annabelle, sighing, took Felicity by the shoulders and said, "Well it's about time you realized how much you loved Gilbert, before you did lose him."

Wide eyed, she whispered, "I never said I loved Gilbert, Annabelle, all I meant was as happy as it was to be reunited with Erasmus, it saddened me to know a dear friend was leaving my life."

"Felicity Robbins-Phelps-Myles, I have stood by for weeks watching you torment yourself and that man, and I'm telling you true, I'm losing my patience with you and your stubbornness and that misguided nobility and loyalty, too."

"Excuse me?"

Not backing down, Annabelle said, "You heard me. And before you get yourself all worked up and start clenching your fists in anger, sit down and hear me out. Then afterwards, if you want to get angry with me then go right ahead, but I'm going to have my say first; and what's more, you are going to listen to me."

Stunned, Felicity glanced at her friend and said, "Fine Annabelle, I'm too tired to argue with you."

Taking a seat across from her, Annabelle sighed, and lovingly took Felicity's hand. "What a dear woman you are. Always extending forgiveness to everyone except yourself. Releasing Erasmus from the pain he had caused you; comforting me after my sister killed your husband, telling me it wasn't my fault; forgiving Anne for bringing that monster back into your life and then thanking her for banishing him back to London. I could go on if you like, to make my point, and list hundreds of times that I've watched you extend such kindness to others, freely and willingly, but I won't. That is unless you make me, by being too stubborn for your own good."

Glancing over at Felicity and seeing she wasn't protesting, she continued. "Now I'm asking you to please Felicity, afford yourself the same courtesy, and for God's sake, stop punishing yourself and Gilbert for living when Miranda and Benjamin died. You had no control over their deaths, but just because their hearts stopped beating, does not mean yours has to. That man loves you and you love him, yet you refuse to let either of you share in any joy because of blind loyalty. I didn't know Miranda very well, but from I have heard about her, she loved her husband too much to let him just exist in the hellish prison you have created for him. And I know without a doubt Benjamin wouldn't want this for the precious wife he loved so dearly. So why, Felicity; why must you keep punishing yourself and Gilbert? Don't let him leave here tomorrow without letting him know he is loved."

Tears streaming down her face, Felicity said numbly, "Gilbert is leaving tomorrow? Where? Why?"

"He is returning to Ireland, and you know somewhere deep inside you the reason why he must go, Felicity. Now I'm going to go downstairs and wait with Anne and Rupert. I pray, Felicity, that you will take this time to think of what it is you truly feel for this man, and then find the courage to follow your heart."

Shortly after Annabelle left her room, pondering everything that had happened, upon hearing the sounds of horses approaching, Felicity leapt from her chair. Glancing from her window and seeing Gilbert entering the house and comforting a distraught Kathleen, she opened the door to her bedroom hesitantly. Taking in a deep breath, her mind racing with her own doubts and Annabelle's words, she lingered before exiting her room, trying to decide if she was ready to speak with Gilbert. Had she seen love for her in his eyes, or had he left her tonight because he now felt obligated to be with Kathleen? Before she could muster enough courage to confront her fears, she heard Gilbert and Kathleen conversing.

"Oh, Gilbert what am I to do? What must you think of me…"

"Don't be worrying about me, lass. Just finish packing and we'll talk tomorrow."

"After tonight, are we still leaving?"

"Aye. Nothing has changed. We both need a fresh start."

~ Twenty-Five ~

Leaning against a tree amidst the thick clearing, to avoid being seen, Felicity listened as Gilbert played his flute that he thought only the birds could appreciate. As the beautiful melody filled the air, she closed her eyes, wishing things between them hadn't become so complicated.

Stepping out of the clearing, Gilbert saw her and he stopped playing abruptly. Apprehensively, she said, "Hello, Gilbert. I hope you're not angry with me for listening to you play without being invited, but I couldn't help myself. I was mesmerized. What song is that? It was lovely."

Standing and hastily putting his flute back inside its felt pouch, he said, "Just an old folk song about a poor fisherman who fell in love with a Merrow."

Felicity's heart ached that he had chosen this song to play on the day he was leaving Brookhaven. Knowing what the Merrow was, he having accused her of being one the day they had returned from Glastonbury. Rather than try to explain her actions as she had done then, she said, "Isn't that the sea maiden who abandons her cloak to come ashore to love a human, only to return to the sea later?"

"Aye, she leaves the fisherman despite his love for her, back to the life she thinks she belongs in." His jaw stiffened and he said defiantly, "But don't be feelin' sorry for the fisherman lass, in the end he finds his way in the world with another, but this time with his own kind."

Hearing his comment, her heart sank. He was telling her he no longer loved her and now loved Kathleen. Swallowing hard, holding back her tears of regret, she softly said, "I see. Well , I'm happy for the fisherman."

"What did ya come by today for, Felicity? Surely not to be speaking about the fairies, which you never believed in to begin with."

His words cut her like a knife, his tone so cold it made her shiver on this warm summer day. Rather than run from him as she had done so often since her accident, Felicity bravely stepped closer, determined not to let him leave Brookhaven on these terms. There had to be a way to resolve their differences without having harsh words again.

"Gilbert, just because I didn't believe in them before, doesn't mean I can't change my mind. People do, from time to time, you know. Not everyone is like you; able to adapt so readily to the unknown; some people need time to accept new things in their lives."

"That may be so lass, but ya either believe in the fairies or ya don't. One can't be making another feel somethin' they don't have it in them to feel, now can they? No matter how much time they are willing to give 'em, some things just aren't meant to be."

Both Gilbert and Felicity knew they weren't discussing the fairies anymore and she searched for the right words to explain what she felt in her heart. It wasn't that she had been ashamed to love a man like him, but rather, that she was ashamed that she had loved another man, period. Suddenly she wondered if it would even matter to him why she had pushed him away from her, or if she had the right to even explain her actions since he had chosen another. Tired of being noble, always trying to do the right thing for the sake of others, she cast all her fears aside, and said, "You're right; I didn't come here today to speak about the fairies…"

"Well then speak your mind lass, we both have other things we need to be tendin' to, now don't we? You got yer brother to welcome back into your life, which ya didn't feel the need to share with me. Havin' to find out after he returned. And we can't be forgettin' that fancy dinner party of yours to get ready for, now can we lass? I'd hate to be makin' ya late for such an important occasion, as celebrating your birthday with those you love."

As she looked at him, she couldn't believe he was the same man who only last night had looked at her with such warmth, then today be angry with her all over again. Annabelle was right, she had tormented him for so long that now he couldn't help but feel bitterness toward her.

"Gilbert, this morning Erasmus gave me this letter from Elise. She sent it along with him since she wanted to be certain I would receive it and not have it get lost in the post. Young Albert had a terrible accident. He fell from a tree and broke his arm. There were complications and they had to amputate part of his arm."

Her words shocked him out of his intolerance to being in her presence, and he began wringing his hands. "Jesus, Mary and Joseph, he's only a child…"

Trembling inside, searching for the courage to speak from her heart, she said, "Gilbert, after reading Elise's letter and crying over what had happened to little Albert, suddenly I realized just how blessed I was. I had to see you today, not to tell you how grateful I am, although I am, Gilbert. More than you will ever know. I owe you so much, not just for caring for me after the accident, but for helping me to restore my life after Ben died. The one thing I had always prided myself on was that through even the darkest times in my life, I was a survivor. But after Ben died, I was barely surviving. I had no idea how to go on, or how to mend my broken heart; until you showed me how. And although I'm still very frightened, and know I have made incredibly bad choices, I've come here today to ask, even plead with you if necessary, if there is any way that we could be friends again." Gilbert said not a word, only gazed deeply into her eyes, and for a brief moment she thought she detected a glimmer of tenderness toward her and she continued. "I promise you Gilbert, I won't come between you and the life you have now found with Kathleen."

Whatever tenderness she had seen vanished instantly, and he spat indignantly, "Kathleen? Is that what you think, I've done? Well lass, as usual you are wrong again. In case it escaped you, she was trying to run off with Will last night, not me."

Felicity's eyes widened; *Did he just say what she thought he said?* Stammering for words, she said, "Gilbert, I'm so confused. I thought you were taking her to Ireland. I heard you say last night that you two were still leaving, to finish packing...."

"Ah, so now the real reason why you came down here comes out. You figured out I was leaving, and you thought Kathleen was comin' with me. Now why doesn't that surprise me?" Shaking his head and snickering under his breath, he said snidely, "You sure have a knack fer gettin' things all mixed up, now don't ya, Felicity? Aye, Kathleen has some packin' to do, but it's not because she's a travelin' to Ireland with me. She's on her way to London. I bought her Annabelle's deceased sister's townhouse so she could start a fresh life."

"London? Is that why you're so angry with me, because last night after her seeing you being so kind to me she got jealous and tried to run off with Will? Well, I swear Gilbert, despite me believing she wasn't right for you and the children after all, I didn't mean to come between you two."

Obviously disgusted with her words, he abruptly interrupted. "Didn't ya just hear me, lass?" Then shaking his head as if tired of trying to explain things to her, he spat, "Felicity, go home. I've got lots to do today and ain't got the time nor the inclination to be tellin' ya again that I don't care where Kathleen Sullivan goes. I look after her because her brother was me mate, and nothin' more."

"Please don't be angry with me. When I heard you were leaving so unexpectedly, I naturally thought you were taking Kathleen back to your homeland so you and she could be alone, but if that's not the case, then why are you leaving here?"

Judging by his menacing glare, she knew her words had further angered him. "Is that the kind of man you think I am? Well listen up lass, if'n I wanted to be alone with that woman, that door was opened for me to waltz on in, the night she arrived. Truth be known, I'm leaving to get away from you!"

Felicity gasped. "Me? Surely, you don't mean that. I know you've been angry with me, but Gilbert, I never dreamt it had come this far. What can I say or do to make you want to stay?"

Taking in a deep breath, he looked at her and rather than continue yelling at her, he calmly said, "Felicity, a long while back, I told ya certain things are better left unsaid. Well this is one of those times, so please just let it go."

Ignoring his request, she looked pleadingly at him. "I can't, Gilbert. I need to know if you are intending to return."

"Stop, woman! I ain't some lap dog you can throw a bone to every now and then. I'm a man, and Felicity, you don't want another man in your life that truly loves you. Lest you forgot, you pushed me away, tellin' me you could never be with me because of our past. So I tried it your way, pretending to court Kathleen, in hopes that it would spark some jealousy in you, but all it sparked was resentment in me. And I don't want to resent you anymore for letting me be with her, or any other woman. I'm tired of fightin' with ya, being angry with ya for being so stubborn. Hell, I've even tried to hate ya for casting me aside; as if what we had didn't matter to ya. But I can't. All I feel is love for you and it hurts watchin' ya from afar, knowin' you ain't never gonna allow yourself to love me because of those we loved in the past. Don't ya see? I have to leave here to try to stop feeling the way I do about ya. Last night when you came down the stairs, I saw the pain in your eyes Felicity, and I can't bear it that I'm the one causing it. So don't be askin' me if I'm coming back or how long I'm going to be gone, because damn it all to hell, I don't know! All I do know is I have to leave if I'm ever to find some peace. So I'm askin' ya again; please Felicity, go home!"

The welled up tears she had been holding back began to fall as her heart raced in her chest. How she ached to be able to say the words she felt in her heart, but her inner fears would not allow her to say them aloud. Instead, she defiantly said, "No! I allowed you to speak your mind Gilbert, now kindly afford me the same opportunity."

"Not that it will be makin' a difference, but go ahead."

Taking in a deep breath to help steady her nerves, knowing she only had this moment to make him understand, she continued. "Gilbert, in Glastonbury when you held me in your arms after we kissed, and said it was a gift from the fairies, I asked them to please let you kiss me again, to make me your own. Then later that night, when we returned and my wish had gone unanswered, I was so ashamed. Imagine asking the fairies for such a thing, not to mention how such a request dishonored the memory of such a fine man as Ben, and a dear woman and friend as Miranda. All because of my own selfishness. And rather then repent, instead, the memory of the first time you kissed me flooded my mind. When you thought I was unconscious after my fall, and you cupped my face in your hands with such a sweetness. I don't think I will ever forget it as long as I live."

His eyes widened and Felicity waited to see if he was going to respond to her confession. Seeing no signs that Gilbert was ready to say anything to her, she bravely went on. "For all these months, every moment since, awake and in my dreams, I've been fighting the guilt of just how much I wanted to feel your lips on mine again. I hated myself for having those desires. Worse, I hated how much I had grown to love you. So you see Gilbert, I lied to you when I said I was not your lady and a second time when you said you had seen the depth of my love for you in my eyes and I denied it."

Pausing to gauge his reaction and detecting none, she meekly added, "The guilt of betraying Benjamin's and Miranda's memories and the love we felt for them consumed me. Don't you see Gilbert; people who fall in love a second time…it's not supposed to be with such depth and passion, it's supposed to be a love of companionship so that the memory of their first love never fades."

"Where do come up with these notions of yours?" Seeing her shake her head, unable to speak any more, he grasped her in his arms and huskily whispered as his mouth came crashing down on hers. "Christ almighty, I love you, M'lady."

Hearing him call her his pet name again, Felicity whispered breathlessly, "Oh Gilbert, I love you, too."

Immediately he pulled her so close to him that it took her breath away and she gasped, feeling his hands groping at her body. She urgently matched his fire and passion, and moaned before pulling her mouth from his lips, and looked into his eyes.

With trembling fingers, she touched his cheek and whispered, "Gilbert, will you please take me to your cabin?"

"Aye, lass; but not today. Not until I'm sure that you won't be finding that cloak and return to the legacy you and Whitney deserve."

Resting her head on his chest, she said softly, "Gilbert I'm not a Merrow, I won't abandon our love once I step back into Brookhaven. Not this time, not ever again."

"I pray that's so, but lass, no matter how much I love you, you need to know that I cannot ever live in the same house where you and Benjamin shared a life. No more than you could live where Miranda and I lived. Their memories would haunt us."

Closing her eyes, knowing his words made sense, she asked, "So where does that leave us, Gilbert?"

"Confused." Pushing her gently from him, he looked deeply into her eyes and said, "Fear not though, M'lady, we can work through our troubles; after all, we got the saints and fairies on our side. You go on and get yourself all pretty for that party of yours tonight and let me tend to what I've got to do —I really have a lot to do today, lest you be forgettin' it's someone's birthday."

Lovingly, she smiled at him, and whispered, "I already have all I need or want. I have your love and I won't ever push that away from me again." Groaning, he leaned his head down and again kissed her tenderly as he held her in his arms.

"I'm starting to believe that, birthday girl."

"Good." Dreamily she laid her head back against his shoulder as if him carrying her were the most natural thing to do. "Gilbert, when is your birthday?"

"Oh, it's come and went already. It was in May."

"May? Why, you didn't say a word. I feel dreadful, I didn't get you anything."

"Sure you did, M'lady; you didn't die on me. And I got to kiss you for the first time."

Her eyes widened, looking up at him. "Surely your birthday wasn't the day of my accident? Why that's awful. You fixed breakfast for me and Whitney, and then the accident. Oh dear, you had a dreadful birthday."

"That's not how I remember it. Why, I think my thirty-seventh birthday was probably the best one of my life. You came to me freely that day, Felicity, on your own accord, wearing your red riding coat and letting me fuss over ya. And like I said, you just didn't give up and die on me after yer fall, instead you fought and stayed alive."

Raising one eyebrow suggestively, and grinning impishly, he added, "Not to mention, I did see you in yer birthday suit before I kissed those sweet lips of yers. So all in all, I'd say it was a perfect day."

Indignantly, she sighed. "How embarrassing that you saw me naked for the first time at my worst, all bloody and mangled up like that, why I'm mortified."

Chuckling softly, he said huskily, "To me, I had just cast my eyes on a delicate angel. The same angel I'm hoping to have another chance to see in all her splendor again, but this time fully awake so she can see how much I appreciate gazing at her loveliness."

Tracing the features of his face lovingly, looking into his eyes, she said softly without hesitation or regrets, "Well, Gilbert O'Flaherty, you could stop being so stubborn and whisk me away to your cabin."

Lifting her in his arms, she began to giggle softly. "Where are you taking me? Your cabin is that way," she said, pointing in the opposite direction from where they were headed.

Shaking his head, grinning as he continued to carry her in his arms, just as he had the day of her accident, he replied lightly, "There'll be no visiting my cabin for you, M'lady, not until we're wed. I waited this long to make ya mine so the way I figure it, I can wait a wee bit longer."

"Ah, so are you proposing to me?"

"Aye. And I just figured out where we're to be wed, too."

"Is that so? And what if I have objections?"

"Now why would ya be havin' objections since ya already said it was an enchanting place?"

"Glastonbury? Oh Gilbert, that's perfect," she purred. "Well now that we've decided where, just when will this glorious event take place?"

"Well that will be depending on you, lass. We can either wait to have our house built, or we can live in the cabin and watch it being built."

"Does that mean we're staying here in England?"

"Aye, this is where we fell in love; it's grown on me some."

"Well in that case, I think it's time for another compromise, Mr. O'Flaherty. And not like our last one, where I didn't really want to win and only pretended to let you win; this time we are going to have to really negotiate."

"Is that right? Well what do you want to negotiate and then I'll be decidin' if it's worth me while?"

Raising her brow, she purred in an Irish brogue, "Oh, I'll be makin' it worth yer while, lad. That, ya can be countin' on."

Glancing down at her and grinning, he said, "Ya wouldn't be usin' a little Irish diplomacy on me, now would ya lass?"

"I woul, indeed," she replied laughing. "Just so long as I get what I want."

"And what that be, M'lady?"

"I want to watch our house being built, as Mrs. O'Flaherty. But I don't want to move all of us into the cabin, it's far too small for the children too, and we can't leave them in Brookhaven alone at night. So, I propose we move your bed and all your lovely furnishings to a vacant room in the house, that we can share as our room. I'll board off the other room if you like, but please Gilbert, don't make us wait any longer. I love you and I don't want to waste another minute not sharing my love with you completely."

Taking a few minutes to consider what she had just said, he shook his head. "Remind me never to negotiate with you again. I don't have it in me, not to be givin' ya what ya want, especially when yer right."

"Oh Gilbert...." Tenderly she kissed him, as he continued to carry her, then whispered, "Thank you."

"There'll be no more of that, lass, or you'll be persuading me not to wait till we're wed, too. So behave yerself, so I can take ya home and be rid of ya."

Wrapping her arms around his neck, she cooed, "Oh you're not going to be rid of me that easily, Mr. O'Flaherty. I can be just as stubborn as you Irish can when I get it in my head."

Chuckling, he said, "As if I didn't know that." His smile faded and his voice trailed off, seeing a coach turn down the long drive leading to Brookhaven. Gently, he lowered Felicity to her feet.

"What's wrong?" Seeing the coach, she sighed and her heart sank. "Oh no, he's back. Why do you suppose James has returned from London?"

Pulling her behind a willow tree where they wouldn't be noticed, he seethed, "I don't know. But I'll hand it to that river rat, he never misses an opportunity to shower you with his attentions, and what better day than on your birthday?"

"No, I'm sure it's something more than that. Anne wouldn't bring him here after we've been reunited unless it was extremely important." Then seeing William step out from the coach, she said, "This has something to do with Kathleen, I think. But why would James be here?"

"Well, we can't find out from behind this tree, that's for sure. You go on ahead and act like nothing has changed. As far as you know, I'm packing to head for Ireland. That way if the river rat has other ideas, it'll be me, takin' him off guard for a change. Now run along, before they come in search of ya."

Shaking her head, not wanting to go, he kissed her lips briefly, then said, "Shh, please Felicity, trust me. We'll not have a moment's peace as long as that man is always lurking around. Now be a good lass and scoot. I won't be long, I just have something to get from the cabin and then I'll join ya."

Kissing Gilbert one last time, Felicity nonchalantly stepped out from behind the tree and began walking to her home through the garden just as Anne and Kathleen stepped out of the study. Seeing her approach, Anne said, "Thank heavens I found you before this woman tried to run off with my son again, prior to him discovering the truth about her, that James was so good as to enlighten me about."

"I hardly think anything James Sterling says would be enlightening. Especially since we know what a vile, despicable bastard, he truly is."

Anne, shoulders squared off and with a superior tone, scolded, "Is that any way a lady of your stature should talk?"

"Trust me Anne, when it comes to him it is. Everything that spiels from his lips are lies, designed only to benefit him. I've come to believe he is truly the devil's spawn."

"Yes, well I hope you're wrong Felicity, since not only does he have startling information regarding this gold-digger, his news includes Gilbert O'Flaherty as well. And I can assure you Felicity, after you hear about what that rogue has done you'll be glad he's leaving for Ireland."

~ Twenty-Six ~

Breathless after running all the way to the cabin, Gilbert headed straight to the chest of drawers and raised it enough so that he could place his arm under it to retrieve something. Having secured what he was in search of, he quickly lowered the chest of drawers back in place and then solemnly looked at the bloody handkerchief in his hands. "Aye, now if this ain't a sight to behold— me mate's blood all over the devil's handiwork."

Unwrapping the bundle carefully, Gilbert stared at the gun that had taken Benjamin's life. "Parson, you up there with the angels know I ain't one to be usin' violence anymore since my mate David died savin' me skin. Ya also know how it came to be that Lavinia got this here fancy gun to shoot ya with."

Tracing the initials engraved J.S. on the edge of the handle, Gilbert continued sadly. "We were lookin' after yer missus so much, we didn't see him blindside ya like he did. And I'm sorry for that, mate. Real sorry, but as I've come to know, it was all meant to be, just like you used to tell me right here in this cabin—you're up there watching over me Mandy girl while I tend to Felicity and yer boy. So if it's agreeable to ya, I sure could be usin' some help today as I stop that evil man from harmin' those we love again."

Then swiftly going to the top drawer of the chest, Gilbert reached for a sock in the far back of the drawer. Turning the sock over, two bullets dropped into his palm. Without hesitation Gilbert loaded them into the chamber then shoved the pistol and handkerchief in his pocket and ran toward Brookhaven.

~

"Oh come now Kathleen, are you suggesting that Gilbert bought you a townhouse in London, just because he wanted to give you a fresh start? And that he didn't know you were with child?"

Looking nervously over at William, Kathleen said, "Mrs. Freeport, just because I went to visit an old woman in town for a stomach ailment doesn't mean I'm with child."

Anne, clearly disgusted, turned to Felicity and spouted, "Surely you aren't naive enough to not see what has been going on right under your own nose, Felicity. Come to your senses and see the two of them for what they really are. Gilbert had his fun with her, and now he wants to rid himself of her so as not to destroy his chances with you. He'll take his respectable children off to Ireland for a few months and then waltz back into your life. With his tart far from here, I'm sure he'll suddenly find it necessary to make a business trip from time to time so he can visit her and his bastard child."

Badly shaken, Felicity remained calm and said, "Nothing you and that man has said," pausing to glare at James Sterling, she continued,"…proves anything Anne. I already knew that Gilbert was visiting Ireland; as a matter of fact, I knew last evening. Annabelle told me. Which is precisely why I went to see Gilbert today—to say goodbye and to see if I could assist him in packing up the children's belongings. Moreover, just because he bought Lavinia's townhouse doesn't mean he's trying to keep a mistress. It makes perfect sense he would try to help Kathleen begin a new life. Why, he's been financially helping her and his late brother, prior to his death, for years. And with Kathleen and he having no other family, he understandably feels a certain obligation to look after her. Furthermore, if Kathleen says she went to that midwife because she was feeling under the weather, I believe her. Why, Catherine had an upset stomach a few weeks past and she certainly isn't with child, so why would you assume the worst simply because James Sterling of all people, has come rushing down from London spreading vile lies? Trust me, I know what a master of deception he is, having fallen victim to one of his schemes myself."

"Oh Felicity, you can't be serious…"

Taking in a deep breath, Felicity glared at James. "This man cannot be trusted – not now, not ever!" Then returning her attention to Anne she added sarcastically, "Surely it's not I who am being naïve here, Anne. Don't you see he's only here to worm his way back into our lives, to wreak further misery? And what better way than to try to help you keep your son away from a woman you despise. Don't believe him, Anne. William loves her, and she loves him. Please don't let him try to discredit good people just so that heathen can try to claim what he thinks he's entitled to."

Directing her attention back to James, she sternly added, "As far as I'm concerned this only proves what a despicable, vile, and contemptuous, low-life you truly are. Now I want you out of my home at once. You disgust me."

Standing, James looked unscathed by Felicity's words. "You forgot barbarian, in your rather colorful description. But fear not, I shall add the other adjectives that you have seen fit to use to describe me, to the others. And although it is true that I desperately want an opportunity to try to make amends for the unconscionable acts that I have committed in the past, this time Felicity, I am not the one deceiving you. It is the Irish potato farmer and his tart, and if you will permit me, I shall retrieve the midwife from the carriage. You can hear from her that Kathleen is with child, and that she admitted from her own mouth that she didn't know who the father was. Will or Gilbert."

Kathleen, hearing his comment began crying, looking pleadingly at Will. "He's lying, I swear he's lying."

James, not relenting said, "Fine then, I shall retrieve her right now. And she can tell us all how you became hysterical when you found out you were with child, and confessed that you didn't know who the father was because you had slept with two men in a fortnight. One out of love, and the other out of revenge. Revenge because you had been hurt, right Kathleen? William cast you aside so you and Gilbert took up with one another."

William, looking over at her, said, "For God's sake, say something. Please tell me it's not true."

Anne, trying to console her son, said, "William, I tried to warn you against the likes of her; she doesn't deserve your love."

Turning to Anne, he glared, gritting his teeth. "Shut up, Mother!" Then looking at Kathleen, he asked in a pleading voice, "Are you with child, Kathleen?"

"Yes," she whispered through her tears.

"See, William, I told you!"

Ignoring his mother, William walked across the room and knelt before her, pleadingly looked into her tear-stained eyes and asked softly, "Tell me Kathleen, is it my child?"

Before she could respond, James said, "Oh please enlighten the poor boy, but I warn you Kathleen, be truthful, because otherwise I'll have to tell him about your insatiable appetite."

Glaring at him, she began shaking her head and looked at William. "Please Will, if I mean anything to you; don't make me answer you here. Let me explain."

William's head slumped to his chest and he hissed under his breath, "Ah, Christ almight Kathleen, you just did." Looking up at her as he stood, he said, "How could you Kathleen, when you said you loved me, too?"

Anne, trying to console her son, reached for him as he rushed from the room, straight into Gilbert. "Get away from me, you cad," he hissed.

Gilbert responded, his voice just above a whisper, "I never bedded her, Will. I swear on everything that is holy. Now you can run off here today with a broken heart, or you can hear me out."

"She lied to me..." Will's voice trailed off as he saw Erasmus exit the cloakroom. "Who are you and what are you doing in my cousin's home?"

C.W. motioned to the younger man, and whispered, "I'm Felicity's brother, so I guess that makes us cousins, too. Now come on in here and listen up to a couple of men who know a thing or two about women and life. Before you lose the best thing that ever happened to ya, lad."

Numbly, William followed Gilbert and the man he had never seen before into the cloakroom.

"Listen up Will, Kathleen didn't betray you," Gilbert said. "If she was with another man, it was before she fell in love with you. Now I ain't got time to be makin' small talk with ya." Pulling two tickets from his jacket that he had just convinced Erasmus to give him for return passage to America, Gilbert said, "This here is your chance to prove just how much you really love that woman in there. Now the way I'm thinkin', that child she's carryin' could just as much be yers as any other. Now you can walk away from them and regret it all the days of yer life; that's your choice and you'll never hear a word from me about it. On the other hand, you can be the man Kathleen thought you were when she told ya she loved ya, and when she told me how much she loved you, too. And Will, I'm tellin ya, after what I've learned about the life she was forced to live just to survive, she ain't never known love before."

Confused, Will mumbled, "But what if it's not mine? How will..."

"Look, Benjamin loved Whitney like he was his, so don't be askin' me how you can do it. It's plain and simple; you do it because you love that woman, who believes in you. Do you want these tickets or don't ya? Cause I'm leavin' out of here to protect the woman I love. Felicity!"

Hesitating for just a second, William grabbed the tickets, and Gilbert patted him on the back. "You won't be sorry Will, I can promise ya that." Looking up at C.W., he said, "Have the lad wait in your coach, then when Kathleen comes out have that driver of yours take them straight to Plymouth." Directing his attention back to Will he continued, "Hide out there 'till ya start your new life with yer wife. Hear me Will, make it legal first. As soon as ya land in New York, head for Chicago. I'll be needin' someone I trust to handle some business out there. C,W. here will tell ya how to get there. Wire if ya need some money."

"I got it covered, O'Flaherty; now go protect my sister from that low-bellied critter you've been tellin' me about."

Rushing outside of the study, Gilbert stood silently and listened to Felicity speaking as he watched Erasmus and William leave through the front door.

"Leave her alone. Haven't you caused enough pain? You got what you wanted. William has left, why must you keep torturing her?" Felicity angrily yelled at Anne and James, while trying to calm Kathleen. "Kathleen, please don't cry. It's not healthy for you to be so upset at a time like this."

James, kneeling before Felicity, whispered, "I can't leave here Felicity, until you face the fact that Gilbert O'Flaherty is nothing but that street beggar we dragged off the streets in New York. He bought her that townhouse with the money he got from your friend's sorrowful death just so he could set himself up with a mistress." Glaring at Kathleen he said, "Tell her Gilbert is the father, or so help me I'll tell her everything I know about you, starting with your fondness for dessert."

Seeing Kathleen's reaction, crying even harder, shaking uncontrollably, with her head in her hands, Felicity snarled, "Dessert? What are you babbling about? Leave her alone."

"Tell her Kathleen or I will!" James demanded.

Kathleen raising her head and looked pleadingly at Felicity. "You and Gilbert have been real good to me, better than anyone has ever treated me in my whole life, and I don't want to hurt you."

Gilbert, walking into the room firmly stated, "Then don't, lass. There ain't no need to be telling lies, just 'cause that river rat thinks he's got ya cornered." Pausing just in front of James who now stood glaring at him, Gilbert said, "Get away from my fiancée!"

James, clearly shocked at hearing Gilbert refer to Felicity in such a manner, sputtered, "Fiancée? You're lying, Felicity would never marry the likes of you!"

Her heart pounded in her chest, grateful that Gilbert had come in when he did; and hearing him refer to her as his fiancée, Felicity beamed with pride. As her eyes locked on to his, revealing all the love she felt for him, Felicity said, "That's where you're wrong, James. Not only am I going to marry this wonderful man, who I trust with all my heart, I thank God he loves me as I love him." Then turning back to James, her tone cold and foreboding, she said, "Now I told you before, get out my home. Either you do, or my soon-to-be-husband will throw you out onto the street, where *you* belong."

"I belong here with you, Felicity…with my son."

Gilbert pushed his shoulder against James, and hissed, "You ain't man enough to be a real father. And you sure the hell ain't fit to wipe the mud off Felicity's boots! You heard my betrothed; she wants the *likes* of *you* out of her home, so Sterling, please give me cause to throw ya out of here bodily."

"This isn't over, you smug street urchin! Wasn't your lustful Irish wench here, lofty enough for you? Oh that's right; you only fancy rich, respectable women to make you feel like a man."

Gilbert, turning to Felicity, in a calm voice said, "M'lady, you take Kathleen on out of here, while me and this river rat have ourselves a little chat." Gilbert turned back to James with squared off shoulders. "I'd be watchin' that tongue of yers if I was you, or maybe these fine folk would like to hear about the gift you left yer demented ex-wife when ya visited her last year."

"What the hell are you babbling about? I never went to see Lavinia. Did that lustful wench of yers tell ya that lie?" James jerked his head around, glaring at Kathleen who was being helped up off the couch by Felicity, then turned back to Gilbert. "Only a fool would believe the words of a whore."

Anne gasped, hearing his latest comment. "What have you done, James? You're lying. You went to see Lavinia last year. Jacque went with you. He told me he waited outside in the coach."

Looking over at Anne then at Gilbert, Felicity said apprehensively, "What's going on Gilbert? What gift? What has he done? What haven't you told me?"

Not taking his eyes off of James, he said calmly, "My beloved Felicity, please be a good lass, and do what I asked. I swear, I'll tell ya everything later, trust me, M'lady."

Beginning to tremble, she whispered, "I do trust you, my love, I don't trust him." Then walking to the door, she softly added, "Come, Kathleen and Anne."

Hearing the door close behind him, Gilbert said in a stern voice, "Kathleen is no whore, but you sure the hell are a depraved, lying bastard. And I got me real proof without blackmailing a poor, frightened woman!" Gilbert reached into his pocket and pulled out the derringer and handkerchief.

James's eyes bulged. "Where did you get that?"

"Benjamin Myles— just before he died. He took it from that ex-wife of yers, just after she shot him. Ya see this here blood, 'tis the blood of me mate that you caused just as sure as if ya shot him yerself. Now you get out of this house and don't you ever try to come near Felicity and that boy again. Or I'll be takin' yer fancy pistol with yer initials engraved on it and shoot ya dead meself. Shouldn't be too hard to convince the local constable that you shot yerself. Face it, river rat, ain't no one gonna care if yer alive or dead or if I come by and piss on yer grave if'n I get me a mind to."

"Is that right, O'Flaherty? Well you don't have the guts to, otherwise you already would have."

Placing the gun in his hand, his index finger hovering over the trigger, Gilbert hissed, "Oh I got me the guts alright, and I'm hopin' yer goin' to give me a chance to prove it."

"That gun's not even loaded, all it had was one bullet in it. Could I help it if Lavinia decided to save it for that swine rather than to end her own pathetic life like I told her too?"

"Oh, it's loaded, alright. Now get the hell out!"

Not giving him a chance to finish his sentence, James lunged for the gun.

Hearing scuffling from outside the study, Felicity froze with fear at the sound of a gunshot. She numbly watched as Erasmus, entering the house, pulled a revolver out from his belt, behind his back, and brushed past her running into the study.

"I wouldn't be doing that if I were you, slick. This here gun will shoot a bullet clean through ya before you can even get a shot off that pea shooter, ya got there."

James, turning to Erasmus, still pointing the gun, hissed, "Who the hell are you?"

"I'm the man who wants ta shoot the head clean off ya, for hurting my baby sister."

Shocked at the scene before her, Felicity inched her way inside the study, witnessing James, aiming the gun at Erasmus; and then her eyes trailed to Gilbert's body on the floor and she screamed.

"Gilbert!" Rushing to him, she threw herself across him. "Shoot me too, you barbarian. I don't want to live without him. Shoot me!"

"As you wish, bitch."

Erasmus, seeing James start to move his hand holding the pistol back toward Felicity, without hesitation fired his gun, the bullet striking James in the chest. As he staggered backward, still trying to fire his pistol, Erasmus shot him again and James slumped to the floor.

Felicity quivered, seeing James's lifeless body no more than three feet in front of her. Laying her head over Gilbert's chest, she cried, "Please God, please don't take him from me, too. I love him." Hearing a heartbeat, she lifted her head, pleading, "Don't you die on me, Gilbert O'Flaherty."

Looking up at Erasmus who was trying to keep Anne and the others from entering, she yelled, while pulling on Gilbert's shirt, loosening it from his trousers. "He's alive! Send Jimmy for Stephen Hix, and have Mrs. Duncan bring me some sheets and water." Then seeing blood coming from below his heart, between two ribs, she tenderly rolled him over to his side and seeing an exit hole, she sighed, "Thank Heavens." Seeing Whitney and Lucas inching their way into the study, staring at James's slain body sprawled out on the study floor, and ripping the shirt from Gilbert's body, buttons popping off in the air, she said, "He'll be fine. But I need your help, boys. Please, run as fast as you can and get that medicine your father used on me."

By this time Fannie had arrived and shrieked, "Bugger me!"

"Fannie, you take the children up to their rooms and tell them that I'm not going to let their papa die."

Seeing the maid still staring at them she yelled, "Fannie, go! Send Mrs. Spencer in here, I need help!"

Erasmus, taking Kathleen by the shoulders, rushed her out the door, and said, "Don't you be crying no more there little lady, here?" Pointing to the carriage, he added, "You got yerself a man in there that wants to be makin' you his wife. Now, hurry on up, before it's too late."

Kathleen, seeing the door of the carriage swing open and Will sitting inside, anxiously waving his hand for her, not saying a word, she ran to him. No sooner had she climbed inside the carriage, it drove off. Erasmus, walking back inside the house, heard Anne crying in the doorway, shaking her head. "I can't, Felicity, I can't." C.W. motioned for Constance to go on inside, while he consoled his cousin.

Constance, rushing to Felicity's side said, "What do you need? I've seen a lot worse than this during the war. Looks like it only grazed him."

Nodding, Felicity said, "Get me something to stop the bleeding."

As Constance balled up pieces of Gilbert's shirt, Felicity gingerly lifted his head and placed it on his wound, and yelled, "Mrs. Duncan, hurry the hell up! I need some water, *now!*""

Opening his eyes, Gilbert said, "Now is that any way for my lady to speak?"

Smiling at him, she whispered, "Well that all depends on the day. Today I'm trying to save the man I love. Are you in pain?"

"Where's James?"

Felicity motioned to the floor in front of them. "Over there, dead. Erasmus killed him."

By then Mrs. Duncan had arrived and Felicity began tenderly washing the blood from his chest as Gilbert tried to say he was fine, just a wee nick and not for her to fuss so much. Wincing, he allowed her to continue tending to his wounds, saying she wasn't taking any chances, as Lucas and Whitney, having returned with the balm, watched silently.

Looking over at Erasmus, then at the dead body of James Sterling now covered with a sheet, Whitney timidly asked, "Uncle C.W., did you shoot him with the gun you used in the war?"

"Sure did, boy. And I ain't sad I did, either. He was a real bad man, shot your pa, Lucas, and then tried to shoot your ma too, Whitney. He's better off meetin' his maker than to hurt anyone else again, I'd say."

Spotting Felicity kissing Gilbert, after finishing binding his ribs, he nodded over at them, and added, "Looks like you boys are goin' to be brothers real soon, by the look of things."

Whitney smiled, and said, "Now I'll be a part of a big family just like the Carmidys."

"Yeah, well I'm still the oldest, so you can start watching *your* little sisters for a change."

Gilbert, hearing the boys, smiled and said, "Come over hear for a minute, lads."

Dutifully, they stepped closer and leaned over Gilbert, and listened. "Now both of you tend to the little ones. And if ya do, I'll let ya both have my cabin as yer own once we get back from Glastonbury."

Whitney, looking wide-eyed, said, "Really, Uncle Gilbert?"

"Aye, lad."

"Da, when are we going?"

"Tomorrow morning."

The boys looking anxiously between them, then smiled. "Are we going on holiday so you can recuperate after being shot, like Mother did after her accident?" Whitney asked.

"Not really, son. I was thinkin' if it's all right with you lad, I'd like to marry your mother at the Tor and make us a real family."

Seriously, Whitney thought about it for a moment, then said, "You have my permission, Uncle Gilbert."

Felicity smiled just as Stephen Hix arrived. Seeing Gilbert still leaning into Felicity's shoulder as she sat behind him on the floor, his shirt off and bandaged around his ribs, Stephen's eyes trailed over to the body on the floor, now covered, and shook his head. "Now why do you call a doctor if you're going to tend to my patient on your own?" Looking at the boys, he said, "Scoot, I need some time alone with Felicity's patient."

Watching the boys running out the door, chattering amongst themselves, Stephen said, "What the hell has happened here? And who is under the sheet?"

Hearing it was James Sterling he said, "What happened? Who shot him?"

Erasmus spoke up, and pulling out his Pinkerton Badge, walked forward. "I did Doc, after he shot this unarmed man and tried to shoot my sister, as she lay over O'Flaherty's body so he wouldn't shoot him again."

"Your sister?" As the two of them exchanged polite introductions and Erasmus answered Stephen's questions, Gilbert turned to look at Felicity. "Jesus, Mary, and Joseph, what were ya thinkin', lass? Why would ya do such a thing?"

Felicity, taking in a deep breath, lovingly caressed his chest. Placing her head next to his ear, so not to be overheard, she whispered, "All I knew was, you weren't going to die on my birthday. Now hush and let Stephen have a look at your wounds, so I can get you in bed; and that, my love, is non-negotiable."

~

After Erasmus was cleared of all charges regarding the death of James Sterling, and the local undertaker had removed his body, Anne said, while sitting in the parlor, "I can't believe this has happened. James dead...I should get home to Jacque, I'm sure he must be wondering what has become of me." Looking over at Erasmus, she said, "So you're certain you saw William take off by foot after he stormed out of the office?"

"That's right Anne, but then all hell done broke loose and to be honest with ya, I was a little preoccupied."

Obviously too distraught to notice that Kathleen had not been seen since the shooting, Anne shook her head. "I don't believe I'll ever forget the sight of him lying there. Surely you aren't intending to use that study after what has happened."

Gilbert, on the couch with a fresh shirt on, resting his right arm around Felicity's shoulder said, "No Anne, as a matter of fact we won't be using Brookhaven at all. Felicity and I are going to start building our own home, past the stream, just as soon as we get back from Glastonbury."

"You are? And what will become of Brookhaven?"

Felicity, looking over at her brother, sheepishly said, "Well, I was hoping that I might be able to convince Erasmus and Constance to stay for awhile. After all Erasmus, this is just as much your home as is it is mine."

"Sis, I came back here for one purpose and that was to see you. We have a good life in San Francisco, but tell ya what, I'd like to stay a spell to help build that house for you and O'Flaherty here. That is if it's alright with the two of you."

Gilbert stood, wincing a little from his wound, extended his hand to Felicity's brother and said, "Sounds good to me, mate."

Erasmus, looking over at Anne said, "Well Anne, I'll see you out, since we're heading over to Rupert's to tell them what's happened and to let them know the birthday celebration has been postponed until after these two get hitched."

Anne, smiling at her cousin said, "I must say, you do have the most unusual way of saying things C.W. Now explain to me again why that is?"

Nodding to Felicity and Gilbert and escorting his cousin and Constance out, he said, "Well, in my line of work...."

Smiling, Felicity wrapped her arm gingerly around Gilbert's waist. "Just because Stephen said you were lucky and it looks like the bullet only knocked the wind out of ya, doesn't mean you should over do it." Pausing as Mrs. Duncan entered the parlor, she said, "Oh good Mrs. Duncan, have the children been fed their dinner?"

"Yes, Mrs. Myles. Montgomery is with them now. Mr. O'Flaherty's room has been made up as you requested. Shall I have Fannie serve both you and Mr. O'Flaherty your dinners there or in the dining room?"

"In Mr. O'Flaherty's room; thank you Mrs. Duncan." Turning to Gilbert, seeing the servant leave the room she said, "Shall we?"

"What will the servants think, M'lady?"

"Why, how lucky I am that you're alive, I should think."

Helping Gilbert climb the stairs, he leaned on her to help steady him, and they went to the room that Felicity had selected for them to share. As she opened the door, a smile crossed her lips noting that the bed she had requested from Gilbert's cabin had been set up and completely made, as it had been in the cabin.

Looking up at him, she timidly said, "Do you approve? I know it's smaller than the other room you had before, but this room has a lovely view overlooking the stream. And I thought we could have that wall removed giving us double the space, since the other room isn't being used."

Huskily he whispered, "It's perfect. How did you get my bed over here in such a short time?"

"Jimmy and Montgomery moved it for me, while you and Erasmus were busy with the constable."

"Hmm, looks to me like I'm goin' to have to be keepin' my eyes on you every second, or there'll be no tellin' what you'll be thinkin' up next."

Getting him settled in a fireside chair, Felicity removed the kerosene lamp, and then moved the end table and the other chair in front of him. "This will have to do for a dinner table for the time being, I'm afraid." Seeing that his eyes were closed and that he was leaning his head against the back of the chair, she asked, "Gilbert, should I send for Stephen?"

"Nah, I'm fine lass. Just thinkin' is all."

Timidly she asked, "Gilbert, the shooting didn't happen like Erasmus told the constable, did it?"

Opening his eyes, he gazed into hers and hoarsely replied, "Now why would ya be thinkin that, M'lady?"

"Because you had the gun before Erasmus pushed me out of the way and went in the study. Where did you get that gun, Gilbert?"

Lifting his hand for her to come closer, she knelt in front of him, resting her head on his lap as he explained everything. Silently, she listened and when he was finished Felicity raised her tear-stained face and looked up at him. "So that was the gun that killed Ben and could have killed you, too?"

Gravely he said, "Aye, lass."

Quivering at such an unimaginable thought, she laid her head back on his lap, and whispered, "Thank you Gilbert, for telling me and especially for not dying. When I saw you lying on the floor, I thought you were dead. You looked so still, so I begged that monster to shoot me too. I just couldn't live, losing you too."

"Well ya not have to be worryin' none about that now, will ya lass? Funny though, after I was shot, I could swear I saw the parson and he said, "Wake up, good friend. It's not your time."

Lifting her head, she said, "Really? You saw Ben?"

"Aye. Before I came back to the house, after getting' the gun, I had me a talk with my mate and told him, I could be usin' his help." Pausing, nodding his head slightly, a smile crossed his lips and he said, "I guess he was listening."

Taking in a deep breath, Felicity closed her eyes and said a silent thank you to her beloved Ben.

~

After Felicity and Gilbert shared a meal, and she had changed his bandages, hearing Fannie knock at the door just as she was helping Gilbert with his shirt, Felicity smiled at the servant as she entered. "Ah, perfect timing, Fannie. Please see to it that the soiled bandages in the basket are burned with the rubbish, and tell the rest of the staff they can retire for the evening. I'll be caring for Mr. O'Flaherty and we don't want to be disturbed, unless one of the children needs us."

"Yes, Mrs. Myles. Montgomery sent me in to tell ya they are all ready to be tucked in fer the night."

Helping Gilbert, who was still stiff, from the edge of the bed, Felicity said, "Thank you Fannie, we'll tend to them straight away."

After Felicity had said goodnight to Whitney, she was surprised that her son had requested time alone with Gilbert. Standing outside his door, she heard Whitney ask if after they were married, if he could call Gilbert 'Da', since his father was in heaven, just like the prayer.

Closing her eyes, recalling how Benjamin had promised to always love and care for her the night he had proposed, she thought, *Even in heaven you kept your promise. Now I will keep my promise to you, and be happy. I love you my darling Ben, and always will.*

Stepping inside her new family's room, Felicity was bombarded with questions. Asking her if they should call her auntie or step-mother after she and their father were married, settling on the English term 'Mum', Felicity saying that she could never replace their real mother. Evidently pleased by her choice, they then wanted to know if they could have their own room, like Whitney. Joey asking for his own pony, Lucas wanting to know if he were now related to Pricilla, and pleased to find out that he wasn't, Felicity smiled realizing he had a crush on Rupert's willful daughter. Then resting her eyes on Suzanne, and seeing her nearly in tears, Felicity asked, "Sugar, what is it?"

"If Papa is going to let Whitney and Lucas have his cabin then where is he going to sleep?"

Stepping from the doorway where he had been standing, listening to Felicity and his children, Gilbert said, "Now don't be worryin' about Da, peanut, I've already got me a room right down the hall. And as soon as we get back, we're going to build us a big house for all of us to live in together."

His daughter smiled, obviously satisfied with his response, and stood up in her bed and stretched out her arms. "Papa, I'll kiss you tonight, since you're hurt."

"Oh, I'm not that hurt to kiss me, Peanut." The other three started giggling as they also stood on their beds for their goodnight kiss. Smiling lovingly at them, he whispered, "Now back under the covers so your auntie can tuck ya in."

Giggles erupted again amongst the O'Flaherty children, as they bounced back into bed, pulling the sheets over them. "Not auntie anymore, Da. Mum."

Anxiously looking for Gilbert's approval, Felicity smiled, hearing him say, "Ah so it's to be Mum, is it?"

Joey eagerly nodded his head. "It tickles my lips, listen..." Exaggerating the sound at the end, he smiled. "Did ya hear that, Da?"

Nodding his head in approval, he added, "Aye, it has a nice ring to it." Standing to the side so that Felicity could tuck them in, just as she had the night they'd arrived, Gilbert smiled lovingly at his family then placed his arm around her as they exited the room.

"Ya know M'lady, I've been thinkin' three sons and three daughters would be nice."

"Funny you should say that because I was thinking the same thing."

"Now that's music to my ears."

Entering the room, she turned up the lamp, then sitting on the edge of the bed, she patted the mattress beside her. "Come my love; let me see if the bleeding has subsided."

"Lass, ya can't be fussin' over me…"

Placing her fingers over his lips, she said, "Oh but I can, just as you did after my accident. Please come let me look at your wounds and then you should get in bed. You need your rest."

Seeing there was no more bleeding from the wounds, she knelt in front of him, and began unlacing his boots. "Felicity, this is nonsense; I can undress meself."

"And how are you proposing to do that when you can't bend over? Stop being so stubborn. Besides, as I recall, you undressed me before."

"Aye, but you were unconscious."

Smiling up at him, she said, "Yes and missed seeing your reaction as you gazed at me for the first time."

Finishing with his boots and socks she looked up at him, and said, "I'll be right back, I'll get your night shirt."

"No need lass, I don't sleep with it on. I just leave it by the bed in case the children wake up in the night."

The thought of him lying in bed naked brought a glimmer to her eyes, and she smiled. "That explains why I couldn't picture you in that gown you lent me." Moving her hands to his trousers, her eyes locked onto his as she began unfastening the buttons from their loops. Seeing his chest rise and fall as his breathing increased, feeling her fingers graze his skin, she whispered, "Gilbert, you'll need to stand so I can remove your pants."

"Aye," he answered huskily. Helping him to his feet, taking in his masculine frame, his arms so muscular, his stomach so taut, Felicity found her own heart racing. Gently placing her fingers on his chest, slowly she let her fingers caress his bare skin. As her hands reached the exposed area of his trousers, she guided her hand slowly around his waist, releasing his trousers over his buttocks and down his thighs. Her eyes taking in all of him, his pants now around his knees, she continued to caress his skin, watching how his manhood enlarged at her touch. Kneeling in front of him, she whispered, "Brace yourself on my shoulder Gilbert, so you can lift your legs."

Removing his trousers, she stood and slowly allowed herself the pleasure of feeling his nakedness, then guided him into bed. Not saying a word, she lowered the lights slightly and standing in plain view of him, she began to disrobe.

Once her clothes had been removed, standing before him, Gilbert whispered, "M'lady, in my coat jacket, in the breast pocket, there's a little something I'll be needin' before you come to me bed. Would you mind gettin' it for me?"

Never had Felicity walked naked in front of a man before, yet despite her uneasiness at being so exposed, she nodded and went to the wardrobe. Feeling a small bundle inside his jacket, she pulled out a laced-edged handkerchief that was bunched around something solid and tied with a red ribbon. Looking over at Gilbert, smiling, realizing this was a gift for her, she said, "You needed this, my love? I don't need for you to give me a gift before I come to you. I'm here because I want to be."

Patting his hand beside him, he said, "Trust me, M'lady."

Smiling warmly at him, Felicity walked over to the bed and gingerly laid beside him, closing her eyes for a moment to feel the splendor of their skin touching as he pulled her closer to him. Slowly moving his hands across her bare skin, he took in a deep breath and said, "Please Felicity, open your birthday present while you're so close to me."

Raising herself and bending her legs beneath her, she sat and waited until he had turned slightly to his side. Gingerly he caressed her face and neck, and Felicity drank in his touch.

"You are an angel, so soft and beautiful."

"I'm glad you think so, my love."

There was no need for any further words, the truth in their eyes as they gazed at each other so freely, said more than any words could have said. Smiling at her he said, "Open yer gift, M'lady."

Lowering her head, seeing the delicate lace-edged handkerchief, she said, "Oh how beautiful. Where did you get such an exquisite hanky?"

"In Glastonbury. Rupert and I passed this small Irish shop and in the window there was this handkerchief and I thought of you."

"Oh Gilbert, you're such a dear man. Why didn't you give it to me then?"

"I was waiting to give it to you when we returned, so you could have a little something of our holiday together with you always."

"But I pushed you away. I'm so sorry."

"No need, you have it now. Look inside, Felicity."

Untying the red ribbon, she gasped upon seeing a wooded hand-carved replica of Glastonbury Tor, with trees near the base and the tower at the top. "Gilbert this is beautiful. Oh look, even the lines of the stones are exactly as I recall." Then seeing the engraving on the base, tears flooded her eyes. Tracing the words with her fingers, she read them aloud. "'An enchanting night.' Oh Gilbert, you made this...."

"Aye, M'lady. So you could remember for always, our magical night in each others arms."

Tears flowed down her cheeks, and he asked, "Do you like it?"

Nodding her head, smiling through her tears, she whispered, "I love it." Leaning closer to him, her lips touched his sensually and tenderly. "I love you. Thank you so much."

"You're welcome, M'lady, but there's more."

Frowning, looking inside the handkerchief, she shook her head. "I'm sorry, but it must have fallen loose in your pocket."

"Nah, lass it's hidden *in* the Tor. Let me show ya." Sliding his thumb across the edge of base Felicity watched in amazement as a section of the base opened, revealing a secret compartment. Her face beamed as he said, "Close your eyes, lass and stretch out your palm. There's a little something inside for you."

Doing as she was told, feeling something fall in her hands, she opened her eyes slowly, seeing paper wrapped around something. "Can I?" she asked, excited, glancing up at Gilbert.

"Aye, just don't tear the paper lass, it's part of the gift, too. And don't read what is written until you see what's inside."

Rolling the paper tenderly, she gasped, seeing three gold rings inside. "Gilbert…" Then with shaking hand, she picked one up. "It's beautiful…"

"They're Claddagh rings. For over three centuries, it has been an expression of love. And I wanted them to be our wedding rings."

Looking at the rings in her hands, she cried softly, "They're perfect…"

Tenderly wiping her tears, he said, "Felicity they were concealed in the Tor, until I was sure that you were ready to give your heart to me fully. When you stood before me taking off your clothes, allowing me to gaze at you fully with no doubts or reservations, I knew you were truly ready to be mine. So M'lady, may I remove the ring from your hand that still binds you to Benjamin and replace it with my ring that will make you my wife? I know the love you shared in your heart for Benjamin will never die, nor should it; so let me place his ring on your other hand, there you can be reminded of both of our love, for all of your remaining days."

Nodding, she watched as Gilbert slid the wedding ring of her ancestors that her dear auntie had given to she and Benjamin on the day of their wedding from her finger and place it tenderly on her right hand.

Gazing lovingly into her eyes, Gilbert said, "Felicity, the ring has two hands holding one heart, with a crown above. With these hands I give you my heart and I crown it with my love."

His words were so heartfelt and beautiful she tenderly caressed his lips with her fingers. Reaching for his hand, she removed the ring that Miranda and he had shared as a token of their love from his left hand, and placed it on his right. Then looking into his eyes, picking up the larger ring from her palm she said, "Gilbert, my love, with these hands I give you my heart freely and I crown it with my love." Slowly she guided it on his finger and watched as he lifted the paper and gazed into hers eyes.

"On this sheet of paper are the traditional Irish wedding vows a bride and a groom pledge to one another, to join them as one. Tonight before we are joined as one physically, Felicity, will you pledge your love to me, just as you came into the world; free from the past, with only the love that we share for one another surrounding you?"

Nodding, not saying a word, she took the paper from his hands, as he took the third ring and cupped it in his palm. Reading the words written on the sheet, tracing them with her fingers before laying the paper next to her, Felicity lifted her head. "To wed me, your promise I must be certain of, so that we may live out our lives in sweet contentment, love."

Gazing deeply into her eyes, Gilbert tenderly took her hand in his, and said, "Here is my hand to hold with you, to bind us for life so that I'll grow old with you."

Placing the third gold ring with five small rubies inlayed, on her finger, Gilbert said, "By the power that Christ brought from heaven, mayst thou love me. As the sun follows its course, mayst thou follow me. As light to the eye, as bread to the hungry, as joy to the heart, may thy presence be with me, O one that I love, till death comes to part us asunder." Then tenderly pulling her closer to him, kissing her lovingly, he said, "I love you, Felicity O'Flaherty."

Returning his kiss, she softly said, "Oh Gilbert, I love you. More than you will ever know, more than I ever dreamt I could."

Smiling, caressing her cheek, he said, "I know M'lady, your eyes have already shown the depth of your love. Now come, lay beside me and let me hold you."

Nodding, she folded the paper inside the Tor replica, sliding the piece of wood back in place, then laid it along with her lace handkerchief on the nightstand. Tenderly returning into his arms, she whispered, "Am I really your wife, Gilbert?"

Wrapping his arm more tightly around her, slowly caressing her skin, he whispered, "Do you feel as if we are one?"

"In my heart, I honestly feel as if I am Mrs. Gilbert O'Flaherty."

"That's because you are, M'lady. Long before they needed someone to preside over the ceremony, a man and woman were joined by pledging themselves to each other before God. I believe from every moment from here on out, God will look at us as one heart."

Raising her hand and gazing at the wedding band on her finger, she whispered, "Oh Gilbert, look, there are five red rubies, one for each of our children."

Kissing her on the forehead, he said, "I know, that's why I chose it."

"Really? What a romantic and thoughtful husband I have." Kissing him lightly, she then asked, "When did you buy these?"

"That day at the shop with Rupert."

Felicity's eyes grew wide. "Rupert knew you wanted to marry me, even back then?"

"Of course. The day following your accident, I told him how I felt and he gave me his blessing to try and win your heart. It only seemed right that he should be there when I picked out the rings that would bind our love."

"You really told Rupert that you loved me that long ago?"

"In truth, he guessed by the way I looked at you or so he claimed. Even then though, I never denied my love, not to him, not to anyone. I would have no other but my precious angel."

Smiling, she rested her head back onto his shoulder and tenderly caressed his chest. "That afternoon following the accident, when Whitney came to visit and you moved me to the side of the bed, I think I knew then how much I loved you. I was just ashamed by how much. You were so close, I felt your breath on my face, and it took my breath away. Don't you recall I became flushed and you thought I had a fever?"

"Aye. Had I known what an effect me holding you brought to ya though lass, I would have sent the lad home so I could lay beside you and fall asleep in your arms just as he did. After all, I had not slept in two days, because of you. The first night praying that you would come to me and not change your mind, and the second night praying to God I wouldn't lose you."

Tenderly they caressed each other's bare skin, not ashamed by their nakedness, enjoying how natural it felt. "Oh Gilbert, and to think I almost missed the chance to know such bliss. Lying here in your arms, enjoying how good your skin feels next to mine..." Suddenly Felicity jerked her head back up. "What if I hadn't come to you this morning and told you I loved you, what then?"

"Lass, you would have received your gift for your birthday. It was made for you. The only difference is I never would have received the gift you just gave me by becoming my wife. Not today anyway, but eventually I believe we would have been brought together. What we have found together is too perfect, not to have been God's plan."

"I finally understand that, my love. You know, your thirty-seventh birthday might have been special to you, but nothing compares to my thirty-second birthday. It was the birth of a new life. A life I'm looking forward to sharing with my wise, attentive, and extremely enticing husband...." Felicity's voice trailed off as she leaned over Gilbert further. Deliberately brushing her breasts against his chest, she seductively added, "Who has stirred a longing in me that I never knew I could possess, except only in my dreams."

Gilbert exhaled deeply; huskily whispering, "It's I who must be dreamin' Felicity, you take my breath away." His words were blocked as Felicity's lips touched his; the tenderness of their kiss sending a desire through her that only matched that of her dreams. Feeling his hands trail over her shoulder and spine, she moaned, eagerly accepting his tongue as it parted her lips. As their lips parted, she suggestively asked, "Do you suppose tonight Gilbert, the fairies will grant me my request, at last?"

Before answering her, he tenderly traced her lips, and as his hand glided down her neck, he watched at how Felicity closed her eyes as she drank in the splendor of his hands. From her expression, Gilbert knew his touch sent waves of pleasure rushing through her. Gingerly she returned to lying beside him, and the two of them continued to leisurely explore the newness of each other's bodies. Hearing her moan softly again as his hands trailed to her breasts, Gilbert huskily whispered, "Aye lass, the fairies saved this enchanting night, just for us."

THE END

A Note from the author, Linda Daly…

Writing each tale from the Doves Collect series has been one the most rewarding experiences of my life. One such moment that stands out is while writing the death scene of one of my favorite characters. Naturally, I cried uncontrollably. My youngest son taking a break from his video game came rushing into my office and asked earnestly, "If it makes you so sad, why are you writing it for?"

Drying my eyes, I tried to explain that just as in real life, my books had to show how tragic and completely unexpected events could happen and so as sad as I was to say goodbye, I must.

From the onset of writing book four, I knew how difficult it would be for me to say goodbye. As any writer knows, this is my baby, yet despite this, I was determined not to fall short from the compelling storylines that I've outlined for the series.

As you bid farewell to those characters you have loved, and those you loved to hate, my sincere hope is that you will look forward to the next installment of Doves Collect, book five:

Doves Flight

THE NEXT GENERATION

As the children and grandchildren of Elise, Felicity, and Miranda try to forge new paths, independent of their ancestry, will it be necessary for our heroines of the first four books to disclose the lies and indiscretions of the past, to protect their loved one's future?

To read more of Ms. Daly's projects, visit www.lindadaly.net or for information regarding LSP Digital, go to www.lspdigital.com.

From the epic "Doves Collect" series...

Virtuous Dove
ISBN-13: 978-0981765471

After a young and naive Abolitionist, witnesses her mother and father's gruesome death; aiding runners in the Underground Railroad, she flees America to Victoria England, the land of her ancestors. Her virtues will be tested when greed, power, and the suppression of the truth test her own belief system.

Rebel Dove
ISBN-13: 978-0979203091

A spirited Southern Spy who believes she is just in aiding the "Southern cause", despite her attraction to a Union major that suspects her of espionage.

Doves Migration
ISBN13: 978-0980073355

The death of an innocent man and the attempts to cover it up spiral out of control. Sequel to Rebel Dove.

For those who enjoy a good who-dun-it...

Sea of Lies
ISBN-13: 978-0981765457

Love is blind and passion can be perilous, especially when personal intrigue and international terrorism stir up a Sea of Lies.

Coming Soon...

Paper Hanger